CRIMSON & CARIUS 2 REAL TRAP LOVE THE FINALE

FINESSED BY: NIKKI NICOLE

Published by Pushing Pen Presents

www.authoressnikkinicole.com

Acknowledgments

Hi, how are you? I'm Nikki Nicole the Pen Goddess. Each time I complete a book I love to write acknowledgements. I love to give a reflection on how I felt about the book. I've been writing for almost three years now and this is my 18th book. When I first started writing I only had one story I wanted to tell and that was Baby I Play for Keeps. Three years later and I've penned a total of 18 books. I appreciate each one of you for taking this journey with me. I'm forever grateful for you believing in me and giving me your continuous support.

Anytime I'm creating I'm in a good space because I'm in another world escaping my current reality. I don't know where to begin, but I'll start here. Crimson & Griff I've spent so much time with them. 111,000 words later we finally have an ending. I love them I miss them already. I ain't gone lie Crimson worked my last fuckin' nerves. I love Camina I swear she's giving Kaniya a run for her money. Mother Dear kept more shit started I swear. I love Cheree and Bone I think you guys will too.

I miss Keondra I swear it'll never be another her. I can't wait for y'all to read it. I know y'all are gonna be at my neck but hey it's whatever.

I want to Thank God for giving me this gift. I can't thank him enough because for years I've always wanted to know what my purpose was. I can do anything with my hands their golden. I've always had a way with words.

I'm a creator if I'm not creating, I'm a mess. I'm an author I love to write. I don't give a fuck where I'm at I'm always writing it doesn't matter. I want to thank my supporters for backing me and believing in me. I love y'all to death. I wouldn't trade y'all for nothing. I promise y'all the wait was worth it. If I haven't dropped a book in 60 days, do trust I'm coming with some major work. In my absence I've been cooking my ass off.

I want to thank my supporters that I haven't met or had a conversation with. I appreciate y'all too. Please email me or contact me on social media. I want to acknowledge you and give you a S/O also.

I dedicate this book to my Queens in the Trap **Nikki Nicole's Readers Trap**. I swear y'all are the best. Y'all go so hard in the paint for me it's insane. Every day we lit. I appreciate y'all more than y'all will ever know. The Trap is going the fuck up on a Sunday. I can't wait for y'all to read it.

It's time for my S/O **Samantha, Tatina, Asha, Shanden (PinkDiva), Padrica, Liza, Aingsley, Trecie, Quack, Shemekia, Toni, Amisha, Tamika, Troy, Pat, Crystal C, Missy, Angela, Latoya, Helene, Tiffany, Lamaka, Reneshia, Charmaine, Misty, Toy, Toi, Shelby, Chanta, Jessica, Snowie, Jessica, Marla Jo, Shay, Anthony, Keyana, Veronica, Shonda J, Sommer, Cathy, Karen, Bria, Kelis, Lisa, Tina, Talisha, Naquisha, Iris, Nicole, Koi, Drea, Rickena, Saderia, Chanae, Shanise, Nacresha, Jalisa, Tamika H, Kendra, Meechie, Avis, Lynette, Pamela, Antoinette, Crystal W, Ivee, Kenyada, Dineshia, Chenee, Jovonda, Jennifer J, Cha, Andrea, Shannon J, Latasha F, Denise, Andrea P, Shelby, Kimberly, Yutanzia, Seanise, Chrishae, Demetria, Jennifer, Shatavia, LaTonya, Dimitra, Kellissa, Jawanda, Renea, Tomeika, Viola, Gigi,**

Barbie, Erica, Shanequa, Dallas, Verona, Catherine, Dominique, Natasha K,

If I named everybody, I will be here all day. Put your name here________ if I missed you. The list goes on. S/O to every member in my reading group, I love y'all to the moon and back. These ladies right here are a hot mess. I love them to death. They go so hard about these books it doesn't make any sense. Sometimes, I feel like I should run and hide.

If you're looking for us meet us in **Nikki Nicole's Readers Trap** on Facebook, we are live and indirect all day.

S/O to My Pen Bae's **Ash ley, Chyna L, Chiquita, T. Miles,** I love them to the moon and back head over to Amazon and grab a book by them also.

Check my out my new favorite Author **Nique Luarks** baby girl can write her ass off. You heard it from me. I love her work! Look her up and go read her catalog!

To my new readers I have five complete series, and three completed standalones available. Here's my catalog if you don't have it.

Cuffed by a Trap God 1-3

I Just Wanna Cuff You (Standalone)

Baby I Play for Keeps 1-3

For My Savage, I Will Ride or Die

He's My Savage, I'm His Ridah

You Don't Miss A Good Thing, Until It's Gone (Standalone)

He's My Savage, I'm His Ridah

Journee & Juelz 1-3

Giselle & Dro (Standalone)

Our Love Is the Hoodest 1-2

Join my readers group **Nikki Nicole's Readers Trap** on **Facebook**

Follow me on Facebook Nikki Taylor

Follow me on Twitter @WatchNikkiwrite

Like my Facebook Page AuthoressNikkiNicole

Instagram @WatchNikkiwrite

GoodReads @authoressnikkinicole

Visit me on the web authoressnikkinicole.com

email me authoressnikkinicole@gmail.com

Join my email contact list for exclusive sneak peaks.

http://eepurl.com/czCbKL

https://music.apple.com/us/album/victory-lap/1316706552

Nikki Nicole
THE PEN GODDESS

Contents

IF YOU GONNA LIVE BY IT; YOU GONNA DIE BY IT.

Dear Crimson Rose,

If you're reading this letter baby it means one of those pussy ass niggas took me out and took me away from you and my babies. I love you, baby, more than life itself. Don't let anybody tell you anything different. Let Cariuna and Camina know I love them, and I'll forever watch over the three of you. Just know I took a few niggas with me. I put that shit on God Crimson. It's a lot of shit that you don't know about me. I never wanted you to be a part of my life in these streets. The less you knew the better. I'm sure you know by now that I was married to Keondra, but we're divorced. The paperwork is attached with the Last Will & Testament. Everything that I own is yours.

If she takes anything from you and my children, go get your shit back now. My lawyer is expecting you. Even in death you and my daughters will forever be straight. I was out here hustling for you. Every bag I secured, it was for you. I vowed to take care of you from my grave. My mission was to make that shit happen. It was accomplished. I love you too much to leave you and my daughters without anything.

There's a safe in the house that's buried underground. It's 20 million inside and, the code is the day we met backwards. Quit that bullshit as job and create your own job. I have two trust funds setup for Cariuna and Camina. Don't let them touch it until they're 21. My only regret is I should've made you my wife. I knew my time was coming because those niggas and Keondra were gunning for me. What goes around comes around. I'll see them again on the other side.

They can't get at me and be able to live in the land of living amongst you and my children. I want you to find love again. I hate to admit it, but I do. I love you for loving me. I love you for being my peace away from the streets. I always told you, you deserve the best because you do. No matter what that bitch says, I was true to you. Dry your tears baby I love you and I'll forever look after you.

Griff

Chapter-1

Keondra

Jacque and I fled from the crime scene. I got my hands a little dirty and I didn't mind being in the trenches with my man. I wouldn't have it any other way. I had his back and he had mine. As soon as we hopped on I-20W. I heard the sirens. I looked out the window and the police were flying down Columbia Drive. My baby had his feet on the gas. He was whipping from lane to lane moving like the true boss he was. Meanwhile, my heart was racing praying that we didn't get caught. I ain't never done shit like this before in my life. I had to make Griff feel me. I'm glad I was there to witness him catch his last breath. We planned this shit out perfect.

Jacque and I worked well together. It was something different about him than any man I've ever been with. I swear he was my Clyde and I was his Bonnie. I love everything about this man. I know the way we met was fucked up, but you can't help who you love. My heart beats for no one else but him. Jacque used to work for Ike. He wasn't from Atlanta so that was a plus. I didn't have to worry about a bitch saying she fucked him. I was the only woman fuckin' him. He was from Brooklyn, New York. He had that New York swag and I loved that about him. My mother adores him. I know I'm playing a dangerous game but oh well it is what it is. I'll play with fire any day when it comes to him. I love me some him.

Jacque was everything to me. He's everything my husband isn't. We went on a few weekend getaways to New York and I met his family and daughter. His baby momma was cool too. He wined and dined the fuck out of me mentally and physically. He always treated me like royalty. Whenever he said my name I came on sight. His voice alone had me mesmerized and sent chills through my body. I love this man I swear he had my heart. His touch was rough and passionate. He set my soul on fire; like a burning torch. Whenever he looks at me my heart skips a beat. He has me doing shit I thought I would never do. I love Jacque. He's from up top and reps the BK. A bitch couldn't tell me I wasn't his Beyoncé when she first wrote I need a soldier. I swear that's how I felt about Jacque.

I'm weak as fuck for him. I'll do anything in this world for him. I'm so crazy in love with him. I'll shoot a nigga dead and leave his bitch and kids sad and crying for him. It ain't no limit what I'll do for him. Jacque was so fuckin' fine. Tall, dark and handsome. He was built so fuckin' nice. His skin was the color of a chocolate Hershey bar and it was blemish free too. Licking his chest was a daily fetish for me and it's one of the things I love to do.

His abs were sculptured nicely. His teeth were white as coke. Long thick and curly locs adorned his head. I kept them freshly twisted. I learned how to do them because I didn't want him sitting between a bitch's legs period. I didn't want a bitch playing in his hair. His eyebrows had the perfect arch. His forehead had the craziest wrinkles when he got mad. Yeah and I'm the ONLY BITCH in his fuckin' bag.

He stayed draped in diamonds and gold. I even stole a few pieces of jewelry from Ike and blessed Jacque with it. He was my king and I was his queen. I'm the only bitch that could sit on his throne. In a matter of weeks, Jacque and I will have the keys to the streets. He'll be the King of East Atlanta. Long Live Griff, motherfucka. I'm obsessed with him. I can't wait to brag and dote on him in public. I know Ike will be mad but that's some shin t he must deal with.

I'll never forget the day I met him. I remember it like it was yesterday. Jacque had been working for Ike for about two months. I never really paid any attention to him, because I was trying to be faithful to Ike. I wanted this marriage to work, unlike my last one. I wasn't even checking for anybody. I was committed to him. One-night Ike didn't come home. He told me he and Baine had to ride out to Macon to handle some business. I log onto my Facebook and my Instagram and I see him, and Baine posted up with a few bitches.

My husband had a bitch in his lap. Jermesha, Mia and Tasha were in VIP with them. I'm at home waiting for him. He's partying with bitches popping bottles. Let's just say he never made it home that night. I found myself in the kitchen crying my eyes out because he didn't come home. This became a habit of his. I spent a lot of time by myself babysitting the couch and fuckin' up my living room sofa and pillows crying my eyes out because of him. I was all cried out. Jacque didn't even acknowledge me, he looked at me as if I disgusted him. So, I was a little surprised when he came on to me.

One night I came in late from hanging with my girls. I was tipsy as fuck. Getting drunk became a habit of mine. I swear I lost myself behind Ike. I had to get drunk because I got tired of him coming home smelling like cheap ass perfume and burnt hair weave. He didn't even try to hide his cheating. His excuse was you knew what type of man I was when you decide to fuck me. He knew what type of bitch I was when he decided to marry me. I beat Ike home. I was under the impression that Jacque or nobody was here in my home. I was glad to have the house to myself. Ike had sent everybody home for the weekend. I didn't understand why he needed this much security. I took a hot shower to get rid of the smoke and club smell.

I walked to the kitchen to grab a bottle of water to dilute some of the alcohol I'd been drinking. My phone was on the island and I grabbed it to call Ike but he didn't answer. I started to throw my phone because I was sick of his shit. I knew he was out doing me dirty. I found myself crying again because Ike wasn't home. I rested my head on the island and tears dripped from my eyes on the counter.

Jacque walked up behind me. He pressed my body up against the island. I had to get ahold of myself because I didn't know what was happening. I could feel the big bulge in his pants. He grabbed a handful of my ass. He was breathing heavily down my neck. My heart was damn near beating out of my chest. I could smell the fresh mint on his breath. My nipples were erect immediately because he was too close. Jacque's whole appearance was threatening and intimidating. My pussy had this tingling sensation and she was begging to be freed. I squeezed my eyes and legs together praying my juices don't slide down the middle of my legs. What the fuck is this man doing to me? Why is he so damn close? What does he want with me? I'm his boss's wife which means I'm off limits.

Whenever he walked in the room, he commanded attention. I was always nervous around him. It's like if you said the wrong thing, he's liable to pop off. I didn't know what to say or do. His cologne invaded my nostrils. His hands roamed my body. It was that moment that I became addicted to his touch. Thoughts of him fuckin' me drove me crazy. I wanted to yell take me now. He asked me why I was crying over him. I didn't even bother to turn around to face him. I knew my face looked a mess. I grabbed the brim of nighty to dry my eyes.

I knew he was tired of seeing me cry. I was tired of him catching me crying over Ike. What fucked me up is when I asked him why did he care? He told me I was too beautiful to be crying over a nigga that didn't give a fuck about me. He also stated if it hurts that bad then I should leave. I turned around to face him that night. He cupped my chin and lifted my nighty over my ass exposing my pussy.

He started playing with my pussy. His hands felt so good playing with my nub. I wanted him to help free the pressure between my legs. A few moans escaped my lips. I quickly got ahold of myself quick and removed his hands.

He grabbed my hands with so much force. He picked me up and laid me across the island. He ate my pussy and fucked me senseless. I was so scared that I was going to get caught. I told him we had to stop because if Ike walked in, we were liable to get caught.

He whispered in my ear that he didn't give a fuck about getting caught. He was willing to take that chance. My pussy was worth the charge and my heart was under arrest. We've been together ever since. I remembered that night like it was yesterday. Jacque and I christened the whole house. He fucked me in the kitchen. We took it upstairs to The Master Suite and fucked up the sheets. When Ike sent a text stating he was on his way home. Jacque and I took it downstairs to the mother in-law-suite. We went at it for hours. Ike called my phone all night long and I was right underneath his nose fuckin' a real savage. I'm pregnant with Jacque's child.

Seven years later and I finally took Griff out. I've been waiting to do this forever, but this is just the beginning. Everything he took from me mentally and physically I'm taking it back from Crimson Rose Tristan and her bastard children. The house, cars, clothes, and cash. My attorney forged documents for me to take over his stuff with a fake divorce decree. I've hired a few fake cops to help execute my plan. I can't fuck with his bank accounts because that's FEDERAL but the safe that's in the house they shared I was coming for that.

I had a million dollars' worth of cash in the backseat. As soon as Ike steps foot in Atlanta he's going to jail for murder. My husband murdered my ex-husband what are the chances of that? Rashad and Baine will be at each other's necks and the heat will be off me. The moment Ike steps foot in jail, I'm divorcing his ass and taking everything. I'm officially a rich ass bitch. I stripped out of my clothes while he eyed me lustfully from the driver's side. I slid my panties off and threw them at his face. He reached over and grabbed a handful of my pussy.

"Pull over I want it right now," I moaned. I wanted him in the worst way, and he knew it.

"Not right now Keondra. Let's get to our destination first." He argued. His eyes fucked me. He knew I couldn't get enough him. I wasn't trying to hear that. I wanted him right now. I leaned over and unfastened his pants. I spat on his dick and started sucking him off foolishly. "You're hardheaded as fuck," he yelled. I tuned him out. He had one hand on the steering wheel. His free hand was palming my ass trying to find my hole he was familiar with.

My ass was tooted up touching the steering wheel. I made that motherfucka clap. Jacque finger fucked me wet. My body shook. I came everywhere. He busted all down my throat. He smacked me on my ass. I politely got back in my seat. I grabbed a wipe out of my purse to wipe the cum off my cheek. I stared out the window. A small smile crept on my face because I couldn't wait to start my new life with Jacque. I finally had a man that was for me and only me. He loved every imperfection and flaw of mine. I slid my black leggings up over my thighs. He was watching lustfully out the corners of his eyes. I grabbed a mint out of my purse. I didn't want my breath smelling like dick. I didn't care because it was my dick. Since I've been fuckin' with Jacque my ass and titties have gotten a little bigger.

"What are you smiling about over there?" He asked. I looked at him and ran my tongue across my lips. If he only knew how much he stayed on my mind. Even while lying in the bed next to Ike my mind stayed on him. I can remember many nights lying in bed wishing I could creep downstairs and fuck him. It got so bad I hated for Ike to even touch me especially in front of Jacque.

“Why does it matter?” I asked.

“I want to know,” he replied. He took his eyes off the road just for a minute to look at me. He gave me a stern look and I bit my bottom lip. He knew that shit turned me on. Jacque cared about me. I could see and feel it. I guess that’s why I was so open with him.

“Why do you always have to bully me? I'm thinking about us and our new life together. I'm thinking about this baby that I'm carrying. I can’t wait to meet him. I hope he's as handsome as his father,” I blushed. I couldn’t wait to meet my son. I knew Jacque and I was meant to be together because he’s the only man that has ever gotten me pregnant with his child and we’ve only been fuckin’ around for three years.

“I haven't begun to bully you yet. My dick is ready to bully that wet as pussy between your legs. We have a long ride ahead of us. Sit back and chill. I'm going pull up to the chop shop and drop this car off. I want to go to our home so we can relax. I want to feed you, eat you and talk to my son,” he explained and while he reached over to grab my thighs. Jacque could say less because I was ready to do all that.

No more sleepless nights and wishing I was with him. I would do that every night. I couldn't wait to get the call from Ike about him being incarcerated for Griff's murder. I loved to see how he would get out of that jam. I'm not even going to pretend that I'm going to help him get out of this jam. I'm divorcing him and taking every fuckin' thing. Tomorrow I'll be at Crimson Rose Tristan's doorstep taking everything from her. I owe that bitch for the old and the new.

I hated Crimson with a passion too. Griff gave that bitch everything he never gave me. Yes, I hold fuckin' grudges. That nigga thought that he couldn't be touched. I touched him. I just wish I was the bitch that pulled the trigger. I wanted my face to be the last thing he fuckin' saw when he took his last breath. I told that nigga he was going to regret the day he fucked me over. Today was his fuckin' expiration date. My beef with Crimson is personal. It's not even about Griff anymore. He was still my husband when she decided to pursue him and fuck him. A bitch can't cross me without any repercussions. I just hate that bitch with a fuckin' passion.

She makes my ass itch. She was to fuckin' perfect. Griff made sure the world knew he was in love with her and his daughters. The youngest daughter looked just like him too. I hated looking at her. She had him wrapped around her fingers. She was always with him. One day we were in Maxine's and he walked in with her. I'll never forget it as long as I live. The little bitch said why do you keep staring at me and my daddy? My eyes bucked. I couldn't believe she said that. It's not nice to stare at people. I wanted to choke her little ass out. Everybody was laughing and just Griff grilled the fuck out of me, begging me to say some slick shit. I knew he wanted to lay his hands on me. I played it off cool and told the little bitch I was admiring how pretty she was. She took my life and lively hood from me. Don't get me wrong, yes, I married Ike and he had bankrolls full of cash too, but it didn't weigh up to when I was married to Griff. Ike was never at home. He threw me money because he was always cheating, and never had time for me.

Chapter-2

Ike

I dipped out early this morning to Jacksonville to handle some business. I wanted to bring Daisy with me but Keondra was tripping. Keondra knew what the deal was between us. Daisy was pregnant by me. I wanted to keep her little ass close to me. Her pussy has been extra wet. I wanted the head and the pussy on the highway. I don't know how I'm going to tell Keondra that she's pregnant. I slipped up one too many times with Daisy and she refuses to get an abortion this time. I couldn't stop fuckin' with her if I wanted too. I didn't want her to have an abortion because I wanted a kid. Keondra barely even gives a nigga the pussy and when she does, she makes sure I strap up. Why do I got to strap up with my wife and I'm strapping up with these bitches out here in the streets?

A lot of shit has changed between Keondra and me in the past few years. I noticed she's gotten thicker and her attitude has gotten worse. I know it's because of me. We haven't been feeling each other lately. She's been keeping her pussy on the preserve. I swear to God if she's fuckin' another nigga I'm gone kill her. I don't give a fuck about what I'm doing she's my fuckin' wife. I'm mad as hell Baine couldn't come with me because Danielle was fuckin' tripping. I don't know why she was pissed anyway. Baine doesn't cheat and that's the difference between him and me. He took his vows seriously and I didn't.

I really didn't want to marry Keondra, but she kept giving me ultimatums and shit. I haven't even been down here for a good four hours and he's been blowing up my phone like crazy. What the fuck could be so important if he didn't come with me to meet our new connect? I know he wanted to play the back and let my face be the head of the operation. We're business partners and his wife need to understand that. Sometimes we got to make last minute trips out of town to handle our business.

I couldn't answer the phone on the spot. We just closed a huge deal out in Jacksonville, Florida. I don't even think that we were ready to see millions by the day. The deal I just secured for us was guaranteed to level us up in a major way.

I didn't really fuck with small towns and country ass shit. Jacksonville has a large port entry and everything in North Florida was our new territory. A nigga couldn't piss or smuggle shit without us signing off on it. The business was first and bullshit was last. I grabbed my phone out my back pocket to hit Baine up to see what the fuck was up. I had eight missed calls from him. Damn, something must be wrong. He's never hit my line these many times unless it was an emergency. He answered on the first ring. Keondra hasn't called me one time to see if a nigga was straight or if I made it safe. If she doesn't want to be my wife, she needs to let me know now. I know plenty of bitches who will play the position.

"Aye Ike where the fuck are you? Please tell me you're in Jacksonville before I go to war with this nigga," he argued. I heard Baine banging up against a wall or something. I looked at my phone because this nigga was talking crazy. I turned my nose up as if he could see me. I don't know who Baine thought he was talking too because I wasn't that nigga. I'm handling our business while he's at home pacifying his wife. I'm out here in these streets taking FED chances for us.

"What the fuck are you talking about? I'm in Jacksonville the same place you're supposed to fuckin' be. My location is always shared with you and you know that. Why the fuck are you questioning my fuckin' moves? We wouldn't even be having this fuckin' conversation if you were here holding up your end of the business," I argued. I could hear Baine huffing and puffing in the background. I'm not with all that talking in circles shit. "Say what the fuck you need to say or get the fuck up off my line," I argued. Baine knows he needs to get straight to the point or get the fuck up off my line.

"Ike chill out for real. It's some real hot ass shit going on out here in these streets. It may be a good thing I stayed. I don't even know how to say this shit," he argued.

"Just fuckin' say it," I argued. Baine and I are never at odds but since he didn't make the trip with me, I felt some type of way. We were married to this paper before he decided to marry Danielle. I don't have shit against Danielle. I'm just curious, how did she think she was able to afford a fuckin' medical clinic to work out of? She's her own fuckin' boss. Her husband selling shit loads of dope provided that for her. I needed him with me at this fuckin' meeting. I could hold my own, but I would've felt more comfortable if my right-hand man was here.

"Aye man, a motherfucka just blew Griff's ass off at the corner of Columbia Drive and Glenwood Road. Your truck is on the fuckin' scene. Man, I don't know how to tell you this shit. They shot Daisy in the head. She's fuckin' dead. She was with Dace and they shot him in the head too. Somebody set you up. I know I'm going to have to fuck around and have to blow Rashad's ass off behind this shit," he argued. I looked at my phone. I couldn't believe this shit. Ain't no fuckin' way this shit went down. I ran my hands across my face. Damn, I knew I should've taken her with me. She was pregnant with my seed. I never wanted anything bad to happen to her. I had a soft spot for Daisy for real. I'm at a loss for words right now.

"Griff got murked and they set me up to take the fall? What the fuck was Daisy doing with Dace? Baine that shit ain't adding up my nigga. Where's Keondra? If Rashad wants to go to war behind some shit, I didn't do then let that nigga join his fuckin' partner. Don't spare him. I ain't got no beef with Griff. I don't know why a motherfucka would want to set me up?" I argued. Griff and Rashad do their thing and we do ours. The fuck I have to take him out for. He ain't got shit that I want. They ain't the only niggas in the city with a bag. Baine and I got a bag too.

"Man, I don't know. This shit is all on the news. They have a warrant out for your arrest. A tip came in they saw you leaving the crime scene. They got a fuckin' witness. Somebody got it out for you. How am I supposed to lay next to my wife and she thinks I may have some shit to do with you killing her best friends' fiancé," he argued and asked. Man, I don't give a fuck what Danielle thinks. I didn't do that shit. Yeah, I married Keondra but Griff and I ain't never had any beef. I know he got a family. I'm not trying to take that man away from his kids.

"Aye Baine miss with that pussy ass shit. You know you and I know where I'm at. We ain't even got to go back and forth about this shit. Nigga, you're worried about the wrong shit. I didn't do that shit. How the fuck can I kill that nigga and I'm in Jacksonville? Call Mike and get him to transfer all my assets to you right now. I'll be home in a few hours. I'll hit you when I touch down. Meet me at Dekalb County Jail when I call," I argued. Baine sounded like he thought I made a move without him and that wasn't the case. We got too much money to be at war with these niggas. It's bad for business on all levels.

"Ike you might not want to turn yourself in. They found a key of dope in your car at the crime scene," he argued. I've been hustling and moving packs all my life. I've never been that fuckin' carless. That's not my fuckin' work. I'm not catching a murder case behind some shit I didn't do. I refuse to let them pussy ass crackers railroad a nigga on a dope charge that carries a maximum of twenty years to life federal.

"A key a dope? Oh, a motherfucka was out to get me. I'm innocent and I'm going to clear my fuckin' name. I hope they catch that motherfucka that did it before I do. I don't play about my fuckin' lively hood. I don't even have any beef with anybody for them to set me up. That's why I'm in the blind about this shit?" I argued. I swear to God and I put this shit on Daisy and my unborn when I catch the motherfucka that orchestrated this setup its lights out for the muthafuckas that birthed them. If you got the balls to get at any nigga be direct about that shit and use your own face card and not mine. Ike Deleon ain't no fuckin' bitch or pussy period. My name holds weight out here in these streets.

"Look man lay low and don't cross that motherfuckin' state line unless you get the okay from me. I'll be out to Jacksonville in about two hours. I'm catching a flight. I got this shit out here in these streets. You can't turn yourself in until Mike gives us the okay. I refuse to have my nigga in the can until I know for a fact that you can walk in that bitch and walk right back out," he argued. Baine and I finished chopping it up. He may have not been my blood, but he was my fuckin' brother. Where was my fuckin' wife? Her ears are always to the streets and she's always in the hood. I grabbed my phone to call Keondra. She didn't answer the fuckin phone. I called her back again and she answered.

"Hello," she moaned. I gripped the steering wheel. I swear to God if she's fuckin' another nigga in my crib, while I was out here making moves to secure our future I'm going to fuckin' kill her. Yeah, I haven't been the best nigga to her, but she knew what it was when she got with me. I was there when that nigga left her broken. I picked her up, helped put back the pieces, and made her my wife. I felt I at least owed her that much.

"Where the fuck are you at and why are you moaning? I've called you twice," I asked and argued? "Keondra I swear to God I'll fuckin' hurt you if you're fuckin' off on me."

"I'm at home where you left me at. Why are you fuckin' threatening me? You want to accuse me of cheating and fuckin' a different nigga because that's what you're fuckin doing. You're the same nigga that brought a bitch to live in our home as help, but she was inside fuckin' pussy. Don't come for me, Ike. I swear you'll fuckin' regret it. I'm not making a fuckin' threat, that's a fuckin' promise. Where are you at since you're questioning me?" She argued. I looked at the phone. She was tripping hard as fuck. She had some shit she wanted to get off her chest.

"You know where the fuck I'm at. Word on the street is your ex got his ass blown off and a motherfucka framed me to do it? You wouldn't know anything about that, would you? Dace and Daisy got shot in the head. They were found at the crime scene too. Last I checked when I left the house Daisy was there with you? Where the fuck were you when Dace picked her up?

She doesn't even fuck around in the hood. I ain't never took her over there. Two muthafuckas that work for me end up dead and your ex-husband is the victim. That shit is crazy," I argued. Keondra got me fucked up. The last thing I need is to be at odds with my wife and got some real shit going on in these streets.

"What the fuck are you trying to say, Ike? Let that shit be known. Correction it's one motherfucka that works for you. You're fuckin' Daisy. That bitch ain't on the payroll. Why are you so hot about that shit? Did you love her or some shit? Did you kill Griff? It's not adding up. Two of your workers are dead. You killed him because

Daisy was fuckin' him?" She argued. I looked at the phone this bitch was really fuckin' playing with me. I swear she acts like she wants to see a nigga down bad. She said this shit over the phone.

"Keondra on everything I fuckin' love, bitch don't play with me. I ain't got to kill no nigga behind no pussy. I ain't got to pay for pussy I get pussy thrown at me on the regular. I curve bitches because I'm not pressed for pussy. Even though my wife ain't giving me pussy. If Daisy was fuckin' him why would I care? She ain't my fuckin' wife you are." I argued.

"Why do I have to be a bitch though, Ike? I just asked you a fuckin' question, the moment you brought that bitch in our lives shit has been fucked up. You know what I'm not even about to do this with you. You woke me up out of my sleep to argue about a bitch you used to fuck and I'm your wife? When will the disrespect ever stop? Goodbye Ike hurry up and bring your ass home so we can have a face to face conversation," she argued and hung up the phone.

I swear to God Keondra better be glad I'm not able to put my hands on her because if I could. I would choke her ass out. I can't believe that bitch said that shit over the phone. In all my years of hustling, I ain't never got caught slipping like that. She acted like she wanted to see me caged up. If I ever catch the motherfucka that did that shit they'll wish they killed me instead of Griff. I'm fucked up behind that shit with Daisy. I cared about lil momma for real. What the fuck am I supposed to tell her mother?

I don't understand how she got caught up with Dace at the crime scene. I guess that's some shit I'll never know. It's crazy because the last words she texted me was how much she loved me and how she wished she could fuck me. It's a shame that I'll never be able to swim in that pussy again. I got a few calls to make. I know Baine could handle the street shit. I know it's about to be war in the city behind Griff. Anytime it was war in the city I wanted to stand in the paint with my nigga. Me and Baine have been through it all together. I couldn't leave my nigga in the streets to fend for himself. Fuck this murder charge, it wasn't going down like that.

Rashad and Baine never saw eye to eye. With Griff being dead and the police looking for me I knew shit was about to go left. I grabbed my phone to check the cameras in the house to see if Keondra was there. I looked in our bedroom and it was empty. Where the fuck was this lying ass bitch at?

I had cameras installed in our house and I never used them. I rewinded the footage back on the camera from the moment I left the crib. Daisy was tip toeing back upstairs in my room. She climbed in the bed and her and Keondra was rolling around in the covers. I had to sit back and adjust my dick.

The two of them were fuckin' each other without me knowing? Keondra always tried to play like she wasn't into it, but this footage displays something different. I fast forward the cameras to see how long it would last and they were going at it for a minute. Dace walked in. What the fuck was he doing in my bedroom watching Keondra and Daisy fuck? I damn near threw my phone because Daisy let that nigga fuck her raw from the back. I grabbed my phone to call Keondra's lying ass back. She answered on the first ring.

"Yo, where are you?" I asked and yelled. I wanted this bitch to tell a lie so I could spas out. I swear to God if she says she's at home and she's not I'm going to fuckin' hurt her. I just told her what the fuck I had going on in these streets. Now isn't the time to be hardheaded because you're mad at me. Being hard-head will fuck around and get you hurt. Being hardheaded means you're a liability. I can't afford a liability.

"I'm at home Ike," she lied. I love Keondra but I ain't never trusted her. She's too smart to be dumb. I know you're not at home that's why I called you back.

"It's funny you would say that because I'm looking at the cameras and bitch I don't fuckin' see you. I thought you didn't like pussy. It seems like I wasn't the only one fuckin' Daisy? I thought you didn't know shit about her and Dace? I saw the little threesome y'all had when I left. Bitch I swear to God I'm not as dumb as you think I am. If you ever think you could play with me, you better think again. I'm not that nigga and I'll show you that I'm not" I argued.

"Oh, so you're going to kill me as you did with Griff?" She asked. I hung up in her face. I got to tell Baine to keep an eye on that bitch. I don't trust her. She's crossed me twice in one day. I live by the street code and she just violated me in the worse way. I don't give a fuck how you may feel about me, but you won't fuckin' cross me and live to tell about it. If my phone was recorded right now her statement alone just raised a red flag. I feel like she's up to something. I never check the cameras in my house but for some odd reason, something told me to do it. She was the last person to see Daisy and Dace alive and they all had a threesome. If that bitch set that shit up for me to take the fall. I put that shit on my life she won't see me fuckin' coming.

Yes, she's my wife but I'll treat her like one of these mutt ass bitches. I ain't never killed a bitch in my life but I won't hesitate to end her fuckin' life. I swear I would give that bitch my last because I had that much love for her. If she crossed me? I'll take the air she fuckin' breathes. I will treat her like a nigga in these streets because she's playing a dangerous game. The last thing she needs is to be at odds with me. I'm gentle with her, but when it comes to the street ain't shit nice about me.

Keondra

The word had traveled fast about my handy work. I heard the hood was jumping. My phone has been blowing up about the shootout that took place. I've been smiling ever since showing all thirty-two of my pearly whites. I logged into social media and everybody was talking about they couldn't believe Griff was dead. I wanted to comment and say bitch I killed him. I wanted to say long live Griff so fuckin' badly but I didn't. I wanted someone else to do it before I did. I ain't tripping off the hood jumping. Once upon a time everybody and they mammy was laughing and pointing fingers at me when that nigga left me to be with another bitch. I got the last laugh now and I'm the head BITCH in charge. It's a new motherfuckin' sheriff in town. CHECKMATE MOTHERFUCKA. He taught me how to play chess. I'm here to collect all that nigga's wealth. I'm about to cash out. Every bitch that counted me out should've counted me in. I warned him but he didn't take heed.

If Ike ain't felt me before he was about to feel me now. How dare that motherfucka sound more concerned about Daisy than me. He had the audacity. He can dream about that bitch from behind bars. He knew I was fuckin' somebody else. I wanted him to know that. Since he's pulling camera's I wish he would go back three years ago to watch me fuckin' Jacque in our home. I wanted him to hear Jacque's grunts and moans. I'll testify against his motherfuckin' ass in court. He's going to prison for life. I got so much shit on him they'll give him a life sentence. He'll never be able to fuck another bitch. I got a few niggas in the cut who couldn't wait to pound Ike's ass and make Ike their bitch. I don't give a fuck. I'm that bitch he'll love to hate. A nigga can't shit on me and think they'll live to tell about it. I shit on niggas and live to tell about it. I'm that bitch these niggas and bitches love to hate.

As he could see Griff is no longer amongst the land of the living. I hope he didn't think he could fuck me over constantly and live to tell about it. Jacque's face was buried deep between my legs while I was on the phone with Ike. I rode his face as my life depended on it. He didn't want me even talking to him. I couldn't help myself. I wanted to bury my face in the pillows because I couldn't take it. Jacque had a big telephone pole dick. Each time he dug deeper and deeper I swear it felt like air got caught up in my chest. I couldn't breathe I wanted to run.

I'm not tripping off Ike because I have a nigga right now sitting in Dekalb County Jail that's willing to take him out. I got 100k on his head and trust me my shooter is ready to cash out the moment he's in there for 30 days or more. He can be mad all he wants to because I don't give a fuck. I stop caring a long time ago. He never gave two fucks about me. I have zero fucks to give.

"Keondra why are you even entertaining him and getting your blood pressure high and you're pregnant with my son? Don't let that nigga bait you. He knows something. Emotions will fuck up everything we just did. If you can't take your emotions out of it, I got to leave you alone sweetheart because I value my life too much. I want to raise Jackie and see my baby girl reach the age of 18. Don't reach for a nigga if he ain't reaching for you.

If you think that shit we did was crazy Keondra, baby girl, you don't want to see me go to war with Ike and Baine and Griff's niggas. I swear to God shorty, this ain't my city but for my life and the child you're carrying I will set this bitch off. These country ass niggas don't want to go war with me. I'm from Brooklyn, New York ma, we get at niggas in the worst fuckin way possible. Remember he hired me to be his muscle? I ain't saying those niggas are pussy because anybody can get touched. It ain't no bitch in me. I play that shit safe because the way you're going about things will bring a lot of heat that you can't handle. If you keep this up, I'll love you from afar and I'll take my son from you and send him to New York so my mother can raise him." He argued. I looked at Jacque like he was crazy. He wasn't taking my son anywhere so another bitch could playhouse with him. He got me fucked up.

"What the fuck is that supposed to mean Jacque? You're trying to leave me too? I can't let him talk to me any kind of way," I cried. I understood everything he was saying. Fuck, Ike, I'm not sparing his feelings because he never spared mine. I love him with all my heart. What about our son he didn't mention him at all? Jacque and I never had an argument like this before. I knew he wanted me to leave Ike alone and I did. I haven't fucked him in months. I won't even let him touch me without a condom. The only thing he can do is to let me sit on his face. I hate lying next to my husband. I haven't been happy with Ike in years.

"You heard what the fuck I said? Do you think I want to leave you? What the fuck did we do all this for? You can't move like that. Its suspect and you're his wife true enough, but at least act like you care until he's behind fuckin' bars. Divorce Ike like I told you to do and you won't have anything to worry about. I don't want to leave you but don't force my hand baiting this nigga. Keondra, I love you and trust me if I didn't, I wouldn't have done any of this shit with you. I need you to trust me. I trust you enough to do this for you. Do what the fuck I say do and we can get far in life. You have a problem listening. I'm not those niggas that you're used to dealing with." He argued and raised up out of our bed. He grabbed his shirt off the chase and put it back on. I jumped up and ran behind him. I grabbed his arms and he pushed me up off him. "Move Keondra," he argued and raised his voice. I jumped because he has never talked to me like that.

"Baby why are you doing this to me and I'm pregnant with your child? I made one mistake Jacque. I love you and I'm sorry. If you leave me now when I need you the most, it proves that you're no better than the niggas I was dealing with. I swear I thought you were different. I was a fool for you. I've risked my life and my fucked-up marriage for you. Who would've known it'll only take one little thing for me to lose you?" I cried. I couldn't stop my tears from falling even if I wanted too. I never thought Jacque could hurt me or treat me this way. I folded my arms across my chest. Tears were running down my face. My heart was beating so fast. Who would've known today might be Jacque and I's last? He let Ike ruin our moment. It's a celebration and we're supposed to be celebrating. Not fussing, fighting, or shit that shouldn't even matter to us. Ike and Griff are history. Jacque and I should've been making new memories.

"I ain't shit like them niggas and you know that shorty. I'm a different fuckin' breed don't ever compare me to those niggas. Just because we're having a disagreement don't do that because I ain't compared you to a bitch I used to fuck with. It ain't no fuckin' comparison. You ain't crying because of me. You're crying because I'm keeping it real with you. I ain't got to cheat on you or do none of that shit. I ain't never fucked another bitch in front you. You don't even know how I much fuckin' love you? I love you, but I'll let you go Keondra, and you can do you. I'll take my son and keep it moving. You got to do shit my way and let me lead or I'm out?" He argued. I'm confused as to where this is coming from. All I've been doing is letting him lead. I've been submissive as fuck to him. He's in his feelings because I answered the phone while he was pleasing me.

"You can leave Jacque I'm not gone beg you to stay," I cried. He walked up on me and cupped my chin. I swatted his hands away. "Move since you want to leave. There's the door since you want to go so bad. It's a problem that I'm defending myself. It's funny you want to leave me how you met me, slumped over after you made love to me and now crying," I cried. I swear to God I love that man with all my heart. I didn't even think I had a heart until I met him. I ain't never loved a man the way I love Jacque. He gets me and he understands me. Why the fuck is he doing this to me? I felt myself getting sick. I ran to the bathroom and threw up.

"Why are you pushing me away? I'm a man baby and it's my job to lead. I swear Keondra, I want to take you to some places that you've never been to before. We got to do it my way and not your way or it'll never work. If by chance this shit comes back to bite you in the ass; it's gone be me that puts my life on the line for you and my son. I need you to think about that. I'm your muscle. I got your front and your back, but I can't if you won't let me lead. I can't do this with you if you're refusing to listen to me. So, what's it going to be?" He asked. Jacque was serious. I could tell he was tired of my shit. I wanted this relationship to work. I'll try things his way for the sake of our unborn and my sanity. He was my future. You know they say the third time a charm. I couldn't wait to rock his last name.

"I'll let you lead," I cried. He pulled me into his arms and cupped my chin. I wrapped my arms around him. He kissed me and my heart started beating. I couldn't take him being mad at me. I ain't never loved nan nigga how I loved Jacque. More of the reason why I need to send the police to Ike's location so they can get the state of Florida to extradite him. I'm ready to start my new life and put this bullshit behind me.

I want to give my son the two-parent home I never had. I cut the shower on. I needed to take a hot shower and clear my mind. Today starts a new day for the rest of my life. Jacque and I are embarking on a new journey and nobody's coming in between that. I had a lot of shit on my mind. Despite what people may think, I loved Griff. We just couldn't co-exist in the same world with each other and we weren't together. I was still madly in love with him. If I couldn't have him it's not a bitch walking that could.

I tried that shit and it didn't work. Crimson had everything that I couldn't give him. He had to go. Everywhere I went Crimson and Griff were always there. He would dote on her like she was so perfect. It irked my fuckin' soul, so I had to take his. His life was perfect with her and I hated that shit. Being with Ike did nothing for me.

I felt Jacque push up behind me. I looked over my shoulder and smiled at him. My head was up under the shower because I needed to wash my hair. Jacque and I were both smiling at each other. I couldn't think of the right words to say. I guess just wanted to take each other in for a minute. I couldn't think of the last time I was able to sleep with him after 4:00 p.m. Since I've been pregnant my hair has grown out so much. My hair touched my shoulders. Jacque yanked my hair back and I gazed up at him and he shoved his tongue down my throat. He was so rough and aggressive with me. He pressed my body up against the shower, forced my hands above my head, and lifted my right leg up. Jacque found my hole and started pounding away at my pussy. I look back at him and smiled. The only sounds you could hear were the sounds of my pussy and water pouring from the shower. I loved being with Jacque. I wasn't anywhere near ready for another round. My pussy was still sore from earlier. I just wanted to lay on his chest and listen to his heartbeat. So much to that.

“You better stop fuckin’ playing with me!” He yelled. I had plans too. He grabbed my loofa and started washing me up. I swear his touch alone soothes me. Being with Jacque is everything to me. I love everything about him. I love how he loves me. “I know you hear me talking to you!” He yelled.

“I hear you and I’m listening. Jacque Fenson. I love you and I don’t want to lose you. I’m willing to play the back and let you lead. Promise me you’ll never hurt me or leave me.”

“I’ll promise you that and more Keondra. Don’t use my government name unless you mean it.”

Chapter-3

Baine

DAmn, shit is looking real crazy out here in these streets. I can't seem to wrap my mind around this shit. Griff and I grew up together. Our fathers were best friends. He wasn't my right man hand, but he was my day one. We were raised as brothers we don't do business together anymore after my father died. We still see each other from time to time because of Danielle and Crimson. I'm caught up because Ike is my best friend and my partner. I know he didn't do that shit, but it looks bad on all levels.

I know how Rashad gives it up and I'll have to fuck around and kill that nigga based off some shit that Ike didn't do. I don't know if I should speak with him first to let it be known Ike didn't do that shit. I can account for his time. To make matters worse, they found a key of coke in the whip. I know how muthafuckas talk so, it'll only be a matter of time before they mention my fuckin' name. I got to holla at Auntie Kaye and Maria before I leave. I owe them that much because Auntie Kaye raised us and I'm here for them. They're my family. Who would set up Ike? We don't have any enemies that I know of. Speaking of Ike, he's calling my phone now. Let me see what's up with him.

“Yo, what's good?” I asked. I hope Ike wasn't calling me back to tell me that he was on his way. I swear that nigga didn't like to listen. He's always a loose fuckin' canon.

“Listen man keep an eye on Keondra she's moving a little funny. I checked the cameras at my house. She was lying like she was at home and she wasn't. I checked the cameras and rewind the footage. She, Daisy, and Dace were having a threesome. It's funny as fuck she’s alive and everybody else is dead except her. You know what she had the nerve to say I killed Griff,” he argued. I had to pull my ear away from the phone. I can't believe any of this shit. I told Ike not to marry that bitch because she was for everybody, but he didn't want to listen. You can't save a hoe nor turn her into a housewife. He didn’t want to listen.

“I hope you're fuckin' lying? I know she wasn't that reckless?” Keondra was an undercover hoe. She tried to throw the pussy at me on numerous occasions before she got with Ike. I knew she was bad news that's why I never pursued her. I was surprised Griff married her. I could never fuck with her off the strength they had some shit going on in the past.

I didn't even like the way she looked at me. Everything about her screamed snake and foul. I don't give a fuck how fine she is. I saw right through that shit.

"I ain't got no reason too. I swear to God Baine when I called her it sounded like she was fuckin. I'm in the process of being jammed up behind some shit that I didn't do and she's fuckin' off and doesn't give a fuck," he argued. Ike loved Keondra but was he in love with her? I don't think so, but he couldn't stop fuckin' off on her. Keondra wasn't in love with him. I never saw it. She was in love with his fuckin' money and street status, that's it.

"I'll put Murda and Beene on her to see what the fuck she's up too" Ike and I finished chopping it up. I hope Keondra ain't moving funny because I'll murk her ass behind my nigga and I put that shit on me. She'll never have the upper hand of having our empire crumble. Bitches came a dime a dozen. I swear to God she'll wish she never crossed a nigga like me. I'm not sparing a bitch when it comes to my fuckin' MONEY. She's costing me MONEY. We just closed a major deal that was liable to make us fuckin' billionaires. See we can't even touch that shit now because they're looking for Ike. He's wanted for murder. One that he didn't fuckin' commit.

I know Danielle is going to trip when I tell her I got to go out of town for a few days. Truth be told I don’t even want to leave but I got to handle this business so she can continue to spend our money however she likes. She was already tripping hard this morning about me riding with Ike. I didn’t leave because I didn’t want her mad at me. Happy wife happy life. I wanted to leave before she made it home. I heard her heels click on the marble floors. I walked up on her and swooped her in my arms and held her. I love Danielle with all my heart. My wife is everything to me.

“Damn baby I missed you.” I kissed on her neck and inhaled her scent. She always smelled so fuckin' good. My wife was beautiful as fuck. I give Danielle the world and if I couldn't I would die trying. I swear I didn't want to leave this for a few days.

We ain’t never apart and making trips out of town wasn’t some shit that I was trying to start. I've fallen back from the streets a lot. I want a few shorty’s running around.

“I missed you too baby,” she cooed. I had a wife. Danielle wasn't a gold digger. She was a fuckin' boss and whatever she says go.

“Nah baby I think I missed you more” I bit the crook of her neck and lifted her skirt up. I wanted to feel my pussy before I dipped out for a few days. “I want to go half on a baby. It's time.” I bit her ear. I had Danielle right where I wanted her.

“Stop baby. I want to make a few babies too. What do you want for dinner,” she moaned and asked. Normally I would be down for whatever Danielle wanted to cook for me, but I can’t even focus on eating because of the shit that’s going on heavy out here in the streets. I know my nigga Ike didn’t do that shit. It’s up to me to prove his innocence. I know Rashad and just because of our past he’s going to insist that he did do that shit. We don’t get down like that. Despite whatever issues we had I ain’t never wished bad on Griff or wanted to see him go out on some sucker free shit. I slid my dick in Danielle's pussy. It was always wet and warm. The moment I dived in it sucked me in and gripped me.

“Baine do you hear me. What do you want for dinner,” she asked and moaned? Dinner is the last thing that’s on my mind. I couldn’t eat if I wanted too.

“Danielle, I don't have an appetite” I continued beating up the pussy. Danielle tried to move from my embrace. My hands were rested on her hips so she wouldn't move. I wasn't about to pull out or stop what I was doing until I busted a nut. I needed to get this motherfucka off right now.

"Move Baine. Since when you don't have an appetite?" She argued. I wasn't even trying to hear it. I busted my nut and pulled out. Danielle grabbed my beard forcing me to look at her. I shoved my tongue down her throat. I knew she was about to go in. No matter how hard I busted my ass in these streets. I always made time for my wife. Every night we had dinner whether it was her cooking or me cooking for her.

"Come here and sit down. I got holla at you for a minute." I explained. Danielle knew me better than I knew myself. She knew something was up. I swear this is one of the hardest things I'll ever have to do in my life. I hate to even repeat these words. Danielle should hear this from Crimson, not from me. I'm her husband and it's a must that she gets nothing but honesty from me. She was looking at me with pleading eyes. She probably thinks I cheated or some shit. It ain't bitch walking that could make me cheat on my wife. Ain't nan bitch worth it when it comes to Danielle Mahone.

“Baby what's wrong?” She asked. She really didn’t want to know the answer to her question. I feel bad for Griff’s kids’ man. Cariuna and Camina are Danielle’s Goddaughters but I rather her hear it from me than someone else. The last thing I wanted was for my wife to think I got some side shit going on behind her back. I don’t move like that.

“A lot. I don't even want to tell you this shit right now but listen to me because I'll never lie to you. My word is the only thing I'll stand on” I explained. Danielle gave me a crazy look. I knew she was about to snap.

“Baine what are you saying? You're scaring me right now. I don't know who should be more afraid; me or you? You're talking in circles” She argued. I don’t want to tell my wife this shit, but I had too, there are no secrets between us. I’ll never tell my wife a lie or leave her in the blind about anything. My wife knew all about my life in the streets and if something was to happen to me, she would know how to move accordingly. It’s important that I let her know what’s going on. I always needed my wife to protect herself if I’m not around.

“Some shit went down today in your hood. Word is Griff got killed and somebody framed Ike to do it” Danielle cut eyes at me and turned her face up. She pointed her index finger at me. She backed up away from me as if I disgusted her. I closed the gap between us. I held her in place. Tears poured down her eyes. I hated to see my baby upset and cry. Especially behind some shit, they're trying to accuse my nigga of. I held her in place so she wouldn't move.

"Baine please tell me this is a lie and a bad fuckin' dream? You wouldn't lie to me baby, would you? You wouldn't fuck up our family, would you? My heart hurt so badly if this is true for Crimson and my babies. I got to go check on my best friend. Ike didn't do it swear to God Baine, put it on your father," she argued and cried? Danielle started shaking she wasn't in any position to go check on Crimson. I couldn't leave the city because my wife was a mess.

"I swear baby, Ike was in Jacksonville. Remember I was supposed to go out there with him this morning. Somebody set my nigga up. I'm about to head down there with him after I make sure you're straight. I need to go speak with Maria and Auntie Kaye. I need to speak with Rashad and let him know Ike didn't do that shit." I argued. This shit hits close to home in more ways than one.

"Baby I don't want you to leave me. Baine your word is the only thing that I'll stand on. I believe you because if you ever lied to me you know off the top that you'll lose me. Ike's your best friend and if he's innocent stand by him. You got to promise me that you'll make it back home to me? Baine, when I pray for love baby, I pray for us," she cried. I don't want my wife crying or doubting anything that I've said whoever killed Griff. I want them muthafuckas dead.

"Baby I'm not going nowhere. We can weather any storm. I'm going to hold you down forever. This shit that's going on ain't got nothing to do with us. Every breath I take baby I'll always fight for us. It ain't a motherfucka breathing that's going to come in between us. I mean it, Danielle Mahone. It's all about us" I explained. I carried Danielle upstairs to our room. She wasn't in any position to cook tonight. I ordered some food. I'll check on Ike the first thing in the morning. My wife comes before anything.

♡

Our food finally came. We ate and I ran Danielle a nice hot long bubble bath. My wife was all over the place. I held her until she fell asleep. After Danielle went to sleep. I whispered in her ear that I was making a run to see Auntie

Kaye. She threw her arms around my neck and told me to be careful and make it back home to her. I leaned and kissed her. Nothing was stopping me from making it back home to her. My wife is my fuckin' energy

I threw on my clothes to go speak with Auntie Kaye and Maria. I hope this shit is a lie. I had Skull to check out Keondra. He hit me up and said that Keondra hasn't been there all day. The Sheriff has been posted up at Ike's waiting to arrest him. Why the fuck isn't she at home. By her and Ike not being at home it makes shit looks suspect. Where the fuck was she at? I need to keep tabs on this bitch because something isn't adding up.

I finally made it over to Auntie Kaye's house. Cars were wrapped around the block. I parked in the yard. I grabbed my piece out the car and tucked it behind my back. Rashad was here so that I could speak with him. As soon as I walked up to the driveway a few of Griff and Rashad's workers were outside on the porch grilling me. I swear these young niggas don't want any fuckin' smoke.

I ain't crazy. I knew them niggas wanted to touch me, but if they did, they'd get touched too. I opened the door to Auntie Kaye's and she was in tears. Rashad looked at me and pulled his gun out. I reached behind my back and grabbed my piece. I made a promise to my wife that I was making it back home and I'll dead this nigga here before I break any promise to Danielle.

"Damn I knew I was gone kill you, but I never thought you were dumb enough to come see me my nigga? This is the last place you should be after the fuck moves your boy pulled today. It's an eye for an eye. Ike caught a body and it's only right I catch yours. I'll drop you right here where the fuck you stand my nigga" He argued. I wasn't threatened by Rashad. It is was it is. I wasn't dying today. If he wanted gunplay, we can shoot it out in this bitch today.

"I'm not a sucka and far from a motherfuckin buster. I know you mad and you have every right to be. I'm not that nigga. You better be careful before you pull that fuckin' trigger. Trust me I won't be the only nigga leaving this world today. I didn't come here for this shit at all. Everything ain't what it, seems" I argued. Auntie Kaye and Maria came in between us. "If he wants to shoot it out, we can but it ain't gone solve shit. We got bigger shit out here that needs to be resolved"

"Rashad don't do that here. Now isn't the time. I got enough shit going on. Baine is family too I can't bear to lose someone else today," she cried. I pulled Auntie Kaye in my arms and Rashad grilled me. I don't give a fuck about the mean mugs or the animosity. Griff is my nigga too and I'll never let one of my niggas touch him. I ain't never give the okay for that. Auntie Kaye broke down in my arms, this shit is fucking with me.

"Auntie Kaye I don't give a fuck, he's responsible for Griff's murder. I don't give a fuck how you may feel about this nigga right here but it's not a nigga walking that could live to say they took my nigga out and I didn't do shit. Wherever I catch him is where I'm going to lay him at," he argued. Rashad cocked his gun back. I heard enough. I'll never let him get the upper hand. I pushed Auntie Kaye behind me.

"Rashad, I don't give a fuck how you may feel about me, but it's not going down like that. Griff was my nigga since the sandbox. We ain't got no fuckin' beef with y'all? If we did do you think I would be here? Somebody set Ike up, he didn't kill Griff.

He's been in Jacksonville since this morning. He didn't do that shit. That's why I'm here. Somebody set him up and Griff in the process." I argued. I grabbed my phone to call Ike. I put him on speaker phone. In all my years of living, I ain't never had to prove shit to nan nigga. Rashad knew we didn't have any beef. We didn't have a reason to get at Griff. Everybody was eating.

"What's up are you on your way?" He asked. I knew Ike was waiting on me and I'm coming but I had to handle this shit first. I don't need a nigga on our backs behind some shit we didn't do.

"Not yet, tomorrow. I had to make sure my WIFE was straight. I'm over here at Auntie Kaye's. Rashad is right here and your on-speaker phone. Clear your name." Ike was explaining himself. We don't have a reason to lie. I heard Rashad mumble some shit under his breath when I mentioned my wife's name. I smiled at him. Danielle Mahone, that's all fuckin' me when you see her in the streets.

"Come on Rashad yeah that's my whip and I was fuckin' Daisy. She was pregnant with my seed. I never wanted to see shawty go out like that. A key was left in the whip. Whoever did this was trying to take me out too. I was on my way back to Atlanta to clear my name, but Baine told me to stand down. Whoever did this y'all two better find them before I do because that's the only fuckin' murder charge I'm catching, and I'll gladly plead guilty to it for the motherfucka that set me up." He argued.

Auntie Kaye wrapped her arms around me. She damn near raised me and Griff together. I never wanted to see my nigga down bad or lying in a casket. Griff was smart ass nigga. He had eyes everywhere. He always moved like a boss the same way our fathers raised us too. I just hope in this case he had the upper hand and was somewhere lying low. If not, I was for damn sure going to carry my nigga and make sure his kids and Crimson were straight.

"Thank you, Baine. I felt it in my heart y'all didn't have anything to do with this. Please find who did this. I want their head on a platter. You and Rashad can team up," she cried and explained. I looked Auntie Kaye like she was crazy I know she meant well but Rashad and I could never work together.

"I'll find out who did it, Auntie Kaye. I don't need any fuckin' help. For his sake and not mine, Ike's better be solid or else I'm going to make this motherfucka clap"

"Stop crying, Auntie Kaye. Whoever did this I'll find them. Make no mistake about it. Rashad doesn't want to work with me and I ain't tripping. I don't take threats lightly. I'll be back through here in a few days." I wasn't working with Rashad. I know he still wanted my wife and that's the real issue. I'm willing to die behind mine. Danielle ain't up for grabs. I laughed at that nigga on my way out.

♡

I made it home to my wife and she was still in bed sleeping peacefully. I pulled the covers back and she was naked as the day she was born. I had to suck on that pussy a few times and make her cum before I hit the road to get up with Ike. I felt her hands run through my hair. Danielle's hands roamed my chest. The tips of her manicured nail sent chills through my body. My dick got hard instantly. I was ready to murder the tight pink wet pussy between her legs.

"Baby I want to feel you," she moaned. Danielle wasn't talking about shit. I wanted to feel her too. I raised up and found her hole. She tugged at my beard. I leaned in and gave her a kiss while stroking her long and deep.

"Slow down baby," she moaned.

"You said you wanted to feel me, so I want you too. I want a kid Danielle we're ready," I grunted.

“I'm ready Mr. Mahone,” she moaned and bit her bottom lip. I never fucked my wife. I always made love to her. I've been in the game for a long time. It's time for me to give this shit up and pass it to my young niggas. I'm ready to have a few kids. I have so much money Danielle can't even spend it all. I'm tired of hustling. I'm blessed to still be alive and able to get out.

Rashad

I've been sitting in front of the trap for about an hour now rocking back and forth. My mind is blown. Dirty sprite is filled to the brim of my Styrofoam cup. I'm not in the right state of mind. I swear to God I'm about to set it off behind my nigga. I don't believe my nigga went out like that; without taking a few pussy ass niggas with him. A motherfucka better tell me something. We got motherfuckin' hitters. I always got eyes on Griff and that nigga got eyes on me. Griff is a paid nigga. Better yet he's a made nigga. How the fuck did Ike catch my nigga and he was that fuckin' sloppy? Dekalb County had the block hot as fuck.

I couldn't even go up there to console Auntie Kaye and Maria. They kept calling my phone, but I refused to answer. I couldn't be front and center on some shit that was supposed to be where they got at Griff. I refused to believe that's him. My partner was a good nigga. Griff being dead ain't my fuckin' reality. If a nigga screamed Long Live Griff, it was lights out. I had to get my shit together because I knew the cops were coming. They found a key of dope on the crime scene and they knew more drugs were near. The last thing I needed was for them to come snooping down here asking questions. How the fuck did Ike kill my nigga and left a brick in the car?

They'll swear it's drug-related and start looking at everybody. I had to find a way to move all this work because trust me the next stop Dekalb County was coming here. I called up my partner Sphinx at Baptiste Funeral home. I needed the Trap God to send his people down here to move this shit to my warehouse out in Ellenwood. He said he was on his way. Nothing was going or coming from Columbia Drive or Glenwood. It was the only way I couldn't get cased up.

This trap house right here ran damn near a million a day. What the fuck am I supposed to tell my Goddaughters. Their father is never going back home. Baine got to see me behind this shit. I swear to God I'm going to bury that nigga. I ain't never trusted that nigga. Its motherfuckin' personal this time. I'm coming for everything that he took for me even DANIELLE. She better pick a side. It's loyalty over royalty.

Danielle

My mind is in a million places. I can't sleep. How could I? I can't even think straight. I don't know what to believe. My husband and I have a bond that could never be broken. We don't lie to each other at all. There are no secrets between us. I know all of Baine and Ike's enemies and Griff wasn't one of them. Crimson hasn't called me, so I don't think it's true. I prayed to God it wasn't because my heart wouldn't be able to take it.

Griff was a good man for real. I can vouch for that. Crimson loved her some Carius Deon Griffey. I was always team them. I kept checking my phone. I didn't have any missed calls from her. I didn't want to be the barrier of bad news. I prayed it wasn't true. I feel like I'm in the middle because of my husband and his best friend. I love my husband, but I'll choose Crimson any day over my husband.

I love Baine with all my heart and everything in me. Crimson is everything to me. Baine could leave today, and she'll still be here. My husband isn't a liar. I believed him when he said that Ike didn't do that. The moment Baine left the house I was scared. If Griff really was dead and they didn't have the person that did it. I knew Rashad would come for him.

The last thing I need is for the two of them to be at each other's head because of accusations. I wouldn't know what to do if I lost Baine at the hands of Rashad. I would be livid. That's why I'm praying it's just a rumor about Griff. I didn't want Baine to leave because I feared for his safety. I know my husband could handle his. I just know how the streets are and Rashad. Who would frame Ike to kill Griff?

"Go to sleep Danielle," he yawned.

"I can't Baine. I've tried," I sighed. He picked me up and laid me on his chest. He lifted my chin and kissed me on my lips.

"Get some rest baby and stop stressing. I got you and I'm not going anywhere. I'm going to shoot out to Jacksonville in the morning, but I promise I'll be back home before you come home. If shit changes than I'll fly you out here with me for a few days"

"It sounds good Baine but if this is true, I got to be there for Crimson and my babies"

Chapter-4

Rashad

I don't know what to believe, but I know I don't trust those niggas. I don’t believe my nigga didn’t catch a body in the process. I don't give a fuck about any of that shit Baine and Ike are spitting. Their word isn't law to me. I don’t abide by that shit. In Griff, I trust that’s the only nigga that could carry me. I’m the only nigga that could carry him. I don’t fuck with those niggas. They ain’t never been my niggas. I don’t give a fuck about that sandbox shit. He wasn’t playing in the sand with me and Griff. He better be glad Auntie Kaye was here or else I would've dropped that nigga dead in her fuckin' living room.

The moment that nigga pulled up to Auntie Kaye's house my shooters sent the G-code to my phone asking me for the okay to light Baine's ass up. I told them to stand down because I wanted to know what he had to say. I owed Baine a bullet anyway. If anybody was to kill him it was going to be me. His WIFE. He said that shit to get up under my skin, and he did. I can’t believe Danielle really married that nigga. I couldn't trip though because that's what she wanted but she couldn't be in the same room with me?

The only thing that made sense was that they wouldn't leave a key of dope in the car. We got our work from the same place. The only difference was ours was packaged differently. Whoever set that up was close to them. Griff didn't beef with niggas. It's crazy for a motherfucka to get at him without him knowing. Whoever it was had been watching him. They knew and studied how we moved. I've been calling Crimson all day and she hasn't answered. I must go check on her and my girls. Griff kept the streets away from Crimson. She knew nothing about what we were involved in. All she knew that it was illegal.

It'll be a long time before I get some sleep. I'll sleep when I'm dead. Sleep wouldn't consume me until I find out what the fuck happened to my partner? I swear to God this shit doesn't seem real. We were supposed to finally get fitted for our tuxes this weekend. My nigga was finally about to jump the broom and say I DO. A pussy ass motherfucka took that from him. I hit up our partner Wire. He handled all our surveillance tapes for every trap.

I needed the footage for the past two months. Ain't no way in hell a motherfucka is going to pull that shit off without me touching them. A dead man can't talk but the motherfucka that did it would be bragging about knocking off a made man. I'll be the motherfucka bragging about ending that pussy ass motherfucka that thought he could live to tell about it. Slap, Wire, and True are supposed to meet me at the spot in a few minutes. My mother had my son. I had to go see him. I'll be in the streets heavy until I get justice, STREET JUSTICE for mine. I'll take him to school in the morning. My young nigga loves to see me before he starts his day.

He hates staying the night over there. I had to see my lil baby Mya before I head over to the spot to see what's up. She's been checking on me all day to make sure I was straight. Mya was my lil baby. She wanted me to commit and leave the streets alone. I would in due time. She was mine and she knew it. I don't know why she wanted me to put a title on it. What's understood doesn't need to be explained.

My mother sent me a text and told me that my son was already asleep. I didn't want to wake him up because he would be asking me to take him home. I couldn't take him home. It's some real shit going on out here in these streets. He couldn't be with me right now. My mother's house was the only place he needed to be. I called Mya and she answered on the first ring.

"Hey Rashad, what's up, how are you," she cooed in the phone. I swear I love the way she says my name. Mya was always checking up on a nigga to make sure I was straight. I had feelings for shorty. I can't even lie. I had to get my shit together because I knew she was tired of waiting for me. I didn't want to miss out on my good thing waiting for someone else.

"I'm good. I appreciate you for checking up on a nigga. I'm about to pull up on you in a few. Unlock the door." I chuckled. I knew she was about to trip. I did it to fuck with her. I don't know why she didn't want to give me a key. I was the only nigga she was fuckin' anyway. I paid all her bills. Whatever she wanted I handled that for her.

"I'm not leaving my door unlocked. I'll put the key under the mat. Just in case you're not here by the time I'm asleep. Have you eaten yet Rashad? If not, I'll put you a plate in the oven" She sassed and sighed. Mya did all the right shit. I had no complaints. She was wifey material for real. I had mad feelings for her. It was time for a nigga to stop playing around.

"Mya I'm on my way don't go to sleep on me lil baby. You know I didn't eat. The only thing I want to eat is that juicy pussy sitting between your legs." I knew she was going to wait up on me. She always does but if she didn't, she knew I was waking her up with some head. Mya had the drip for real.

"Stop calling me baby Rashad. I'll try to wait up on you but I'm not making any promises. I can't allow you to do that because sex complicates things. If that's what you're coming by for, go home. I'm glad you're safe. I can't keep doing this shit with you." She sighed.

"Why I can't call you baby? You know you mine Mya. Why you are tripping? You belong to me. It ain't shit you can say that can change that," I argued.

"Rashad you heard what I said. I want to be your baby but you ain't ready for that. In order for me to your baby, we would have to be together and we're not. Your words, not mine and I'm cool with that. I accepted that years ago. If we're not together then we shouldn't even be fuckin'. I'm practicing celibacy. I'm not fuckin' a man that I'm not with. I don't even want you to suck on me if we're not together," she argued. Mya was tripping for real. The last thing I needed was to be at odds with her. I had enough shit going on out here in these streets. Mya and my son were my peace away from the bullshit and I wanted to keep it that.

"Mya, are we really going there? Who do you think we're about to be fuckin'?" I argued. Mya knew better than to ever give my pussy away. She wasn't crazy. She knew I was a reckless ass nigga. Ain't shit changed.

"Get here and if I'm up we'll talk later," she sassed and hung up the phone. Mya was tripping hard and that's the last thing I needed. I knew she was in her feelings. I'll deal with her later. I got what she wants. I just need her to be a little more patient with me. She has been patient with me. She deserves more than what I'm giving her. I planned on giving it to her. She's been holding me down for a minute.

The money wasn't enough. She wanted time and me. It's hard for me to juggle the streets and make time for her. It's about to be hectic if Griff was gone everything is on me. I refused to replace my right-hand man, that's a position that could never be filled.

♡

I finally made it to Mya's house. I checked under the mat and the key was there like she said it would be. Whatever Mya cooked smelled good as fuck. I didn't have an appetite though. Murder was on my mind and this little bull shit Mya was spitting had a nigga tripping. I headed upstairs to her room. Her light was on and she was reading her kindle. I politely snatched the kindle out of her hand. I hated when she would read those books. She was more into the books than me. I would always be catching her smiling and shit. Every week she had a new book bae. The fuck is a book bae? I'm her bae. I was the only bae she needed. As much as she reads, she needs to write a book about us.

"Stop Rashad, I was reading that." She sassed and sucked her teeth. She folded her arms across her chest. I didn't give a fuck about her being mad. It's our time now. Her book could wait.

"You're always reading. I came over here for you to read me." She was naked as the day she was born. Her nipples were erect begging me to suck them. I couldn't wait too. She knew to put that kindle up when I was coming over. I stripped out of my clothes. I pulled Mya to the edge of the bed and hovered over her. I bit her bottom lip. I shoved my tongue down her throat. She had an attitude. She wasn't even trying to kiss me back.

I ain't done shit but keep it real. I was breaking down a few walls tonight. She was breathing heavy and trying wiggle from underneath me so I wouldn't play with her pussy. I pried her legs open. I finger fucked her wet. Lil baby came on sight. Her mouth said one thing, but her pussy was singing an entirely different song. I primed that pussy before I murdered it. “Can I eat Mya?” She didn’t say anything.

“Stop Rashad please you’re complicating things,” she moaned. She knew I wasn't about to stop. I put my stamp on this pussy years ago. It's nothing that she could say to make me stop. We’ve been complicated why switch up now?

“I'm here Mya say what you got to say. You ain't about to be fuckin' who if we’re not together,” I asked. I wanted her to repeat that shit. Believe it or not just because we're not together. I wasn't out here fuckin' nobody else but her. She was the only one that got my time. She was the only one I was bussing down for. Whenever I made an appearance she was on my arm. What more did she want? Everybody knew she was special to me. She knew it.

“I said what I had to say. Can you get off me,” she asked.

“Nope, I’m not. We gone talk now. You know I like to beat my pussy up at the edge of the bed. You naked for a reason. You knew I was coming home. You knew the only thing I wanted was you. Why are you tripping Mya? You know what it is between us. I love you and we are gone be together. We are together. Tell me what I got to do to make shit right between us? It ain’t shit that I won’t do for you. I spoil you lil baby and I adore you. Lil baby you got a nigga weak as fuck for you.”

“Rashad, I want more from you. I give you all of me and you only give me half of you. I don’t care about what you do for me because I don’t need it. I can pay my own bills and pamper myself. I can buy a few dildos and fuck myself. I want the real deal. I want the title confirming what we are. How is that fair to me? Do you care if I date someone while I’m waiting for you? I want you to hold me every night and make love to me or fuck me until I fall asleep” She argued.

“Mya what are you saying? You’re talking in circles right now. I know you want more, and I have every intention of giving you more. Lil baby you’re fuckin’ with a real street nigga. I make real gang moves. I'm a crime boss lil baby. I rather keep it real with you then lead you on. Right now, I'm not ready. My best friend might be dead. After I leave here baby, I don't know when I'll see you again, because I'm about to fuck these streets up to find out what the fuck happened to my nigga. I may never come back to you, but for my nigga Mya, I'm gone ride till I fuckin' die. If I die today, it'll be a Trap Holiday.

I live a life of sin and tomorrow ain't promised to a nigga like me. If this would've been last week and my partner would've been alive yeah, I would have given you the title, but I can't do that right now. I'm going to leave Mya because I shouldn't even be here. I got to focus and taking my frustrations out on your pussy right now will complicate things" I raised up off Mya and started putting my clothes back on. I shouldn't even be here. I needed to check on Crimson and my goddaughters. Pussy is the last thing a nigga like me needs right now.

Mya had an attitude and right now I ain't got time for that shit. She grabbed my shoulder and I politely snatched my arm away from her. I'm not pressed for pussy. I could fuck any bitch I wanted but Mya was the only bitch worthy of riding my dick. She had a problem with what we're doing. We ain't got to do this shit no more.

"Rashad don't leave please," she begged. She's making shit complicated. One minute she wants me gone and now she wants me to stay.

"I got to go Mya. I would love to stay lil baby, but I can't. I'll see you when I see you" I kissed Mya on her forehead and dropped her key on the dresser. I liked Mya a lot, but I refused to be forced into another relationship. I'm too deep in these streets to be committed. I rather keep it real than lie and get her hopes up. Some females are used to niggas lying and leading them on but I'm not that nigga.

"Wait Rashad you didn't even eat. I'm sorry" She begged and pouted. Mya gave me pleadings eyes. She was in her feelings now because a nigga was leaving. I wanted to be here, but she didn't want me here, so I had to jugg.

"I'm good. I'll grab me something on my way. What are you sorry for? You didn't do shit but speak on how you feel?"

"I know but I know you're going through some things and I should've been a little more considerate." Mya needed to trust me. I wasn't out in these streets fuckin' off or giving a bitch hope that it could be us. She was the only female besides my mother and Goddaughters that got my time.

"It's cool Mya I'll hit you up tomorrow" It's nothing that she could say to me right now that could make me stay. I was on my way out. Mya grabbed my hand, she backed me up into the base of the door and unbuckled my pants. She wanted this pipe between my legs. If she freed this motherfucka I was for damn sure gone give it to her. Right here and right now.

"What are you doing lil baby. I'm not trying to complicate shit" I explained. She didn't want me to suck on that juicy motherfucka between her legs. I wasn't about to turn down any head.

"I'm giving you something to think about when you're out there in those streets" She sassed. Mya dropped to her knees. She pulled my dick out of my boxers and spat on it. I knew she was about to act a fool. She wrapped her pretty ass lips around my shit. I grabbed her ponytail. I couldn't wait to fuck her face since she was being disrespectful.

Her mouth was wet as fuck. She ran her tongue across the tip playing with me and shit. "Aye stop playing and suck this motherfucka like you got some sense" I argued. I ain't got time for all the extra shit, I got shit to do. If she wanted to fuck and suck on me we could've been doing that.

"Be careful what you ask for Rashad" She sassed. Mya raised her nighty over her head and tossed it on the counter. She bent over and made her ass clap. She pointed her index finger at me telling me to follow her. She grabbed my hand and led me to her bedroom. Mya gave me a devilish smirk. She pushed me on her bed and started undressing me. I knew she was about to go in. I rested my hands behind my head. I swear I'm going to punish her ass for playing games with me. She knew I wanted the pussy and the head. I had to go through all this bullshit to get it.

Mya was stacked like a motherfucka too. Her skin was the color of a chocolate kiss. Her breasts were perfect. Her thighs were thick as fuck too. Her ass sat up like a stallion and I was the only nigga hitting her from the back. I stroked my dick. Mya better stop playing with me. I motioned with my hands for her to get down here and do her fuckin' job. She stood in between my legs and done a split on my dick.

"You're showing out now" I grunted. I smacked her on her ass and she bit her bottom lip. She hopped up off me and her head got lost between my legs. She was teasing the fuck out of me sucking and licking the tip of my dick. I grabbed her hair roughly. I had one hand on her ass cheek. I had a death grip on that fat motherfucka. I started fucking her face. I wanted that ratchet pussy head. She swallowed my dick and felt my dick touch the back of her throat. I tightened my grip on her hair and ass.

I was about bust my kids all down her throat. I felt her gag a little bit, so I eased up. She ran her tongue up and down the vein of my dick. She deep throated me again. She started humming on my shit. I blessed her with all my kids. She raised up went to the bathroom to brush her teeth. I knew what that mouth did. I wanted to feel that pussy all of it. Mya walked out the bathroom and made her way to me.

"Get your ass up here and ride this motherfuckin' dick!" Mya always rode my shit with no fuckin' hands. She always fucked me like a porn star.

Chapter-5

♡

Crimson

I've been tossing and turning all night. For some odd reason, sleep wouldn't consume me. I prayed to God that whatever was stopping me from sleeping would past me by soon. I had an early day tomorrow. These past few days I've been extra tired with school and my clinicals. I knew Carius would wake me up when he made it home. As soon as I fed the girls and gave them a bath I was done. I tried to wait up on him for as long as I could, but it wasn't happening. I would've never gone to sleep if he wasn't home. Anytime I had a problem with sleeping Carius would pick me up and lay me on his chest. If I didn't have a problem sleeping, I would still end up on his chest. I'm wondering why he hasn't done that. As much tossing and turning that I've done I should've been felt him caress me. I patted the spot next to me and it was empty. I jumped up instantly because he wasn't here. I searched the house for him, and he wasn't here. Where the fuck was he? We never go to sleep without each other.

He knows I don't play that shit. I can't even think of the last time the love of my life wasn't lying next to me.

He's not here and he's the reason why I couldn't sleep. He should've been home hours ago. He's always home by 9:00 p.m. no later than 10:00 p.m. I looked at the clock on my nightstand and it's after 1:00 a.m. It just feels like something is wrong. An eerie feeling crept over me. I knew Griff was heavy in the streets. He always kept the streets away from me. Whenever he left the house, I always prayed that he made it back home to us. I grabbed my cell phone off my nightstand. I needed to check and see if I had any missed calls from him and I didn't have anything. I had a ton of missed calls from everybody else. That's what was strange because he would've called me by now to let me know what's going on.

He should've been home by now. I grabbed my phone to call him and he didn't answer. That's not like him not to answer his phone. I dialed his number again and he didn't answer. He got me fucked up. We're about to get married in a few months and now isn't the time to try some new shit on me. Thank God nothing is wrong. He was calling me right back. I answered the phone instantly and started cursing him out instantly. I wasn't even waiting for an explanation.

"Griff do you know what fuckin' time it is? You should've been home by now. It's after 1:00 a.m. What has you so tied up that you can't bring your ass home?" I asked and argued. If I was sleepy before I'm wide awake now. "Say something Griff why aren't you at home and you're breathing all fuckin' heavy?" I screamed praying not to wake my children up.

"Excuse me ma'am this isn't Griff, but this may be his phone? You just called a phone that was found at the crime scene for a victim whose case we're trying to solve." He stated. Victim, what type of crazy shit is going on? I know I didn't dial the wrong number. Who was this and why did they have Griff's phone? What fuckin' crime scene? My heart dropped instantly. I hope Griff isn't in any trouble. I refuse to think the worst so I'm going to pray for the best.

"It must be a mistake sir this is my fiancé's phone, Griff" I sighed. If this was the police, I wasn't about to give them his full name. For all, I knew they could be trying to take him away from his family. I really need to get off this phone and call Rashad.

"Miss, I hate to be the one to tell you this, but Carius Deon Griffey, Daisy Michelle Andrews, and Dace

Ipaye is the name of the victims that were gunned down this afternoon in East Atlanta off Columbia Drive and Glenwood Road. His murder and the others were ruled a homicide and drug-related. His wallet and this phone were left at the crime scene. It's how we were able to identify him," he explained. "Your fiancé, did he have any enemies that you know of? You can come down to identify his body but it's hard to recognize him with the damage that was done"

"What? Gunned down? No this must be a mistake." I cried. Tears flooded my eyes. I couldn't even stop them from falling if I wanted too. I wanted to rip my lashes right off my fuckin' eyes. I wish I could pull my eyes out of its socket. I wish I could stab a knife in my chest. My chest caved in and my knees started to get weak. Please Lord, don't let this be happening to me. Carius Deon Griffey is everything to me. He's the air I breathe and the only person besides my children that completes me. I fell to the floor instantly. The phone slipped from my hand. My heart rate sped up and skipped a few beats. This shit couldn't be happening to me. I stood up and grabbed the phone off the floor beside me.

I ran to the bathroom, cut the faucet on, and filled the Styrofoam cup up with cold water. I threw the water in my face. I looked in the mirror. This had to be a bad dream and now would be the perfect time for me to wake up. I walked into our room and the bed was still empty. My phone was still in my hand and the time on it was still counting. I knew something was wrong but not this. He swore he would never leave me not like this. Who would do this to me and my family?

"Excuse me, is everything okay? Are you still there," he asked. I looked at the phone and ended the call. He called right back, and I cleared him out. He called back again, and I answered the phone.

"Hello," I cried. I couldn't utter another world. I couldn't continue this conversation. Just the thought of living without Griff seems inevitable. I only had two people I could call and that was Rashad and Danielle. I called Danielle first and she answered on the first ring.

"Hello," she answered.

"Danielle, I need you right now" I cried and screamed.

“I’m on my way.” I hung up the phone and called Rashad. He answered on the first ring.

“Rashad, what’s going on? Is it true? Is he gone? Please tell me it’s a lie. Why hasn’t anybody called me? Why did you let them take him from me and my babies?” I cried. “Rashad say something please, tell me it’s a lie” I couldn’t even catch my breath. I started hyperventilating.

“Crimson, I can’t talk over the phone but I’m on my way.” He explained. I got a bad headache. My whole body is shaking. Between my head and my heart aching, I don’t know if I’ll be able to make it until they get here. I’m ready to check out at any giving minute. I can’t live with this nor will I accept this. I can’t live without him. I won’t live without him. My heart beats for him. If his heart stopped today, I want mine to stop too. I don’t know what I’ll do. Oh God, I don’t know what to do. “Cariuna and Camina mommy loves you” Carius why did you leave me alone in this world without you? If you can hear me, baby, you know I love you. Those were the last words I told you. Damn, why did they have to take you? Why couldn’t you stay at home? “Why the streets never loved you, your family needs you” I cried.

Chapter-6

Danielle

My heart hurts so bad for Crimson and my babies. They were about to get married in a few months. She was done and I could hear the pain in her voice. I could feel the pain too. Crimson was my sister. Blood couldn't even make us any closer. I guess it's true, I've been praying that it wasn't true. I prayed so hard and I was hoping that God heard me. I wanted him to keep his hands-on Griff. I guess he needed Griff more than we did. I stayed awake for a reason; this is the reason why I didn't go to sleep. I was waiting on her to call me to confirm if the rumors were true. Without a call, my mind was still in limbo. Baine didn't say anything about what happened when he went over to Auntie Kaye's. I thank God that he made it back home safe.

I couldn't wait to come running and hold Crimson in my arms. We've been through it all together. I don't know how we're going to be able to get through this. I know God will make a way. I don't know what it's like to lose a loved one. I finally mustered up enough strength. I had to be here for my girl. I jumped up out of bed hoping not to wake up Mr. Mahone. He was right on my heels. I grabbed a tracksuit out the closet and threw it on. I felt my husband walk up behind me. He held me in place and I just broke down in his arms. He picked me up and carried me to the bathroom.

"Not now Baine give me a minute. I'm good." I can't believe Griff's gone.

"Stop crying baby I'm not even going to tell you it's going to be okay because it's not. I know you'll have to be there for Crimson. You're supposed too. It's late at night and I can't let you leave this house upset because anything could happen to you. I'm not trying to live this life without you. I know she needs you but you're in no position to drive. Do you want me to drive you?" he asked.

"No, I'm good baby I just had a moment I'll be fine. Get some rest because you have a long day ahead of you." Baine and I both are in a fucked-up position. I know he wanted to be strong for me, but I had to be strong for him too. I had to be strong for Crimson and my babies. I had to get these tears out the way before I even made it over there to her

Rashad

Lord have mercy on my soul. When I catch the motherfucka that put out a hit on my nigga its lights out and I'm wiping out a whole fuckin' bloodline for mine. God can take me now because the pussy ass nigga that did this won't live to tell about it. These past twenty-four hours have been crazy. I got my ears to the streets looking for a lead. My shooters got their feet to the street and their steel in the air. It's about to be real live Guerrilla warfare. It's about to be an early summer. I got nothing but heat for the muthafuckas that took my boy from me.

I should've been at Griff's house hours ago. Mya was making it really hard for a nigga not to leave. I needed to relive all my stress on her. Hearing Crimson cry that shit did something to me. I had to pound my fist in my chest because the thought of losing my best friend was my fuckin' reality. It wasn't a fuckin' mirror image it was the truth. I haven't had time to even look at the footage to see where all roads lead to. I should've been the one to give Crimson the news and not anyone else. That's my fault. Griff knows I'm going to take care of his family like their mine because they are mine.

♡

I finally made it to Griff's spot and there was an Audi A8 in the driveway. Crimson wasn't expecting anyone. I grabbed my piece from behind my back and made sure I had one in the chamber just in case I had to air a motherfucka out for fuckin' with my family. I had a key, so I didn't have to knock. I heard Crimson's cries throughout the house. I made my way upstairs. I checked on my goddaughters and they were still asleep. I heard the cries coming from Crimson and Griff's room. I made my way in there and Danielle was holding her. Danielle and I locked eyes with each other. She tapped Crimson on her shoulder. Crimson looked up at me and started crying even harder. I swear to God her fuckin' tears broke me. Danielle held her and rubbed her back.

"Why him Rashad? Why did somebody have to take his life? Griff doesn't bother any fuckin' body. What the fuck am I supposed to tell my kids?" She argued and cried.

"Crimson I can't give you the whys right now but just know the motherfucka that touched him gone die behind him. I got y'all. Never question that it ain't nothing in this world that I wouldn't do for him or you. I got you and we're going to get justice. I can guarantee you that. If I gotta kill wives, and all associates, I don't give a fuck," I argued. My eyes were trained on Danielle. She was giving me evil glares. I meant what the fuck I said too. She's not excluded because she's guilty by association. I guess she didn't tell Crimson that fuck niggas best friend was the suspect and he's on the run. Yeah, I heard everything Ike said but I don't believe that shit. A nigga will say anything to keep the heat off they ass. It took everything in me not to murder Baine in Auntie Kaye's tonight. I wonder how Crimson found out.

"Who done it, Rashad? I know you know something?" She cried and asked. Danielle gave me pleading eyes. I wasn't about to lie to Crimson. I'm going to keep it real with her.

"Crimson they said Ike did it, but I spoke with Baine and Ike said somebody set him up," I explained. Crimson turned around to face Danielle to search her face for a lie.

"Danielle, you knew Griff was dead this whole time and didn't say anything to me or call me? Ike? What does he have against Griff? Who would set him up?" She argued and asked.

"Crimson don't do that. I heard it but I didn't believe it was true. I prayed to God that it wasn't true. I was waiting for you to give me the call. I wasn't about to call you with bad news if it wasn't true. I'm here now that's all that matters and I'm not going anywhere. Trust me if Baine and Ike had anything to do with that. Our MARRIAGE would be a wrap. He knows that. My loyalty lies with you. Niggas come and go especially FUCK NIGGAS. I NEVER HAD A PROBLEM WITH REPLACING ANYBODY. I don't take threats lightly for my husband. I'm going to fuckin' ride and let that clip loose if need be," Danielle argued. She kept her eyes trained on me.

"Danielle and Rashad, you should've both told me. I would've rather heard it from you than the police," she cried.

"I'm sorry. Stop crying Crimson you're going to make yourself sick. Please. My husband and I got you and the kids. Never question that. I'm going to make some tea. Danielle got up and headed toward the kitchen. I was right on her heels. I don't give a fuck about all that tough ass shit she's talking.

I hurt her ass and be ready to kill that bitch ass motherfucka she's married too. I want a reason to kill him and she's the reason. Danielle grabbed the tea kettle and as soon as she knelt. I wrapped her my hand around her throat. I knelt and whispered in her ear.

"You better tread lightly with me, because I'm not that nigga. Your husband will be lying next to my nigga. If you want to shoot it out with a nigga like me. Let me know something" I argued.

"Rashad you better keep your fuckin' hands off me. Don't fuckin' touch me. If you want to keep those hands, I suggest you ease those muthafuckas up off my neck. I said what the fuck I said. My husband ain't got shit to do with that. If you touch him, I'll touch you and I mean that fuckin' shit" Danielle didn't scare me. I wasn't releasing shit. Her body tensed up. I could feel the hairs rise from her neck. We never cross paths and always moved around each other. She didn't want to be in the room with me. She didn't have a choice now. I whispered in her ear.

"I need a reason to kill Baine. I owe him one and you're the reason. You only married him out of spite to get over me. You don't love that nigga. You just tolerate him. If I find out it's some funny shit going on with him and Ike, its lights out. You know I'll kill him and you heard it from me"

"I'm only going to ask you one more time to raise up off me and leave me the fuck alone. My husband ain't got shit to do with whatever is going on, but if you keep fuckin' with me I'll let him know the two of you have a problem because you can't keep your hands to yourself." She argued. Danielle better watch her mouth. Griff won't be the only reason her husband has a bullet with his name on it. I shoot to kill. I don't even know why I'm letting shawty get to me. I knelt and whispered in her ear. "I wish that motherfucka would."

"Leave Rashad. I got it from here and don't fuckin' come back. I mean it because the next time I won't be as nice." She argued and sassed and pushed me up off her.

"Call him up right now and tell him. I'm begging you too. The only reason why he made it back home is because Auntie Kaye stopped me from pushing his shit back. If she wasn't there, he would've been dead the moment he stepped out the car."

Danielle

I couldn't believe Rashad. I'm not even surprised. I swear I hate him. Hate is a strong word to use but I do for the old and new. It took everything in me not to elbow him or grab his nuts so he can back the fuck up off me. I didn't want him to get aroused by my touch. I knew he was mad about Griff. Hell, so was I. Griff was the brother I never had. Baine knew if Ike had anything to do with that it was a wrap between us. I love Baine with all my heart, but my heart would have to suffer because of my best friend and her future husband. If Ike had anything to do with that, Baine and I couldn't be together because he's guilty by association. I couldn't let Rashad disrespect my husband and not say anything. I refused to let that happen.

We haven't spoken in years and I prefer to keep it that way. We never crossed paths with each other. If the girls had a party, I always arrived so early to see them and leave before Rashad had a chance to step foot in the door. I was okay with that. I gave him what he gave me and that was nothing. I didn't care to speak with him now. I knew he was going to follow me in the kitchen. I could feel it.

Every word that he spoke he was staring me in the eyes. I refused to move out of this spot until I knew he was gone. The tears from my eyes dropped in the spot in front of me. I had to make Crimson some tea. I can't believe I really let this nigga get to me. It's already a lot of shit going on and I didn't need the extra stress dealing with him. I love Baine and I'm not trying to lose him to Rashad. I didn't marry Baine to get over Rashad. He swept me off my feet and the rest is history. Why couldn't he respect what the fuck I had going on?

We've been done for years. I knew he wanted to hurt my husband, but I wasn't about to let that happen if I could help it. I went back upstairs to check on Crimson. She was lying in bed and she was staring at the ceiling. I grabbed some tissue from the bathroom. I climbed in bed right beside her.

"I don't know the right words to say but I'm sorry Crimson. I know what heartbreak feels like. I'm here every step of the way. I know I should've been the one to give you the news, but I didn't believe it. Baine had to catch me because I broke down.

Griff was my brother and I swear to God I prayed what I heard wasn't real. Telling you that Griff was gone was one of the hardest things I would ever have to do in my life. Whoever did this I want in. If they took Griff away from us, we're taking something away from them and that's a promise. Baine wanted to come to support you, but he had to go speak with Ike in Jacksonville. I don't think Ike did it. I can tell when Baine is lying, and he said somebody set him up. I'm glad Baine didn't come with me because Rashad is acting really stupid"

"Thank you for coming, I appreciate you. Promise me you'll never leave me, Danielle. It hurts so badly. What I am going to do? I feel like giving up. I don't want to live this life without Griff. What am I going to tell my babies? They love their father so much? What happened to the tea?" She asked and cried?

"I'm not going anywhere you know that I got you. Baine better be prepared to lay by himself because I'm moving in. You can't give up because my babies need you. I need you. We've been through a lot and overcame every obstacle that was thrown at us. We overcame it no matter what. I swear it gets greater later. God wouldn't bring you this far to leave you. Girl, I couldn't even make the tea. It's still brewing. Rashad called himself choking me out in the kitchen. He was making threats about killing Baine. He had the nerve to say I married Baine just to get over him and I don't love my husband. He's crazy. I don’t know if I can stay here if keeps up with this shit?” I explained. Crimson was laughing. I don't see what the fuck was so funny. He's trying to handle me like I was the one that fucked up. “I'm married HAPPILY.” I'm glad Crimson can laugh at my expense.

“Girl you've been avoiding him for years. He’s never got to properly explain himself and apologize. When he heard you and Baine had gotten married he was pissed. He still cares about you. He never got the chance to right his wrongs. You were the one that got away. I'll talk to him and let him know to leave you alone. I saw the way he was looking at you and bitch I saw the way you were looking at him. He doesn't bring any females around. Every event he looks to see if he'll run into you. I be wanting to say you just missed her. Talk to him Danielle because you'll be seeing a lot of him. I need both of you right now.” She explained. How dare Crimson say that to me. Yes, I was looking at him because he was talking crazy and throwing jabs at my husband.

"Crimson I'm happily married. Rashad and I don't have anything to talk about. He fucked up and he needs to live with it and move on. I'm thankful he fucked up because Baine stepped it all the way up and wifed me. I can't talk to him because he has a problem with my husband, and he doesn't respect what we have going on. He needs to move on. I know you need us Crimson and I'm here for you. Rashad needs to move on because I can't do this with him. I'm trying to keep the peace and not tell Baine he put his hands on me because he tried the fuck out of me."

"Danielle, I swear this feels like Deja Vu minus my heart being taken away from me. I rather talk about your life than mine. Who are you trying to convince, Rashad or me? He wants you bad. Baine is my brother but so is Rashad. You got that drip just hear that man out. I think you still care about him or else you would tell your husband. I secretly rooted for y'all to get back together but that didn't work out." She laughed. Crimson and I finished talking. I swear I missed nights like this when we could lay up and chill. I hate that it's under these circumstances. Every now and then she would break down and cry.

Crimson drifted off to sleep. My mind drifted off to Rashad. It's too late. What we had was done a long time ago and it's because of him, not me. I've already said I do. I can't be in the same vicinity as him. I closed my eyes and drifted off to sleep. My mind was in a million places. I was tired and I prayed that sleep would consume me. I felt a presence over me. I didn't pay it no mind until I felt a pair of lips connect with mine. I prayed I was dreaming because I dozed off early. "Wake up I know you're not asleep. How long has she been asleep?" He asked. I refused to open my eyes and acknowledge him. "I know you hear me fuckin' talking to you." I pray he would leave me alone and go on about his business. He shoved his tongue down my throat. I pushed him up off me. I wish he wouldn't have done that. He's making me cheat on my husband.

"Leave me alone," I whispered and pushed him. I didn't want to wake Crimson up but he's trying me. He lifted me up and carried me to the next room. I kept kicking my legs, but he was too strong for me. He had a death grip on my legs. He was feeling me up.

"I wish you would stop fighting me. You've been fighting and hiding for too long. You knew I was coming back to you. If you were smart Danielle, you should've taken your ass back home. Call that nigga up and tell him it's a wrap." He explained. Rashad is crazy and he's lost his fuckin' mind. As soon as he lets me go, I'm going home. I shouldn't be here. Baine would trip if he knew Rashad did this much. I got to go.

"I'm married Rashad and you're overstepping your boundaries. Please just leave me alone," I argued and pouted. I can't even be here for my best friend like I need too because he's doing all this stuff. Damn, he's inconsiderate as fuck.

"I don't give a fuck about your marriage. I don't respect that shit at all. You belong to me. I don't give a fuck about what that piece of paper says. You can do shit my way or you're going to learn the hard way. Either you divorce him or I'll make him divorce you." He argued. I wasn't even about to sit here and argue with him. It was pointless

"Are we done here? I care about my marriage and I respect it. I take my vows seriously. I belong to Baine Mahone, not you. You and I were done years ago. Make this your last time fuckin' touching me. I'm not divorcing him. Tell Crimson I'm going home, and I'll see her tomorrow." I argued. I pushed passed him fast, not giving him a chance to talk. I ran into Crimson and Griff's room and locked the door. I don't know how this was going to work. I want to be here for Crimson while she's going through her stuff with Griff's death, but Rashad is going to make that extremely hard.

I avoided him all these years because I didn't want any of this. I refuse to live in the past with him. Crimson was finally asleep. I'm tripping off Rashad and all the anger he has built up against me. Last I remember he cheated not me. I moved on and the weak ass apology that he gave me years ago was enough. He couldn't keep his dick in his pants. Instead of him being honest, he chose not to say nothing at all. He only wanted to explain himself when he saw Baine in the picture. If Baine wasn't in the picture, he wouldn't have said anything. If Crimson and Griff didn't hook up, I would've never seen his ass again.

"Danielle, what were you and Rashad doing in my guest room?" She asked. I tapped Crimson on her shoulder. She turned around and looked at me.

"Bitch I thought you were asleep? We didn't do anything. He was talking crazy. Girl if I had my knife on me, I would've stabbed his ass for invading my personal space."

"Please don't do that Danielle, I can't take another death. I'll be sure to talk to him." She explained. "I know

Crimson. It's him, not me. I'm not going anywhere I'll just steer clear of him. When he's here I'll leave and when he leaves I'll come back." I explained. Crimson and I finished talking until we both dozed off.

THE NEXT DAY

Chapter-7

Crimson

Reality finally set in that Griff and I will never be able to see each other again. Just the thought of him not holding me and lying on his chest at night does something to me. I'll cherish those moments because I will not able to get them back. Griff was the realest man I've ever known. Who would want to hurt him and why? Tears soaked my pillow every time I thought about it. His scent was still lingering in our room. I wish this was a bad dream that I could wake up from. I hope it would leave soon.

My heart hurts and I don't know if I can exist in this world without him. I couldn't sleep if I wanted to. I wish my heart could stop beating. I would give anything just to hear him say I love you. My eyes are closed but I'm not asleep. I can't believe the Lord would let them take Griff away from me. I know I shouldn't question God but why him? It doesn't seem real at all. I guess you'll have to see it to believe it. I heard Camina and Cariuna come into our room. I know they would be asking questions.

"Mommy and God Mommy Danielle, where's my daddy? He didn't wake us up." Camina squealed. She was looking all around the room for Griff. It's going to hurt Camina the worst because she's his mini-me and she's always looking for her father. How am I supposed to tell my baby that her father is never coming back? I raised up from the bed taking in Cariuna and Camina. We made some beautiful babies. Even through my tears, my babies brings a smile to my face.

"Camina and Cariuna I have something to tell you," I sighed. I blinked my eyes twice to stop the tears from falling. My voice started to crack. I couldn't hold back my tears even if I wanted too. Danielle grabbed me a tissue.

"What's wrong mommy?" My oldest daughter Cariuna asked. I wiped my eyes with the back of my hand. I had to tell them the truth. It was now or never even though it's still fresh. It hurts to say this. I had to go and identify Griff's body at the morgue later. I couldn't take my babies with me. I'm next to kin.

I motioned with my hands for Camina and Cariuna to come and join me. They walked over to me. I knelt in front of them. My words were getting caught in my throat. I hate to even repeat this, but I had to tell them the truth.

“Daddy was hurt really bad and he won't be coming back any time soon.” I cried. Cariuna and Camina cried also. I tried to keep it together, but I couldn't. Griff was my soul mate. We were about to get married in a few months. They don't make them like him anymore.

“Who hurt my daddy mommy? He's tough. He would never leave me and not come back.” My youngest daughter Camina argued and pouted. Griff leaving would be hard on Camina because Griff lets her do whatever she wants. He could never tell her no.

“I don't know who did it Camina, but they hurt him badly and he won't be coming back home. He loves you, never forget that.” I cried.

“Mommy stop crying. Give me your phone. I need to call my uncle Rashad, he knows who hurt my daddy. I want my daddy back NOW.” She cried and pouted. I wish I had half the heart Camina has. She was determined to find her father's killer. She told me to stop crying and call her uncle Rashad. She grabbed my phone and called her uncle Rashad. Danielle looked at me and laughed. Camina was calling the shots and she was only four years old. Rashad answered on the first ring.

"Uncle Rashad, I want my daddy. Where is he and who hurt my daddy? How come you didn't help him. Come and get me so we can find them." She argued and pouted. She had Rashad on speakerphone. He was chuckling in the background. Camina was serious as fuck too.

"Camina, I got you. Never question that. I'll be by there to see you in a few. Whoever hurt your daddy I'm bringing their head back to you. They won't get away with hurting your daddy. I put my life on it. I love you and Cariuna."

"We love you, Uncle Rashad." Camina and Cariuna beamed and cried. Rashad hung up the phone with the girls. I needed to get dressed and take them to school. Danielle was going with me to the morgue. I couldn't go there by myself but first I needed to feed my babies and myself. Cooking always soothes me and it'll help me get my mind off Griff and everything that's going on around me. I went into that bathroom and grabbed my face towel.

I looked in the mirror and my eyes were swollen. I looked a mess I've been crying all night since I got the news that he passed away. He didn't deserve to be killed. Damn Griff, why did they have to take you? Since we've been together I never thought about living this life without you. He was my soul mate he was my everything. I handled my hygiene. I didn't look my best, but this will have to do until later.

I went downstairs and grabbed the sausage links out the refrigerator and some fresh fruit. Danielle was mixing up some pancakes. Cariuna was setting the table. Camina was sitting in the corner with her headphones on. Her cheeks were red, and her little eyes were puffy. My baby was sad her daddy was gone. I walked over to her. I knelt in front of her.

"Come here Camina, tell mommy what's wrong?" I asked. She took her headphones off and stomped her feet when she walked over to me. She folded her arms across her chest and poked out her bottom lip. Camina had an attitude and it had everything to do with Griff being gone.

“I want my daddy mommy. He promised me he’ll never leave me. Daddy doesn’t make promises that he can’t keep. Why would someone want to hurt my daddy and he can’t come home, mommy?” She asked and cried. I wish I had the answers, but I don’t. I can only pray that it’ll get better. Whoever killed Griff and took him from me and our kids. I swear I’ll shoot them dead. I’m not a violent person but to ease my pain and my daughters’ pain, I’ll do it. My baby was in her feelings behind her father. I was too but I had to be strong for her because she needed me. I finished cooking breakfast and fed my girls. Camina had a fit because she had to go to school today.

Griff never made her go that's another reason why she was mad. Her days hanging with her father and Uncle Rashad were over. She’s taking her ass to school. I knew she was going to be my problem child. I combed her and Cariuna's hair and got them dressed for school. Camina showed her ass. I jumped in the shower to handle my hygiene. My clothes were already laid out. It's the beginning of fall and the weather hasn't changed a bit. I washed my hair. I was rocking my afro today. Maria and Auntie Kaye called my phone. I’ll go there later. I wasn't in the mood to talk. I needed to get this over with.

I dried off and I was debating rather or not I wanted to air dry my hair or not. I grabbed my Blueberry lemonade Trap Sweets lotion. It smelled so good. Griff loved to smell this on me. My eyes were still puffy from all the crying. I grabbed my Shea butter from underneath the sink and applied a little under my eyes hopefully it'll take down the swelling and not leave marks. I didn't wear make-up, so I was throwing on my big face Chanel glasses on. I grabbed my Marathon cut off sweatshirt with the matching joggers. I oiled my feet with some Almond Oil. My lips were chapped, so I grabbed my nude lip gloss off the sink and painted my lips. The girls and Danielle were sitting on my bed waiting for me. I tossed Danielle my keys because she was driving.

"Mommy can I please stay with you today?" Camina asked. I would let her, but I didn't want her there to see her father's body. I will pick her up from school early and spend extra time with her. Her father was her everything.

"No Camina, you have to go to school. I'll come and get you early." I explained. She pouted and whined. Cariuna told her to be a big girl and Camina pushed her. She's pushing it now. I feel like whooping her ass. I know she was in her feelings but that didn’t give her a reason to put your hands on her sister.

♡

An hour later Danielle and I were headed to the morgue. We dropped Camina and Cariuna off to school and we were headed right over there. I was nervous as fuck. I don't know if I’m going to be able to do this, but I had too. I’m all Griff has. His mother and father are both dead beside Auntie Kaye, BeBe, and Maria I’m it. Danielle pulled up to Dekalb County Coroners and Medical Examiner’s office. I was nervous as fuck. I started shaking. I got hot instantly and she gave me bottled water.

“Are you alright?” she asked. I gave her a faint smile. She knew I wasn’t fuckin all right. Bitch, I just lost the love of my fuckin’ life. I wouldn’t wish this feeling on my worst fuckin’ enemy. It was now or never. I had to begin the process. Danielle grabbed my hand and led me in the building. I was so nervous. I’m sure she could feel my body shaking. I don’t want to do this. I feel like turning around and running as far as my feet could take me. As soon as we entered the building a rush of emotions came over me. I walked up to the front desk.

"Hi, welcome to the Dekalb County Medical Examiner's Office. How may I help you?" She sassed and asked. She had a nasty attitude. She looked me up and down as if she knew me from somewhere. I swear I'm not beat for anybody's shit.

"Hi, my name is Crimson Rose Tristan. My fiancé' Carius Deon Griffey Jr. was brought here. I came to identify his body." I cried and sniffled. Danielle handed me a tissue. She gave me a nasty smirk. What the fuck was that about? I knew when someone is being malicious, I could feel it.

"Okay, no problem let me look it up and I'll be right with you." She stated. I heard her mumble something up under her breath. Danielle and I took a seat in the waiting area. The receptionist keyed a few things in on her computer.

"Ms. Tristan, can I speak with you for a few minutes?" She asked and sassed? Her tone was firm, and I didn't like it. Danielle and I approached the front desk. I was already on go mode because it feels like she's trying my fuckin' patience. Everything about her seemed conniving.

"How can I help you," I asked. Danielle knew I was about to spaz out because she handed me the water. This bitch had an attitude and I don't even call females bitches. I was giving her what she gave me.

"I hate to break it to you Ms. Tristan but Mr. Griffey's wife was here this morning to identify his body. We've been giving strict instructions not to allow any family members besides herself to see him and gather his belongings. She's handling all his funeral arrangements." She sassed and explained. I looked at her like she was crazy. I knew it was a mistake.

"It has to be some mistake. He wasn't married because we were engaged." I argued and said with so much confidence. "I know you motherfuckin' lying. Griff wasn't married to any fuckin' body. Can I speak with your supervisor," I asked and argued.

"I am the supervisor. I'm filling in for the receptionist today. I hate to be the one to break it you Ms. Tristan but Carius a.k.a Griff married my cousin Keondra Griffey. She stakes claim to him and all his possessions." She argued. I looked at Danielle. I cocked my fist back and Danielle grabbed me because I was about to go to jail. I knew something was up with this bitch.

I could tell by the way she looked at me this shit was motherfuckin' personal. I could feel it. Everything she stated and how she stated it was personal. She was dripping with hate and venom. I wasn't even about to argue with this bitch. I couldn’t let her get the best of me. I stormed off and Danielle was right behind me. I made it to my car and I swear if this shit was true, Griff better be glad I wasn't the one to kill his ass. Danielle and I locked eyes with each other because she knew I was mad. She could look at my face and tell. She hit unlock on the car and I slid in and kicked the dashboard in my car. To say I was pissed was a fuckin' understatement. If it ain't one thing it's something else.

“Crimson calm down, do you want to talk about?” She asked. I can’t calm down if I wanted to. That’s a huge blow. MARRIED!

“Of course, I want to fuckin' talk about it. Married to Keondra? How was he able to pull that off? Was I a fuckin' joke to him? I feel so fuckin' low. Her words ate me up Danielle. Take me to Auntie Kay's house. Let me call Rashad. He got me so fucked up. I'm tired of muthafuckas trying to play me, Danielle.” I argued.

“Calm down Crimson. I don't believe he was married to her. Don't let these bitches take you out of character. You and I both know what the fuck you meant to him. Griff ain't dumb. He would never play you like that. Keondra is married to Ike bitch. You can’t be married to two people, come on now.” She explained. I hope so. I grabbed my phone to call Rashad. He answered on the first ring.

“What's up Crimson? How are you feeling today?” He asked. If he only knew I was about to blow his ear off.

“I'm good. I could be better. Let me ask you this Rashad and I want you to be honest with me. I went to the morgue to claim Griff's body and guess what, I couldn't. The bitch at the front desk said his wife Keondra Griffey has already claimed his body and she’s making funeral arrangements. I know like hell you haven't been smiling in my face and he's married to her.” I argued. He got me fucked up. Don’t smile in my face and think you can play me.

“Calm down Crimson. Griff ain't married to that bitch. It's some bullshit going on. He was married to her. I know for a fact he divorced her. I can’t prove it now but trust me; my nigga handled his business. Don't take heed to what the fuck is going on around you. Let me handle the bullshit and the beef that's going on in these streets." Rashad and I finished talking. I heard him but I wasn't hearing him. Why would Griff keep that he was married to her away from me?

"Don't trip Crimson but let me call my husband to put a bug in his ear." She stated. Baine answered on the first ring.

"Hey, baby I missed you. How's your day going?" He asked. Danielle was blushing like a schoolgirl. I was so happy for her. How did she get married before me? I always wondered that. Now I know that motherfucka was married to someone else.

"I miss you too baby. It's going okay it could be better. Where's Ike if you don't mind me asking?" She asked and cooed. Danielle was about to drop the ball on Keondra.

"He's right here what's up? Is everything okay?" He asked. Danielle tapped me on my shoulder and smirked.

"No it's not baby, shit is fucked up. Where's Ike? Put me on speaker phone?"

“He's right here. What's up Danielle, did somebody touch you or threaten you?” he asked.

“No baby, it's nothing like that. I went with Crimson to the Coroner’s office to identify Griff's body and to gather his stuff but his wife KEONDRA GRIFFEY beat us there.”

“Say what Danielle, repeat that shit again, so IKE can hear.” He argued. Danielle repeated herself and IKE was tripping.

“Aye Danielle and Crimson, that bitch ain't married to him. We're married and we have been for a year now. I don't know what the fuck shawty got going on, but I didn't kill Griff and she shouldn't be claiming nobody's fuckin' body if we're married.” Ike argued. Danielle and Baine finished talking. My mind was in a million places. I don't know what to believe. Ike was just as upset as I was. Why would she do that and she's married to someone else. I just need to go home and lay down.

Chapter-8

Keondra

Sometimes I crack myself up. I was feeling myself, I can't even lie. It feels good to take a Kingpin like Griff down. My nigga and I are about to take these streets by storm. We had a million dollars of Griff's hard-earned cash. I couldn't wait to buss it down and deposit it in my savings account. My cousin Cutie called me and told me Crimson came down there to identify Griff's body. I shut that shit down. Cutie said that bitch was hot. All them muthafuckas are about to feel me. They think this shit is a fuckin' game. Jacque had stepped out to make a few runs. Ike was blowing my phone up like crazy. I decided to answer to see what the fuck he wanted.

"Hello," I sighed. Why was he even calling me? Bring your ass home so I can call the cops, so you could go to jail. I wasn't even about to play like I was at home since he's checking cameras and shit now. Fuck Ike. The moment he steps foot inside the jail he'll see it's fuck him.

"What's up with you? Where the fuck did you lay your head at last night? What the fuck are you trying to pull

Keondra?" He asked and argued? I had time today to argue with Ike because Jacque wasn't here. If he wants smoke, I got that shit for him. Don't call me questioning my fuckin' moves. Where did he stay last night and who was he with? I don't even care anymore.

"Ike lower your fuckin' voice when you're talking to me. Since when have you been clocking my moves? It's funny how the tables have turned. I used to be on the phone clocking your moves begging you to come home and you never came. It doesn't feel good when that shoe is on the foot does it? Why would I need to be at home and you're not there? You want me to be at the house and get killed when they run in there looking for you because you killed Griff?" I chuckled. Yeah motherfucka if the FEDS were listening, they would get an ear full just because you call yourself coming for me.

"Keondra you want me to fuckin' hurt you? Listen bitch I ain't kill Griff but the way you moving it seems like you fuckin' did. I'm a paid nigga and any fuckin' move you make I know about it. Your mouth is really fuckin' smart right now. Peep this bitch, I heard about you going to the coroner's office and claiming you're Griff's wife. What's up with that? If you want a divorce bitch, I'll give you that. I'll divorce you just like that nigga did. Watch who the fuck you cross because if I ever find out you're playing with me bitch, I'll hurt you and fuckin kill you for playing with my sanity. I'll be glad to catch a murder charge behind your stupid ass. I'll show you how ignorant and stupid I am. I'm a stupid ass nigga if you provoke me.

I'm not making any threats. It's a fuckin' promise. Since you don't want to be at home you ain't got to be. I'll have Baine pack up your shit and drop it off in the hood." He argued and hung up the phone. I didn't even get to say the shit I wanted to say. Baine better not drop shit of mine any fuckin' where. I threw my phone on the couch. Before I could even take a seat. I felt a pair of arms around me. I jumped instantly. When did he come back and how much did he hear?

"Keondra, shorty, you're playing a dangerous fuckin' game. I heard everything that nigga fuckin' said. Why would you do that shit? I just told you yesterday about that shit. I got to move around shorty I'm not about to keep doing this with you. Griff just died yesterday. Why in the fuck would you do that shit at the coroner's office? If they investigate that shit, his murder will lead back to you. Damn, do you even think before you do shit? You must be ready to fuckin' die?" He argued. Why did he have to hear that conversation?

"Jacque stop tripping, please. I know what the fuck I'm doing. A lot of my plans were already in motion before you came in the picture. I have my ducks in a row. You want to leave me so bad you can leave. I love you but I'm not going to beg you to stay. I can fend for myself out here in these streets. I'm the queen of fraud and finessing. I need a nigga that's gone be down to ride. I don't need a nigga that's not going to fold under pressure." I argued. I'm sick of arguing with him about simple shit. I know what the fuck I'm doing.

"I need me a woman that's gone listen. You want me to leave Keondra? Is that what the fuck you want? Speak up now because we can end this shit today shorty. I'm not in the business to keep a woman that doesn't want to be kept. What's so hard about you fuckin' listening? You're so smart that you're fuckin' dumb. The man died yesterday his death is still fresh.

Why in the fuck would you deny his girl the rights to claim his body? You ain't his fuckin' wife. Damn, are you still in love with him or some shit? You got me out here looking like a fool. If you want the world to know you killed that man, do that. I move in silence shorty. If you want those niggas at your head, let's pull up on the block right now and let Rashad know. Call Ike back and let him know you set him up. You won't be able to reap the benefits of what the fuck we just did. I'm tired of talking. I'm out of here." He argued. Jacque started packing his shit up. I wasn't about to stop him. I love him but I got to do shit my way. I want them muthafuckas to feel me.

"Jacque!" Before I could even say anything else, he cut me off.

"If you ever try to play me how you played those niggas. I will kill your whole fuckin' family. I'm that nigga that will deliver your skull to your mother and father. I put that on my unborn son you're carrying and for your sake and not mine the child your carrying better be mine." He argued. How dare him to say that our son might not be his.

Tears poured down my face. I can't believe we have come to this. I wasn't even about to try to explain myself to him. It was pointless. His mind was already made up. He wanted to leave. Jacque grabbed the last of his things. He looked over his shoulder at me one last time. He knew he was hurting me by leaving but he didn't give a fuck. I grabbed my phone to call my cousin Cutie. I wanted to know who came to the Coroner's office with Crimson. She answered on the first ring.

"CUTIE who came to the office with Crimson this morning," I asked. Ike knew too much in a short period of time.

"Keondra, bitch, I had that hoe hot this morning. I recorded it for you. She had some light skin bitch with blonde hair with her. She was bougie as fuck. I just knew I was about to tag those hoes. I've been waiting for you to call me. I just knew I was about to do those hoes. The bitch said it must be a fuckin' mistake. No bitch you were the mistake. Girl, that hoe was about to cry she stormed off. What's up though?" She asked. I love my cousin Cutie. I knew she served Crimson. I'm glad she felt all that! Bitch I still stake claim to Griff. He could never get rid of me. Even in death, that nigga will feel me lying right next to his mother.

"Girl, what's not up? Jacque is tripping hard. Crimson must have been with Danielle that bitch called Baine and told him what happened. I should've known that bitch wouldn't have the balls to go there by herself. I'll never know what he saw in her. Now I know that's why Ike called me with the shit. Okay, it made sense now. I got something for that bitch. She thinks her HUSBAND is perfect. I think the FUCK not. If I didn't send for a bitch, she should've never sent for me. Keep my name out your fuckin' mouth. I apply pressure. Sweep around your own front door first. I hate them, bitches. God bless those bitches." I argued. Bitches are always worried about the next motherfucka. Worry about yourself. The last bitch that was worried about me, I shot her ass.

"What happened Keondra?" She asked. Cutie was with the shits too. Our fathers were brothers. She was down for me.

"Enough bitch. Too much to even talk about. You better be ready to ride." I knew Cutie was down since we linked up five years ago. She's never switched up on me. She's the sister I never had. I'm thankful for our bond!

"Keondra, don't do me! You're my fuckin' blood. I got your back until the death of me. I'm not them weak ass bitches that you call your friends. I'm loyal. You'll never have to question me. I don't need anything from you. I always got my own. I'm gone always ride for you," she argued. I felt that shit too.

"I know Cutie. I appreciate you and I got you. You're all I have besides Jermesha. Jacque packed his shit and left." I sighed and explained. I thought he was different. He knows me. He didn't even know if that shit was true or not. He's just taking Ike's word for it.

"Are you serious?" She asked. Cutie knew I wasn't lying. I had no reason too. I could keep it real with Cutie.

"Yes, bitch I am." I gave Cutie of the rundown of what happened. She was livid. We finished talking before her boss came in. Cutie worked for Dekalb County Medical and Examiner's office. Her boss signs off on all the bodies. All she had to do was use his credentials. He never went behind her to check her work. She's been there for years.

Jermesha was calling my phone now. It was time to really get shit in motion since Jacque was out the picture. Jermesha knew were Crimson and Griff lived. I needed an address. That bitch would no longer live in that castle. I had the paperwork drawn up to get Crimson put out of Griff's house. I knew the safe was there. I was coming for it all. My paperwork was legit. My cousin worked for the county she knew a few sheriffs that would help with the eviction. I paid all five of them $1,000 apiece. I answered for Jermesha to see what she wanted.

"What's up? I heard somebody killed Griff" She laughed and asked. I swear I needed a good laugh. Jermesha was it for me. She was bubbly and in good spirits.

"I heard that too. Your cousin, has she made it to Mother Dear's yet," I asked and laughed. I knew Crimson was livid. I couldn't wait to see her. That's what she gets for fuckin' with a nigga that never belonged to her.

"No, not yet. I haven't been by there today, but you know I'll post up over there for a few hours just to see if she shows up. I'm ready to make the next move. When are we doing that?" She asked. Crimson and Jermesha were blood but that didn't mean shit because Jermesha was team me she didn't give a fuck who knows it.

"In a few days, I'll make my move. I don't want to hit the bitch all at once but fuck it I might change my mind. Danielle tried me. She called herself telling Baine about what happened at the Coroner's office. Ike called himself spazzing on me. I'll fuck with her first and then I'll fuck with Crimson before the week is out." I argued a bitch can't send for me without repercussions.

"Fuck Danielle and Crimson! I ain't never liked them, bitches. She always thought she was better than somebody. The day she trapped Baine with that tuna fish pussy she thought she was better than everybody. She married a DRUG LORD and a whore. I can name plenty of bitches that fucked him. She better be glad you and I both didn't fuck him. Hurt that bitches' feelings today. Let that bitch know her husband ain't shit. Embarrass her at her little clinic. Let that bitch know you calling the shots. We're breaking up homes. Fuck she thought.

If I marry any nigga, I bet over thirty bitches won't be able to say they fuck him!" Jermesha was my bitch I don't give a fuck. I knew she couldn't fight but I'll put a gun in her hand, and I bet she would be quick to shoot. If Danielle only knew what I had in store for her ass. I thought about what Jermesha said. Fuck it, I might as well go in. We finished talking and plotting. Danielle was going to feel me tomorrow or maybe today. I'm not going to let that slide. I knew these pictures would come in handy. I just didn't know today would be that.

I ain't got shit to lose. I never sent for Danielle but the moment she thought it was cool to tell my husband what the fuck I had going on she put a target on her fuckin' back. It's hell to get a beast like me off you. Ike and Baine are best friends, but Danielle and I never clicked. We went out on a few double dates, but we never said one word to each other. I was cool with that because she wasn't my bitch and I wasn't hers. My little cousin Ashley, Cutie's sister, worked for JJL a process server in Atlanta. I know she wouldn't mind serving Danielle for me. I'll pay her more than her job pays her. I grabbed my phone to Facetime Ashley.

"Hey Keondra, what's up?" She beamed and smiled through the phone.

"Hey lil Cutie I need you to do something for me and I'm paying." I smiled. I loved my little cousin. I was so proud of her. She has a great head on her shoulders. I'm glad she's not in the streets.

"I'll do it. You don't have to pay me just give me the location and I'll serve whoever. I'll get the job done we're family." I knew she wouldn't take the money but I'm paying anyway that's just me. I never wanted anybody to do anything free for me.

"Thank you, Ashley. You know I'm your big cousin and I got to look out for you. I'm paying you and it's not up for debate." I had to pay her for doing a job that was about to shake some shit up.

"Okay if you insist. Do you want me to swing by and pick it up or do you want to drop it off at my house and I'll deliver it tomorrow?" She asked. I gave Ashley the details. Tomorrow it was going down. Little Mrs. Mahone will feel me. Let the fuckin' games begin.

Chapter-9

Crimson

I'm so over this fuckin' day. I never pictured my morning would be like this. I knew I was going to have some problems because I wasn't ready to face the reality that Griff was gone. I never saw this coming. I don't think I've ever been so humiliated in my fuckin' life. To say I was embarrassed was a fuckin' understatement. Danielle and I decided to have lunch. I needed to eat something since I didn't really eat that much for breakfast. I picked over my food. Griff being married to someone that's not me fucked with my mind mentally. It was written all over my face. I felt so fuckin' defeated. I knew he fucked with her, but I didn't know he was married to her. Rashad confirmed that they were married.

"Welcome to Julissa's can I take your order?" The waiter asked then took our order. Why would he keep that from me? I'm feeling some type of way? I can't stop thinking about it. I trusted him with my fuckin' heart and look at how he repaid me. I guess the saying is true "everything comes out when you die." We were dining in at Julissa's. It's a cute little spot downtown by Piedmont.

They have the best soul food. Danielle knew it was my favorite. It cheered me up to come here. The atmosphere was cool and I loved the vibe. Griff and I knew the owners, Journee and her husband Juelz. She could cook her ass off. I love her fried fish plates with potatoes and onions. That's what I was having today. She came out to greet us. I loved her spirit. She was always cool. She gave me a hug, I needed that. I didn't know if I was going or coming.

"Crimson, hey love. Hey Danielle! I'm glad to see the two of you. I heard about Griff last night. I don't believe that shit man. My heart dropped when my husband told me. Your family has my condolences. Your food is on the house. Anything you want or need it's on me. Griff was a good man, I can vouch for that. I loved the way he looked at you. I told my husband he better start looking at me like that.

You need to comb the streets to get justice for him. I'm going to write my number down. Call me if you need me for anything. I'm down to ride. We can set it off. If you want me to get the girls, I'll keep them for as long as you need me too. I'm here for you and I mean that shit literally." She explained. She got teary-eyed just talking about him. I miss my love so much.

“Thank you Journee, I appreciate you so much. I swear it's hard I don't know what to do. I'm lost without him. He was everything to me. He held the keys to my happiness and soul. For someone to take that away from me. I refuse to accept that. Why him? He would give you his last. I swear I will never love another man as I love him. I don't want too. My babies miss him so much,” I sniffled. I had to blink my eyes twice to stop the tears from falling. I couldn’t help it.

“It's okay to cry Crimson. Crying is releasing. Griff loved you and the world knows that. Trust me he’ll be your guardian and he’ll always watch over you and your babies. You have his two beautiful daughters. You have a piece of him with you every day. Death isn’t easy, trust me I know. I lost my mother when I was sixteen. I had to raise my brother and sister all by myself. It never gets easy. I’m just keeping it real. I miss my mother and it’s not a day that goes by that I don’t think about her. I’ll pray for you every day, Crimson. I will do that and if you use my number I’ll come whenever you call.” She explained.

“Thank you.” While we waited for our food Danielle and I listened to Journee drop some jewels. I've never experienced death before. I didn’t know my mother or father. All I had was Mother Dear, Danielle, Griff, and my kids. I've been with this man for the past seven years and he's all I knew.

We finished eating our food and Journee gave me a hug on the way out. I slid back in the passenger seat. I had a few texts from Auntie Kaye and BeBe. I'll call them back later. I wasn't in the mood to talk. Mother Dear called me too. I'll go by there because I needed to see her face to face. My Facebook notifications were going off like crazy. I don't even use it that much unless one of my favorite authors were releasing a book. I just wanted to keep up with future releases nothing more nothing less. Someone tagged me in a picture.

I logged in to see who it was. It was the marriage certificate of Griff and Keondra and their wedding pictures. My heart was crushed. It felt like my heart was beating out of my chest. I threw my phone up against the window. I couldn't take it. Why would he do this to me? I started shaking. I placed my hand on my heart. Why now, why did she want me to know now?

“Crimson what's wrong?” She asked. I couldn't even say anything. I couldn't form a sentence. She grabbed my phone to look and see what was going on. I started fanning my face. I couldn't take it. I never did anything to that girl. I don't understand why she keeps fuckin' with me. I could've sworn Griff cleared it up years ago. Why wait until he's dead?

"Danielle I can't do this. My heart hurts so badly and I feel like it's about to beat out of my chest. I'm stressed out." I cried and screamed. Next thing I know everything went black.

Chapter-10

Danielle

I stay in my lane I promise you I do. I've been on my grown woman shit for a long time now. I've come a long way from Snapfinger Road. It ain't shit for me to revert to my old ways to address a bitch. Don't let this lab coat, stethoscope, and these Christian Louboutin heels fool you. I've been begging for a bitch to bring me out of retirement for a long time. Guess what, KEONDRA is that BITCH. The moment a bitch swerve in my lane and fuck with my sister it's a motherfuckin' problem because she doesn't bother anybody. I'm your fuckin' issue. I'm going to do what Crimson won't do. I'm at your fuckin' neck and you're going to respect me. It's either given or I'll take it. See Keondra thinks she's bad and can't be touched. I know I'm bad because I walk it like I talk it. I'm not BeBe. I heard about that shit she did years ago. I wish a bitch would. If she shoots me, then she better make sure she kills me. If I shoot her, I'm guaranteed to kill her. The choice is yours. Keondra gone fuckin' feel me and that's a fuckin' understatement. I owe that bitch one from years ago.

Crimson doesn't bother anybody but me BITCH, I'm a fuckin' BULLY. I'll beat your fuckin' skull in until I see white meat. My best friend's blood pressure was 280, due to the level of stress she's been dealing with. She's in a medically induced coma. All because you're jealous. I don't know why Ike married that bitch. I'm fuckin' livid right now. She got me fucked up. I'll touch that bitch and hit her where it hurts. I put that shit on God. I hate when a bitch keeps poking and poking without any consequences. Enough is enough and bitch you gone catch these motherfuckin' hands behind mine. I swear this is one call I hate to make to Mother Dear. Mother Dear is too old to be dealing with this. My sister has to make it. I don't know what I would do without her. I grabbed my phone out of my back pocket and I dialed Mother Dear's number.

"Good Afternoon Danielle, how are you? I've been trying to reach Crimson all morning, have you heard from her? I heard about what happened to Griff and I know she needs me now more than ever. I'm headed to her house." She explained. I could hear the concern in her voice. I kept telling Crimson to call her. She was worried sick about her.

"Mother Dear I've been with her since last night and she's not doing well at all. We went to identify his body this morning and everything went downhill from there. She passed out and her blood pressure was extremely high. They put her in an induced medical coma to get her blood pressure down. I need you to come quick," I cried. "We're at Emory Crawford Long."

I tried to hold back my tears, but I couldn't. Crimson is my heart and she has been for years. That'll never change. I've been by her side since they took her back there. I'm a registered nurse and I wasn't leaving the fuckin' room at all.

"Danielle, why are you just now calling me? I'm on my way. Please stay there until I get there. I need you to get Cariuna and Camina for me from school and take them to my house. Where's Rashad? See if he can pick them up. Do you have his number, if not I'll shoot it to you?"

"I'll pick them up. I'll leave as soon as you get here." I finished speaking with Mother. Ain't no way in hell I was calling Rashad from my damn phone. I know Mother Dear is upset but me calling Rashad is out the fuckin' question. Crimson was resting in her room. I climbed in the bed and laid beside her. I had a long talk with God. I needed her to pull through because her babies need her. I need her. Death isn't easy, but it'll get better one day at a time. I know what Griff meant to her and I feel her pain. I can't wait until she wakes up.

I have some good news for her. They ran a urine test on her and she's eight weeks pregnant. What are the chances of that? God works in mysterious ways. If it's not one thing it's something else. I feel a bad storm coming. I sent my husband a text. I needed to catch a nap before Mother Dear made it. My mind was in a million places. It'll be a while before I get any sleep with everything that's going on.

Mr. Mahone - I love you and I miss you. Be careful, please.

My Heart - I love you too baby. I'll be home soon. Do you want me to fly you out?

I would love to catch a flight out and be with him but Crimson needed me more than he does. I couldn't leave her side at all. My Godbabies need me since Crimson is down and Griff is gone. Who killed Griff and why? I'm sorry but none of this sits right with me. Griff was too smart to get caught slipping. I wish this was a bad dream.

I don’t know what I would do if I lost Baine? I’d go crazy that’s why I was bothered when Rashad was talking reckless about my husband. Baine has my heart and I don’t want to lose him because Rashad is out for blood. Mother Dear and my grandmother finally made it. I told them I would bring the girls by to see her and I’ll take them home with me. I had to swing by the office. Michelle said a process server served me with some certified papers. I was curious to see why I was getting served because I don't owe anyone. I rushed over to my office as fast as I could to see what was going on, but the traffic was heavy.

I had to grab Cariuna and Camina first. Of course, they were looking for their mother and I told them she was at the hospital. She ate something that made her sick. I stopped by Cold Stone Creamery to get the two of them an ice cream cone. Camina’s teacher said she had two fights today. I don't know what we're going to do with Camina. I’m not having it and she knows that. We'll worry about that later. I pulled up to my office and got Camina out of her car seat. Cariuna grabbed her hand and she snatched it from her. I swear this little girl is going to make me spank her tale. She knows I will if she keeps pushing me.

“Camina that's not nice, she's just grabbing your hand, so you won’t run off,” I explained. Camina turned her nose up at Cariuna. Poor thing, she’s just trying to be the big sister. I can see how I’m probably going to have to whip her tale before the week is out because she keeps trying it. I know she’s acting out because her father is gone. She needs discipline bad.

“I'm a big girl God mommy Danielle. I'm not a baby. Let me see your phone so I can call my Uncle Rashad to come and get me.” She pouted and whined. Crimson needs to get a good grip on her. Hell, no she ain't using my phone to call him. Camina was spoiled rotten between Griff and Rashad. The two of them let her do whatever she wants to do. No ma’am not me. She hates to come to my house because she knows I don’t play that shit at all. She probably was fighting because she was mad she had to go to school. I grabbed both of their hands and walked in my office. Michelle greeted us at the door.

“Hi, Danielle, Cariuna and little Ms. Camina.” She beamed. Michelle was a great assistant and I’m grateful to have her. I wasn’t worried about being away from the office because she had it.

"Hi, Michelle." They beamed and smiled. She waived at them and we headed into office. I wanted to see what was up with these papers! I walked to my office quickly.

Camina and Cariuna took a seat on the sectional in my office. Camina grabbed their I-pads from underneath the pillows. I swear she was a little demon. She threw the other iPad at Cariuna.

"Oops." She laughed. I swear I'm going to beat her ass. I don't give a damn how cute she is. There was manila folder on my desk with Tuna Fish written over it. I knew a bitch was playing games. Tuna fish, bitch, please. I don't play games. The only games I play are with these two little girls. I tore open the manila folder to see what was inside. It was a few pictures of Baine and Ike and two females. I swear these bitches ain't got shit better to do. I'm so fuckin' confident about where I stand in my husband's life. Too bad the jokes on whoever sent these. There was a cute little note attached with.

Dear Tuna Fish

Don't Ever Send for A Bitch That Ain't Coming for You. Keep My Name Out Your Fuckin' Mouth. What I Do on My Time Is My Fuckin' Business. Since

You Made My Business Your Business. Now You and Me You got Beef. You Don't Want to Go to War with A Bitch Like Me. You have Been Warned. Your Husband Ain't Shit Just Like My Husband Ain't Shit. I Thought You Should Know That. Check Out These Pictures of Your Piece of Shit Ass Husband. Oh, And Ask Him How My Pussy Feels. Tread Lightly When You Are mentioning Me.

Keondra Griffey

I know this bitch didn't come for me. I swear to God she'll fuckin' regret it. Keondra is so fuckin' dumb she's stupid. She wishes her last name was Griffey. If Griff did marry her, he did the right thing and divorced her. Get the fuck out of here with this clown ass shit. I grabbed my phone and took pictures of the photos and the letter. I sent them to Baine and told him to tell Ike he better get a grip or a good hold of his dumb ass wife because she won't live to suck or fuck him another day. I don't play games at all but she's fuckin' reaching. I can guarantee you when I clap, I'm going to clap that ass. The two girls in the photos Ike fucks with the two of them. Normally I don't condone men cheating on their wives or cheating period because I've been cheated on. Not by my husband but my EX. I don’t like what being cheated on feels like.

Honestly, I never liked Keondra and it doesn't have shit to do with Crimson. We just didn't click. I'm big on vibes and we didn't vibe. I could never be cordial with a bitch that didn’t like my sister. I don’t give a fuck. It’s loyalty over royalty. Ike and Baine are best friends and I would never disrespect his wife because of the bond they have. I just chose not to deal with her. All that shit went out the window TODAY. That bitch can get it wherever the fuck I see her at. I rushed over to my office thinking it was something important and this bitch wants to send pictures of two bitches that her husband is fuckin'. Not mine but hers. I need to be with my fuckin’ sister and not here looking at this whack ass shit.

See bitches think they know a lot, but they don’t know enough. Baine and I had lunch with them. I knew they were having problems at home. I never asked Baine what was going on because she wasn’t my concern. She wasn't my bitch and I wasn’t hers. This is the reason why; she's childish ass fuck. She's not on my level, but I’ll get hers. Baine called me and I answered on the first ring.

"Hey, baby, what's that all about?" He asked. I looked at the phone and smiled. Baine knew I was pissed that's why he used that approach. I hate for a bitch to try me and I can't do anything about it. If I didn't have Camina and Cariuna I would've rode out and started looking for the bitch.

"You know why, I don't appreciate her coming for me because I was looking out for Ike and Crimson. You know I don't bother anybody, Baine? She had these pictures and letter sent certified. I thought it was something important. Who does that? What if I didn't know Keionna and Rita and I thought you were cheating on me? You would've been one and done. You see she shouldn't be causing problems with us. Why do I have to be the bigger person? Can I just show my ass one fuckin' time?"

"Danielle Mahone you know me better than that? I don't make any moves in the streets unless you're with me. It's funny because you were there also. I guess you went to the bathroom or something. So, I'm guessing she didn't witness the part when you were there? I guess she wasn't able to snap you in the picture! The moment we made it official I was done with all that bull shit. Fuck her she because mad. Don't even stoop to her level. Baby you got too much to lose and entertaining her isn't worth your energy." He explained. He always wanted me to be the one to take the high road. I couldn't do that with Keondra. She's tried it one too many fuckin' times.

"I don't care Baine my best friend is in the hospital because of her. I'm sick of this bitch. She tried the right fuckin' one. She's the one who wants to play games. I'll play along with her and drag that bitch to the finish line. Don't fuck with my family." I argued. I don't care what he says, I'm not letting that bitch slide. I refuse too. A bitch can't try me and live to tell about it. I don't have much family so the ones that I do have I'll protect them at all cost.

"Danielle, I feel where you're coming from trust me, I do. Keondra is up to something and I don't want to kill her before we find out what's going on. I need you to chill because if she starts fuckin' with you then I won't hesitate to touch her for fuckin' with my wife. Please let that shit go. Do I need to come and get you to make sure you don't do anything you'll regret later? I need my wife to keep her hands clean. It's my job to get my hands dirty. I love you and I want you to listen to me." He explained.

"I love you too." Baine and I finished talking. I heard him but I wasn't trying to hear him. I looked at the pictures one more time. I just shook my head because misery loves company. I know I have a lot to lose but she'll lose a lot fuckin' with a bitch like me. Don't include me and my husband in your bullshit. I trashed the pictures in my shredder. I tapped Camina and Cariuna on their shoulders to let them know it was time to go. I grabbed their hands, so we go to the hospital to see their mother before visitation hours are over.

I checked my phone and Mother Dear sent me a text telling me not to bring the girls because she didn't want them to see their mother like that. I understood where she was coming from but if she hears her babies, I think she'll wake up. The last thing she wants is for Camina and Cariuna to grow up without a mother since we didn't have that.

"God mommy Danielle, I'm hungry can we get something to eat? Is it okay if we stay at our house tonight, so we can stay in our own room?" Cariuna asked. Cariuna read my mind because I was hungry too. I needed to feed them and redirect my energy somewhere else. Keondra got me on one.

"Sure baby, we can do that! What do you want to eat," I asked. Camina and Cariuna decided they wanted some spaghetti and corn on the cob with garlic bread. We stopped by Publix and grabbed all the things we needed.

♡

The next stop I made was my house to check the mail and grab a few things that I would need for a few days.

I put my things in the guest room, and it smelled just like Rashad. Ugh, I would be lying if I said the Creed cologne that was in this room didn't smell good. I grabbed the Febreze out the hall closet and aired it out. I had to change the sheets. I couldn't smell him all night. Camina and Cariuna were getting ready for their bath. I took a shower before I started cooking dinner for them. I called Mother Dear and my grandmother to check on Crimson. Her blood pressure was down some but it was still high. Its good news but not the news that I wanted to hear. Real bitches never tap out. I need my girl to shake that shit. We got bigger issues at hand.

I dried off and went downstairs to start our dinner. I laid out everything before I took a shower. Cariuna grabbed the pots for me. Camina's bad ass was sitting at the table with her headphones on. Her face was buried in her IPad.

She looked up at me and I could've sworn she gave me an evil smirk. It's always the cutest kids that are bad as hell.

"God mommy Danielle my God daddy Rashad is on his way. Can you fix him a plate too? Pretty please, thank you." Camina stated and cooed. Then she placed her headphones back on her ear. I walked over to this demon child and took her headphones off. She looked up at me and batted her eyelashes she with the biggest smiled on her face.

"Yes God mommy Danielle?" She asked and beamed. She hasn't been this nice all day which means she's up to something. She'll be the death of me.

"Why is Rashad coming over here? Who invited him?" I asked. The last thing I needed was to be alone with him in this house and Crimson and Griff are nowhere in sight. I trust myself, but I just don't trust him after what happened last night.

"I did God mommy Danielle. I miss my daddy and my God daddy Rashad. I asked him to come and see me." She laughed. I looked at Camina like she was crazy. My eyes got wide. I know the fuck she didn't. On her daddy, I feel like she's trying to play me. I'll lock myself in the guest room. I'm not trying to go there with him today.

I started cooking dinner. Spaghetti was a quick dish to cook. It'll take about an hour. I took a seat at the island and poured myself a glass of wine because I needed it. The ground beef hadn't started to brown yet. Camina and Cariuna ran to the door. I started to get up behind them, but I figure it was Rashad so there was no need to greet his ass. He had a key just like I had a key. He swaggered in the kitchen. I continued cooking not pay his ass any mind.

Camina was grabbing his hand leading him to the table meanwhile I could feel his eyes focused on me. I couldn't wait to finish cooking this food so I can go to the guest room and lock this fuckin' door. I couldn't wait to tell Crimson about her child. Just the thought brings a smile to my face. I knew she would trip. I hope he doesn't start a conversation with me. Camina called him over here, he needs to tend to her.

Crimson - Bitch you need to wake the fuck up NOW! Girl my day has been so fucked up. I need you here to help me weave through all the bullshit. I got so much to tell you. CAMINA is bad as hell and that's a fuckin' understatement. Your daughter is trying to ruin my marriage. Where did she come from? I miss you and I love you!!

I started crying and I didn't even realize it. My best friend didn't deserve anything that's happening to her. I'm crying for Griff too because he was real as nigga. I don't know what Keondra is up too, but that bitch is coming hard which has me looking at her like a suspect. You haven't been with Griff in years and the moment he dies you're on some good bullshit? It doesn't take a rocket scientist to figure out what's up? She set her husband Ike to take the fall and he was in Jacksonville. It's a reason why you went to the Coroner's office to claim that body. You're hiding something and I'm going to figure out what it is. Bitch I'm on to you. I fuckin' mean it. If she killed Griff, I swear to God Crimson better kill that bitch. She needs a slow horrible death. She fucked with the wrong one. For her sake and not mine, her steps better be in order. The ground beef was finally brown. I drained the beef and added my spaghetti sauce in it. Rashad walked up behind me and wrapped his hands around my waist. I stopped him.

"Don't do that and keep your hands to yourself please. I'm married and it's disrespectful to my husband," I explained. Camina was staring at me giving me an evil look. I swear this child is bad as hell. I busted out laughing. Why couldn't she be like Cariuna? She's really about to be mad her mother is expecting another child. I hope it's a boy.

Chapter-11

Rashad

I got a call from Mother Dear telling me what happened to Crimson. I damn near lost it. I couldn't even drive because I was ready to fuck something up. I'm failing big time out here in these streets. First Griff now Crimson. I refused to go out like this. None of this shit was supposed to happen a motherfucka is going to pay for all this shit. I just need a name and it's on. For my nigga, I'm wiping out fuckin' bloodlines. I swear to God if it ain't one thing it's something else. I know sis is having it hard because Griff is gone. Shit, I am too.

I need her to fight because her daughters need her. I got to get to the bottom of what happened. Mother Dear told me Danielle had the girls. I didn't have a number on Danielle. I asked Mother Dear for it, but she wasn't budging. She said I was a little too eager and Danielle is married. If she only knew that was the farthest from my mind. I was surprised when Camina Facetime me from her iPad and asked me to come over. I needed to speak with Danielle anyway to see what happened that caused

Crimson's blood pressure to be so high. I love the fuck out of Danielle. I never stopped. She was the one that got away.

I swear Camina was my child. Danielle tried to front like she didn't want a nigga, but I knew better. She kept throwing it up in my face about her being married to him. I wasn't tripping off that. I was about to put an end to all that shit.

"I need to speak with you about what happened earlier. I don't give a fuck about your husband. I ain't got no respect for him." I heard her mumble something underneath her breath. "Speak up I can't hear you."

"We can talk after I feed them and myself, but after that, you need to go home." She argued. Danielle was tripping. I wasn't trying to hear anything she was saying. She knew I was staying the night. I had to protect my Goddaughters and her. I don't know whose out here calling shots, but I'm protecting mine. I watched Danielle move around the kitchen. She fixed everybody a plate but me. I swear she was petty as hell. Camina watched her like a hawk. She folded her arms across her chest. I swear my baby was about to turn up. Danielle sat down and was about say grace. Camina poked her lips out and cut her off.

"Excuse me God mommy Danielle, but you didn't fix God father Rashad a plate for dinner. That's RUDE." She pouted. Danielle cut her eyes at me. Shit, I didn't say nothing Camina did. She got my back and I got hers. Cariuna and Camina were night and day. I swear when she grows up, she's going to be a force to be reckoned with. Griff and I have had this discussion numerous times. She's nothing like her mother. She refuses to go to daycare. Griff couldn't even collect from the trap twice a week because Camina was always with him. It was crazy because yesterday was the pickup day and the time Griff got hit, he would've been leaving to pick up Camina, but Crimson picked her up instead. Damn what a coincidence.

"I'm sorry Camina, I forgot he was here. I didn't mean to be rude. I'll fix his plate. Rashad, do you eat spaghetti? Would you like some?" Danielle asked. Camina straightened her ass out. Danielle's crazy as hell. She knew she cooked this for me before when we were fuckin' around. It still smells the same. She knew I wanted some. She petty as fuck. I'm sure Camina relayed my message.

"Yeah, I want some you know that." I chuckled. Danielle raised up from the table to fix my plate. Camina looked at me and smiled. I walked up behind Danielle as she was fixing my plate. I could hear her breathing heavy. I don't give a fuck about any of that shit. Danielle handed me my plate. I sat down and she said grace. We ate our food and afterward I put Cariuna to bed. Camina wasn't having it. She was trying to go with me. I told her I wasn't leaving and I'll be here when she wakes up in the morning. Danielle was cleaning the kitchen up when I walked up behind her and grabbed the towel that she was drying the counter off with. She turned around to face me. She had a mean scowl on her face. I cupped her chin and she swatted my hand away. Danielle was beautiful as fuck. Baine was an ignorant as nigga to leave her in arms reach of me. I'm a taker and I got plans to take what rightfully belongs to me. I couldn't keep my eyes or hands off her.

"What Rashad? Stop touching me. Do you not see that I'm cleaning up?" She asked. Of course, I could see what she's doing but we got to have a conversation. That shit can wait. I needed to know what the fuck is up. Ain't no tiptoeing around shit.

"Damn Danielle, I know the way shit ended for us was bad years ago. Lil shawty I'm grown, ass man. I'm sorry, but we got to communicate on behalf of our Godchildren and Crimson. It's some real shit out here going on in these streets and I'm playing for keeps behind my nigga. My best friend is gone and yours in the hospital. I need justice. Street justice.

I know you'll never forgive me or forget but we got to move on." I argued. I know I fucked up, but that shit was years ago. I can't do anything about that. She needs to let that go so I can mend her heart. Danielle was looking at me crazy. She had her hands on her hips grilling me. She pierced her lips together. I know she was about to say some fly shit that I wouldn't like.

"BOY I'm not tripping off you. I hope you didn't think you were that special. I was YOUNG and DUMB. I was good on you the moment, I said I do. We can communicate for them and that's it. I don't want you in my personal space. Can you respect that?" She asked. She dangled her ring in my face. I didn't say anything. She better be glad I got moves to make or else I'll snatch her ass up and make her eat those words.

"Yeah, that's what I thought. If you're going to be here tonight. I'll leave and come back in the morning to take them to school." She explained. Danielle was throwing her cheap shots as she always does. If you're happily married, you don't have to talk about it. I can end all that shit that she and that pussy ass nigga got going on. I got to find out who put a hit out on my nigga. That's more important.

"Nah you're not going anywhere. Dead that shit. It's too late for you to be out. Tell me what happened earlier." I argued. She knew she wasn't going anywhere. That's out the fuckin' question. Danielle ran down to me about everything that happened. I pinched the bridge of my nose. Sweat appeared on my forehead. Veins popped on the side of my head. My heart was pumping, and my face was dripping with venom. Damn Keondra's coming hard as fuck. I ain't never liked that bitch. I don't even call females bitches. She's playing a dangerous game fuckin' with a nigga like me. What's her motive? I swear to God Ike better not had set this shit up. I knew Danielle could tell I was hot. I don't give a fuck. I can't hide my emotions.

"What's wrong Rashad? What's going on? Why are you looking like that?" She asked. Danielle was asking as if she was concerned. I'm a street nigga and I'm Griff's muscle out here in these streets. I enforce everything. I bring the fuckin' pain and apply pressure.

"I don't hit women, but I'll fuck around and murk Keondra. She has some shit going on. I can't believe that bitch pulled that shit. I ain't never liked that bitch or trusted her. I know for a fact Griff divorced her. I bonded him out of jail the day they got the divorce. She tried to set him up that day. She lied and said he shot BeBe and Ms. Carolyn.

I got to make some moves right quick. Be careful out here when you're with my Goddaughters! Thanks for the food." I would love to sit here and lay up with Danielle, but I can't. I got to find out what's going on out here in these streets. My nigga ain't even been laid to rest yet and everybody is calling the shots but me. I got to stay away from anything that's clouding my judgment. That would be Danielle and Mya.

"Be careful Rashad." She sighed. I had to look over my shoulders to see if she meant that.

"I will. Danielle, do you care or were you just saying that?" Danielle just looked at me and shook her head. I asked her a question. I needed a valid response, not a shrug of the shoulder and her shaking her head from side to side. I care about her and I can't even lie. I always wondered how she's been. I never wished badly on her. I wish she didn't marry that nigga. I wish I could've right my wrongs. I wish she was my wife and not his.

“I care Rashad. If it didn’t, I wouldn’t have said anything. Damn, I don’t wish bad on you. I don’t want anything bad to happen to you. Crimson and her daughters can’t take any more losses. I want you to be careful.” She stated. I could rock with that. I wanted to pry some more but I couldn’t. Not right now anyway.

“I’ll see you around Danielle, be careful. Tell Camina to call me if she needs me.” I explained. I looked at Danielle one last time before I made a few moves. I had plans to harass her tonight, but with the shit she just dropped on me I couldn’t. I had to get at whoever’s responsible. It couldn’t wait another day. I had access to the tapes from yesterday. Wire had that shit waiting on me. I hit up Slap and Wire and told those niggas to meet me at the trap. I just haven't had the time to look at them. Tonight is the night I got a feeling some shit isn't adding up. Keondra's making moves like she's entitled to something and she's not. I’m sure I'll find something, if I don’t, I’m at her fuckin’ crib tomorrow. I can’t wait to see where these roads lead too. I needed Danielle and Crimson to be careful.

♡

I made it to the spot in about forty-five minutes. Slap and Wire were sitting on the porch waiting on me. I stepped out of the car and slapped hands with my niggas. We checked our surroundings and made sure security was airtight out this motherfucka. Wired pulled the tapes out his duffel bag. It was a shit load of tapes. It got to be some clues.

Whoever pulled this off had to be watching us for a minute. They caught Griff slipping which means they've been watching him for a minute. Slap rolled up the weed and Wire poured up a few shots. I mixed up the lean. We studied these tapes with a fine tooth comb. The only thing that was out the ordinary was the truck that was posted down the street at the same time every morning for the past two months. I got to get the tag on that truck tomorrow. I got to see who it's registered too. We checked the surveillance tapes from yesterday. Griff wasn't the one that came and got the count. I knew my nigga's body structure and walk like that back of my hand. That wasn't him. Slap and Wire both agreed. Who was in my fuckin' trap house without me knowing? Whoever the nigga was he made sure his face couldn't be recognized on camera.

It was cameras all in the house. Griff never showed up that day. It was somebody else. If that wasn't Griff than where the fuck is he and who was that? Some shit ain't adding up. We finished looking at the tapes. The strangest thing I noticed was nobody was at the trap house working that day. It was supposed to be four niggas there when Griff picked up the bag to make sure the count was right. It wasn't him. I watched whoever it was removing a big duffel bag. Our duffel bags always weigh up to a million plus. I cleared the trap before the police swarmed down here asking questions. Yesterday's count was in the basement hidden in the stash spot. It was a million dollars in cash. If the cash wasn't in the duffel bag, then what was? The video shows whoever it was walking out. If that wasn't Griff that walked out of here then who was it? Damn these tapes just blew my fuckin' mind. Slap and Wire dapped me up.

We made plans to see each other tomorrow. Wire had to get the tag information so we could pull up. They had to take it in because they were both married. Mya was blowing up my phone. I knew she wanted me to come through. I could but I wanted to slide back through Griff's to push up on Danielle. Mya was blowing me up again. I answered because I knew she was worried about a nigga. I at least owed her that.

"Hey, baby I miss you. I haven't heard from you all day. I was checking on you. Have you eaten? I cooked, can you come through?" She asked. I hate to hurt Mya feelings because she always looked out for a nigga and made sure I was straight.

"I miss you too. I've been busy as fuck. I meant to hit you back earlier. I ate but since you cooked for me and you asked I'll slide through."

"How's Crimson and the girls? Who fed you? I don't need anybody doing my job." She asked. Mya knew of Crimson, but she hasn't met her. It couldn't bring anybody around my family if I wasn't for sure if we're serious are not. I got love for Mya, but I couldn't give her my heart because it's with someone else.

"Man, Crimson is in the hospital. Shit is really bad right now." I sighed.

"Damn I hate to hear that. Who has the girls? She asked. Mya knew nothing about Danielle, and I wanted to keep it that way.

"They're with their grandmother. Camina called me earlier pouting. I pulled up on her. I plan on pulling up on Crimson tomorrow to see what's up."

"What did you eat?" She asked. Damn Mya was nosey as fuck and she was asking a lot of questions. I already ate what's the big deal.

"Spaghetti, corn on the cob and a salad." Damn that shit was good as fuck too. Just thinking about it brought a smile to my face.

"It must have been good because you're smiling, I can hear it in your voice. If you already ate, then you don't have to come through. I just wanted to make sure you ate because I know you have a lot on your plate. Be careful Rashad. I was just thinking about you. I won't hold you up." She sighed. I knew Mya was in her feelings, but she asked the question. I ain't trying to hurt her feelings that's why I won't commit to her. I'm not trying to do that. I refuse to break another female's heart. That shit ain't in me. I've been paying for the shit I did to Danielle for years now. She's the reason I can't love another.

"Dan, Mya, don't do that. If you want me to come through I will. Why are you tripping on me? I thought we were good. We kissed and made up yesterday. I ate earlier but I've been smoking and drinking I'm sure I could eat again."

"Were you about to call me another woman's name Rashad? You're so fuckin' disrespectful." She argued. I was hoping that she didn't catch that.

"Mya you're tripping for real. I was about to say damn but I didn't want to cuss or start an argument with you about nothing. Look I'm about to slide through there. Unlock lock the door and don't have nothing on." I hung up on her before she could say anything else. Mya knew some shit was up. I wish she would just fall back for a minute. I wasn't stringing her along because she knew what it was between us. Damn, she's calling back.

"Rashad, why did you hang up in my face? I'm not stupid at all. I knew a bitch cooked for you. I'm good enough to fuck, but I'm not good enough to commit too. Is it okay if I fuck someone else?" She asked. I had to look at the phone because Mya was tripping hard.

"Look don't start. I'm on my way. We'll talk about it when I pull up." I argued. I'm not even trying to go there with her. I shouldn't have answered the phone. I had plans anyway and now she's was killing my vibe.

"Don't come. Whatever bitch got you smiling and cooking for you go there. I'm good." She argued and hung up. Mya was tripping hard. Was it that obvious? I had plans and she ain't said nothing but a thang. Back to my regular scheduled activities. I couldn't wait to be alone with Danielle. All I need is one night alone with her. Mya called my phone back, but I wasn't about to answer. She said what she had to say. I need to stop fuckin' with her because she wants more, and I can't give her. We connect on a sexual level and that's it. It could be more but it's not.

Ike

In all my years of living. I ain't never in my life second-guessed any move I made. My steps have always been ordered and calculated. I'm second guessing everything now leading up to this moment right here. Where the fuck did we go wrong? Yes, I cheated multiple times, but she knew what it was when we go together. I only agreed to marry her if the marriage was open. She was supposed to be my down ass bitch. I married this bitch and gave her my last fuckin' name. On my road to riches, she was the only bitch that I could depend on to have my back out here in the streets besides my nigga. Whenever I counted a check, she counted with me. Did I trust her? Hell no but she would never know that.

I loved and trusted her enough to make her my wife. Keondra was on some real bullshit. What's her fuckin' motive? That's what I'm not understanding? To claim this nigga body at the Coroners and you're married to me is disrespectful. I can't let that shit slide or slip my fuckin' mind. Yeah, I was out here doing my dirt, but home was always with her. I had that bitch living lavishly. She had access to everything. Whatever she wanted I cashed the fuck out. I don't like anybody disrespecting me. I gave this bitch everything. We've been married for four years now.

To make matters worse you're fuckin' with Danielle and Baine on some bullshit, and your signature said, Mrs. Griffey. I knew she wanted to fuck Baine years ago, but he passed it up. We used to laugh about that shit, and I ended up getting stuck with her. I'm tripping off the letter when she referenced him feeling her up years ago. Damn was she still thinking about that shit and she's being lying next to me all these years? I swear to God I want to hurt that bitch. I feel like she had Griff killed and set me up to take the fall.

I can't shake the thought. It makes sense by her fuckin' moves. I knew a motherfucka set me up, but I would've never thought she would be the one behind it. She really wanted the police to hide me. Your wife is supposed to be there when shit is looking bad, but that bitch ain't nowhere to be found. She got it out for nigga. She switched up quick. If a motherfucka would've told me this shit would've happened yesterday morning I wouldn't have believed them. Baine knew I was tripping. I was ready to kill something.

"Aye Ike, don't sweat that shit for real. If she's moving like this ain't no telling what she'll do. Chill out.

We got to lay low for a minute. We can't go to the city right now. If Keondra set you up she'll hang herself." He argued. I heard everything Baine was saying but I wanted to be that nigga that hangs her if she crossed me.

"Baine, it's easier said than done. I married the wrong bitch. Out of all the women I ran through I cut off some good women for her. She was the one that fucked me over. My own fuckin' wife set me up and is out to get me. She's still reminiscing about fuckin' you on the low. I'm not a pussy ass nigga and I ain't never ran from nan nigga. If I did anything, I'm always out in these streets holding fuckin' court. I'm out here hiding behind some shit I didn't do. It hurts. I know I wasn't the best nigga to her, but I would never be grimy and do no shit like this." I argued. I'm out here losing big time. She's fuckin' with my money and my sanity.

"I know how you feel. Trust me I do. We're human and it's okay to feel hurt and betrayed because that's what it is. We can't change that, but what we can do is play the same game that bitch is playing. Fuck hiding out we can ride back to the city and you can lay low in our territory. Let's fuckin' ride. You know I ain't never wanted to fuck her, because I saw right through her. I tried to tell you but you weren't hearing me. Let's clear this motherfucka. We've never hidden from anything and we're always on the front line."

"About fuckin' time." Baine and I slapped hands with each other. I tossed him the fuckin' keys. He was driving and I was lying in the backseat. I couldn't hide out. It makes me look like I'm guilty and I'm not. I refuse to go to jail. I needed to see what the fuck was going on. Keondra was calculated, but I need to sit back and watch my prey. I'm glad I had my attorney to take her name off everything. I decided to call to see where her head was at. She answered on the first ring.

"Aye hoe where you at? I want you to come and see me."

"I'm not a hoe. You need to turn yourself in for killing Griff." She laughed. I had that bitch on speakerphone so Baine could hear.

"Why would I do that if I didn't kill nobody? I'll talk to you later." Baine looked at me and shook his head. Keondra was with the shits.

Chapter-12

Danielle

Sleep wouldn't consume me. I've been tossing and turning all night. Baine sent me a text stating that he would be home in a few hours. I missed him already and he hasn't been gone that long. I couldn't get Rashad off my mind. From what he told me Griff and Keondra were married. I never knew. Shit, Crimson never knew. I guess that's what hurts the most. I think Keondra had Griff killed and she was behind it. A person ain't moving like that and she's married to somebody else. What did Griff do to make her do the shit she's doing?

Keondra is a crazy bitch. I swear to God if I find out that she had something to do with Griff getting killed I'm on that bitch's ass. I wanted to pick some more information from Rashad, but I guess that'll have to wait. The door opened to the guest bedroom and I looked up to see who it was. I rolled my eyes because it was Camina. Lord this child needs to go to bed because she has to go to school tomorrow. I guess she couldn't sleep either.

“God Mommy Danielle I miss my mommy and daddy. My mommy, is she coming back? I know my daddy isn’t coming back he's gone, but he's going to come back and get me.” She asked. I swear Camina is too smart.

“I miss your mommy and daddy too. Your mommy she'll be back home in a few days. Maybe tomorrow. You have to go to bed because you have to go to school tomorrow.” Thinking about Crimson and Griff both brought tears to my eyes. Crimson is the strongest person I know. She can beat this. She has too. I guess Camina noticed me crying because she started wiping my tears with her tiny hands.

“Stop crying God mommy Danielle. I don't want to go to school tomorrow. I need to go see my mommy and look for my daddy.” She stated. She looked at me with wide eyes demanding not to go to school. Lord, I don’t know what I’m going to do with this child.

“I'll take you to see your mother but after that, you're going to school.” I sighed. Camina gave me the biggest smile. Her ass was up to something. She’s going to school tomorrow. I don’t care if she shows her ass but she’s going.

"Okay but my Uncle Rashad is going to come and get me, so I don't have to go to school. Why don't you like my God father Rashad?" She asked and pouted. I wasn't about to sit here with Camina and discuss Rashad. She needs to go to bed and stay out of grown folk's business.

"Camina you have to go to school. You're too smart not to be at school learning. I do like your Godfather." I wish I could tell her the truth. I can't stand that cheating fine ass motherfucka. Camina gave me a big smile. I don't trust this child. She's a little cute manipulator.

"Good night God mommy Danielle. I'm going to sleep. Can you make me some French toast and eggs in the morning?" She asked. Camina was using me. She didn't fool with me tough. Her badass had to know I knew she called Rashad because she didn't want to listen to anything I had to say. Crimson told me if she told her no, she'll pout and cry to her father to get her way.

"Yes, I can Camina, good night." She wiggled her little badass out the room. I looked at the time on my cell phone and it was after 12:00 a.m. It's way past my bedtime. I threw the pillows on the floor and got a little more comfortable. My eyes were getting heavy. I guess sleep wanted me as bad as I wanted it and I finally drifted off to sleep. I felt my toes being sucked and my night shorts being slid down my legs. I always wanted Baine to have easy access. I didn't pay it no mind because I missed Baine. My husband was a freak. He sucked my pussy as if his life depended on it. I was so into it. I hope the door was closed because I didn't want Camina and Cariuna to see me buck my hips while having a wet dream. I always ran my hands through Baines dreads whenever I sat on his face. I attempted to grab his dreads and they were non-existent. I ran my hands across his head. I just felt deep waves. I know Baine didn't cut his hair. The flick of his tongue sped up. I was on the verge of coming.

"Let that shit go. Damn, that pussy still tastes good." He stated. I jumped up fast. Ain't no way in hell I was dreaming about Rashad? I tried to raise up and I couldn't move my legs. He had a death grip on my legs. I looked between my legs and it was him. He gave me a devilish smile. My heart started beating fast. I just cheated on my husband. He's trying to get me killed.

"Rashad why would you do that? You violated me! I'm married, do you understand that?" I argued and cried. I'm crying my eyes out and he's fuckin' laughing.

“I wanted too. I don’t care about you being married. Divorce him.” He argued and laughed. Tears poured down my face. My heart was hurting. I just cheated on my husband by force and not by choice. Rashad was never supposed to be this close to me. I'm married, why can't he understand that. I feel so violated.

“Why are you crying, Danielle?” He asked. He tried to wipe the tears that were falling down my cheeks. I smacked the shit out of him. I looked at him as if he was crazy. You got to be fuckin' kidding me.

“Leave Rashad. The reason why I’m crying doesn't even matter to you. I just cheated on my fuckin' husband. I don't cheat. I’m not a fuckin' cheater. Why would you do that? It's plenty of females out here that's willing but I’m not.” I argued. I tried to raise up out the bed, but he wouldn't let me get up. He had a hold on me. “Please just let me go.” I cried.

“I can't do that. I won't do it. For the record, I don't give a fuck about these other females out here. I could be there, but I want to be here. How do you think I feel Danielle? You're not supposed to be married to him? You were never supposed to do that. I ain't sorry. I wanted it and you did too.” He argued.

"No, I didn't. You took the pussy. I don't want your mouth on me." I argued.

"I didn't take the pussy. I tasted it and you fed me the rest, it's a difference. You wanted me to suck on you." He chuckled. I swear this motherfucka done lost his damn mind. I can't stand him. I can't stay here at this home with him. He doesn't give a fuck about anything. I'm married.

"Move Rashad," I argued.

"I'm not going anywhere Danielle you can forget about it and neither are you." He wasn't trying to hear anything I was saying. This was wrong on all levels. He kept trying to kiss me and I refused to do this with him. I kept moving my face. He freed my breasts from my sports bra and started sucking on my nipples. He knew that was my spot.

"Stop Please," I begged and moaned. His head got lost between my legs again. He sucked every hole on body. I couldn't take it. I grabbed the pillow off the floor to muffle my screams. He snatched it out of my hand and threw it on the floor. I couldn't take it. I just came all on his face. I'm going to hell.

He was eating me as if I were his last meal. He was doing things to my body that I couldn't even explain. My heart and pussy both had a mind of their own. I couldn't control it if I wanted too. Why me? Why couldn’t he do right? This is the reason why I stayed away from him all these years because I was afraid of all this.

I might as well enjoy myself and pray this moment never comes back to bite me in my ass. My mind was saying no but my heart was saying something else. I heard a knock at the door. I didn’t pay it any mind. I was so in the moment.

“God mommy Danielle what's going on in here and why are you screaming?” She asked. My heart dropped. Damn, Camina's grown ass don't miss a beat. Rashad stopped moving. We were caught. If you not doing anything you should be you shouldn't be doing it. I was taking this night to the grave with me. If Crimson isn't home, then Camina and Cariuna will be at my house. I can't stay here.

“I'm sorry I didn't mean to wake you up. I was having a horrible dream. A nightmare.” I panicked. It wasn't a complete lie because I was having a dream about my husband being down there, not him.

"Oh okay. Who is that in the bed with you?" She asked. Take your ass to bed. Rashad wasn't making shit any better because he was finger fuckin' me. I couldn't take it.

"No one, it's my body pillow." Rashad pulled my body to the middle of the bed and slid his dick in. So fuckin' disrespectful. Thank God it's dark in here. He started pounding me.

"Oh, well whose shoes are those on the floor? My God daddy Rashad has the same shoes."

"They're my shoes I brought the wrong ones over here. Go back to bed Camina we have to get up early in the morning." Camina did as she was told. Rashad flipped me on my back side, and we went at it until the wee hours in the morning.

"You know it ain't no turning back after this? You better not fuck that nigga either." He argued. I knew he was crazy. Little did Rashad know he'll never see me again. Morning came quick. I was exhausted and I couldn't wait to leave this house and never come back. I woke up to an empty bed. I had to wash the covers. Crimson would kill me. I checked my phone to look at the time. It was a little after 7:00 a.m. I snatched the covers off the bed. Fuck it I'll trash these. I don't need any evidence reminding me of what I did.

I stepped into the bathroom to handle my hygiene. I took a long hot shower. My mind was a wreck. I had no business doing that. I can't wait until Crimson wakes up. I headed downstairs to cook Camina and Cariuna breakfast. Rashad beat me to it.

He looked at me and I refused to look at him. I wanted to get as far away from him as possible. I played it cool. Baine called me and I stepped out to take the call. I guess Baine and I's conversation lasted longer than I expected it too. Rashad walked up behind me and started kissing me on my neck. I pushed him off me. He pushed me in the corner and grabbed my phone and hung up on Baine. He was sucking on my neck. I know he was about to leave a passion mark that I wouldn't be able to hide. He was so fuckin' disrespectful.

"You can't be doing that," I argued and pouted. He closed the gap between us and invaded my personal space. He cupped my chin forcing me to look at him.

"I do what the fuck I want. You're on my time now, so end that shit now. Let's go. I cooked your breakfast." He argued. I can't stand him. Baine called back.

“My bad baby, my call dropped. Let me fix the kids breakfast and I’ll see you in a few.” I beamed. Rashad was breathing down my neck.

“You heard what the fuck I said.” He argued. I can't wait to eat and get up out of here. Rashad fixed our plates. Camina was on the right of me and Cariuna was on the left. Rashad sat right in front of me. He slid us our plates. It smelled and looked good. I couldn't eat because he was staring a hole in me. I said grace and ate our food. I offered to do the dishes. I wanted Rashad as far away from me as possible. His phone was blowing up. He wouldn't answer it. Camina and Cariuna went upstairs to put their clothes on. Rashad was grilling me. I attempted to walk upstairs but Rashad grabbed me. I gave him a nasty scowl.

“Aye Danielle, don't do that. I want to see you later. Call me if you need me.”

“You won't be seeing me later. I'm married. What happened between us will never happen again,” I argued.

“Is that what you think? Your mouth says one thing, but your heart and your pussy said its mine. I'll see you later. Think about that.” I took Camina and Cariuna to see Crimson. She was sleeping peacefully. I told Mother Dear she could go home.

After I dropped the girls off I made it back to see Crimson. I climbed right in the bed with her. Mother Dear was still here. She gave me a funny look and I didn't know what that meant.

"Danielle you ain't slick. You better get your shit together. Camina called me from her IPad last night and told me Rashad was in the bed with you." She laughed. My heart caved in. Any life I had in my face was drained. I couldn't take this child to my house. I just held my head down. I was so fuckin' embarrassed. I swear Crimson better wake up. She needs her ass whopped. I tried to ignore Mother Dear because I didn't want to talk about this. I just wanted to forget that it ever happened.

"Danielle, are you really going to sit here and ignore me? Please tell me you didn't?" she asked. I rose up so she could see me. My face was soaked with tears because I didn't want to reveal or talk. I just wanted to be alone without Crimson and tell her about all the bullshit that happened without Mother Dear prying in my damn business.

"Technically I didn't. He took it from me. I feel so bad because I have a wonderful husband's who's perfect and he didn't deserve that. I can't keep the kid's at

Crimson's or my house because I don't want Camina to get me killed. I guess that's what I get for being a good friend and God Mother. I'm getting the shitty end of the stick. I knew the first night I shouldn't have stayed there because of the way he acted." I sobbed. Mother Dear gave me a nasty look.

"Stop crying when you were screaming last night. You weren't crying. Baine is a good man and Rashad is too, but you should've never closed the door on Rashad. You weren't over him. Rashad never stopped loving you, and Baine loves you too, but you're playing a dangerous game. Tell Baine what you did or walk away. Don't cheat on him. I raised you better than that." She explained. I looked at Mother Dear as if she was crazy. I wasn't telling Baine that. God I could beat Camina's ass right now. Crimson needs to do something about her.

"I can't tell him that I cheated on him and I'm not walking away from my husband." Baine and I have been married for five years. I'm not throwing away my marriage for a one-night stand. I hate I did that.

"Danielle do you actually think Rashad is just going to accept that and be cool about it? He didn't care that you were married. I'm not saying leave your husband but how do you think this is going to play out?" She asked. I heard Mother Dear, but I wasn't listening. Not now anyway. My heart already hurts that it went that far. He crossed a line that he shouldn't have. I feel so guilty because I enjoyed it. I had plans to take that to the grave with me.

Chapter-13

Keondra

Time wasn't on my side. I had to start planning Griff's funeral immediately. I wanted to wait until the weekend, but I couldn't. Auntie Kaye and that bitch Auntie BeBe kept calling my phone asking me what type of games I was playing. That's for me to know and for them to never find out. Marie fake ass was calling me too. Why are y'all on my phone now though? I'm not with that fake shit. I just hung up in their face. Stop calling my phone. Jermesha told me Crimson was in the hospital. I'm not done with that bitch either.

The same way they treated me when he was alive, they need to act the same way now that's he's dead. Bitch, I'm his fuckin' wife. Last I checked Crimson wasn't. I had to get this show on the road. It's been a few days now and it's time for me cash out. I didn't even want to deposit this cash until he was good in the ground. I need to put this million dollars in the bank.

I couldn't take Griff's body to Willie Watkin's Funeral Home because he knows their whole family. I didn't want anybody viewing Griff's body. He was fucked up really bad. Baptiste and Son's is the next best thing. I had to call my bitch Jermesha and my cousin Cutie to see if they wanted to ride with me. I called Jermesha first.

"What's up bestie, what's the move?" She asked. Jermesha was my rider. I don't give a damn. Whenever I call her, she's always there. I know I can depend on her no matter what. She crossed her own family out for me. That action alone speaks volumes.

"Hold on Jermesha let me merge Cutie in." I beamed. I needed my girls to ride with me. Even though I killed Griff this is one of the hardest things I'll ever have to do. I loved him, but he should've just given me another chance and we wouldn't even be here. I was supposed to have his kids not her. He was my meal ticket.

"What's up Keondra?" Cutie asked. If she only knew the day I had between Ike tripping and Jacque leaving, it's been a mess. I'm trying not to stress myself because I'm pregnant. I want this baby even though Jacque is tripping.

We need to have a conversation about where we stand. I know I was moving hot, but I don't give a fuck. Griff is dead and he ain't coming back. I got moves to make. I refuse to hold up the process. The sooner I get this nigga in the ground and Ike behind bars the happier I'll be.

"Everything! I'm about to ride to Baptiste & Son's Funeral Home. I wanted to see if y'all wanted to ride with me?" I asked. Jermesha and Cutie were lit. What the fuck did I miss? "Calm down it's just a funeral home." I laughed. Jermesha and Cutie where both trying to talk at the same time. Jermesha just had to speak her piece first.

"Keondra what time are you pulling up? I'm picking out my outfit now. Give me about an hour to get dressed. Baptiste Funeral Home, bitch, you must not know who owns that? Sphinx and Vell bitch. You know I wanted that man for years. He would never give me the time of day. I heard he was married now, but that ain't got shit to do with me. I just want to borrow him for a few days or hours." Jermesha beamed. Damn, I forgot they did own it. Oh yeah, I need to get cleaned up real nice. Sphinx and Vell were both easy on the eyes.

"Jermesha, you ain't never lied. I went to school with Vell's fine ass. It ain't nothing but dope boys up through there. I'm choosing today and it's nice outside too. Let me find me a cute sundress to grip this ass and curves. I bet I cuff me something." Cutie stated. We finished talking for a few minutes. I needed to get dressed too. I had a little pudge, but I wasn't showing just yet. Normally I would be down, but I want Jacque so bad and I miss him. After I have the funeral and put Crimson out, I'm going to California to spend a few months with my mom. I'm praying that Jacque and I will be back together by then. I missed him so much. I didn't sleep at all last night because he wasn't in arm's length. I called him last night and he cleared me out. I sent him a long text and he read it but didn't respond.

♡

It took us over an hour to get ready. I looked at my watch and it was after 2:00 p.m. I pulled up on Jermesha and Cutie, doing a once over and we were killing it. I knew Jermesha and Cutie where with the shits. They both had on a pair of shorts that stopped at their ass. If they bent over everything was hanging out. They had that drip for sale. Cutie had on a cute crop top and Jermesha had on a sports bra to match her shorts. I threw me on a cute little sundress that stopped at my thighs. I felt overdressed. These bitches were out doing me today.

We pulled up at Baptiste Funeral Home. I don't know what the fuck was going on, but there were niggas posted up outside in Bentley's, Bugatti's and Maybach's. Damn! You name it these niggas was pushing it. Every nigga out here was dripping. I couldn't even throw the car in park good because Jermesha and Cutie were ready to hop out. As soon as our feet touched the pavement all eyes were on us. You couldn't miss the lustful stares. I made sure what little ass I had I threw it in a circle. I grabbed my Chanel frames out my purse and threw them on my face. I didn't want to openly eye fuck anyone but damn. I couldn't help but to eye fuck this one nigga. He was tall dark and handsome. Dreads adorned his head. Big Gold Chains draped his neck. He had the eyes of a killer. He grabbed his dick when I walked past. Damn, I almost fainted.

"Bitch, that's Mauve'," Jermesha whispered where only I could hear. The name sounded familiar, but I couldn't remember where I knew him from. We finally made it inside the funeral home, and it was nice as fuck. The receptionist greeted us.

"Welcome to Baptiste and Son Funeral Home. How can I help you?" She asked.

"I wanted to make some arrangements for my husband. Can you assist me? Is the funeral director here?"

"Sure, I need you to fill out some paperwork. You can pick out the casket and we'll handle the rest." I filled out the paperwork. Jermesha and Cutie went with me to pick out the casket. Damn, I can't believe I'm really doing this. I tear slid down my face.

"Excuse me, Mrs. Deleon, Mr. Baptiste will see you now." She stated. The door on the right opened and damn I never seen a God in the flesh. He was so damn fine. Jermesha made her way over there immediately. Cutie was right behind her. He held the door open for us. As soon as we got seated, it was another nigga in there also. He was fine as fuck too. He wasn't as dark, but I could tell they were brothers. His dreads were long and he was dripping. Damn, I should've killed Griff sooner if I were able to be in the presence of these two. No wonder Jermesha and Cutie were on go.

"Thank you for choosing Baptiste and Son Funeral Home. I'm Sphinx and this is my brother Vell. We'll assist you with all your arrangements." He explained. He was rude.

No handshake or nothing. He took a seat back behind his desk and got busy with his laptop.

Jermesha took that as her queue to fuck with him. "Aye shawty, you need to back the fuck up. I don't want you in my personal space." He argued. Cutie was eye fuckin' Vell. I gave him the rundown of how I wanted the funeral.

"Okay, I heard about Griff. He was a good nigga. I hate he went out like that. Let me hit up Rashad first to see if he okay's this because I was under the impression that he was handling the funeral arrangements. Who are you to Griff?" He asked. I looked at him like he was crazy.

"I'm his wife," I argued. Vell looked at me and chuckled. He gave me an evil grin. I gave him a nasty glare too. "I'm calling the fuckin' shots. Rashad can't tell me what the fuck I can and can't do." I argued.

"Oh yeah, well let's see about that?" He argued. I heard the door to his office open. Two bitches walked in and gave us an evil glare. Vell shook his head and Sphinx never looked up. I don't know who these bitches are, but I can feel it's about to be a problem because neither one of them said anything.

“Vell, what the fuck is going on in here.” She asked. She placed a bag of food in his hands. She straddled him on his lap. She gave us an evil glare. Cutie looked at me and laughed. “What's funny?” She asked. Neither one of us spoke up. I didn't have time to argue with anybody. I’m pregnant.

“I’m working baby. I’m trying to see if this funeral is about to happen or not. Since you’re here I’ll let you take it from here.” He explained. The small tiny one she marched over to where Sphinx was and pushed Jermesha into the wall. My eyes got wide as hell. I know the fuck she didn't. What type of business is this? Can he at least say something? Jermesha couldn’t even stand on her feet because whoever this bitch was rammed her face in the wall. I stood up to break it up. Sphinx closed his laptop and he gave me a hateful glare.

“I wish the fuck you would!” He yelled and looked directly at me.

“Is that a threat,” I asked.

“Shawty, I don’t make threats. I make shit happen!” He yelled. His tone was so threatening and powerful I felt that shit.

"Bitch, you're too fuckin' close to him. When you see him, bitch, know that's me. If you don't, every time I see you, bitch, I'll touch you so you'll know that's me. You need to back the fuck up before I plan your fuckin' funeral. If my husband told you once to back up take heed to what the fuck he's saying." She argued. Sphinx pulled his wife down on his lap and wrapped his arms around her waist. He was whispering something in her ear to calm her down. Vell put his phone on speaker.

"Aye Rashad, I got this chick up in here claiming to be Griff's wife. She's trying to have his funeral. Did you sign off on that?" He asked.

"Is it Crimson, if not tell that bitch KEONDRA it's a fuckin' no. I'm about to pull up, keep that bitch there so I can holla at her. She ain't married to him. HE DIVORCED HER. I'm on my way VELL don't let that bitch bust a move." He argued. I grabbed my purse. I don't have time for his shit. All eyes were on us.

"Don't leave now. Have a seat and wait on Rashad to get here." Vell laughed. I looked at him and cracked a faint smile.

"I'm out your services are no longer needed. I thought you niggas, liked to make money? I guess not," I laughed. His wife stepped in my face. I took a step back.

"Watch your mouth lil bitch before I put something in it. I'm not talking about my niggas. The one that you and your bitches thought you could come in here suck. I caught all that. We got money and it's clean. We don't fuck with dirty money. Whatever games you got going on in these streets you better watch your fuckin' back. You can never walk in our business and talk shit about how we do business without me putting my hands on you." She argued. She cocked her fist back and punched me in the jaw. Oh hell no. I drew back my hand and Vell grabbed it and pulled it back damn near out of the socket. I winced in pain.

"You're hurting me and I'm pregnant." I sobbed. Damn these are some ruthless ass niggas.

"Leah that's enough. We don't tolerate disrespect at all. You got about three minutes tops to leave and if not bitch you're going to be embalmed. Rashad signed off on that." He argued. We ran out of there so damn fast. I almost tripped on my feet. I swear I didn't expect my visit to go like that. We hopped in my car and pulled out as fast as we could.

Rashad

On God I wasn't expecting to hear from OG Vell. I knew it was business and important because we don't even talk on the phone. We talk in person. Slap and Wire ran the tags on the truck that was parked on the street. We followed the address to where the vehicle was registered too. It led to the Jamaican niggas that worked for Ike. It was music to my fuckin' ears. Slap and I pulled up on the block they hustled on and we lit that bitch up. I was on my feet airing that motherfucka out. Straight headshots. I didn't give a fuck. I wasn't leaving this motherfucka until I laid every nigga affiliated with Ike and Baine down. Baine and Ike ain't talking about shit. They ordered the hit. Nobody can tell me otherwise. My phone rang and it was Vell calling back.

"Yo!" I yelled through the phone. OG Vell was laughing in the background. He already knew I was on some hot ass shit. Those niggas were talking that big boy gang shit about how they touched mine. I couldn't wait to drop those niggas. The same way they gave, that's how I gave it. No fuckin' smoke man.

"Aye Shad. Keondra just left. Shawty got some shit with her. I don't know what she's up to but she's up to something. Do you know this bitch brought two hoes in here with her? After we denied her service, she wanted to talk shit. My wife rocked her in her shit. Jermesha hoe ass came up in here all on Sphinx and shit. Malone rocked her ass. Hold up, Cutie was with the bitch too. You know I used to fuck with that hoe years ago.

Remember I almost killed that bitch at Chit Chat because she was acting stupid. I hit my wife up and told her to pull up now because I knew they were on some good bullshit. Cutie knows not to come in my fuckin' presence. It took everything in me not to drop that bitch in my office." He argued. Keondra was a hoe just like them bitches she ran with. I ain't surprised at all. Clearly, those bitches didn't know they were walking into a death trap, but Cutie knew.

"I already knew that bitch is up to something. She knows I'm on her ass. I know that bitch and her nigga set my nigga up but it's cool. I put it on my life I ain't leaving out this motherfucka until I take those muthafuckas with me." I could always depend on him and Sphinx no matter what.

Baine

It felt good to be back in the city. I can't wait to see my wife. I've only been away from her for two days and that's too long. I couldn't move around like I wanted to because Ike was wanted for murder and my nigga wasn't going down like that. I got a call from my nigga Kato saying Rashad, Slap, and Wire lit up the block on feet. Eight of my soldiers were dead. I told that nigga we didn't have shit to do with that. It's about to be a full-fledged war.

My Jamaican niggas were some ruthless and dangerous niggas. Rashad had to catch them off guard. Ain't no way he pulled up on my block and it went down like that and he's still moving around out here. Ike was ducked off in our old Condo out west in Powder Springs on some real low-key shit. He was dying to get back on the block. That shit couldn't happen unless he was ready to go to jail. I can't have my nigga going to jail. Ike wasn't hearing shit I had to say.

"Baine fuck that. I hear you, nigga but I don't. My niggas died behind some shit I didn't fuckin' do. Get Rashad on the phone so I can speak with that nigga face to face. If I go to jail, I just go to fuckin jail. Bond me right out because I'm going to handle my fuckin' business. I'm not a pussy ass nigga if those crackers hide me for a little bit, but then that's what it is. I'm not guilty and no matter what they have on me, it won't hold. I ain't never ran from shit and I'm not about to start. If they catch me before you can prove that I'm not guilty, oh well. Until then I'm gone ball until I fall. I'm in these streets with you." He argued and explained.

"I hear you Ike and I respect everything you just said. I know how you are and I knew laying low was never going to fly with you. It is what it is." We've been following Keondra all day and so far, nothing. I'm tripping because she's really trying to have Griff a funeral and she's not his wife. It took everything in Ike not to run up in there to shut all that shit down. I had to grab him to keep him from going in there. Our soldier's that we had following Keondra shot us an address to check out. Her car has been sitting there overnight. Now we know where she's been staying at.

Ike and I were headed that way now. We stopped by the corner store that wasn't too far from the house. It was a nice low-key area but what the fuck was she doing over here. She was married and had a home. Ike and I pulled back up on the block.

We parked four houses down from the address that was given. A black G-Wagon Mercedes pulled up. Ike pushed me trying to get my attention.

"What the fuck was that for?" I asked. I turned around to see what the fuck Ike was getting at. We both saw the G-wagon so what. It dawned on me that it was Jacque's piece. He used to work for us up until a few months ago.

"Turn the fuckin' car around. That was Jacque. What the fuck is he doing over here?" He argued. I turned the car around. Ike was still sitting in the back seat. I did as I was told. Jacque stepped out the G-wagon checking his surroundings. He checked the mailbox. That's a sign he lived there. He got back in the G-wagon and pulled in the garage. Keondra came flying down the street. Ike and I both looked at each other. I could tell he was frustrated.

"Aye Baine, this shit isn't coincidental. I swear to God if that bitch was fuckin' this nigga while he was working for me. I'm killing the two of them. I'm going, in let's go. I want to hear what's going on inside of that house." He argued. Ike opened the back door and I opened the front. As soon as our feet touched the pavement. The garage door went up and Jacque was backing out the garage fast. Keondra was running out the garage. She picked up a brick and threw it at his car. Whatever happened, it had her mad as hell. Tears were running down her face. Jacque raised down the window and he said something to her. Ike was kicking the back seat. Keondra a real hoe out here for real. That's why her attitude changed. I couldn't do shit but shake my head.

"Baine, pull off before I jump out the car and hurt this bitch in broad daylight." He argued. I was pulling off anyway. I already knew what time it was. He kept his hands on the door. I can't even believe she's giving it up like this, but I'm not surprised. I wish he would've seen this shit years ago. I felt sorry for Ike for real. If it ain't one thing it's something else. Keondra keeps hitting him where it hurts.

"Ike, she ain't even worth it. Don't let her provoke you. She wants you to touch her so she can get you cased up."

"Baine, I know I haven't been the best man to her but you know what it ain't even no buts. I would never do that shit to her. I paid this nigga. He was on payroll but sleeping with my wife right under my nose." He argued.

"I know but at least you can sit back and watch what's going on. You know now that she was cheating. Let's see what else she got going on. Whatever she's doing it'll lead us to the answers that we're looking for."

"True but I want to come back through here tonight. She got to feel me though. I know she's setting me up. On God, Baine, I'll kill this bitch. If you wanted to cheat and still be a hoe you could've spoken up earlier. She always thought she could do what the fuck she wanted, because I was cheating. She was a fuckin' saint. I could've been divorced her. We wouldn't even be here. Jacque gone feel me too."

Chapter-14

Keondra

I swear this day couldn't get any worse. First, it's the little shit that popped off at the funeral home. I was looking forward to putting that little shit behind me. Jermesha, Cutie, and I decided to get something to eat and drink after all the bull shit popped off. I couldn't even eat my food or take a sip of my tea because Jacque called me going off. He told me to meet him at the house. I thought we were finally about to make up and move on. Boy was I wrong. We couldn't even have a decent conversation. I didn't get him either. You're with me or you're not. He wasn't even here a good five minutes and he left. He started going in on me instantly. I made sure he felt me. I left a nice dent in his G-wagon. I can't deal with him right now.

I had to bury Griff so I can make some serious moves. I had to find a place to have this funeral quick. Who knew planning a funeral could be this hard? I went to identify Griff's body after I dropped Jermesha off. Cutie escorted me back there. Damn, he's fucked up bad. I was still having an open casket. I wanted people to see how I took out this pussy ass motherfucka. Crimson won't be allowed to view anything pertaining to him. Security will be airtight. Rashad better hope I let him in. The sooner I get him in the ground the better things will be. I guess I'll have to check with some of the funeral homes outside of Metro Atlanta.

After everything that happened at Baptiste and Son today, I'm fuckin' done. Sphinx and Vell both were too aggressive. It was a turn-off but they had me turned on. My mother was calling me, and I haven't heard from her in a few days. She knew I was pregnant. She told me I needed to tell Ike or leave because she didn't see it working out well for me. I've been avoiding her calls because I didn't want to be lectured. I went ahead and decided to answer.

"Hi mommy. I miss you," I sighed. I tried to sound as sad as possible because I didn't want her to go in on me.

"Keondra don't do that. What's going on with you baby girl? I've been calling your phone for the past three days and you haven't answered. I just find it funny that you can post on social media all day, but you can't answer any of my calls. I heard about Griff passing. I'll be down there to pay my respects. My flight leaves Sunday. Why are you posting all those pictures of you and Griff and you know that what the two of you had was years ago?

Girl, you're so disrespectful. What does Ike have to say about that? Have you told him you're pregnant by Jacque yet?" She asked. I shouldn't have answered the phone, but I didn't want her to worry about me. I know she means well but I'll cross that line when I get there. Fuck Crimson, I'm not sparing that bitch period.

"Mommy no I haven't told Ike yet. It's complicated. Why would you want to come to Griff's funeral? I loved Griff and I still do. True love will never die. I don't care how Ike feels. I know how I feel." I argued. My mother loved Griff no matter what we went through.

"Griff was a great man. It's not my fault it didn't work out. You should've kept your legs closed. Keondra, I need you to grow up, you have a child on the way. Thank God it's a boy. Haven't you learned anything from your past mistakes? It's this thing called Karma. I'm sure you've heard of her. She always comes back around when you least expect. You got to stop treating people wrong and fuckin' over them. You got to much pride just to walk away. Your pride is what's going to get you hurt." She argued. I had to look at my phone to make sure I was talking to the correct person. I knew she would come once she heard the news. It reminds me I need to delete her off my social media. She's just too nosey.

"Mommy, whose side are you on? I have learned some lessons. You can't help who you love. I made a lot of mistakes. I don't regret my son. I hate that Ike isn't the father. I made my bed, so I'll deal with it. I just don't know when, but I will. I just want you to have my back mommy, that's all. I know Ike will be upset and I'm not ready to go through the extra emotions on top of being pregnant. We're already not in a good space because he killed Griff." I sighed I was laying it on real thick too.

"Keondra what's really going on? You need to be honest with that man. I know things between you and Ike were Rocky but the moment you call yourself having Jacque's child and being head over hills for him you should've walked away.

Why would Ike kill Griff that doesn't seem right? What did you do Keondra? I always got your back right or wrong but I'm still going to let you know how I feel. I just don't want you to get hurt. I don't want anybody trying to hurt people you love because of the things you do." She sighed. I finished talking to my mother. We've been having the same conversation for a few weeks now. I love Ike. Am

I in love with him, no? I was waiting on him to get locked up so I can break the news.

Ike

Keondra played me for real. I can't even lie. It hurts watching her crying behind another man that's not me. It didn't feel good at all. My chest got tight as fuck. I don't even know how I missed the signs. I should've known something was up when she stopped letting me fuck her raw and we were married. It's not that I was even in the blind. I wasn't paying attention. Just off the strength that she had the balls to fuck with a nigga that worked for me right under my nose is foul. I knew they were fuckin' around heavy because his car was programmed to the garage. She was crying so I knew it was something personal behind it. She's emotional and she only cries when she's hurt. I just didn't give a fuck. She should've given a nigga the heads-up years ago. We wouldn't even be here if she had.

Things have been bad between us for years and I wanted to walk away. She begged me to stay. I stayed and I tried to work shit out. I didn't want to be that nigga to give up on my marriage and to leave without trying to see if it would work. Shit was all good for a minute and then it went back the same. I'm not even surprised because my mother always told me the same way you gain them is how you lose them. When I met her she was married to Griff. He wasn't my nigga, but we knew each other.

Keondra and I got together off the strength she was going through some shit with Griff and I was there. She had a situation and I had a few. Don't get me wrong, Baine is my nigga and his word is law, but I couldn't let Keondra slide. I had to touch her because if you give a bitch an inch, they'll take a mile. I couldn't give her another mile. If Baine knew me like I think he does. He knows I'm headed over here. I knew she was at the house because the living room light was on and her car hasn't moved since we left. I've been waiting to make my move. I wanted to run in there and drag her ass out.

Kato and Drake were posted up on the block. The streetlights were already on and that was a bonus. It was time to make my move. In all my years of living, I ain't never put my hands-on a female but Keondra would be the first. It took everything in me not to jump out of the car and murk the two of them in broad daylight. It had to be a God somewhere because the devil was on my back telling me, young nigga kill that bitch.

I tried to shake that monkey off my back, but I couldn't. Jacque crossed me. I don't give a fuck I got to touch him too. Can't no nigga eat at my table and fuck my wife right under my nose. There wasn't much movement on the street. Kato picked the back door and left it unlocked for me. I stepped out the car checking my surroundings. Everything looked good. I threw my hat up at Kato. He nodded his head at me giving me the okay to go in.

I made my way in the house. Keondra really moved out and called herself living with this nigga. Her clothes were everywhere. I tiptoed in and she was in a heated conversation with someone. I stood still so I could hear everything she was saying.

"Mommy I promise I'll tell Ike soon, that the child I'm carrying isn't his. It's not as easy as it sounds," she cried. Damn, I didn't even know that she was pregnant. This bitch was really trying to play me. She finished up the conversation she was having with her mother. I waited until she dropped the phone down. I walked up behind her and tapped her on her shoulder. I pressed the gun to the back of her head. I could see the hairs raise up. Damn did she think I was that dumb?

“Drop that fuckin' phone bitch. What are you scared to tell me? Keondra ain’t scared of shit last I checked. Nah better yet give me that shit right now. I bet you're surprised to see me huh,” I asked and chuckled? She was talking a lot of shit over the phone. She placed the phone in my hand. I slid it in my back pocket. I cocked my Glock back because I wasn't playing with this bitch. She flinched. Don’t get scared now.

“Ike, what are you doing here?” She asked and cried. She turned around to face me and my gun was pointed directly in her face. She looked at me with wide eyes. I don’t give a fuck about her tears. That shit doesn’t move me. I don’t feel sorry for her. She was playing a dangerous game now she needs to deal with the cards she dealt. She’s in a fucked-up situation and that ain’t got shit to do with me. It’s all on her.

“Nah bitch don't cry. Save those tears for another fuckin' day. You're pregnant by who if I'm not the father? Bitch you got me fucked up. You've been fuckin' with Jacque behind my back. How long?” I asked. She couldn’t even look me in the face. I know now though.

“Ike you don’t understand.” She cried. I understand it all. I see what it is.

"I asked you who. You fucked the help, you really got me out here looking like a fool. I don't even know you anymore. Who the fuck are you? You've always had hoe tendencies but this shit right here I'm tripping off. You're reminiscing about my nigga finger fuckin' you in the club years ago? How do you think that shit made me feel? You're acting as if you're Griff's wife, but you got my last name." I argued. She doesn't fuckin' understand. I understand she was playing me and now she's caught. Explain yourself.

"Can you please put the gun down?" She asked and cried. Keondra couldn't guilt trip me. I wasn't putting shit down. I shoved the gun in her face. Look at everything she's done to me. She doesn't deserve to keep breathing. She already knows how I give it up. The worst thing she could've ever done to me was attempted to fuck me over.

"Why should I Keondra? Give me a fuckin' reason why I shouldn't? You said a whole bunch of shit over the phone. I'm here in the flesh now say what the fuck you got to say. You're not in any position to ask questions, I am. I ain't putting shit down." I argued.

"Ike, I fucked up and I'm sorry. I didn't know how to tell you. It takes two but you, you did this to me with all the constant cheating and lying. I made a mistake and I got caught up." She cried. I did this. Nah, bitch, you did this. Cheating is only fun when you don't get caught. Why are you crying? It was all fun and games before I showed up.

"How long Keondra? If you fucked up why couldn't you say that? I ain't never fucked a bitch that you were cool with. Do you know how many bitches smile in your face every day that want to fuck me? It's boundaries but I would never give a bitch that smiles up in your face that much power to say they fucked me. I loved you enough not to do that. Love isn't a factor here. It's level to this shit. He stayed in my home, was on my payroll, and he fucked my wife.

It's not going down like that. You know I'm not sucker and that nigga won't live to talk about what the two of you had going on. Whose baby is it? How many months are you?" I asked. I knew it wasn't mine. I just wanted her to tell me to my face.

"Can you please put the gun down?" She asked and cried. I lowered the gun out of her face. "I'm pregnant by Jacque and I'm three months." She cried. I just shook my head. I can't believe this bitch. I cupped her cheek roughly. She was really having this niggas' baby.

"Three months. What the fuck are you crying for? Damn, I wanted kids for the longest. You wouldn't even let me touch you, but you've been fuckin' this nigga raw for months while laying up under me. Bitch, you ain't even worth this bullet. It's a fuckin' wrap Keondra. Everything that you own at my house I'm getting rid of that shit. It's over. You ain't shit. I should've left you where I found you at. I should've kept you as a fuck," I argued.

"I'm sorry Ike. I never meant to hurt you." She cried. I raised my hand up and backhanded her. She should be glad that's all I've done. It's taking everything in me not to pull the trigger.

"Bitch stop lying. Shut the fuck up. You talk too much," I argued. My phone alerted me that I had a text. I looked at my phone and Kato said we got company. Jacque. Just the nigga I wanted to see. I heard the door open. Keondra looked at me and I gave her a hateful glare. I wish she would let that nigga know I'm here. I'm catching a body today.

"Keondra, where the fuck are you? I'm going to fuckin' hurt you." He argued. Oh, that nigga was coming back through here. They really had a full-blown relationship going on behind my back. At least he had the balls to stop working for me, but I still want that niggas' head. Ain't no way around me.

"I'm in here." She sobbed. I stood back and hid behind the door. I didn't want that nigga to see me, but he's going to feel me. He stepped toward the door and I pushed the door open as hard as I could. I rushed his ass and he fell to the floor. He gave me an icy grill. He knew what time it was. It's on and it's not even about her. It's the fuckin' principle.

"Oh, bitch you set me up after I did your dirty work." He argued and spat blood from his mouth. I laughed at his stupid ass. I rushed him again because he got me fucked up. He shoved me toward the wall, and I shoved him back.

"Nah nigga you set yourself up fucking my wife and working for me," I argued. I picked him up and slammed him on the floor. I raised my foot up I kept stomping the fuck out of him. He grabbed me by my leg and we started going at it blow for blow. I started going in on his ass. He crossed me so he had to feel me. I gave that nigga my best work. I was killing him with my bare hands.

"Ike that's enough." She stated. I looked over my shoulder. I snarled my face up at her. I smacked the fuck out of Keondra. She should be glad it wasn't her ass on the floor. A motherfucka can't play me and live to talk about it.

"Aye keep your hands off her, it's between you and me. She's pregnant with my child." He spat. I was done talking to this nigga. I grabbed my Glock from behind my back. I cocked it back. Jacque tried to run but I shot his ass in the back and he dropped to the ground. I ran up on him and shot his ass in the head twice. He fucked up coming back here. He wasn't walking out of here alive. Keondra was crying in the background. Did she think she was about to be with him and I was going to allow that? I hope she wasn't that dumb.

"You love that nigga huh? I killed that motherfucka. Call the police now bitch, you're accessory to fuckin' murder. I wish the fuck you would. I can survive in jail. I'll get out because I'll plead insanity. I'm not cleaning up this body. You better dispose of it and make sure it never comes back to bite you in the ass." I argued. Fuck Keondra! She crossed the wrong one. I'm going out the same way I came in.

Keondra

I couldn't stop the tears from falling or stop my heart from aching even if I wanted too. Not even the sharp pains from hurting my stomach. I looked between my legs and notices specks of blood. I couldn't stop the blood from flowing between my legs. Oh God, I hope I'm not having a miscarriage. I never thought about how I would feel if I lost him too. Oh God, what did I just do? Every time I would wipe my eyes, more tears would start forming in the brim of my eyes. Lying in front of me was Jacque's body. He was lying there, and his eyes were wide open looking at me. It's the pain in his face that has me heartbroken. He thought I set him up, but I didn't.

I wish could stop the death scent from lingering in my nostrils. Ike was never supposed to catch me slipping. My life flashed before my eyes. Never have I ever been held at gunpoint. How did he find me? I was so shaken up I didn't know what to do. Ike finally found out about my truth. My heart hurts so badly. I hate Jacque came back here even though I asked him to. He died trying to protect me and our son. I don't know the first thing about cleaning up a body. Ike was a crazy motherfucka. I hate that he had one up on me.

What the fuck am I supposed to do? Jacque was the only man that loved me for me. It wasn't supposed to go down like this. Oh Lord, why would you shatter my world like this? I heard a few footsteps come in. I looked up and it was Ike and Kato and the clean-up crew. They looked at me as if they were disgusted. Ike was staring at me. I refused to look at him and give him the satisfaction of the day. He tapped me on shoulders roughly. I turned around to look at him to see what he wanted. He pointed a gun to my face.

"Go ahead and kill me if that's what you came to do!" I cried and yelled. I'm over Ike. He can do everything to me, but I can't do anything to him. He should've acted like he cared a long time ago.

"Killing you is to fuckin' easy. You deserve a long painful death. You want to be a boss and a ruthless motherfucka? Let's start by cleaning this body up. I hope you didn't think I was doing it for you. Nah, bitch, you are since you like to call the cops and shit." He argued and tossed me some gloves. I had blood pouring between my legs and he wanted me to do this shit.

"Keondra hurry the fuck, you got to fuckin' move quicker than that. Why the fuck is that blood coming from between your legs?" He asked and pointed I thought he would never ask. I'm not cleaning up this body. I'm in some serious pain.

"Ike, I'm having a fuckin' miscarriage. I can't clean up his body while my body is aching and I'm having unbearable cramps," I cried and screamed. It hurts so fuckin' bad. I need to get to the hospital and see a doctor. My heart was beating so fast and I was having hot flashes. I started hyperventilating. He walked up to me and cocked his fist back. I just knew he was about to punch me in my face. He cupped my chin roughly. I could feel my jaws touch my teeth. He was hurting me.

"Shut the fuck up and stop crying. I need you to walk it like it you fuckin' talk it. You don't tell me what to do Keondra. You're going to clean up whatever I fuckin' tell you to clean up. You should be glad I give a fuck. I don't give a fuck about any of that shit. You crossed the wrong motherfucka and I'm not sparing you because you're a female.

Everything you're going through right now you brought that on yourself. I don't give a fuck about you having a miscarriage. Why should I? It wasn't fuckin' mine. You see this niggas blood is on your fuckin' hands, not mine. You're the cause of all of this. I don't feel bad for you or the baby you lost. These are the cards you dealt. Play them right and clean this body up. After that, you can go to the hospital and do whatever the fuck you need to do." He argued. Kato told me everything to do. Ike recorded me cleaning the body. I threw up so many times I almost passed out. Ike kept throwing water on me. Each time I would move slowly he would smack me in my face and tell me to pick up the pace. Kato grabbed Jacque's chain and tossed it to Ike. Ike looked at it and grilled me.

"Bitch I know you didn't give this nigga my jewelry. On everything I love bitch you better be glad I don't care about you or else. I would slaughter your ass the same I made you slaughter him." He argued. Jacque's phone started ringing. Ike looked at me and laughed. He snatched the phone and slid it to Kato. I swear this day couldn't get any worse.

Jermesha

Time wasn't my friend today. I looked at the clock and it was after 3:00 p.m. already. I had a nail appointment at 3:30 p.m. I had to get my sew-in tightened and styled at 6:00 p.m. I've been posted up at Mother Dear's house for the past two hours and she hasn't made it here yet. I've been calling her phone for the last hour and she keeps saying that she's on her way. I moved out of Mother Dear's house a few years ago and got my own spot.

My children's father wanted to get our kids for the weekend so of course, I was dropping their ass off. Mother Dear's house was the drop-off spot. I didn't want my baby daddy knowing where I laid my head at. I don't care how much you pay a month in child support or what you buy, it wasn't happening. Mother Dear finally pulled up. My smile instantly turned into a frown. I was surprised to see Camina and Cariuna. They were beautiful little girls. I just didn't care for their mother.

Cariuna was Crimson all over again but Camina, ugh she's bad as hell. If she ever comes to my house I will beat her ass so good she'll never forget me if she lives. I can't believe Crimson and Griff are her parents. Mother Dear wants to talk about everybody kids being bad. I opened Mother Dear's car door to help her out. I see she had a few bags.

"Mother Dear is everything okay I've been calling you for the past hour. Where's Crimson and why do you have her kids?" I asked. I could give two fucks about Crimson. I just wanted to be nosey.

"Why are you worried about it? I have your kid's now. Why can't he know where you lay your head at? She's in the hospital. She'll be out in a few days. I decided to help with the girls. Somebody killed Griff. I hope whoever did that shit rots in hell." She argued. Mother Dear loved Griff and she didn't care who knew it. I'm glad he's dead and I can't wait to see Crimson be knocked off her high horse. I brought front row tickets to the show.

"Oh okay is she alright? I'm sorry to hear that. I heard about Griff but that comes with the territory when you're the biggest Kingpin in the city. On the news, they stated it was drug-related." I had to rub that part in. Mother Dear looked at me and rolled her eyes.

"No, she's not okay but she will be. She's in a coma but she's strong, so I know she'll push through. She's going through a lot and she's pregnant again. Don't believe everything you see on the news. No matter how Griff got his money he took care of his family. That defined him. He was a good man and he didn't deserve that shit at all." She argued. Thank God my children's father pulled up. I wasn't about to go back and forth with Mother Dear about Griff.

"Your breath stink," Camina mumbled under her breath. Cariuna was laughing too. Oh, she got me fucked up. I'll beat her little ass today. I have ten minutes to spare.

"Camina what did you say? Were you talking to me?" I asked. I was all up in her face. She started laughing and waving her hand in front of her nose.

"Your breath smell like boo-boo," Camina laughed. I snatched her up by her shirt. Mother Dear smacked in the back of my head. I turned around and looked at her to see what the fuck was that for.

"Jermesha, get your motherfuckin' hands off her. If your breath smells like shit take your ass in the house and brush your teeth. Be glad she told you before, you take your ass to the nail shop and bitches be laughing at you instead of with you." She argued. I did the breath test and it was a little strong. Maybe it was because my mouth was dry. Camina should be glad Mother Dear saved her ass.

Chapter-15

Mother Dear

Something has to give. I feel so bad for my baby. She loves Griff so much she couldn't take living without him. I need Crimson to pull through because her babies need her. Shit, the baby that's growing inside of her needs her. The moment Cheree dropped Crimson off on my front porch and never looked back I ain't never asked her for shit and I should've made her handle her fuckin' responsibilities. I need her right fuckin' now. Her daughter is fighting for her life and her grandchildren fuckin' need her. I don't give a fuck what she got going on. I need her to bring her ass. I grabbed my phone off the nightstand and hit the dial button. Cheree lived in California and I didn't give a fuck about the time difference.

Hey, momma is everything okay?" She asked. I rolled my eyes just listening to her. I could tell she was concerned, and she should be. If everything was okay, I wouldn't be calling her this time of the fuckin' night.

“No Cheree, everything isn't okay. I need you here right now. Crimson in a coma and it isn't looking good,” I explained. I heard Cheree gasp. Now isn't the time. Please don't ask any questions. Just come home, please. Knowing Cheree that’s too much like right.

“Say what momma? What happened?” She asked. If I could reach through this phone and touch Cheree I fuckin’ would. If I tell you to come home, you shouldn’t even be asking any questions. Catch a flight and come and see about yours.

“Cheree, I ain't got time to explain to you what happened. It's a lot that's happened. Bring your motherfuckin' ass home now to see about your child and your grandchildren. You ain't never did shit for Crimson her whole fuckin' life, but right now you need to come and see about yours. It's only so much I can fuckin' do but you Cheree can do more than fuckin' me. She needs you,” I argued.

“Momma Crimson hates me. What the fuck can I do?” She argued and cried. She wanted to cry now. Save those fuckin’ tears. You can start by bringing your ass home to see about yours. You got to start somewhere. I swear to God this child of mine is driving me crazy.

It's too late for me to be even raising my voice or getting my blood pressure high. Leave it to Cheree to take me fuckin' there.

"Cheree Ava Tristan, bitch let me tell you one motherfuckin thang. I have never been the one to repeat myself fuckin' twice. I don't give a fuck what you got going on. I need you to bring your ASS home. DO YOU FUCKIN' HEAR ME.? Cheree, CRIMSON didn't ask to fuckin' come here. I wasn't fuckin her father, you were. You should be tired of fuckin' running from your responsibilities. So what if she hates you. Make her fuckin' love you by being there when she needs you. This shit ain't up for debate. Get here now because if I have to catch a flight to come and get you it's gone be some motherfuckin' problems. Ain't shit changed but my fuckin' age. I refused to leave Sherry and Jermesha alone with Crimson's kids. So they can torture them and be mean to them," I argued.

"Momma, what the fuck you mean Sherry and Jermesha will torture my fuckin' grandchildren? Sherry doesn't want to fuckin' see me. I swear to God I will drag that bitch and her fuckin' daughter for fuckin' with mine. My kids and grandkids ain't got shit to do with our beef.

I'm the bitch she doesn't want to fuckin' see." She argued. I had Cheree right where I wanted her.

"You heard what the fuck I said Cheree. I need you to come here. I can't sit at the hospital with your daughter and your grandkids. I don't have a choice but to leave them at the house with Sherry and Jermesha. Cariuna and Camina already said Sherry and Jermesha were whipping their ass just for the hell of it. Crimson been in a coma for 3 days and their father got killed a few days ago. I'm all they have until Crimson wakes up."

"Momma I'm on my way. I'll be there in about four hours. I put this on Crimson Rose Tristan. Sherry is going to regret the day she ever laid hands on a child of mine. I know that's your daughter but when I see her it's going to be hell to pay. She'll be the next bitch lying in a coma. I'll be at your house in the morning. Let me call Crimson's father so he can be on his fuckin' way too." She argued. I knew just what to say to get Cheree riled up. When she gets here, I can't let her beat the shit out of Sherry. It ain't happening but Jermesha she needs her ass beat by her Aunt Cheree.

Cheree

I knew something was wrong because my mother would never call me this late at night. I always kept the phone close because she was older. I knew my sister wasn't concerned about her well-being. I was hoping and praying that it wasn't anything wrong with her. God answered that prayer. My mother is my everything and I'm forever grateful for her. I never thought it would be my baby Crimson she was calling about. My heart dropped instantly. If I lost Crimson, I would go crazy. A mother never wants to be on the receiving end of a call like that. I guess it was finally time for me to go home.

I haven't stepped foot in East Atlanta in years. I hate it's on these terms, but it is what it is. I can't wait to see my baby and her babies. I wanted to come back home years ago, but I didn't. I couldn't. Too much shit had happened to me. Crimson's father was my high school sweetheart and my everything at once upon a time. Bone was a few years older than me. I knew Sherry was jealous of me, but I brushed that shit off because I knew my sister would never cross me. I just didn't believe it. Sherry started to switch up when Bone and I started dating.

Bone was heavy in the streets and so was I. I never forget the day Bone and I met. We were in Techwood on New Year's and with this nigga, I use to fuck with name Chino. I had no business fuckin' him. It was something about him I couldn't stop fuckin' with him. Chino was that nigga and he had it. He was selling Coke for twenty-two five. He was mixed with Puerto Rican and black. He had long braids. Chino was paid like a motherfucka too. I snuck out of the house every night to be with him. We were in the middle of the projects and he handed me an AK. He told me to let that motherfucka rip and my grown ass did it.

You couldn't tell me shit. Bone was sitting off in the cut watching me. He would never say anything to me. He would just watch. I told Chino to watch that nigga. I didn't trust him. It was some grimy ass niggas out in Techwood. Chino and I were leaving the projects. He was taking me back home because Mother Dear was blowing my pager up. She worked nights and she had no clue that I snuck out the house.

I always locked my door and cut the radio up. I knew Sherry had to rain on my parade. Chino and I were at the red light and his car was ambushed. I was scared as hell. I just knew I was about to die. Chino always had a lot of cash on him and he was flashy ass nigga. He was used to getting robbed and flexing on a nigga the next day. I just had a bad feeling that this wouldn't end right. The doors were being snatched open.

Chino and I were thrown out the car. I never felt so violated in my life. One of the robbers touched every part of my body. The robbers wanted cash. Chino gave them everything he had. They wanted his jewelry and he gave that shit up too. They grabbed the AK out the backseat and pointed at Chino's head. I was shaking because I wasn't ready to die yet. I just started living my life. I was in the right place at the wrong time. One of the robbers pulled me to the front of the car by my hair. My mother raised me not to fear anyone but God. I had a mug on my face.

He said I want you to shoot this motherfucka in his head the same way you were letting that bitch rip a few minutes ago in my hood. My heart dropped because I knew his voice from anywhere. It was Bone. I wasn't doing it. If Bone wanted to kill Chino then he could, but I wasn't. I told him no. I told Chino I didn't trust his ass and I meant that shit too and, therefore he died by the hands of that nigga. He put the gun to my head and asked me did I want to die? I told him to do what the fuck he had to do. Bone shot

Chino dead in his fuckin' head. His blood was all over me. I was fucked up behind Bone doing that to him. Bone took me to his house to change clothes. He was so fuckin' rude to me. I hated his ass. He took me home that night and threw me his phone. My mother beat my ass when I got in the house. Sherry stood in the corner and laughed. I took that ass whooping like a G though.

I curved him for a few weeks. I didn't want to be seen with another man because Chino's family was already snooping around asking questions because I was the last person to see him alive. Bone wasn't making shit easy by popping up. I didn't need anybody to connect the dots. Sherry was so happy when she heard Chino got killed.

One day I was walking home from school with Daniel. He pulled up on me and threw his car in park and hopped out. I was shaking because Bone wasn't my man. I don't know why he was acting as if he was. I folded my arms across my chest and just listened to him. He was showing his ass.

I got in the car with him to keep confusion down because the last thing we needed was the police to pull up or one of the enemies. I didn't want his blood on my hands.

My life changed the moment I got in the car with Bone for better and worse.

I was fuckin' with a Techwood Vet. Mother Dear put my hot ass out. I moved in with him and I ended up getting pregnant with Crimson. Crimson's father Bone was the dope man. He ran Techwood with Goldie Danielle's father. Bone was a great man and a provider, but he became ruthless as fuck the moment we got together. Everything changed. He didn't want me in the streets. It's crazy because we met each other in the streets. I couldn't chill in Techwood with him. Yeah, he brought his money but that wasn't enough for me. I wanted his time because before I got pregnant, I had all of that. The moment I got pregnant everything changed.

I'll never forget that day as long as I live. Bone had brought me a brand-new Mustang GT drop top convertible. A bitch couldn't tell me shit. The same day he brought me the Mustang he never came home. I knew him and Goldie was going out. It's after 3:00 a.m. and he should've been home. I called his cell phone and paged him. He didn't return any of my calls. I jumped up and threw my clothes on because he had me fucked up.

I pulled up in Techwood and his Cadillac was parked on Front Street. J-Boy was a dope fiend he knew. He said, “Cheree give me a rock and I’ll tell you which apartment he's in.” I didn't have any rocks on me. I gave his ass a $50.00 bill. He pointed me right to the door. I knocked on that motherfucka like I was the God damn police. A bitch came to the door. I recognized the hoe because she hangs with Sherry and this was her apartment. She was a stripper.

I asked that hoe was Bone in there and she said yes. She pointed me back to the room. Bone was fuckin' Sherry on the floor. I swear this nigga and this bitch was trifling as fuck. My fuckin' sister to make matters worse. Y'all fuckin' in somebody else's shit on the floor on a mattress and water is running out the fuckin' bathroom.

I walked up on his ass and kicked him in the back of the head with all my might. He turned around and looked at me. He hopped up quick. I dragged Sherry all through old girls fuckin' apartment. I beat her fuckin' ass. Bone couldn't keep me off that bitch. As soon as I got outside, I popped my trunk. I grabbed my crowbar and busted the windows on his Cadillac. He ran up on me and grabbed me. I swung the crowbar at him and hit him in his face.

I went to work on his ass too. He still has the scar to this day. I was fuckin' done with him. After that Sherry was running around telling everybody she was pregnant by him. Bone swore Jermesha wasn't his, but I didn't give a fuck though. She looked like him to me. I moved out of the house we shared and back in with my mother. Bone didn't owe me any loyalty, but Sherry did.

We were pregnant at the same time. I knew for a fact Crimson was Bone's because he was the only one I was sleeping with. I despised that bitch. I washed my hands with the two of them. The moment I had Crimson I let Bone see her so he could get a good look at her because I didn't want him to have anything to do with her. I had to leave Atlanta and my daughter behind because Chino's family had found a dope fiend that saw what happened to Chino and told them. When I had Crimson Chinos' family came to the hospital and questioned me. His family was well connected. They threatened to take my daughter and kill both of us. The nurse that was in my room that witnessed it came in and asked what was going on? They found her dead the next day behind the hospital. The police questioned me about her murder. I knew his family wasn't to be fucked with. I didn't want my daughter or myself to die because of some shit her father done. I left her with my mother and never looked back. She was safe with her and not me. I've been on the run for over twenty years. Every now and then somebody affiliated with Chino's family will run down on me and I'll have to move. I swear Sherry knew somebody affiliated with them because only two people knew my moves and that was my mother and the Lord himself.

Bone and I kept in touch over the years because he paid for all my living expenses. He's the reason why I'm on the run. I know I should never question God but why my baby? Why her? I hate to even call her father, but I had too. It was late and he was probably laid up with his bitch. I don't give a fuck. I hated making this call.

“Why are you calling my phone this time of night? You’re causing fuckin' problems. I just sent you some fuckin' money.” He argued. I hated calling I swear to God I do. If it was such a problem, why did he answer the fuckin’ phone? Don’t nobody want his old ass but Sherry and some bitches that don’t know any better. He was trying to show out.

“Bone lower your motherfuckin' voice and watch how you talk to me. Send me some more money trick. We got bigger problems besides the bitch that's at your neck.

My child is in a fuckin' coma. Get your ass to fuckin' Emory Hospital right now and don't leave until I fuckin' get there." I argued. That's the only thing I need him to do. Nothing more nothing less.

"What the fuck you mean my daughter is in a fuckin' coma? What the fuck happened to her. Cheree if them pussy ass motherfuckin' Puerto Ricans touched my daughter I'm killing every fuckin' thing." He argued. I could tell he was upset. I didn't have time to go back and forth with him. He heard what the fuck I said. I hung up in his face. I had to get to the airport to see my child. I wasn't even packing a bag. I'll buy whatever I need when I get there.

Bone called my phone back and I cleared his ass out. I said what I had to say. He needed to get the hospital instead of calling me. He called back again, and I cleared him out. He kept calling back until I finally answered.

"Bone, I'm trying to get my things. I said what I had to say. Just get to the hospital to look after my child." I argued. As soon as I get there, he can take his ass on. I don't need him being there when she wakes up.

"Who's picking you up from the airport? I'll have my driver pick you up. What time does your flight arrive?"

He asked. He's asking too many questions that I refused to give him the answer to.

"No one. I'll catch an Uber. I don't know when my flights arriving, but I'll meet you at the hospital. Is there anything else you want to know," I argued.

"Why the fuck did you hang up and I was still talking to you? Where are you staying at?" He asked. He sure is asking a lot of questions for a nigga that got plenty hoes.

"Because I can. When I called you it was a fuckin' problem. You of all people know I'm not calling to have a conversation with you. Trust me if my daughter was in a coma you wouldn't have a courtesy call. I said what I had to say. Does it matter where I'm staying? You don't need to know that."

"You know what Cheree I'm not about to argue with you. I see you're still on that bullshit. Bring your ass because if something happens to my daughter it's on you since you denied me the chance to know her. You can spend my money, but you can't hold a conversation. Fuck out of here with that shit." He argued. Every time we have a disagreement, he throws that shit up. I don't have to mention it all. A hit dog will always holler.

"Whatever Bone, I'm not tripping off shit. Trust me I hate spending your money, but you owe me because I could've dropped the dime on you years ago and I didn't. I should've because I didn't owe you any loyalty and you didn't owe me any. I ain't in the business of helping nan motherfucka do they job. I don't need your money I told you years ago to stop sending it, but you insisted. You ain't got to front my shit. Bone, I've always brought my own. You met me in the streets ain't shit changed." I argued. I hated calling Bone because our conversations always led here. He knows I don't need his fuckin' money.

He kept sending it to keep tabs on me. Bone likes bitches that want to be kept. He knew he couldn't keep me. I was one and done. He hung up the phone in my face. I don't care long as he takes his ass to the hospital, I'm cool. I called my mother back to let her know I was on my way. I pray for peace but if Sherry and her daughter touched my grandkids I swear to God I'm drawing blood. I don't care if we share the same blood. That shit went out the window years ago. If Sherry pops slick at the mouth, it's going to take more than momma to keep me off her ass. I play a lot of games but please don't fuck with mine because you don't like me. You have no reason to. If Bone wanted to continue to fuck you, he could but I would never fuck him again.

I haven't seen my family in years, but I know as soon as I step foot in East Atlanta a lot of shit is about to change. I'm looking forward to reuniting with my daughter. I know it'll be a lot of static between us, but I'll just have to deal with it and pray she forgives me. I can't wait to see my mother. Sherry got one time to say some shit out the way to me or even make a slick comment and I'm beating her ass.

Chapter-16

♡

Bone

Cheree knows she's a fuckin' trip. I swear some shit never changes. Usually, when a motherfucka gets older they let go of all the bullshit and stop holding grudges. Too bad that'll never be the case with Cheree Tristan. Now isn't the time to be acting like a fuckin' eighteen-year-old. You're grown as fuck. We should be able to have a civil conversation. I know I did some fucked up shit years ago, but I was young and dumb trying to prove a point. I can't change any of that shit. If I could I would.

I'm older and wiser now. Yeah, I got Cheree caught up in my shit years ago, but I wasn't afraid of those niggas. If they wanted to go to war than we could get to it. I was ready for it. It is what it is. They knew not to fuck with me. Chino was involved in a lot of shit. For the right price anybody can get touched. I just so happen to be the nigga that touched him.

Cheree shouldn't have been with that nigga no way. It's always been whatever with me. Ain't shit changed. I'm still Bone a Techwood Vet. My name holds weight out here in these streets. If they wanted me, they knew where to find me. I ain't hard to find. They knew I was fuckin' with her heavy. It wasn't a secret. Whenever you saw her you saw me.

I just find it funny that everybody could point her out on camera, but I wasn't identified. I was waiting on them niggas. On top of that, the shit that happened with Sherry was a deal breaker. I never knew her and Cheree were sisters if so that shit would've never gone down. When a woman is scorned it ain't shit you can do about it. I agreed to stay away from Crimson, but I shouldn't have. I slipped up a few times. I regretted that shit every day. Jermesha, Sherry's daughter wasn't mine. We had a DNA test done. I told Cheree but she didn't give a fuck. I had two sons', but Crimson was my firstborn. I got a lot of explaining to do. I know Cheree wanted me to be at Crimson's room when she made it there but I couldn't. I had my security team looking after her.

We had a lot of questions that needed to be answered. I wasn't answering shit if Cheree wasn't there because she caused all of this. I wanted to be in my daughter's life, but her mother didn't want me too.

Whenever I saw Mother Dear in passing, I would always give her wads of cash for Crimson, but she wouldn't accept it. I knew her loyalty was with her daughters. I had no choice but to accept that. Sherry approached me. I didn't approach her. She knew who I was though. I didn't know her. Every now and then we cross paths and she tries to push up on me. I pass every fuckin' time because she fucked up my life. Nothing good came from me fuckin' with her. I had bad luck for a long ass time. She was a beautiful distraction with a rotten soul. I lost two things that meant the most to me because of her.

I'm sure my daughter thinks the worse of me but I'm not a dead beat. It's her mother's fault and I shouldn't have agreed to it because Cheree was in her feelings about some shit I done. If I lose my daughter, I'll never forgive Cheree and she won't live another day holding a grudge against me. That's a promise. Cheree wanted to be sneaky and sneak in town without me knowing where she was laying her head at. I kept tabs on Cheree. I knew she was seeing someone that's why she told me to stop sending her money. I never did it. She'll never be happy if it's not with me. I'm a selfish ass nigga. She was single for a reason. Every time she thought she had somebody that she thought was going to be permanent in her life. I made sure they disappeared. If she couldn't be with me, she wouldn't be with anyone.

I knew she was up to something because she didn't want to give me any flight information. If she knew me, she knew I was coming for her ass. I've been posted up at Hartsfield Jackson Airport since I hung up on her. I brought a ticket knowing damn well I wasn't going anywhere. I wanted to be at the gate when she stepped off that plane to snatch her ass up.

♡

It was a little after 3:30 a.m. and the flight from LAX just arrived. The passengers haven't been cleared to leave the plane yet. I was posted in the corner waiting on Cheree to exit. I had the tip of my hat covering my face. As soon as she steps off the plane it's on. The passengers finally started coming off the plane. I kept my eyes on everyone that exited the plane and Cheree finally walked out. She hasn't aged a bit. She was too busy on her phone smiling at shit and she didn't even notice me. Never paying attention to her surroundings. I walked up right behind her and wrapped my arms around her waist. She turned around to face me and she gave me a hateful glare. I snatched her phone. I knew she was about to show her ass. She's mean as hell, ain't shit changed.

"What's up baby momma? Long time no see. Shut up and don't say shit before I make a scene." I argued and continued to push her toward the exit. She stopped walking. I know she wasn't going out like that without some slick shit coming from her mouth.

"Look Bone I ain't got time for your shit. Leave me the fuck alone. Why are you here? I told you I had a ride. That's why I declined the offer. Stalking is against the law shouldn't you be looking after my daughter like I asked you too? You should be there and not here. I asked you to do one thing and you couldn't even do that." She argued.

"Cheree, come on and shut up. We shouldn't even be doing this at the airport. Let's go so I can see my child. I hope you didn't think I was going up there without you. If she's anything like her mother I know she's not trying to hear anything I have to say. I know you said you had a ride, but I don't give a fuck. You swiped my card to pay for the ticket so I'm here to escort you to wherever you're going. Where the fuck is you staying at," I argued.

Her phone started ringing and it was a nigga calling by the name of IRV. "Who the fuck is IRV Cheree?"

"Bone just leave. I'll meet you at the hospital. Here's your money for the ticket and here's your credit card back. I swiped the wrong fuckin' card. Why are you so worried about me? I got me last I checked. I was interrupting shit REMEMBER? Keep that same energy you had over the phone because clearly, I am. Please don't worry about me and where I'm staying. Don't worry about who IRV is. Just know he'll never fuck a bitch that shares the same blood as me. If Crimson is anything like me, and you hate my ways, why are you in my presence? I don't need an answer, but I'll see you around." She argued. She counted out the cash and placed my black card on top of it. I put it back in her hand.

"Why are you giving it back now? I ain't worried about you Cheree. I'm just looking out for you. I know what the fuck I said but listen to me. You can take it how you want too. Stop fuckin' playing with me because I'm not that nigga. My daughter is lying in a fuckin' coma so I ain't got time to argue with you, about shit that doesn't matter. If it ain't about Crimson I don't want to fuckin' hear about it. Wherever you think you're staying at cancel that shit, you're staying wherever the fuck I want you to stay at.

I ain't never said I hate your ways. Don't put words in my mouth. For the record, I never fucked a bitch that shared the same blood as you twice. Once I found out it was a wrap and you know that. Tell IRV it's a fuckin' wrap too, you're on my time and not his. Last I checked I paid your phone bill and I don't want that pussy ass nigga calling a phone that I pay for," I argued.

"You know what Bone fuck you. You ain't got to pay shit for me. I don't need your money. I'm giving you your card back because my man doesn't want me spending another man's fuckin' money when I can spend his. Real niggas do real things. That some shit you may never know about. You can't tell me what I can and can't do. You tried that and it never worked. Take me to the hospital. I'm tired of arguing with an old ass hating motherfucka like you." She argued. I escorted Cheree to the car and she slammed the door. I just shook my head and laughed at her ass. The tension was thick between us. The driver was out front waiting on us. I don't give a fuck about her being mad. She wanted to rub it in my face about her man. Too bad her man will be a thing of the pass in a few days once I found out who he is and where he lives.

"Give me my phone Bone I need to call my mother and tell her I made it." She argued and sucked her teeth. She held her hand out for her phone. I dropped mine in her hand. She smacked the shit out of me and I laughed at her ass.

"Watch your hands. You can use mine. I don't give a fuck about you having an attitude. If you want to call your mother here's my phone. She knows my number," I laughed. Mother Dear was the one that told me what time her flight arrives.

"Fuck you Bone and stop talking to my mother. Hate is a strong word to use and I shouldn't even give you this much of my energy. You and fuck nigga shouldn't even be in the same category, but you're acting like a fuck nigga. God, I hate being in the same space as you. You irk my fuckin' soul right now." She argued.

"Fuck you too Cheree, you know I ain't never been a fuck nigga. I saved you from a fuck nigga. I get what I want. You can't hate somebody that you love, remember that," I chuckled. That shit made her mad as hell. She mumbled some shit under her breath. I still wasn't giving her phone back. Just like that Cheree is disrupting my world again but this time I refused to let her leave. I won't let her get away. I owe her a nice life.

Cheree

The infamous Bone Stephens a Techwood vet was still checking for little old me, but I'm interrupting shit. I didn't even get the chance to take him in good. He ruined a perfect moment. I could tell by the clothes he wore he was someone important. I could tell by the Salvatore Ferragamo's that adorned his feet. The white Versace button down that fitted his frame to perfection. The black Versace slacks displayed. He had the perfect build. I knew stepping back in East Atlanta was going to be hard for me. I had to deal with it. It's time to face my past so I can have a new future with my daughter and granddaughters.

Bone wasn't the first person I wanted to see when I stepped foot in Atlanta. We had to cross paths. He disgusts me. I always check my surroundings. I saw the guy in the corner. I just didn't expect it to be him. He had his hat tilted low covering his face. He hasn't aged a bit. His skin was the color of a dark Snicker bar blemish-free skin. Except for the permanent scar I gave him. His teeth were white as snow. He just had the salt and pepper look going on with his beard. Whenever he was mad, he wanted to let the world know. It's this thing he does with this eyes and lips that lets you know he's ready to snap. Don't take your problems out on me. I don't care about him being mad. I am too. When I look at my daughter for the first time in person after twenty-nine years, it's going to remind me of what I gave up loving him. That's what hurts the most.

He's been talking reckless over the phone for years. Whenever we had a conversation, things always went bad. I'm not the least bit surprised this happened as soon as we saw each other. He never apologized for anything, but he's the first person I see when I step off the plane. I don't know how I feel about that. We haven't seen each other in years.

Seeing him in his prime brings back memories. Some that I would love to forget about. He brought out a lot of emotions and feelings that I had hidden, resurfaced. I won't ever lie and say that I don't think about him because I do. Bone was my one true love, but he fucked that up. I lost a lot dealing with him.

I always wondered why Bone and I cross paths just to have a daughter and not be able to raise her. I never knew one person to fuck up your life for a long time. He was that person. Nothing ever got easy with time. Yeah, I had money but so what. I wanted to fall in love and get married. None of that ever happened for me. Anything that I thought would be permanent disappeared. I wanted more kids, but I could never have any more if I couldn't raise Crimson. I knew whenever we met again, she would probably wonder that.

Our entire ride was silent. I had so much shit on my mind its crazy. I could feel the tension between us. The bubbly butterflies in my stomach made things extremely worse. I could feel him staring a hole on the side of my face. I wasn't going to address it so, I chose to ignore it. He tapped me on my shoulder and I ignored him. He tapped me again. I turned around to face him to see what he wanted. He cupped my chin roughly. I rolled my eyes because I wasn't ready for this. He's coming on too strong and aggressive.

"Do you want to address it, or do you want to continue to act like WE never happened? I know you feel it because I can. This is what it's supposed to be between us because I can feel it. Whenever we get in the same room with each other this happens. Stop fighting it. It hurts so bad that you choose to ignore it. Yes, I fucked up Cheree I was young and dumb back then. Relationships were never my thing. You were the first for me. I'm not a saint. What you see is what you get with me. The moment I lost you I was willing to do everything right and be the perfect man for you. If you would've allowed me too. I never got the chance. I fucked up a few times, but I'm willing to bet you I'll get it right this time. I know shit got bad between us and I'm the cause of our daughter not being in our lives. I'm man enough to admit I was wrong, and I can never apologize enough.

I've run across a lot of women and entertained many, but none of them were you. I'm coming for everything. I NEED and LOVE you. I don't give a fuck. I won't let you fuck it up because you want to be stubborn and not forgive me. Think about that, keep that on your mind. I'm letting you know how I feel and what it's going to be." He explained and dug in my soul. Tears slid down my face. I wiped them with my free hand. Why did he do this? I felt everything he was saying and that's scary. His words held so much power. Why did he have to go there?

"I hear you but I'm not listening. We could NEVER be. I'm not thinking about you. Feelings don't matter to me. I go by actions. Live your life Bone because I'm living mine. It's good seeing you though. I just hate it's on these terms, but it is what it is," I whispered. He gave me a threatening stare. His eyes were trying to dig into my soul. Every time I would blink my eyes, he would still be looking at me. I can't take it. My heart was beating out my chest and the butterflies were burning a hole in my stomach. He ran his tongue across my lips. Chills ran through my body. He slid his tongue in my mouth and I welcomed it.

“You heard what I said Cheree I’m not playing with you.” He argued and continued to kiss me. I quickly pushed him off me. We shouldn't even be doing this. Bone stroked his beard and started laughing. I couldn't be around him because I knew this will happen. As soon as Crimson gets better, he'll be a thing of the past.

We finally made it to the hospital. Bone took me to breakfast before we came here. I needed to grab a blanket because I wasn't leaving her side until she woke up. He grabbed one too. He escorted me upstairs to her room. His men were posted up outside of her room. I was impressed because he did everything, I asked him too. I knew Bone was moving major weight, but this setup lets me know his street status has leveled up. Now I was scared to go in. I’m sure her pictures wouldn't do her any justice. Bone and I walked in her room.

We approached her bed and she was so beautiful. Tears poured down my face I can't believe I'm in arms reach of her. I just wanted to hug and hold her. I knelt on my knees and grabbed her hand and started praying for her. I hated it's on these terms, but I swear to God I will do anything he asks me to. Just to bring my daughter out of this state she's currently in.

"She's beautiful." He stated. Yes, she was. That's me. Tell me something I don't know. She looks exactly like her mother. Pregnant again. I can't wait to meet my new grandchild. I climbed in the bed right beside her. Gosh she was everything. I couldn't stop looking at her. Bone kissed me on my forehead and advised that he'll back in a few. He had a few errands to run.

"It's cool you don't have to check in with me. We're not together. Thank you for making sure I got here safe and looking after her until I made it here."

"I want to though. You know what it is." He stated and smiled.

I watched him walk out the door. I couldn't stop looking at her. She smelled so good I couldn't stop inhaling her scent. I placed my hand on her heart and I felt it beating. I was tired the moment my face touched the pillow I drifted off to sleep.

♡

I was sleeping well until I felt somebody standing over me. I wiped my eyes with my free hand. I had the biggest smile on my face. It was my mother. I haven't seen her in years. Tears poured down my face instantly because it's been so long. She's so beautiful.

"I thought that was you. I wasn't for sure, but I know just anybody wouldn't be lying in bed with my baby. How are you? Stand up so I can see you. I guess Bone put you to sleep." She laughed. My mother was a trip. I hated when she teased me. I tried to hide my smile.

"Momma stop it, please. I don't appreciate you selling me out. Why didn't you tell me that you were still in contact with him?" I asked. My mother was sneaky. Why was she still in contact with him? Her loyalty is supposed to always be with me. I stood up to give her a hug. I missed her so much. I noticed two little girls in the corner looking at me. It must be them. They were so beautiful. They looked just like their mother. I waived at them. The smaller one kept grilling me.

“I don't have to tell you everything Cheree. Last I checked I was your mother and not the other way around. Of course, he keeps in contact with me when he wants to know a few things about you and Crimson. Cariuna and Camina come here. I have someone I want you to meet.” She explained. They walked over to us. The youngest one folded her arms across her chest. I could tell she was the boss and a little hot head.

“Yes, Mother Dear.” They beamed and smiled. They were respectful with good manners. She's raising them right. Mother Dear looked at me giving me the okay to tell them who I am.

“Hi I’m Cheree. Your mother's mother. I'm your grandmother. It's nice to meet you. What are your names?” I asked.

“Hi grandma, I'm Cariuna. It's nice to meet you. I think my mommy will be happy to see you.” She beamed.

“Hi, I’m Camina. Why were you in my mommy's bed? Did she say you could get in there with her?” She asked. I let out a small laugh. I knew she had a lot of spunk.

Mother Dear looked at me and laughed. I'm sure she gives her mother a hard time. She reminds me of myself when I was younger. I see it and it's bad.

"It's nice to meet the both of you. No Camina she didn't tell me I could lay in her bed, but I wanted too. Is that okay with you?" I asked. I got acquainted with the girls. I can't wait to spoil them. Camina was sitting on my lap playing in my hair.

"Grandma I don't want to go to school today. Can I stay with you and my mommy?" She pouted and whined? Of course, she could I wasn't about to tell her no. Her mother may never let me see her again. I couldn't blame her but at least she'll remember me.

"Sure, Camina you can stay with me," I beamed. Mother Dear cut her eyes at me. I threw my hands up, shit I didn't know. Crimson's door opened and it was a tall slender female that walked in. She was beautiful. Her skin was the color of honey and her hair was a few shades of blonde and it was bouncy with big curls. Her eyes scanned the room and they landed on me. She sized me up. Who was this?

"Hi God mommy Danielle. I'm ready for school. Camina isn't coming she's staying with my grandmother and mommy." Cariuna beamed. Camina laid her head on my chest and rolled her eyes at Danielle. She looks just like Daniela her aura screams bossy and bitchy.

"Danielle, I want you to meet Crimson's mother Cheree." My mother explained. I reached out my hand to shake hands with her. Camina refused to look at her. I guess it's safe to say Camina doesn't like God mommy Danielle.

"It's nice to meet you too. Sorry I kept staring at you. It's just she looks just like you and you like her. I thought that was her. She'll be happy to see you. She'll give you a hard time at first but don't let her run you off. She needs you now more than ever. I can't wait until she wakes up. Thank you for coming. Watch out for Camina she's already getting you under her spell. Tomorrow she's going to school. I don't care." She beamed and grabbed Camina's arm. Camina snatched it from her.

"Leave me alone God mommy Danielle. Bye take Cariuna to school." Camina pouted.

I finished talking to Danielle because she had to get Cariuna to school. Danielle looks just like her mother. I haven't heard from Daniela in a few months.

I snapped a picture of Danielle. She was perfect. I wanted Daniela to see her. I attached a caption your mini-me. It's fucked up we couldn't be in our daughter's lives because of the men we love, well in my case loved. I guess that's what get for being ride or die chicks. Daniela sent me a text back.

Daniela - Good morning! How did you get that? She's perfect, where are you?

Cheree - Home?

Daniela - Home is EVERYTHING OKAY?

Cheree - No

Daniela - Give me about an hour. I'm going to check in.

Cheree - Okay

Daniela and I have always kept in touch throughout the years. Her situation was way different than mine. They had to leave Danielle. They didn't have a choice. Danielle's father Gary, he was and still is a ruthless ass nigga. Bone and Gary were best friends. Gary robbed the connect and Daniela helped him. They stopped being cool because of that. Bone got caught up in it because that was his right-hand man. I don't even know how he made it out alive but he did some type of way.

I was long gone by then. I'll never forget that day as long as I live. My momma called me and told me how the Dula Cartel terrorized the city. The Dula Cartel were killing any and everybody associated with Gary. One day I guess they got tired of looking for Gary and somebody told them were Daniela's mother stayed. They headed to Ms. Gladys house to look for Daniela and Gary. They ended up coming to my mother's house looking for them. They thought Daniela's house was our house. The police ended up being on the street the same time they pulled up. An officer recognized a few members of the Dula Cartel and arrested them.

They had the wrong house and thank God the police confirmed that. My mother cussed me and Daniela both out. She told us both to stay as far away as possible. Dealing with the men we loved is dangerous and putting both of our families in jeopardy. This is what the fuck happens when you disobey your parents and deal with dangerous criminals.

Whenever she was in Cali, she always came to visit me. She lives in Hawaii, but they have homes everywhere.

They're never in the same place for a long period. It's crazy because Danielle and Crimson are still best friends and their life is a mirror image of ours minus the bullshit and crime. We were deeply involved in their fathers' business.

Hell, we ran it. Whenever they were holding court in the streets, we were too. I can't wait to speak with her. I know she has a ton of questions. Now would be the perfect time for her to show her face. I need her to help me get through this too. I know Bone and Gary will never see eye to eye but that has nothing to do with me. My mother was looking at me.

"Yes mother, why are you staring at me?" I asked.

"You look good Cheree. You're thick. It's good to finally see you. I missed you. I'll be better when your child wakes up. I'm glad you came. How was it seeing Bone after all these years? I'm sure he had you hot and bothered?" She asked while laughing. My mother was searching my face for the truth.

"Thank you. Momma, why are you coming for me? I'm good on Bone. We could never be I'm in a relationship and he has some shit going on. In case you forgot Crimson is damn near thirty. I don't have to deal with him. We don't have any ties with each other. Why would he have me hot and bothered?" I asked.

"You're in a relationship? Funny Cheree, I ain't never known for you to tell a lie but damn every time you tell me you have a man he ends up missing and you never see him again. You and I both know Bone doesn't care what type of relationship you're in he'll DEAD that shit. I know y'all did something because I can tell by your facial expression.

"Momma you're messy and we did not. He kissed me and I didn't kiss him back. I didn't come home to circle back. I came to look after Crimson Rose Tristan and you. Let's talk about what I want you to cook for me while I'm here. I want some liver & onions, smothered potatoes, greens, and some cornbread. I want a chocolate cake too." Crimson had a sofa in her room. I laid across it with Camina and talked to my mom.

Chapter-17

Sherry

My mind had to be playing tricks on me. I know that wasn't him standing in my mother's door. I guess he finally came to his senses that I was the one for him after all these years. I squinted my eyes to get a better look. That was him. I would know him from anywhere. I fixed my breasts by pushing them up a little bit. I looked in the mirror to make sure my make-up was on point. I knew I was the shit. A young bitch couldn't fuck with me on my worst day. You better ask Jermesha. When we go out who pull the most niggas, me or her? I wanted him to see me. It's been a minute since we've seen each other. I jumped out of the car quick. I know his stature from anywhere. Bone had a big ass dick too. You could always see the print in his pants. He was making his way out the front door. He wasn't leaving here without me saying what the fuck I need to say.

If Bone was snooping around here it had to mean one thing. Cheree was in town and he was snooping around to see her. I don't know what the fuck she was coming back home for. You haven't been here for her so, why now? I guess because the little bitch is in a coma. Guess what that's what the fuck she gets for trying to run in the big leagues. Her weak ass momma couldn't handle it and she can't either. I bumped him on purpose. He turned around and looked at me. I blew a kiss at him and he gave me an evil glare.

"Watch yourself." He argued and turned his face up. I sucked my teeth. That wasn't the reaction I was looking for. He needs to watch his hands.

"And if I don't what the fuck are you going to do about it," I argued. He kept walking to his car and ignoring me. I ran up on him. He turned around and pushed me off him.

"What the fuck do you want from me? I ain't got to fuckin' speak to you. Keep your hands off me. I don't hit women, but I'll hit you. I'm not beat for your shit." He argued. He'll beat me for whatever I give him. He knows what I want from him.

"I see what type of shit your own. I was good enough to fuck but I guess since she's back on the scene, its fucks me. Any other time we see each other you're cordial.

Why are you at my mother's house? Are you here for me?" I asked and argued. I wanted him to admit it. I hope she catches us. Once a dog always a dog.

"What type of shit am I on? I don't fuck with you and you know that. Yeah, I'm cordial when you speak to me. I threw my hands up that's my way of speaking to you. When you try your hardest to throw your pussy at me, I curve you every fuckin' time. I fucked you one time and I was done after that. The only thing in my life I ever regretted was fuckin' you." He argued. I had to blink my eyes twice to stop from crying.

"Fuck you Bone and fuck that bitch. Fuck your daughter too. That's why I made sure I made her life a living fuckin hell," I argued. He snatched me up and grabbed me by my neck. I don't care. He wanted to talk shit, well I'm going to talk mine.

"Watch your fuckin' mouth and take your bitter ass on. If I ever find out you've done any harm to my daughter I will fuck you up and I mean that shit. Stay out my face and leave me the fuck alone. I've killed bitches for less and you don't want to be one of those bitches added to my list." He argued. I got something for his ass. I stormed off and headed into my mother's house. My grandchildren and

Crimsons' children were sitting at the table eating. My mother looked at me and didn't say anything.

"Hey mother, are you acting funny too? What was Bone doing here?" I asked. Cheree was always my mother's favorite. I wanted to see if she would be honest with me.

"Hi Sherry, how are you? Why would I need to act funny with you? He was here to see Cheree and his grandchildren of course. Why were you up in his face though? Don't do that ghetto ass shit in front of my house. You're too old to be carrying on the way you do. Leave him alone." She argued. If Cheree thought she could come back to East Atlanta to be with her baby daddy she's sadly mistaken. I kept her away from here for years. This time it'll be permanent.

I'm the reason that bitch is on the run. I told Chico's father that Cheree had him killed so Bone could take over and they believed that shit. Every time she thought she was comfortable I made sure them niggas popped up, but this time they may need to finish the job. I'm not sparing this bitch and I don't care. I heard some footsteps come down the stairs. We locked eyes with each other, and it was her. She grilled me and I grilled her. She still looked the same.

I'll give it to her, she's still a bad bitch, but she's not hotter than me. We were only eighteen months apart.

"Are y'all really going to sit here and not even acknowledge each other? The two of you are sister's same mother and father. BLOOD!" My mother argued. Cheree ain't got to speak to me because I wasn't about to speak to her either.

"Momma please don't do this in front of Cariuna and Camina. Blood doesn't make you family. Loyalty does. Do I have to speak to her? She has one time to talk outside of her neck and I'm passing out ass whooping's. Who wants them? I don't want to speak to her but to make you happy I'll speak. Hey Sherry." Cheree explained. I sucked my teeth and rolled my eyes at the bitch. She wanted to be slick with her comments I'm about to shut her up.

"Fuck you too Cheree. She knows nothing about loyalty. I guess she's still mad because her baby daddy wanted to see what Big sis pussy was hitting for. Excuse my language ma. It's the truth, deal with it. Cheree, he still wants me. You cut off your family to be with a nigga that ain't shit. You've got to be the dumbest woman I know," I laughed.

"You know what Sherry I'm not about to go back and forth with you. If you want Bone, bitch you can have him. The same day I caught him fuckin' you on an air mattress in somebody else's filthy ass apartment like a hoe I was done. I told that nigga he could have you if he wanted you. Y'all had plenty of time to be together, but he still wants you? The difference between me and you are I'm not worried about nan nigga I used to fuck with in the '90s. Gets the fuck out of here. Every nigga I fucked with in the 90's still checking for me. Loyalty you know nothing about that. You were my sister and you fucked behind me; he didn't owe me any loyalty you did. I ain't tripping. I'm good." Cheree argued.

"Is that what you think Cheree? You're dumber than you look. You're still smiling up in his face after he slept with me." I argued. I had to hit that bitch where it hurts. I heard the door open. I look toward the front door and it was Bone coming back. He made his way to the kitchen. I kept my eyes trained on him. He wouldn't even look at me. He knows I was about to cut up and show my ass.

"Mother, I'm taking the girls with me. It was good seeing you Sherry. You got one more time to let some slick shit escape your lips and I’m going to give you everything you’re asking for. I'm begging you to fuckin' try me.

My mother is the only reason you're not on the floor leaking. I don’t want my princess’ thinking it's okay to fight their blood. I got enough respect for her not to beat your ass in front of your grandchildren. Try me and I'll drag your ass all up and through this house.

You hate me so bad, but I’ll treat you like a bitch on the street.” She argued. Oh, Cheree wants to talk her shit because Bone walked in. She caught me off guard back then because her man was standing all up in this pussy, but today she can get it. I busted out laughing. I started clapping my hands. Cheree’s mouth has always been fly but mine is flyer.

“Bravo Cheree. You found your voice because Bone is here? I wish you would've seen him when he was pushing up on me when I walked in. Don't let Bone get your ass whooped, because that’s exactly what’s about to happen. The only reason you beat my ass the last time was that your man was nailing my pussy to the wall and I was in an awkward position. I wanted you to watch me fuck him. I laughed all in your face. Momma let her go so I can tap her ass.” I argued and clapped my hands.

"Sherry, what the fuck is wrong with you? Damn, I didn't raise you to be this way. You're so fuckin' evil and vindictive. You've passed your ways down to your fuckin' daughter. You should be ashamed of yourself. Out of all the men that fucked you or the one's you fucked. You're caught up on your sister's ex. Wake up because you're old enough to realize when you're in the wrong. Apologize, Sherry. Nothing good came from what you've done. You've had nothing but bad luck since you did that. He didn't want you Sherry, and you never had a chance with him. You just ruined our fuckin family being selfish. That's what all three of you get. I'm sick of y'all shit. I'm too damn old to be the referee for bullshit.

The love the Bone and Cheree have for each other is deeper than any fuck you can remember. Bone and Cheree both of y'all are stupid. All these years and y'all let her keep y'all apart? She won by keeping y'all apart. I guess I'm a different breed and I bred the two of you. I would've killed Sherry with kindness. I would've forgiven my man and moved the fuck on. One fuck wouldn't have ruined a lifetime of happiness for me. You know why because I would've killed you softly and continue to be with him. You would've watched him love me. Wishing that you were me. You can't compete where you don't compare.

That’s the problem with your generation now. Y’all so quick to say fuck it instead of talking out y’all problems and working it out. What did you get out of it, Sherry? Nothing. Jermesha wasn't his and he still wouldn’t be with you? Ask yourself was it worth it? You blocked all your blessings being selfish.” She argued.

“Momma you're always taking up for her. I'm not trying to hear none of that right now.” I argued. I hated when she did this. I knew she was going to act differently once Cheree came back.

“That's your problem Sherry, you don't want to fuckin' listen. I'm taking up for who? Don't get the truth mixed up with me taking up for anyone.” I don’t want to hear the truth. What’s understood doesn’t need to be explained.

“Bone take my babies to the car. I don't want them to witness me beating her ass. Momma I tried, but I don't have another try in me. Move out my way. I don't bother anybody, but she still wants to talk about old shit. Do you see why I wasn't going to speak?

I knew she was going to do this. I didn't come here to deal with her or him. I came here for Crimson and these two.” Cheree argued. She wanted to be the mommy of the year. My mother always gave her a pass. I don't appreciate her always taking up for her. Cheree could do no wrong in her eyes and neither could Crimson.

"Cheree let's go. She ain't fuckin' worth it. Sherry, I already told you once that I wasn't beat for your shit. I'm not going to tell you again. I don't make fuckin' threats and that's a promise. Off the strength and respect for your mother, I'll keep all my comments to myself. Mother Dear I'm sorry for bringing all the confusion to your home. If I would've known that she was here. I wouldn't have come here." He argued.

"Let that bitch go. It doesn't matter to me. I always win Cheree. You heard it from momma first." I laughed. Cheree walked past me. I cocked my fist back and punched her in her head. She wanted to talk her shit about what she'll do to me. She looked over her shoulder and laughed.

"Bitch, you had to get me while my back was turned?" Cheree asked. She tried to break free from Bone, but he was still holding her.

"Let that bitch go so you can watch me beat her ass for the old and new," I argued.

“Bone take them to the car. If you love me, you'll let me go so I can tap her ass.” Cheree argued. Bone stepped out the way and freed Cheree. It was on and fuckin' popping. Cheree was quick. I wouldn't dare let her get the upper hand on me. I ran up on her and she swung. I tried to duck but her fist connected with my face. I pushed her off me. She drew back and kept tagging me in my face. I started throwing my hands wildly. Blood poured down my nose instantly messing up my clothes. I couldn't stop the blood from running down my nose. I wiped my nose with my free hand. Cheree grabbed my arm and drug me to the floor. We both fell. I tried to cover my face up, but she kept tagging me. I felt lightheaded. She lifted my head and pounded my head into the kitchen floor.

“Bitch you ain't gone be satisfied until I kill you. Sherry leave me the fuck alone. Stop sending for me if I’m not sending for you.” Cheree argued. Jermesha's kids were crying.

“That's enough Cheree. Sherry are you fuckin' satisfied now.” My mother asked and pulled Cheree off me. I watched Bone from the corners of my eyes. He stood in the corner and shook his head. Cheree stormed off and kicked me in my face. My mother helped me off the floor.

“Sit up, so I can clean up your fuckin' face-up.” She argued. I don't know why she was mad at me. It takes two to fight. All she did was tell Cheree to get off me. Not once did she break it up.

“Momma why didn't you break it up?” I asked. My mother just stood there and let Cheree get away with it.

“Sherry don't start that shit, because you started all of this shit. I wanted to see your little sister beat your ass because you needed it. It was long overdue. I don't ask you for much and I’m never in your business. Leave Bone the fuck alone. I watched you the moment you stepped out of the car. I knew it was going to be a problem. Sherry, you're so beautiful and you can have any man you want. Your sister's man should've been off-limits. Why did you go for him and you knew he was with Cheree? I hate to say it, but happiness is going to find you soon and you're going to fall hard, but it's going to be taken from you.

You know why because of everything that you've done to make someone else miserable. I'm telling you now to stop it and let it go because I won’t be here to always pick you up after you've started shit that you couldn't finish.” She argued. I heard everything my mother was saying but this is far from over. Cheree put her hands on me for the last fuckin' time. Let's see how she likes it when Chino's people snatch her ass up.

ONE WEEK LATER

Chapter-18

Cheree

I've been back home for almost a week now. It felt good being back in my city. I loved everything about Atlanta. It was my stomping ground. I used to wreak havoc out here in these streets. I knew it was going to be some problems when I touched down but not as soon as I touched down. I knew I was going to have to beat Sherry's ass but not this soon. I regret putting my hands on her because I almost killed her, and she wasn't worth it. She just wouldn't shut up. I've never beat anyone's ass before and regretted it afterward. Bone and I had a few words after it happened. It's his fault. He should've kept his dick in his pants. If bitches were acting crazy and they only fucked him one time and they're still thinking about it over twenty years later. I don't want to fuck with him. I can only imagine how the bitches that are fuckin' him now act. I stayed on the phone with Daniela all night talking about Sherry's dumb ass.

I hated to do that in front of my mother, but I refused to be disrespected by anyone. Sherry tried me for the last fuckin' time. I couldn't let that bitch slide for another minute; because she wouldn't have let it go. She thought I wasn't going to do shit. I'm grown and I've grown up. I'll still get shit popping if need be. Crimson still hasn't woken up yet. I'm at the hospital every day checking on her. The doctor said she was doing well and it's only a matter of time. I've been staying at Crimson's house with the girls. I felt uncomfortable staying in her house, and she doesn't know it yet or know me. She had good taste. I decided to get me a spot until she comes home. Staying at my mother's house was out the question.

Staying with Bone was out the question too. I haven't said anything to him since we had a few words a week ago. I've been steering clear of my mother's house because I'm not trying to run into Sherry. Her energy is bad, and I don't like negative shit around me. My mother decided to have a cookout, and she wanted me to bring the girls. I declined but Cariuna and Camina begged me to go. I swear they have me wrapped around their fingers.

I agreed to go just for a few hours. It was Saturday and we didn't have anything planned after seeing their mother. I wanted to take them to Atlantic Station to get some ice cream and see a movie. Bone gave me a car to drive because I refuse to ride anywhere with him. I didn’t like what he was trying to do to me. I caught on to him. He threw me the keys to a BLACK BMW X5. The License plate was customized BNE WFE. I just shook my head looking at him. I started to object, but I didn't feel like arguing with him. Our arguments are too intense.

♡

We pulled up to my mother's house. It was a few people on the porch. Cariuna couldn't wait to get out of the car. I stepped out the car so I could unfasten their seat belts. Cariuna hopped out quickly and started skipping toward the porch. Camina waited on me. She grabbed my hand tight. I knelt in front of her to see what's wrong. If somebody is bothering her, I’m putting a stop to it today.

“What's wrong Camina?” I asked. I knelt in front of her so she could tell me what was going on. I love this little girl so much. I’ll do anything to protect her.

"Jermesha is always hollering and being mean to me." She pouted. I swear it felt like I grew an extra neck. I wish she would fuck with my granddaughter while I was here. Camina and I walked up toward the house. All eyes were on us. Jermesha looked just like her mother. She was beautiful I can't deny that, but I couldn't miss the hate dripping from her pores. Why bother to even speak and I know her mother has filled her head with a bunch of lies about me. She got one fuckin' time to try me and I'll beat her ass like her momma should've. The ice cream man pulled up. I grabbed a few bills out my purse to give to Cariuna and Camina and they took off running.

"Slow down before you hurt yourself," I yelled. I felt a tap on my shoulder. It was my mother and my brother Tommy. I haven't seen him since I've been here. I jumped up and gave him a hug.

"I thought I wasn't going to be able to see you. I see Bone pulled down on you." He teased.

"Whatever Tommy, you know I was going to come and see you. I have just been staying out the way," I laughed.

"Yeah, momma told me you and Sherry fucked up her kitchen." He laughed. Tommy was always the instigator when we were growing up. Nothing's changed. We're talking and catching up.

"Mother Dear do you want anything from the store I'm about to make a run really quick?" Jermesha asked.

"No, I'm good but I do want you to meet your Aunt Cheree," she stated. Jermesha sized me up. Tommy looked at me and laughed.

"Oh hey," Jermesha stated. I waived. I wasn't about to speak. I don't know what her momma told her about me, and I really don't care but I hope she told her I would beat her ass. Mother Dear asked me to help her in the kitchen. I didn't have a problem with it. I told Camina and Cariuna I would be in the house if they need me. I lifted the living room window so a breeze could come through. I patted out the ground beef and turkey for the burgers and made a salad. I took a seat on the sofa. Bone was texting my phone telling me he was about to pull up because we needed to talk, and I told him no. I couldn't even focus on Bone because the conversation that was going on outside had all my attention.

"What are you looking at me for with your octopus face, stop staring at me," Camina asked and laughed. What fucked me up was the response that she got back.

“That’s why your daddy is dead.” I stood in front of the window to see who was talking Camina like that because it wasn’t a child. It was an adult.

“No, my daddy ain’t dead! Your momma dead octopus face,” Camina laughed and argued. My granddaughter has so much heart.

“You better watch your mouth little girl before I beat your ass like your mammy needs too.” I heard enough. It’s not a bitch walking that can talk to mine like that. I stepped outside on the porch and walked up in the bitch’s face that was talking crazy to my granddaughter.

“You’ll beat whose ass? I know you weren’t talking to my granddaughter like that. She’s a kid, MINE at that. I don’t know how you talk to these other kids around here, but BITCH watch your fuckin’ mouth about how you talk to MINE. I’ll beat your ass for looking at MINE wrong,” I argued and pointed at Camina and Cariuna.

“Keondra let me handle this. I don’t know who this bitch thinks she’s talking too. She better asks her daughter that’s lying in a coma how we give it up,” she laughed and slapped hands with the chick Keondra. I tapped Camina and Cariuna on their shoulder and told them to go in the house. They did as they were told. Tommy already knew what it was with me. I tossed him my phone and clutch and cracked my knuckles. A bitch can't disrespect me, or my grandchildren let along my daughter without any repercussions. I stepped in Jermesha's personal space. I smiled at her showing all thirty-two.

"I don't know what your mother told you about me but let me tell you a little bit about me. I don't tolerate disrespect at all from no one. Blood or not. It ain't nan bitch that's gone disrespect me or my daughter to my face and laugh about it to my face without getting their ass whooped. My mother raised me to respect my elders and your mother should've raised you the same way. Since you're comfortable calling me a bitch and letting this bitch here disrespect your cousin and my grandchildren without speaking up, I'll treat you like a bitch. Oh, and JERMESHA I AM THAT BITCH," I argued. She was saying something slick.

"FUCK YOU AND FUCK CRIM…" I didn't even let her finish another word. I wanted to be directly in front of her when I beat the shit out of her. I drew my arm back and my fist connected with her cheekbone. She held her hand over her cheek. I swung and she ducked. I swung again and my fist connected with the same cheek. I knew I cracked the bones in her face. She fell back instantly. I wasn't about to spare her ass. I stood over her and started tagging her. She was trying to cover her face up. I drug her ass off the porch. Sherry should've taught her weak ass daughter how to fight. All bark and no bite. She got too much mouth like her momma and can't fight.

"Jermesha this is not a fuckin' game you better ask your MOTHER about me. I got a bad temper and Keondra you gonna beat who ass? You want some if so, tag your motherfuckin' ass in. I got some work for you too," I argued. I don't play games or tolerate disrespect. I don't give a fuck who you are. My mother stood in the door and shook her head at me. This here is why I didn't want to come. I didn't want to put my hands on anybody, but she deserved it for disrespecting my daughter. I hope Crimson wasn't letting these, lame ass bitch's punk her. I wasn't done with Jermesha's ass. I hate fuckin' bullies. I grabbed her face roughly. I wanted her to look me in my face.

"Call your momma and let her know I beat your ass. If you ever disrespect me again. I'll make sure your ass is laid up in a coma." I felt a strong pair of hands lift me in the air and off her.

"Why are you out here showing your ass? You know better than that." He argued. I inhaled his scent. He sent chills through my body. My mother and Tommy picked Jermesha up off the ground. She was leaking and I grilled her ass. The worse thing a bitch can do is become an enemy of mine, blood or not. My mother was smiling from ear to ear. She set this up. She knew how I would react if that girl said one thing to me.

"Put me down NOW," I sassed. He held me even tighter. I could feel his heartbeat. He refused to listen.

"I'm not because you know better. Why are you out here fighting children?" He asked.

"Because they were fuckin' with my grandchild and disrespecting my daughter and me. You already know I don't tolerate any form of disrespect. Why are you here," I asked.

"You know why I'm here. I was coming rather you wanted me to or not. We need to talk today and not tomorrow." He argued.

"About what Bone?" I asked. I know what he wants to talk about, but I wasn't up to it. He's been trying to have this conversation for a week now. I have a situation and he does too.

"Take a ride with me and I'll tell you." I couldn't be in a car alone with him. I already know where we would end up. Some things are better left unsaid. I moved on and so has he. He's made that clear on numerous occasions. If Crimson wasn't in a coma, we wouldn't even be this close to each other.

"Can I decline? I can't leave them here." Bone likes to be in control and I'm one female that he couldn't control. I don't care how much money he had. I'll never change me to coincide with his lifestyle.

"Declining isn't an option. Mother Dear has them and nobody's going to fuck with them since you're passing out ass whooping's." He chuckled.

"Whatever, I'm heading back up to the hospital so I can see my baby for visitation hours are over." He grabbed my hand and led me to his car. I stood in front of it because I wasn't getting in.

"Get in Cheree and stop playing." He gave me an evil look. He opened the door for me. I slid in because I could tell he was about to make a scene. He grabbed my hand and pulled off. I looked at him like he was crazy. I'm not about to do this with him.

"What do we need to talk about?" I asked. He sighed heavily. What was that for?

"Us." I turned around to face him to see what he had to say. We should never be a conversation that we needed to have. It's best to leave the past where it's at.

"There is no us, so why would we need to talk about us?" I sighed and asked.

"Why can't it be us? Why can't we give us another try? I've been taking care of you, your whole life. I know I'm not a saint and I ain't never wanted to be. What your mother said last week has been tugging at my heart ever since. If everybody around us can see it Cheree, why can't you? I did some foul shit to you, but I didn't know. That's the truth. I ain't never circled back. How long are you going to put up this front that you don't want me? I know you still care about me because I care about you. I've been watching you with girls. Damn, I hate Crimson never got that chance with you. You're the perfect grandmother." He explained.

"Thank you, but it'll never work Bone. I never said that I didn't care about you. I just don't fuck with you. I forgave you years ago and I'm not tripping off that. Leave us in the past. We both moved on and once our daughter is out of a coma our lives can go back to how they were." He pulled over on the side of the road and hopped out. He opened the car door for me, and I stepped out. I folded my arms across my chest and we just stared at each other. He stepped in my personal space. I couldn't back up because the car was my support. He cupped my chin forcing me to look at him.

"Stop playing with me. How do you know we would never work if you don't take that chance? You're still letting Sherry win. We will work if you stop fighting it. When my daughter wakes up, you're not leaving Atlanta." He argued and explained. I'm going back home. The only thing I've accomplished since I've been here is spending time with my grand-daughters and beating Sherry and her daughter's ass.

"Whatever Bone." He bit my bottom lip and slid his tongue in my mouth. I refused to kiss him back. He grabbed my head and ran his hands through my hair.

"Stop kissing me. I don't know where your lips have been," I argued. I knew Bone had someone. Where is she because I don't want him in my face?

He knows I'm never playing second to anyone. I know he has bitches stashed somewhere.

"My lips haven't been anywhere. I want them on you though." He chuckled. Bone is full of shit. I can't take him seriously and I don't appreciate my mother shedding light on our past.

"They could never be. I told you I got a situation and I don't cheat. We have to stop all this." I sighed. I'm seeing someone and I'm not trying risk what I have going on for him.

"What situation? Tell him daddy's home, or I'll find him myself and tell him. You've been single all these years for a reason Cheree think about that. I'm shooting my shot. You can either give me a chance or I'm taking it. I gave you a choice.

"What's changed Bone, why now? Just a week ago I was interrupting shit. We couldn't stand each other but now you want to be with me?" I asked. His stare was so much intense. He was searching for something. I pray he doesn't find what he's looking for.

"We changed. You're worried about the wrong shit. Worry about right now. I always wanted to be with you, and you know that." He explained and leaned in and deepened the kiss. I couldn't hold back even if I wanted too. I had to stop myself. I'm not supposed to be doing this with him. He grabbed me by my thighs and lifted me up. Bone was always so aggressive. His touch always sent chills through my body. He was turning me on. I wrapped my legs around his waist. I stopped the kiss. We stared at each other for a moment taking each other in. I buried my head in his chest. Getting lost in his scent. He started whispering sweet nothings in my ear.

"Damn, I've been wanting to do this for a long time now." He stated. I didn't know what to say. "Cheree, do you hear me?" He asked. I didn't say anything. Bone put me down and grilled me.

"What Bone, what do you want me to say? I missed you too, but I never imagined myself in your arms again. I knew we would see each other but I didn't think we would be doing this. I'm scared Bone that we're moving too fast. I'm not trying to end up hurt because you think you want something," I explained.

"I'm not trying to hurt you Cheree. I WANT YOU and I NEED YOU. I let you get away once, but it won't happen again." He explained. His eyes dug into my soul. I knew Bone was serious. This is one of the reasons why I didn't want to be alone with him. I knew he would do this. When we first got together, he came at me the same way. I'm speechless.

“I hear you, but actions speak louder than words. Only time will tell.” I sighed.

“I plan on showing you. I'm all about action and you know that. Dead that nigga before I do. I don't want any distractions while we're getting to know each other again. Why are you looking for a place to stay and you can come and stay with me?” He asked.

“I want my own spot. I don't feel comfortable lying in her home and she doesn't know me. Of course, I want to be gone before she wakes up. I'm sure she hates me. I'm not staying at my mother's house. That's out the question. Why would I stay with you Bone? I'm sure you have a few females running up behind you. Are you threatening me or telling me, because I didn't agree to anything.”

“I'm telling you. You don't have to agree to anything. I already told you what it is with me. If you want to know do I have something going on with someone else just ask me. I have a few friends, but it's nothing serious. I live alone for now. I would prefer you to stay at my residence. I don't want you running around the city giving niggas the impression that you're single and you're not. We'll work on Crimson together. It won't be easy but I'm not giving up. I want to make up for lost times with you and her and our grandchildren. I want her to meet her brothers." He explained. I knew Bone had two sons and they were a few years younger than Crimson.

I wasn't having another child or getting involved with a man that had kids if I couldn't raise Crimson. I only wanted one and she was it. I never got the chance to spoil her so it's only right I give her children the world. I could give it to her if she allows me to.

A DAY LATER

Chapter-19

Rashad

I had a long night last night. Shit hasn't been the same since the day they took my nigga away from me. Apart of me left too. It's like the world stopped. No matter how many bodies I've dropped I still felt the same. I couldn't bring my nigga back. I don't know if I'm going or coming, but either way, I've been sending some niggas back to their creator. I haven't seen my son in a week and that's a first for me. It's killing me but shit is hectic out here in these streets. Anybody can get caught slipping. If I get caught I don't want my son with me.

I've painted the city red behind Griff. I haven't heard from Camina or Cariuna. Camina must be cool because she hasn't called me. Crimson's mom has the girls. I'm sure Camina is driving her crazy. I need to get a number on her so I can get her for a few hours. Crimson's still in a coma. I need her to bounce back. I need her out here. I received a text from a strange number telling me to meet him at the spot. I looked at the number and I didn't recognize it. It's only one nigga that I know that tells me to meet him at the spot and he's dead.

I don't know if somebody was playing a game, but they don't want to fuck with me. I'm not the nigga to fuck with. Danielle's been heavy on my mind too. I was serious. I want her to leave Baine. She doesn't have a choice. I hope I knocked her ass up too. I don't know what to do about Mya because we've been kicking it for a while now. She wants more from me, but I can't give her that. I don't want to continue to waste her time so I'm going to slide. My phone alerted me that I had another text from the same number that texted me earlier.

770-682-4688- Aye meet at the spot ASAP

I didn't bother to text back. It could be a setup but if so, I would never give those niggas the upper hand to drop me. They wouldn't see me coming. I sent Slap and Wire a text to let them know I was headed to the spot and if they don't hear from me in an hour to pull up. I didn't bother to wait on them to text me back. I know they were pulling up either way.

♡

I finally made my way to the spot and everything looked normal. Slap and Wire were already there waiting on me. I checked the back and nothing seemed out the ordinary. I hopped out the car and slapped hands with Slap and Wire. They followed me inside. What type of joke was this? We headed to the conference room and I could smell some loud as Kush coming from the room. Marathon OG. Slap and Wire both looked at me. We had our guns drawn. I kicked the door in, and it was Griff sitting at the head of the conference table with his feet posted up laughing. I didn't know rather I wanted to be mad or sad but either way I was glad my partner was alive. We approached each other and embraced. Griff slapped hands with Slap and Wire. We took our seats at the conference table. I wasn't waiting on Griff to speak up. I need to know what the fuck the deal was.

"Aye the next time you want to fake your death give me the heads up. What's up, if that wasn't you then who was that? Who ordered the hit? Do you know how many bodies I've dropped since you've been gone?" I asked. Griff had some explaining to do.

"I'm telling you now because the streets are too hot because of you. We got money to make. If it's hot, we can't get paid. Keondra ordered the hit, that bitch has been on me hard. Ike and Baine didn't have anything to do with it. Peep game though. The nigga she got caught fuckin' on tape years ago was Dre? Remember he used to work for us. I always watch my surroundings no matter what. I couldn't tell you what was going on until I figured it out. I ran into Dre one day when I was coming out of Maxine's. I couldn't really talk to him because I had Camina with me. I wanted to hear what he had to say.

I left Camina with Maria. Dre, Honcho, and I pulled off. He gave me the rundown of everything that Keondra was up too. He told me that he was the one on the tape. Do you know this bitch was the one behind my mother's murder?

She played a part in taking my mother from me. I could never trust a nigga that would bite the hand that fed him. I used that to my advantage. Every play that bitch setup he knew about it and it was on point. It just so happens the day they decided to make a move. I set him up on a dummy drop and she made a move. I knew something was up because she had eyes on the trap from sunup to sundown. The day she made a move they came later than they normally would, and it was an hour before it was time to make the drop.

I wanted to test his loyalty to see what he would do if he had to transport a million dollars in cash. The money was fake. As soon as he made it to the stop sign. I heard tires screech and guns clapping. I got to give it to her, she had that shit setup perfect. I got something for her ass." He explained. Keondra has to get it. No wonder that bitch was doing the most.

"I knew that bitch was up to something. Griff, she has to go." I argued. Actions speak louder than words. She was moving funny because she had something to gain.

"I know but she deserves a slow painful death. Killing her is too easy. I'm going to hit her where it hurts the most. Everything she took from me I'm going to take from her. We need to switch up everything. Let her have the lil funeral she's trying to throw. Make sure you're in attendance. It's time to switch everything up. Here's the layout and the locations to the new traps. I need the work moved and these spots setup ASAP. We got a huge shipment coming in this month. I need shit to go as smooth as possible. Rashad no more bodies but the Jamaican niggas had to go, they were working for Baine and Ike but Keondra had them on payroll." He explained.

"Okay so when are you coming out of hiding. I see you've been working. Where the fuck are you staying at?" I asked. Griff had shit figured out and planned to perfection.

"Soon but we need to find out what else she's up too. I've been staying at home in the basement. Don't tell anybody I'm alive. Stop fuckin' Danielle in my house nigga. I don't want no parts in that." He laughed. I don't appreciate him airing my shit out.

"Fuck you and fuck Baine too. I don't like you having one up on me. What about Crimson?" I asked. Crimson was going through it. Hearing that Griff was alive, she would love it.

"Don't tell her. I'll protect my family at all cost. Once Keondra is dead she'll see me." Griff, Slap, Wire, and I finished looking at the layouts.

THREE DAYS LATER

Chapter-20

Crimson

"Aye Beautiful you need to wake the fuck up TODAY. I don't give a fuck what you got going on out here. You need to shake this shit. You got two beautiful daughters and another child on the way who needs you. I didn't give birth to a weak ass bitch. My blood pumps through you." She argued. I kept hearing this same voice for the past few days, but I couldn't get up. My body didn't want too. Whoever she was, was rude as fuck. I didn't think nurses talked like this. What does she mean she didn't give birth to a weak ass bitch? I hope that's not who I think it is.

"Cheree shut the fuck up and don't talk to her like that. She's resting and she doesn't like Camina and Cariuna to hear a lot of cussing," Mother Dear argued. Who the fuck is Cheree and why are my children around her? I need to wake to see who this Cheree lady is and why does Mother Dear have her around my children. I don't play that shit and why is she talking to me like she knows me.

"Momma I don't care, that's my daughter lying there with tubes in her. She needs to wake the fuck up. I didn't raise her but I'm not going to pacify her either." She argued and explained. Who was this woman talking to Mother Dear like they were crazy? Momma? What daughter did Mother Dear have besides Sherry? I opened my eyes to see who Mother Dear was talking too. I tried to say something, but I couldn't talk. Who was this man staring at me? I had tubes on my stomach. I banged on the bed to get their attention. Mother Dear turned around and looked at me. She had the biggest smile on her face. Tears were running down her eyes. I couldn't talk and I wanted to talk. Where am I and what am I doing here?

"God I'm glad you're up Crimson. Let me go get the nurse so she can remove the tubes out your throat." What the fuck is going on? Why do I have tubes in my throat and where are my children? Who is the lady and man that keeps looking at me? The nurse came in and removed the tubes out of my mouth. She gave me a glass of water. My mouth was dry as hell and I'm hungry.

"Mother Dear what happened? Where are my kids and who are these people in my fuckin' room? What happened to the lady that was talking crazy to you a few minutes ago? That's why I woke up." I argued. "Why is this baby monitor in here? Who's pregnant?"

"Crimson, Danielle has the girls. I'll call her and tell her to bring them up here to you. Your blood pressure was high after you looked at the stuff on Facebook. You fainted and they had to put you in a medically induced coma until your blood pressure went down. You're pregnant again Crimson. I'll let these two people tell you who they are." It makes sense now. I've been here since Keondra tagged me in that bullshit. Pregnant? I know Griff didn't leave me here alone to raise his three kids. I'm good enough to have your three kids but not good enough to marry.

"Hi, Crimson. I'm Cheree Tristan your mother and this is your father Brian Stephens." She explained. I know she didn't say what the fuck I thought she said. This isn't a fuckin' family reunion. My mother? Looking at her is like looking at myself. I took another sip of my water. My throat was still dry. How dare they come up in here like shit was all good. I always wondered what I would say to the two of them if I had the chance to see them again. My mother doesn't look like she had a hard life. She looks as if she's a few years older than me. My father, he looks good for his age too. I wondered if they've been together this whole time.

"Why are you here? You see that door right there; you belong on the outside of it. I'm thirty years old. In all my years of living, you ain't never showed your fuckin' face. No birthday's no holiday's nothing. I don't even fuckin' recognize you. It's bad when you don't recognize your own parents. Your dead to me, haven't I always been dead to you?" I argued, asked and cried. I shouldn't even let this bitch and this nigga get to me.

"Crimson, I understand that you're mad and you have every right to be. I can't change the way you feel, and I won't. I'm mad too. I wanted to be there for you, but I couldn't. I probably shouldn't be here now but I am. I'm not leaving here until I make sure you're good.

My mother called me and told me it wasn't looking good for you and I needed to bring my ass home, so I'm here in the flesh. You ain't never been dead to me. I wasn't in your life for a reason. If I was you and I both probably wouldn't be breathing. I would be less than a mother to allow someone to kill my child if I could do something about it.

I left you with my mother. I've been running all my life and it's time for me to face my reality. We all got to die someday so if I die while I'm here at least I get to see you and my grand-daughters. I'm content with that." She explained. I ain't trying to hear shit she's saying. She looks perfectly fine to me. Hell, she looks as if she could be my sister. Where's Danielle with my fuckin' kids I'm sure she's killed Camina already. My so-called father decided to speak up. I could tell he had some shit with him.

"I don't have an excuse as to why I wasn't around. Your mother didn't want me around so I'm a dead beat by choice. She thought it was best that I stayed away from you because we had a lot of disagreements. She made permanent decisions on temporary emotions. I respected her wishes." He explained. I don't have time for this shit at all. Two grown ass muthafuckas that don't give a fuck about shit but y'all think I want y'all apart of my life now.

"I don't care what y'all got on period. It was fuck me from day one so it's fuck y'all too. I always wanted to tell the two of you that and I mean that shit. I had a hard fuckin' life dealing with Aunt Sherry. Y'all knew about me, but y'all here now? Thank y'all for coming, but y'all can leave and go back to wherever the fuck y'all came from. I'm good on excuses. There's no need for an apology," I argued. It felt good to get that shit off my chest. My mother wasn't budging. She climbed in the bed right behind me. My father stood in the same seat and didn't move. I turned around to look at her. We just stared at each other. I said what I had to say. Now, what did she have to say?

"I know you're upset Crimson and I am too. I'm not leaving you until you're 100%. You might not need me now, because you're grown but I need you. I love you and I want you to know that." She stated. I couldn't even respond to her because Danielle walked in with Camina and Cariuna. Danielle was looking at me smiling. Cariuna gave my father a hug, and Camina ran to my mother and climbed in the bed between us.

"Mommy you're up." She beamed, grabbed my cheeks, and kissed me.

"I missed you to Camina. Have you been a good girl while I've been gone?" I asked.

"Yep, I've been good ask grandma? She's been, bad mommy. She beat up Auntie Sherry and she beat up

Jermesha too." She laughed. Damn, I must've been out for a minute. I've missed everything. Danielle approached the bed and smiled at me.

"I missed you so much. I'm glad you're awake. When are you leaving because Keondra's having Griff's funeral and I've been praying every day that you wake up before they had it? They're showing his body tomorrow." She sighed.

"Are you serious, hopefully, today or tomorrow. I don't know because it hasn't been discussed yet." I got to get out of here.

"Excuse me Crimson and Danielle. I hate to interrupt your conversation and be nosey, but Keondra is she the one that runs with Jermesha?" Cheree asked.

"Yeah, why?" I sassed and asked. Why is she still here and being nosey while Danielle and I are talking? I wasn't in the mood to hear her voice. I hated that she was even this close to me. I can't wait until she leaves so, I can talk about her ass with Mother Dear and Danielle.

"I asked because the day I tapped Jermesha's ass, she was there talking out the side of her neck to Camina. The ass whooping was intended for her but Jermesha took the charge. I asked her if she wanted some too if so, she can tag herself in. It makes sense now. Please assure me you don't be letting these weak ass hoes punk you?" Cheree asked. Danielle looked at me and I looked at her.

"They could never punk me. Have we had words, yes." I explained. I didn't know Cheree to be telling her my business. I can tell she's very protective. I wish I would've seen Sherry and Jermesha get their ass whooped. I'm sure they deserved it. Camina's telling it all.

"Oh, okay I was just checking because I don't tolerate disrespect in any form. You may not know me and excuse my language, but a bitch can't disrespect me or anything that's related to me without any repercussions. They got one time and one time only and it's a motherfuckin' wrap. Momma stop letting people sit on your porch if they don't like my child. I don't give a damn if she's with Jermesha. She was to comfortable talking shit. The next time I see Jermesha I'll be sure to let her know that." Cheree argued.

"Grandma, can I stay with you today? I don't want to go to school because the kids be picking with me. Can you beat them up the same way you did Jermesha," Camina asked, whined and pouted? I can see now Camina has her wrapped around her fingers the same way she has her father.

"It's perfectly fine with me, ask your mother is it okay," Cheree asked and looked at me? What could I say the damage was already done?

"It's okay mommy right," Camina beamed. She knew I wasn't going to say no. Especially since she's been with her already.

"Of course, you can." I smiled. Camina wrapped her arms around my neck and laid her head on my chest. She was using me since Griff wasn't around.

"God mommy Danielle you don't have to come back and get me I'm staying with my grandma." Camina explained and rolled her eyes. We all started laughing.

"Danielle what did you do to my child?" I asked. Danielle and Camina never got along. I'm sure she's whooped my baby by now.

"Nothing. What she has done to me is the better question." She laughed. Cheree and Brian took Camina and Cariuna with them. My kids have attached to them already, now that's crazy. As soon as my door was closed, I couldn't wait to dig into their ass. Don't be using my kids to get close to me.

"Mother Dear why did you call them? I don't even know her, and you thought it was okay for her to keep my kids while I was down and out? She couldn't even keep me." I argued. I hated to go there but I had too.

"Calm down Crimson. I called her because I wanted too. It was time for the two of you to meet. It's been too long and I'm not going to always be here Crimson. I'm getting up in age and you need your mother. I know you don't like it, but it is what it is. Yes, she's been keeping them because I didn't want to have to fuck Sherry and Jermesha up myself for fuckin', with your kids. So, I called your mother who would do it without blinking an eye. Besides, in order to save Danielle's marriage, it's best that she came because Camina said she saw Rashad in the bed with Danielle and she was screaming." Mother Dear laughed.

Mother Dear was with the shit for real and Danielle's not off the hook. I looked at Danielle. She had a lot of explaining to do. I hope she didn't fuck Rashad. Danielle couldn't even look at me. I'll be sure to ask her what that was about.

“I don't care Mother Dear I would've handled them myself. I feel violated. I wish you wouldn't have done that. Why does she feel so comfortable to lay in my bed as if we're cool because we fuckin ain’t? I don’t want to hear excuses period.

Let your daughter know I’m 100% so she can go back to wherever the fuck she came from. I wish you would quit saying you won't always be around. I bet you're going to outlive everyone. You knew I wouldn't be okay with this,” I argued. Mother Dear knows she tried me.

“Crimson watch your damn mouth. I know you're upset, and you should be, but everything ain't what it seems. She's not going anywhere until she sees for herself that you're straight. She's comfortable because she had you. I'm not going to always be here. Crimson I want to sell my house and cruise the world. Your daughters love her especially that damn Camina. If you never hear her out, I know you'll listen to me. She didn't want to come because she knew how you would react because you two are the same. I told her to bring her ass and she came. Trust me as much as you missed her growing up, she missed the fuck out of you too.

The only difference between you and her is that Cheree didn't listen to nothing I had to say. She lived her life and did whatever she wanted to do no matter if I liked it or not. She didn't listen and she found herself involved with some dangerous criminals. She was in too deep. They wanted her head and yours too. So, I did what I was supposed to do and told her to get the fuck on and as far away from you as possible.

She gave up EVERYTHING she loved to save your life. She's at the point where if they come, she doesn't give a fuck about dying. I'm not taking up for her because I don't do that. I state facts but that's what the fuck you get when you don't honor and obey your mother and father. Bad shit happens and that goes for your mother to Danielle." She argued and explained and pointed her finger at us. I hated when Mother Dear got to preaching and stating facts, she always made me feel bad like I'm in the wrong and I haven't done shit wrong. It ain't my fault she wanted to be grown and not listen to her.

"So, what's his story since you're airing out everybody's dirty laundry?" I asked. Mother Dear knew everybody's damn business. I swear this lady knows everything. Since when has she wanted to sell her house and travel the world?

"He wanted to be around he didn't give a damn if the Puerto Ricans came, he was willing to stand in the paint for Cheree, but she didn't want to have anything to do with him because of SHERRY.

Brian a.k.a Bone to the streets, was good guy. He just got caught up with the wrong pussy and your mother has a zero tolerance for any bullshit. It was a wrap. That's where you get it from." Mother Dear laughed. Damn Sherry has been hating for a long time.

"What did Sherry do?" I asked.

"Crimson, ask your mother. She'll be glad to tell you. You already know what Sherry did. It's the same shit Jermesha will do to you. She fucked your daddy and your mother caught them and beat the hell out of Sherry and him too. If you ever look him in the face, you'll see the permanent tattoo on his face from her." Mother Dear laughed. Ugh I can't stand Sherry or Jermesha. It makes sense now why those bitches didn't like me. I'm not even surprised. Damn they're always fuckin' somebody's man.

"Mother Dear, who won the fight?" I asked and laughed. Cheree is to pretty to fight but her mouth is nasty.

"Your mother did of course and know I didn't break it up because Sherry deserved that shit. The moment she saw your father walk out the house she was pushing up on him, doing that ghetto ass shit. She knew he wasn't there for her, but she just had to try her luck.

Your mother don't bother anybody. She minds her business, but Sherry was digging and talking her shit. In return your mother tapped that ass. I thought she was going to kill her. You should've saw Jermesha get her ass handed to her. It was everything. She cracked the bones in Jermesha's face. I was praying she got Keondra's ass too. After she seen Jermesha get whooped, she ran to her car and pulled off." Mother Dear laughed. We finished talking I didn't even get to hug my baby Cariuna.

I hope they come back through. I missed my babies. It seems like everybody has been having fun without me. I got to get out of here. I want to see Griff one last time before they lay him to rest.

Chapter-21

Cheree

God is good all the time. She finally woke up and I'm very thankful for that. I knew she would respond the way she did. I wouldn't expect anything less from her. I can't even be mad because I would've done the same thing. She's stubborn as hell. I can tell she's going through a lot. I just want to be there for her if she allows me to. I know I don't look like what I've been through, but I been through it. After having Crimson I had to give her up to my mother, I suffered postpartum depression. I didn't have anybody to lean on. Yes, my mother was one call way, but I needed her in the flesh. I missed my child every day.

I longed for Bone so much back then, but he would never know that. He was the reason that I couldn't be with her. It took me years to get over that. I wanted to hear her voice and to protect her from the world. I knew she was lying about Keondra, I just felt it. I put this on my life if I find out that Keondra has been fuckin' with Crimson I will bury that bitch alive. You can call me what you want to but it is what it is. Bone tapped me on the shoulder and I turned around to look at him. He was so fuckin' sexy. Damn, he's gotten better with time. I couldn't be with him. I don't care how much he pushes up on me. It'll never happen.

"What's up?" I asked. He was searching my face for an explanation, but I didn't have one to give. I had a lot on my mind. Crimson was the only thing that consumed it.

"You. Are you okay?" He asked. He knew I was in my feelings. I've been waiting on this day for years. I wish I could change back the hands of time, but I can't. If I could I would've done a lot of shit different. I do have regrets. I wish I wouldn't have crossed paths with them, but I did. I love everything about Crimson.

"Yeah, I'm good. What about you?" I lied. I'm not ready to open up to Bone about how I feel. I'm not there yet. A lot has happened between us. I can't sit here and act as if we're cool. I'm not holding a grudge, but I never got the chance to raise my child. It was taken away from me because of him. He had other kids that he was able to watch grow up. I never got that, because they were at my neck behind some shit he did.

Yeah, I had his money and I was able to spend however I wanted to, but it wasn't about that. I longed for

Crimson. Hearing about her through my mother did nothing for me.

“I’m good. I just want to make sure you’re straight. She’ll come around but I think you should try to talk to her again. When I look at Crimson, I see you. She acts like you. I wanted to laugh. It was hard as hell holding that shit in when she let fuck you and I mean that shit escape her lips. You ruined her and she doesn’t even know it” he chuckled. At least he found some humor in it, but I didn't. It hurt to hear her say that, but that's how she feels and to be honest, I don't know how to approach her. Mother Dear said she was an angel and sweet as pie. Shit, she left that shit out. She was on the defense straight out the gate.

“I know I see it too. My mother said she has peculiar ways. I just didn’t know that was one of them so, I guess I had to see it for myself. I wouldn’t expect anything less from her. I want to talk to her again Bone but I’m not going to sweat her though.” I explained. I know she needs time and I’ll have to give her that, but we’ll have to talk. I'm sure she had questions about the hints I threw out there but it's the truth. What choice did I have?

“You’re not sweating her Cheree, you’re her mother. I can’t change the past, but I can help mold the future. You’ve come too far to give up. Go back up there and talk to her. She wants you there. You’re the reason she woke up.” He explained. I took Bone’s advice. I know I’m the reason she woke up. I had to talk to her that way so she would wake up. She's a fighter. I heard Camina telling her to wake up it's time to come home. So, I incorporated that. She was looking at me. I wonder did she know who I was. We had locked eyes immediately.

The girls and I stopped by the gift shop to get their mother some flowers, chocolate and ice cream. I grabbed me a charger to charge my Kindle. I grabbed me a journal to write a few things down. It's been so much going on I haven't had time to write. Here goes nothing, wish me luck. We made it back upstairs to Crimson’s room and she was alone. Cariuna and Camina ran to her bedside. She was a great mother. I sat in the chair in the corner. Camina and Cariuna climbed in the bed with her. They grabbed the remote and flipped it on the cartoons. Crimson was trying to get out of the bed. I ran to her side to help her.

“I got it.” She explained. I knew she would say that. She knew I would help her no matter what she had to say. She's strong despite the few minor setbacks. I meant to ask her what she saw on Facebook that had her blood pressure high.

“Let me help you Crimson, you haven’t been on your feet in days. Do you want anything good to eat? I can order you some food” I asked. I could already tell she was about to decline, but I wasn't having that. She needs some real food. She's been on a liquid diet for a week now. It's important that she eats. A good meal would give her strength. She has a baby growing inside of her.

“I’m fine. I got to pee. I want to take a shower and wash my hair.” She explained. I see now this tip-toeing shit around her feelings ain't going to work. I know she's mad at me, but I’m not about to pacify her. Tough love is the best love and that's exactly what she's about to get from me. I'm not about to dumb it down for her. What you see is what you get with me.

“Okay, let me call a nurse. They need to unhook this baby thing.” I've been washing her ass for the past week and her hair. I didn't have to do it, but I did because I don't trust a motherfucka around mine period. I don't give a damn what your profession is.

“Okay, if you insist. I can do it myself I went to school for this.” She sassed and stated. Crimson is trying me for real. I swear I'm not beat for it. I don't have any patience, but for her, I'll try.

"I heard but let them do their job. What do you want a boy or another girl?" I asked. She didn't need another girl. I'm praying she has a boy. I just wonder how Camina was going to adjust with having another child in the picture. She's spoiled rotten. She's so cute. You can't help but do it, and she's bad as hell. Cariuna is a princess. She's perfect and respectful.

"Neither," she sighed. I wonder why she would say that. Children are a beautiful thing. Especially if it's by someone you love. I checked out the pictures in her home and I could tell Griff loved her by the way he looked at her.

"Why not? I can tell you're a great mother." I had to ask? It took her a minute to answer but I had time. I understand that he's gone but he left another piece of him with you that's a blessing within itself. I don't know what she's going through, but I can feel her pain.

"I just don't. Do you have any other kids?" She asked. She looked at me with wide eyes. I knew she was ready to set me straight if I had other kids that alone lets me know I made the right decision.

“Nope, just you. I only wanted one. If I couldn’t raise you, I refuse to raise another. I could never give another child, what I couldn't give you. I want to give your children what I couldn't give you. If you would allow me too. I know none of this is easy for you Crimson. I know I’m late, but I’m on time. I got you, all of you if you would allow me to.” I stated. Crimson looked at me and tears poured down her face. I wiped her tears with my thumbs.

“It's hard Cheree, I swear to God it is. I want to call you momma, but I can't. I’m not there yet. I've longed for you for so long and now you're finally here and I don't know what to do. I lost my soul mate and it's hurt so bad. I'm begging God to please take the pain away. For some reason, I can never do people how they do me. My heart won't allow it. I guess I’m not built like that. As bad as I wish I could shut you out. I can't.

Suddenly you appear after all these years. I'm not going to sit here and act like I don't need you because I do, but you got one time and one time only to fuck me over and I’m done.” She cried. I wrapped my arms around her, and she hugged me so tight. She was crying and I started crying too. I'm glad we were able to get here.

“Thank you Crimson for giving me a fair chance. I swear I won't fuck it up. Besides my mother and brother, you and your children are all I have. I need you. Crimson, I need you more than you need me. Thank you for giving me a chance. Thank you for not judging me. I appreciate you for not pushing me away. I expected worse. Thank you for proving me wrong and I'm forever grateful for that.” I cried.

THE WAKE

Chapter-22

Keondra

These past few days have been rough. After the whole blow-up at Mother Dear's house, I was done. I don't know who told that bitch to ear hustle. I wanted to pinch the fuck out of Camina's little badass. How dare she call me an octopus face. I should've told her to call her mother that. I wasn't even about to fight with her old ass grand momma. After she tapped Jermesha's ass and Mother Dear's eyes were trained on me. I noticed she kept reaching in her purse. I knew she wanted to shoot me. It was best that I left to avoid dying before I had the chance to shit on Crimson. I just had a miscarriage, so I knew Ike was lurking in the shadows waiting to fuck me up. Ike was a ruthless ass nigga. I had no clue that he was that heartless. He scared the fuck out of me. I can't believe he made me clean up that body. I have nightmares and flashbacks about what he did to Jacque.

I finally found a funeral home to do the services for Griff's funeral. Eppinger Funeral Home in Cartersville, Georgia. Thank God because nobody in the city would do it for me. It was beginning to piss me off, but finally, they agreed to do it. They did a great job. Boy, I fucked Griff up. I couldn't wait until these muthafuckas saw my handy work. I can't dwell on that right now. It's time to bury this nigga and cash out. The streets were already talking about they couldn't wait to see Griff.

Jermesha already told me Crimson was out the hospital. If she thinks she's about to view his body, she has another thing coming. Not on my fuckin' watch is that going to happen. I was giving the hood something to talk about. If they wanted to take pictures, post him on Facebook, and make memes of his death they could. I don't care I'm here for it. I was a day away from being a rich ass bitch, courtesy of him.

Jacque's mom has been calling me for the past few days. I finally answered my phone and told her I haven't heard from him because he broke up with me. That was the truth. I hope she doesn't dig into it. I don't know what Ike did with his phone. My mother came down like she agreed to. She was very upset about me having Griff's body shown because of the condition it was in. She kept telling me don't show his body to the public. I wasn't hearing anything that she was saying. It's bigger than how he looks. Everybody thought that Griff couldn't be touched. Well, I touched him and I wanted muthafuckas to see. The wake was scheduled to start in an hour and I was dressed to impress. I was drippin with an all-white Chanel fitted dress even though I'm not pregnant anymore.

My breasts were fuller and what little ass I had was sitting up like a stallion. My pixie cut was tapered and styled to perfection. I still had some of Griff's jewelry that I stole from when we were together. I couldn't sell it because Griff had specific pieces and insurance on his shit. Somebody would've recognized it and told him. Today I'm wearing it. My mother looked nice also. Our ride was quiet. I knew she had some things that she wanted to say but right now wasn't the time. I cut my radio up to avoid hearing her. She cut the radio down.

"Keondra, I'm going to ask you one more time. Could you please not show his body," she asked and argued. Thank God we came to a stop light. I lowered my shades on my face so we could be eye level with each other. I bucked my eyes at her. I know she lying.

"Momma, I'm doing it. He would've wanted me too," I sassed and gave her a devilish smirk. She God damn lie. I was doing this and nothing could change that.

"Keondra, are you actually going to sit here and lie in my damn face. If that was you lying in that casket, I would never let a motherfucka see you fucked up like that. What the fuck are you up to? Griff wouldn't want that. Hell, he wasn't even with you. You're a different type of crazy. Griff divorced you years ago and made a family with somebody else.

Move the fuck on. You're married to Ike and you were pregnant by Jacque. Why are you so invested in this man? How were you able to pull this off and he was with someone else," she asked. I looked at my mother as if she was crazy. I couldn't believe she let that shit escape from her mouth.

"Mommy, whose side are you on? I'm your daughter. Griff and I weren't together but I have rights. He never remarried after we had a divorce. I'm doing this because I want too and ain't nobody going to fuckin' stop me. Ike and I aren't together. He made it clear he wants a divorce and Jacque and I broke up," I explained. I don't even know why I'm explaining myself because I don't care what Ike or anyone else thinks.

"I understand that Keondra. I'm not fuckin' dumb. How do you think Griff's woman feels? This is her job, not yours. You shouldn't even be doing this. God sits high and he looks low. I know you better than you know yourself. You have something going on. Whatever it is, I don't feel good about it at all. I pray this shit doesn't blow up in your face," she explained. I'm glad we finally made it to Praying Hands on Your Baptist Church. I threw my car in park. I swear I hated to do this. I ain't never disrespected my mother before but today was the day.

"Mommy excuse my language, but I don't give a fuck about HER. He married ME and HE NEVER MARRIED HER, so I don't give a fuck how she feels. I always deal with the cards I've been dealt." I argued. I stepped out of my car and straightened my dress. I grabbed my purse out the back seats and threw my Chanel frames on. My momma stepped out and slammed the door. I hit the alarm and strutted to the door ignoring her. The parking lot was filling up fast. I didn't bother to hire security because the only bitch I wanted to check at the door was Crimson. Jermesha and Cutie were already waiting for me.

The whole hood came out to see Griff. I wasn't surprised that I heard so many gasps and laughs after they saw his body. I couldn't hold the laughter in even if I wanted to. I felt a tap on my shoulder. It was Maria, Auntie Kaye, and Auntie BeBe. The smile I once had on my face was replaced. Jermesha and Cutie elbowed me. I don't know how I let the three of them pass me bye. Auntie BeBe cleared her throat. We never liked each other and I knew she had some slick shit she wanted to say.

"Keondra, you are wrong as fuck for allowing the public to see Griff's body," she argued. I had to choose my words wisely.

"What's your point, Auntie BeBe? What's done is done. I can't take it back and I'm not taking it back," I argued. I don't give a fuck what they think. It doesn't fuckin' matter to me because on Monday morning I'll be a rich ass bitch.

"You know what Keondra, I ain't never wished bad on a bitch before, but the way you're moving it's wrong on all levels. You're having a funeral for my fuckin' nephew and his family and children aren't involved. I got a fuckin' problem with that. What goes around comes around. Every

BITCH has their day coming and guess what, yours is coming soon," she argued and walked off. My mother stood in the corner and shook her head. Fuck all of them. Jermesha, Cutie, and I finished talking and started greeting the guest that came to pay their respect. Cutie and Jermesha both sucked their teeth. I looked in their direction and it was Crimson and Danielle. I know shit was about to get real and I was ready for it. Danielle and Crimson attempted to walk toward the mortuary, but I stopped them.

"Excuse me, can you get the fuck out my way so I can see my fiancé," she argued. We sized each other up. She won't be seeing Griff today.

"Fiancé'? I'm not moving because you're not allowed to fuckin' see him. In case you forgot bitch, I was his wife and I'm calling all the fuckin' shots. No, you're not allowed to fuckin' see him. I hate to rain on your parade but it's not happening today." I argued. Crimson took her glasses off her face. So I took mine off too. I meant what the fuck I said. Everybody was looking at us. We had a crowd now. I tossed Jermesha my purse and Cutie my phone. Her cheeks were red. She pointed her finger in my face and stepped in my personal space. I gave her an evil glare because she was pushing it.

"Look, BITCH, I'm sick of you. Yes, he was my fiancé and you and I both know it. You're childish as fuck. Do you remember he proposed to me in your fuckin' face? I remember like it was yesterday. Whatever games you're playing you can keep playing them because I ain't got fuckin' time. You're bitter and fuckin' miserable. You're doing this for what because everybody knows the truth. He fuckin' despised you. I don't have to see him I know what we had. I don't have to put on for no fuckin' body. I'm going to tell you one time and one time fuckin' only.

Leave me the fuck alone. The next time I hear about you talking crazy to my daughter bitch, you gone fuckin' see me," she argued and punched me in my face. I raised my arm to draw back at her. My mother grabbed my arm and stopped me. I looked at her like she is crazy.

"Let it go Keondra. You've done enough," my mommy argued.

"Ms. let her go. I wish you would. I got so much anger in me bitch you will be lying in that casket right next to him. I'm begging you to fuckin' try me," she argued. I tried to get around my mother to get at her. Crimson had me fucked up. Danielle grabbed her and rolled her eyes at me. They walked toward the exit.

“Mommy why did you do that,” I argued. I’m sick of her and I’ve been trying to be respectful, but she’s tried me for the last time today.

“You’re doing way too much Keondra. I may be a lot of things but this whole damn setup is fuckery and you know it. I raised you better than that. Muthafuckas are already talking about you. I don’t care how much you hate that girl, it’s not going to change shit. Everybody came to pay their respects, see Griff, take their pictures, and talk their shit. But guess what, these muthafuckas are talking about you. Nobody in their right mind would show that body. Do you think muthafuckas want to remember him like that? I heard you snickering with them. I hate to say it baby girl but Lord have mercy on your soul. I didn’t raise you like this. Whatever is coming to you I hope they take it easy on you. You can only do bullshit for so long. When it finally catches up to you, I hope you’re prepared.

I’ll see you around, I changed my flight. I’m leaving tonight. I don’t condone bullshit and fuckery. I never thought I would have to distance myself from you, but you drew the fuckin’ line with this shit. I’m out,” she argued and stomped her feet out the mortuary. I don’t have to explain myself to anybody. It is what it is. Griff’s wake was almost over. I'm surprised Rashad and Griff's crew didn't come to pay their respects. I'll see them tomorrow. The show must go on. I can't believe my mother. We've never had it out like this before.

THE FUNERAL

Chapter-23

Crimson

I've only been out of the hospital for a few days and I haven't had any sleep. I've been catching up with the girls and my mother. I thought tonight would be different, but I guess I was wrong. I couldn't sleep for some reason. Maybe it's because I've been in a coma and all I was doing was sleeping. I missed Griff so much despite all the bullshit. I've been going through it since he's been gone. I wish I could kiss him. I wish he could hold me in his arms one last time. Him telling me how much he loves me, and that everything was going to be okay, but that's wishful thinking.

Hate is a strong word to use but I swear to God I hate Keondra. I don't get why does she have it out for me? She doesn't even know me. If I was throwing Griff's funeral, I wouldn't deny her to see him. I would allow her to pay her respects because I know what we have. It took everything in me not to kill her earlier at The Wake for Griff. She brought me out of character. I wanted to see my baby one last time and she denied me of that. I'm glad I didn't bring Camina and Cariuna with me. I wanted them to remember their father just the way he was. His funeral is less than eight hours away. How am I going to be able to see him? I feel his energy and I smell him. I heard a knock at my door, and it was my mother. I'm glad she's here. I need her to help me with the girls.

"Come in Cheree," I sighed. She took a seat beside me. I swear she's a great listener.

"Crimson you need to get some rest. Why are you still up? I noticed you've been going non-stop since you made it home. You need to relax. The girls and I need you. So does that baby that's growing inside of you," she explained. I know but I've been down for so long. I had to catch up with everything I've missed.

"I know but I can't. Griff's funeral is in a few hours and I won't be able to attend it. That's why I can't even sleep." I sighed and held my head down. I'm so fuckin' frustrated. I feel so damn defeated it's ridiculous. I felt my mother raise up from my bed. She stood in front of me and cupped my face. I looked at her and smiled.

"Crimson don't ever put your head down. What doesn't kill you makes you stronger. Why can't you go to Griff's funeral," she asked. I gave my momma the rundown of what happened. I knew she was about to go off. I could tell by her facial expressions.

"Crimson I thought you said she wasn't a fuckin' problem when I asked you that a few days ago? I knew you were lying, but she got you fucked up. I'm glad you didn't let that bitch punk you in front of all those people. She ain't stopping shit if you want to go to Griff's funeral you can and you fuckin' will. Just disguise yourself as someone else. That's all you'll have to do. The only person she's checking for is you and Danielle," she explained. Damn, I should've told her that earlier. The biggest smile appeared on my face.

"I need the perfect disguise." I beamed.

"A Muslim so you can cover your entire face with a Hajib. I'll go get you and Danielle one in the morning. What color do you want," she asked and beamed?

"White." My mother and I finished talking. I love having her around and I can't lie. She climbed in bed right beside me. I grabbed the remote to find something on Netflix to watch. Her phone was going off. I wondered if it was my father. He's been on her heavy. She looked at her phone and rolled her eyes.

"Cheree, what's up with you and Brian," I asked and laughed. She turned around and looked at me. She grabbed my cheeks.

"Nothing is up with us Crimson. I forgive him but I can't be with him. I just can't. I wish he would stop trying and move on," she explained.

"I hear you Cheree. Have you told him that? I don't see him just moving on because you want him to. He's going to wear you down," I laughed. My mother and I finished talking. My father called her phone back and I told him she was asleep. He told me my mother was too old to have me to lie for her.

Rashad

Today was the day Keondra was throwing this bullshit as funeral that she was having for Griff. Auntie Kaye and Maria already told me how she was acting yesterday at the wake. I'm not surprised. I'm glad he's alive but damn I really didn't want to go to this shit. I ain't never wanted to murk a bitch as bad as I wanted to murk her. The only reason why I was going was that he asked me to. I don't know why Griff wanted us to go through with this shit and it's not even him lying in that casket. The block was talking heavy about how fucked up Griff looked, and how she had his body shown to the public and shit. I had to play it cool so nobody would suspect anything different. Keondra should count her last fuckin' days because her time is coming. She already knew to steer clear of me.

Slap, Wire, and I suited up so we could be in attendance. Mya was coming with me. For some reason, I wanted to show her off. I wanted her by my side today. I tried to call Crimson to see if she wanted to ride with us, but she said she wasn't going. She wasn't allowed to come to the funeral. She didn't need to come anyway because that wasn't my nigga lying in that casket. Mya fixed my tie. I grabbed her hand and we headed out.

♡

We pulled up to the funeral and it was packed. It took me at least five minutes to park. Auntie Kaye, Auntie BeBe, and Maria were already in there. I opened the door up for Mya and grabbed her hand. I know we were headed inside the church, but my glasses weren't leaving my face. Slap and Wire were right behind us. I swear I didn't want to do this. It's disrespectful as fuck, but it's time to get this shit on the road so we can make our next move and dead this bitch ASAP. Mya grabbed my hand and I looked at her. Mya was bad as fuck, I can't lie. I'm going to try and get my shit together so we can do something since my nigga is back. She has been rocking out with me for a minute. I might go ahead and give this relationship shit a try.

"Rashad is everything okay?" She asked. I'm good I just didn't want to be here pretending that it was my nigga lying in that casket. I couldn't tell Mya that. The less she knew the better.

"I'm good Mya," I smiled. We entered the church and grabbed an obituary. I shook my head flipping through this shit. Keondra didn't put one fuckin' picture of me or his kids in the program. It makes sense now that bitch was up to something. I told Griff to let me do her. I looked to the left and Keondra had her whole crew up front. Auntie Kaye, Auntie BeBe, and Maria were sitting a few rows back. Mya and I made our way up front to view the body. I damn near jumped looking at this shit. Mya grabbed my hand when she saw me jump.

I could've sworn I heard a few laughs coming from the area Keondra was sitting in. I looked over at her and she gave me a devilish smirk. I gave that bitch an evil smirk. All this was funny to her and I couldn't wait to kill her. We took our seats because the funeral was scheduled to start in about fifteen minutes. The last few people were coming in to view the body before they closed the casket. I looked toward the aisle to see how many more people were coming. There were about thirty more people. It was two females that stood out the most. They were draped in all white. Hijabs were covering their faces. Big chunky gold jewelry draped their necks.

They were Muslims. Their faces were covered but it's like I knew them. Griff didn't know any Muslims that I knew of. Something about them seemed familiar. I noticed one of them kept scanning the room taking in her surroundings. Our eyes locked with each other and its like time stood still. I knew her eyes anywhere. It was Danielle and I'm sure the other one was Crimson. A small smile crept on my face. Mya tapped me on my shoulder. I tried to ignore her because my eyes were trained on Danielle. We haven't seen each other since we explored each other. Our eyes were having a conversation of it's on.

"Rashad who is that and why she keeping looking at you like that does," she asked. Mya was getting on my last fuckin' nerves. We're at a funeral. Did it ever occur to her that they may know me?

"I don't know," I lied. Danielle quickly turned her head. Danielle and Crimson finally made their way toward the casket. I knew Crimson was about to break down. I got up out of my seat to help her. Slap got up right behind me. As soon as she placed her hand on the casket. She let out a loud piercing scream, the body raised up from the casket and everybody started running, even her and Danielle. I swear that was the funniest shit I ever saw. It looked like a hood track team. I ain't never saw black folks run that fast if it wasn't the police.

"Don't run young people. To be absent from the body is to be present with the Lord," the preacher stated. "The dead can't hurt you it's the living." Shit Black folks don't give a damn about that. If a dead body raised up out the casket, they weren't staying around to see what was about to happen next. Fuck the food and everything else.

Crimson and Danielle ran trying to get away and they fell too. I scooped Danielle up in my arms, and Slap helped Crimson off the floor. Danielle and I locked eyes with each other. Slap looked at me to see what was going on. Danielle knew she was mine. I don't give a fuck where we're at. I'm letting that shit be known. I don't give a fuck if Baine was in the room or not.

"Put me down Rashad," she argued. I wasn't and she already knew that. Fuck this funeral. This shit was a dub anyway. Everybody was leaving. I'm glad too because I didn't want to sit here with this pretending shit. Mya tapped me on my shoulder. Danielle was still in my arms. Mya was grilling Danielle, and Danielle was grilling her back. I put Danielle down to keep the confusion down. Danielle and Crimson marched off and headed to their car. I slapped hands with Slap and Wire. We had plans to link up with Griff later to see what the next move was. As soon as we made it to the car. I closed Mya's door and she couldn't wait to go in on me.

"Rashad who was that? I asked you earlier and you fuckin' lied. The moment they walked in the door your eyes stayed on her. The moment they went to view his body you were right up there too. To make matters worse I'm here with you and instead of looking for me after everybody ran out, you're up in her face holding her bridal style. So, who is she because she has your fuckin' attention?" She asked. I pinched the bridge of nose. I threw my Benz in park.

"Mya you're tripping for real and guess what, I ain't got time for that shit at all. If I did all that it's somebody I know. That was Crimson and her mother. Keondra wouldn't let her come to the funeral so they came in a disguise. I went up there with her because I knew she would take it hard. Is that okay with you?" I asked. I wouldn't dare tell her that was Danielle. She didn't need to know that.

"I'm sorry," she mumbled. She wasn't sorry mind your business and not mine.

“You can keep the apology. Think before you talk to me.” I argued and pulled off. I was dropping Mya’s ass right at home. She could forget about chilling with me.

Crimson

I'm so fuckin' nervous my hearts beating extra fast. I'm trying to calm down but it's hard. I tried to keep it together, but I couldn't. I lost it when I saw him lying in that casket. It didn't look like him at all. I couldn't even feel him. Keondra is an evil bitch. I would've never shown his body to the public like that. It's so fuckin disrespectful. Soon as his body rose up from the casket I damn near lost it. I never experienced anything like that before. His obituary didn't mention his children at all. I trashed it. I'm so glad I didn't allow my children to come to this fuckery. Danielle and I made it to my car. I tossed her the key so she could drive. I needed a few more minutes to get myself together.

"Are you okay? Where too," she asked and sighed. I could tell Danielle was going through a lot of shit, but she didn't care to share. It doesn't work like that. She's always there for me no matter what. It's only right I'm there for her in return.

"It doesn't matter I'm hungry let's get something to eat. I don't give a damn what kind of disguise you have on

Rashad knows you. Danielle, if it's something you need to get off your chest you can. I'm here and I'm all ears. Girl who was the girl that tapped him on his shoulder. I noticed how she looked at you." I don't know what Danielle and Rashad got going on but it's something. I can feel and see it. I wasn't the only one that picked up on it.

"Okay, I want some soul food from Julissa's! I don't have anything to tell you yet. I'm not ready. I'm embarrassed. I don't know who she is. Ask Rashad. Fuck him I wish he would stay out of my face. Let's talk about this shotgun funeral. Bitch, that didn't look like Griff. It looked like one of those bodies from tales from the hood.

I damn near pissed on myself and broke my fuckin' ankle when the body rose up from the casket. I was done. Why did that shit happen when we went up there? Griff wanted to hug you one more time. He didn't give a damn," she laughed. Danielle and I finished talking and catching up on our way to Julissa's. Despite all the bullshit I still had a lot to smile about.

TWO WEEKS LATER

Chapter-24

Keondra

Griff's funeral was two weeks ago. It's time to get this show on the fuckin' road. His funeral was ruined the moment some Muslim bitch stopped in front of his casket and started crying. Who was she, because his body rose up from the casket and everybody left? I don't know if she did voodoo or not, but she did something. I wanted to stop that bitch dead in her tracks, but I couldn't because I ran too. I thought he was coming for me. I paid for a funeral that nobody got the chance to attend. The funeral home said they didn't put enough embalming fluid in the body. I didn't care because I had shit to do. They hauled his body off to the burial site. I didn't attend. I just wanted to get the shit over with. Guess who's not getting paid? Them muthafuckas because they ruined everything. I had fuckin' setup.

I tried to let shit blow over before I made my next moves, but today was the fuckin' day. Crimson was leaving from that house. I needed to get inside of there to get ahold of the safe. Cutie had her friends from the Sheriff department waiting on me. They were sitting in front of my house on standby. I'm waiting on Jermesha to pull up so we can get this show on the road.

It was a little after 10:00 a.m. I don't give a fuck if she was still asleep or not, but she had to fuckin' go. Jermesha finally pulled up. I was waiting for her so we could make our move. She wanted to be there to witness me shit on Crimson and kick her out of my mansion. I needed somebody to record it. It was the middle of fall so it wasn't that cold or too hot outside, but I was covered up and dressed to the nines. Jermesha hopped out her car and in with me. She bought me an ice coffee from Starbucks, and it was on. I checked my mirror to make sure I was on point and I was. It's time for me to live the life that I was fuckin' promised and today solidifies that.

♡

We finally made it to Griffs' palace. He had this bitch living lavishly. It's too bad I was about to take all this shit from her. She tried me at the wake, but today I was serving that bitch with the comeback. I was coming for all this shit. I'm taking every fuckin' thing. I want it all.

Griff fucked up by never marrying her and allowing me to catch him up. Killing him wasn't easy because it took time and patience but obtaining all of this was easy as fuck. I had the gene to finesse. I was for damn sure about to use it. I had all my ducks in a row. Crimson wasn't as smart as me. Jermesha confirmed that. Griff lived in a gated community. You couldn't even gain access to his property unless you had the code. Thank God I had the Sheriff's department with me because we bypassed all that bullshit.

Griff had an extra security code for the entrance of his house. I had the Sheriff to buzz the intercom and the gate opened immediately. Her voice irks the fuck out of me. We made it onto his premises and this bitch was living lavish as fuck. I stepped out my car and banged on her door like I was the fuckin' police. The Sheriffs, Cutie, and Jermesha stood right behind me. The door swung open and I was face to face with Crimson. Her two daughters were standing right behind her looking at me. She gave me an evil smirk. Camina was grilling me. I can't stand her.

"How can I help you?" She asked. Our eyes were trained on each other.

I let the Sheriff's do all the talking before I said anything. I wanted this bitch to see how real shit got fuckin' with a bitch like me. The biggest mistake she ever made was laying eyes on Griff. He was mine forever. I'm ready to show her how she made the wrong fuckin' decision.

"Ms. Tristan we're here because you have to vacate the premises according to this divorce decree. This property belongs to Keondra Griffey," the sheriff stated. Crimson smiled at me and I smiled back showing all thirty-two of my pearly whites.

"You heard what the fuck he said. It's time to roll," I argued and sucked my teeth.

"Camina and Cariuna go get grandma and go to your room and don't come back until I ask you too," she explained. Mother Dear or her mother was here. The Sheriff looked at me for an answer. I didn't have one because I wanted this bitch off my property. Crimson's mother came and stood right behind her. She smiled and moved from behind Crimson and stood right in front of me and Jermesha and Cutie.

"Crimson do we have a motherfuckin' problem? If so, call the police because these muthafuckas can be imposters. The worst thing a bitch can do is fuck with a child of mine or send for a motherfucka that's not sending for them. Y'all trespassing and this is fuckin' private property. Jermesha you fuckin' disgust me. I don't want to even beat your ass. I want the bitch that gave you the balls to bring your ass over here on some bullshit. You bitch's better ask about me. Y'all fuckin' with the right one," her mother argued.

"Excuse me sheriff but there must be some mistake because Griff and I bought this house together. My name is on the deed and not his. This is my house. I own all of this. I'm not going anywhere, but my attorney and the police are on the way to clarify any issues you have. Can I look at your divorce decree? You can look up the owner at Dekalb County tax accessor. It'll verify that Crimson Rose Tristan is the only name on the fuckin' deed," she explained.

It has to be some fuckin' mistake. There's no way Griff brought her this house and her name is the only one on it. The police and her attorney were coming in the driveway. Crimson had the biggest smile on her face and her mother did too. I noticed Cutie got in the car and a few of the Sheriff's tried to leave but Crimson closed the gate to stop them from leaving. I had a bad feeling about all of this. Her mother walked to the car and made sure they all got out.

"Don't leave NOW the party has just begun," she laughed. Crimson's attorney, the Sheriff's, and few Deputy's came and looked at the paperwork. They compared it to the documents that her attorney had. They looked at me and approached me. I had a bad feeling about this. The Sheriff placed handcuffs around my wrist.

"What is this for?" I asked. I wasn't going to jail. I've never been to jail before.

"Keondra Deleon you're under arrest for falsifying a divorce decree. You're trespassing on private property. You don't have any rights to this property or anything associated with Carius Deon Griffey Jr. This property belongs to Crimson Rose Tristan and his name isn't even on the deed. You're one of the dumbest criminals I have ever laid eyes on. It's best to do your research. It would've saved you time and money. Every one of you that attempted to help her pull this off, you're fired and will be tried in a court of law. You will never be able to work in law enforcement in the United States if I have anything to do with it.

I need your badges NOW and they key to the vehicles. You all are under arrest for bribery and using your position to help a criminal contain property that isn't hers. Its fraud and you're on the clock using our vehicles. Ms. Tristan, would you like to press charges?" He asked. Crimson looked at me and smiled.

"Of course I would, and I want a restraining order also," she beamed and smiled. The Sheriff placed me, Jermesha and Cutie behind the police car. Cutie was livid. She just lost her job. I'm sorry I didn't know this was about to happen. Jermesha was crying too because we've never been in jail. My truck was being towed and I needed to get my purse out of there so I could bond us out of jail. I couldn't get ahold of the safe or the house, but I still had a million dollars' worth of cash that needed to be dumped in my account. I knew where Griffs' traps were. I would hit them bitches up to get some more fuckin' money. It's not over until I say it's over. This won't be the last time

Crimson sees me. Game on bitch. You got me this time but it won't be another.

"Keondra I just lost my fuckin' job behind this? What the fuck am I supposed to do now? I had $100,000.00 in there and now and I won't be able to get access to any of that since I'm fired. How am I supposed to live? I thought you had all of this figured out. We've all lost our job. If she decides to press charges which I'm sure she will my life is over. I won't be able to provide for myself," my cousin Cutie explained.

"I'm sorry, I got you. Don't worry I'll figure something out. I have some money stashed. I'll pay you for your 401k." I explained. I feel bad Cutie got caught up in my shit and now she lost her job. It wasn't supposed to go down like this. I should've left the moment she said her attorney and the police were on the way. Now I'm headed to jail behind this shit.

"Keondra my purse is in your car. I only have $700.00 to my name and that's for my car payment and to buy groceries for my children. I have to pick them up from school by 3:00 p.m. Do you think we'll be out by then." she asked.

"I got you. I'll bond you out, trust me. I don't know if we'll be out by then. You get one phone call. Call your baby daddy to get them. You know they're going to call Mother Dear and tell her what happened," I explained. The Deputy brought our purses. I watched the tow-truck remove my vehicle from the property.

Crimson

Oh my God if it's not one thing it's something else. I can't believe this bitch tried me. What the fuck was up with that? I don't even call females bitches but that's exactly what she was. She really wanted my house. She had this whole thing figured out. I thought something serious had happened because the Sheriff was at the gate. I knew something was up when I opened the door and she was standing right behind them with an evil smirk on her face. Jermesha's dumb ass was right along with her. God don't like ugly because I got the last laugh.

Griff bought this house for me right after I had Cariuna. He didn't put his name on it because if he ever got caught up, he didn't want them to seize it and take it from me. This Keondra chick is a different type of crazy. Jermesha never seems to amaze me. She's running up behind this crazy ass girl and now she's going to jail right with her for trespassing. I couldn't wait to call Mother Dear and tell her.

Thank God my mother was here because I didn't know what to do. My mother walked into my room and took a seat beside me. I swear of all this extra shit I can't deal with it. I guess it's true when people die folks start coming from everywhere claiming shit that's not theirs. Had I known he was involved with someone like this I would've never fucked with him. I mean that shit.

"Crimson you got a problem on your hands. She has it out for you and trust me it's not going to stop there. Long as I'm here I won't let any of those tricks fuck with you. The only reason why I didn't tap they ass is that the police were here. She's tried you one too many fuckin' times. It's only one way to get rid of a bitch like that and it's to kill her," she explained.

"Cheree, I can't do that. I've never done that before." I explained. I knew she was crazy, but damn I'm not killing anyone. Her facial expression didn't change. Oh, she was serious.

"I don't give a damn. I wouldn't be surprised if she had Griff killed the way she's acting. I don't trust her, and she doesn't deserve to walk this earth with you. You don't have to do it, but I fuckin' will and that's a promise. A bitch can't come to my house calling shots without any repercussions. After we take the girls to the school, we're going to the gun range to buy you a gun so you can protect yourself if I'm not around.

We shoot first and ask questions later. If it was just the three of them without the Sheriff, the coroner would've carried those muthafuckas out of here today. Jermesha is my niece but I don't give a fuck. She's not excluded either, because she decided to go against you. I'm serious Crimson. She was too comfortable coming to your house. It can't happen again," she argued. We finished talking and getting the girls ready.

A MONTH LATER

Chapter-25

Jermesha

I've been going through it and lying low these past few weeks. Ever since I went to jail and got caught up with Keondra my life has been a mess ever since. They charged me with fraud and conspiracy and tampering with a divorce decree. It's a felony and I've never been in trouble before besides a few parking tickets. I don't have the money to get a paid lawyer yet, so I'm using a public defender. They won't allow me to participate in the first offender's program because we had actual sheriffs involved with the crime. The judge wouldn't allow it at. I was fucked. I've never wanted to turn back the hands of time until now. Going to Crimson's with that fake divorce decree was a disaster and I wish I wouldn't have done it.

To make matters worse my children's father or my mother never answered the phone that day to pick my kids up from school. I had to call Mother Dear to get them so the daycare wouldn't call DFACS. Thank God Mother Dear answered and got them for me. She didn't want to do it, because Cheree and Crimson told her what I had done. I was so embarrassed and ashamed. I'm grateful that she didn't turn her back on me.

We ended up getting released from prison later that night around midnight. Keondra didn't get released because they wanted to question her about Jacque's disappearance. His mother came down from New York and filed a missing person's report. They were one the same phone plan and the last call he made was to Keondra and the last location his cell phone pinged was the house they shared together.

They were holding her regarding his murder. The police asked me did I know anything about it, and I didn't. Thank God. If it wasn't for Griff's murder I would've still been in jail. Keondra is supposed to be released today.

I got her car out the pound like she asked me to and parked it at her house in the garage. I put money on her books every week. I went to see her every Wednesday, that's the least I could do. I didn't want to leave her down and out when she needed me the most. I haven't seen or heard from Cutie since we were released. I called and sent a text just to check up on her and she never hit me back. I got the picture she wasn't fuckin' with me.

Keondra was scheduled to be released today and I was going to pick her up from jail. I love Keondra. That's my girl, but I got to fall back. I got three children to look out for. I can't do that behind bars. It was fun until the police got involved and I'm going back and forth to court every week. I'm on probation and paying them every week.

I'll have to find a job because this probation officer is a real bitch. Any little thing I do she's on me. It's a requirement of hers that I have a job. I've been interviewing every week but so far nothing has come through. I really want to sit down and talk to Crimson to see if she'll drop the charges. I asked Mother Dear if she could set it up, but she declined. I know I haven't been the best cousin to her or her children but I'm sorry. I can't live like this.

I wish I would've never ridden with her that day. My mind was all over the place. I've been sitting in front of the jail waiting on Keondra for the past thirty minutes and she hasn't come out yet. I heard a knock at my window, and it was her. I hit unlock and she hopped in. I gave her a big hug. It was good seeing her despite all the bullshit.

"About time they freed a real one," I beamed. I'm glad she's out. I hope she gets her shit together. I can't participate in this type of activities anymore.

"I know. Thank you for staying down and being true to me. Cutie ain't fuckin' with me. I haven't heard from my mother. I've been calling her all month and she hasn't answered one call. I know she was mad at me about the funeral and stuff, but I need her." She cried. I felt bad for Keondra, but she brought this shit on herself.

"She's probably trying to teach you a lesson. Do you want to get something to eat before I take you home?" I asked.

"I really don't feel like being out. I want to go home, change clothes, get my hair and nails done, and go shopping. I can't let anyone see me like this," she beamed. I was cool with that because I really didn't have the money to treat her.

My man has been blowing up my phone ever since I left the house and told him where I was headed. He doesn't want me fooling with Keondra since the police are popping up at our house every week. The last thing I wanted to do was hear his mouth. We almost broke up behind me going to jail. Keondra and I caught up with each other on our way to her house. I dropped her off at home and I headed back to the house. I don't know when I would see her again. I might even get my number changed.

I hope and pray she gets her life together and leave Griff's things alone. I wasn't going to jail for anybody. I couldn't get involved with her and anything illegal. I need my freedom. I swung by Mother Dear's house. Before I went in I noticed that Crimson and Danielle were already here. I threw my car in park because I really needed to have this conversation with her. I approached the porch and I heard them inside talking. I could smell food. Mother Dear must have cooked breakfast. I made my way to the kitchen and everybody was sitting down talking. As soon as I walked in they stopped talking.

"Excuse me, was I interrupting something?" I asked. Auntie Cheree looked at me and cut her eyes. Danielle rolled hers and Crimson didn't even look up from her plate. Mother Dear looked at me and motioned with her hands for me to have a seat.

“Sit Jermesha, we’re eating breakfast, or should I say brunch. Would you like a plate?” Mother Dear asked. Of course, I wanted to eat. Mother Dear cooked salmon croquette, eggs, grits, sausage, French toast, and she sliced strawberries and apples.

“Yes ma’am,” I beamed. No matter what I did Mother Dear never turned her back on me. She didn’t agree with what I did, but she always checked me when I was wrong. It was a lot of tension in the room and now was the perfect time to clear it. My man sent me a text asking me, where was I? I replied and said Mother Dear. Auntie Cheree was burning a hole in the side of my face. I know she wanted to slap me or beat my ass. I washed my hands and took a seat.

Mother Dear fixed my plate and slid it in front of me. Mother Dear said grace, and everybody started to stuff their face. I took a few bites of my food. I couldn’t enjoy my food like I wanted too because the tension was so thick.

“Auntie Cheree,” I pouted. She looked at me with wide eyes and turned her face up at me. I just wanted to make peace that’s it.

“Yes Jermesha, how can I help you?” She asked. She set her fork down and focused her attention on me. I wasn't trying to fight her. I just wanted to apologize, that's it.

"I just wanted to say I'm sorry about the way I acted a few months ago. I was in the wrong and I should've never disrespected you. You may not accept my apology, but I owe you one. I just wanted to get that out. I hate that it's so much tension between us," I explained. All eyes were on me even Crimson's. I was sorry and I didn't realize it until I was placed in a fucked-up situation because of my actions.

"I appreciate that but why the sudden change of heart?" She stated then asked. I knew this question was coming. I had to be honest because being vindictive and heartless placed me in a bad situation that damn near took my kids from me.

"A lot. Sometimes certain situations give you a wakeup call. I just wanted to apologize. Crimson can I talk to you in private," I asked. She looked at me and rolled her eyes. I knew she wouldn't be so forgiving. I've done too much stuff to her and I shouldn't have.

"No, you can't talk to me in private. Whatever you have to say to me you can say it right here in front of family," she argued. At least she wanted to hear me out. I wasn't expecting to even get here. The worst feeling in the world is when your past comes back to bite you in the ass.

"Crimson, I'm sorry for everything. I know you may never forgive me, but I'm sorry. I mean it from the bottom of my heart. Everything I've done to you wasn't right and I shouldn't have done it. I should've never treated you how I treated you. You've been nothing but good to me and my kids. I know I may be pushing it, but is there any way that you can drop the charges against me? I almost lost my kids to DFACS.

I'm on probation and my probation officer is hard on me. If I don't find a job by the end of the month, she's going to revoke my probation and I could lose my kids," I cried. Crimson looked at me as if I were crazy. Her face lacked any emotion.

"Jermesha stop crying. I'll never forgive you and I'll never forget. If you knew everything that you were doing was wrong, then why in the fuck did you do it? Mother Dear always said blood was thicker than water, but that's not true. You and your mother made my life a living hell for as long as I can remember.

I was a mother to your kids while you were running the streets. I took them to school and made sure they had their shots and physicals, but where were you? I don't feel sorry for you because you brought this shit on yourself. No, I'm not dropping the charges against you because you should've never been riding that hard for her and I'm your fuckin' cousin.

When were you ever going to ride for me? Never, if you wouldn't have gone to jail. We wouldn't even be having this conversation. It would still be fuck me. If you do go to jail just know I'll look after your kids that's about all I can do. I shouldn't even do that, but I would never do you how you did me," she argued.

"Crimson-" that's was all I was able to get out before she cut me off.

"You don't even have a reason to why you did all that shit to me. I always treat people how I want to be treated. You fucked me over numerous times, but I never fucked you over," she argued. I can't even be mad at Crimson because I brought everything on myself. I don't even have a response because there's no excuse for my actions.

"Crimson, just think about it," Mother Dear told her. I smiled. I knew Mother Dear could talk her into it.

She was always looking out for me, and she didn't have to because I did this to myself.

"I have and I'm not dropping the charges. It's time for Jermesha to grow up. Mother Dear stop enabling her. Her probation officer wants her to find a job. That's something she should have anyway had to provide for her and her children. I'm not making her life easy and she fucked up riding with her best friend. She chose her over me every time.

Real friends do real things. Danielle would never put me in a fucked-up situation were losing my kids was a possibility. Ask your friend to take your charge that she got you in the mess, not me." She argued. I hope I find me a job before the month is up or else, I'll violate my probation. I finished eating my food and caught up with Mother Dear. The vibe was still off between everyone but that's my fault. I should've never crossed my own family.

Chapter-26

♡

Keondra

It feels good to be finally released from jail. I never intended on being in there that long. Jail was no place for me. It was filthy and disgusting. I was scared to touch anything. Every pound I gained from my pregnancy I lost because I wasn't eating as I should. As soon as we made it, I had a bondsman waiting to bond me out. I was confused as to why they had a hold on me. I didn't have any parking tickets or warrants out for my arrest. I've never been in trouble before or to jail. I should've been in and out. I had no plans of making jail a permanent residence of mine. I thought I wasn't ever going to be able to make it out. My heart dropped instantly when they questioned me about Jacque. I had no clue that's why they were holding me until after I was there for three days. I'm sure the detective could tell I was nervous I was stuttering and shit.

I just knew Ike had leaked those pictures or made his body appear. I knew I was about to rot in jail and be charged with his murder. Just the thought alone fucked me up because a month or so ago I was taunting him about

Griff and somehow, I managed to find myself behind bars with no one to depend on. It's funny how the table had turned. Thank God I dodged that bullet for now. I knew questioning from Jacque's disappearance was far from over.

Jacque's mom filed a fuckin' missing person's report and dropped my name to the police, so they've been holding me for that. I knew his body wouldn't pop up. I just had to play it safe. They finally let me leave because they didn't have anything, they could hold me on. Let's just say these past few weeks have been hell. I had the cellmate from hell and an annoying ass detective that would pop up every day asking me different questions about Jacque and me. I played it safe. I hope they don't harass me anymore. I didn't feel comfortable talking to them alone. I knew they were trying to catch me up.

I tried to call Ike, but he changed his number. I need to go by the house to get my clothes and a few other things that I left. I still wanted to get ahold to Griff's safe. I don't know how I'm going to be able to do that.

Crimson pressed charges and took out an order of protection on me. Maybe I can hire someone to break in and do a home invasion. I haven't heard from Cutie. I called her a few times while I was locked up. I wrote to her and she never answered the phone for me or responded. I knew she was still mad about what happened but it's nothing that I could do to change that. What's done is done and I agreed to pay her 401k or retirement. Since she was acting like a bitch I'm not paying her shit and we don't have to talk anymore. I'm thankful Jermesha held it down for me while I was away. She was the only one I had in my corner. My mother wasn't even there for me. Jermesha wasn't herself today. Something felt different about her. I can't put my finger on what it is but it's something. It's too late now, she's the only person I have in my corner, and it's too late to switch up.

I'm hungry as hell and I can't wait to have a nice meal. I had a million dollars in cash that I can't wait to deposit into my account. Soon as I made it home, I took me a nice hot shower. My pixie cut has grown out. I needed a good trim, but that would have to wait for a few hours. I need to see an available balance in my account for a million dollars. I grabbed me a cute sweater dress out the closet with the matching booties. I beat my face to perfection and sprayed my body down with perfume. I grabbed the duffel bag full of money and my next stop was to SunTrust.

♡

I finally made it to the Bank. It was packed because it's lunchtime. As soon as I stepped in the bank all eyes were on me. I hated coming inside of the bank. I swear every time I'm here they always give me a hassle. It's like they've never seen a young black woman getting money before. If they asked me where I got this much cash from, I had plans to tell them I was a stripper. After waiting in line for about five minutes. I finally approached the counter.

"Welcome to SunTrust how may I help you?" The clerk asked. About fuckin' time. It's time to get this show on the fuckin' road.

"I would like to make a deposit." I beamed. I sat the duffel bag on the counter. The clerk advised me that a banker would be right with me. A banker approached me and led me to a separate office. I noticed Ike coming in as I entered the office with the banker. We locked eyes with each other. He had an evil smirk on his face. I broke eye contact with him immediately. Just the thought of how he acted a few weeks ago turned me off.

"Hi Mrs. Deleon, I'm Dominique. How may I help you?" The banker asked. I didn't like this Banker. Whenever Ike and I came in here together she always undressed him with her eyes. I knew she wanted him. If I could request another banker I would. I just want to cash out and get the fuck on. I'll catch this bitch another day, but not today.

"Hi, I wanted to make a deposit," I explained. She looked me up and down. I know she saw Ike outside. He saw us walk in here. You couldn't miss him. He was the finest motherfucka in the building.

"Okay great. I can help you with that. Mr. Deleon, will he be joining you? I need your account number and how much you're depositing," she explained. I didn't even respond. I provided her with the information she asked for. Her eyes grew wide when I told her how much. Just deposit my money so I can get the fuck on.

She counted the bills and ran them through the money counter. It was one point one million dollars to be exact. Griff was getting money. It's too bad he won't be able to spend it anymore. The banker took the bills to deposit the money. I was waiting for her to come back with my deposit. I knew it was going to be a few minutes, so I checked my social media to see what the hood was gossiping about. It was the same shit different day. I snapped a picture for Instagram, Snapchat and Facebook.

My caption was #RICHBITCH. In a matter of minutes, I'll be a million dollars richer.

I looked up and the banker was coming back with the police. Everybody was looking this way. The banker and the police entered the room. I started getting hot and nervous instantly. I didn't know what the fuck was going on. I waited for her to speak first before I said anything. I knew I didn't like this bitch for a reason.

"Mrs. Deleon, I'm sorry but I was unable to make your deposit. The money was counterfeit. That's why the police are here. They want to take you in and ask you some questions," she explained and gave me a nasty smirk that I couldn't miss. My heart dropped instantly. COUNTERFEIT? I'm already on probation and another charge would violate me.

"It must be some mistake. I got this money last night from work. I'm a stripper," I explained. The banker and the police gave me a dirty look. I couldn't go to jail again. I just got.

"Okay, no problem. I still have to take you in. Long as your story checks out you'll be free to leave if not you're going to jail for criminal fraud," the officer explained. He slapped some handcuffs on my wrists. I was so fuckin' embarrassed to be escorted out the bank like this. The police officer wanted to embarrass me. He walked me out through the front door. I locked eyes with Ike on my way out. He shook his head at me.

My phone alerted me that I had a text from an unknown number. The officer shoved me in the backseat. I looked at the picture that was sent to my phone. CHECKMATE BITCH was the caption. My stomach dropped and air filled my chest. I couldn't breathe. I let out a loud piercing scream. The police officer looked back at me to see what was going on.

"They killed my momma," I cried and screamed. No wonder she didn't answer the phone for me. She's dead. Who would do this to her, because she doesn't bother anybody? This day couldn't get any worse. I can't win for losing. I called Jermesha.

"Jermesha, where are you?" I asked and cried. I needed her. What am I going to do without my mother?

"Calm down Keondra, what's wrong?" She asked. I tried to catch my breath, but I couldn't.

"I'm on my way to jail and somebody killed my momma. If I don't call you within an hour meet me at Cobb

County jail," I explained. The police office snatched my phone out my hand and disconnected the call.

TWO MONTHS LATER

Chapter-27

Crimson

I swear to God I feel like giving up. My grandmother always told me God gives his toughest battles to the strongest people. I know I don't look like what I've been through. My appearance is just a mirror image of my soul. I wish I could place this battle in the palm of his hands so he could fight it for me. I know God didn't bring me this far just to leave me. Giving up is too easy and not an option for me. I know I should never question God but sometimes I wonder why me? Why Crimson Rose Tristan? Since birth, I've been dealt a bad hand. My mother dropped me off on my grandmother's porch when I was four days old. In the middle of August and never looked back. I use to wonder why she did that.

No letters, pictures or anything. For as long as I could remember I couldn't point my mother out in a line up if I was asked to. I always wondered what she looked like and how did she smell. I use to dream about her, but I never had a clear vision of her. All that changed recently. It's safe to say when I see her, I see an older version of me. She smells heavenly. Her touch and nutriment mean everything to me. I love how she has my back no matter what without asking me. Thank you, God, for bringing her back to me. I finally met my father too and the two of them together is a beautiful sight to see. I use to think that none of my parents gave two fucks about me. Boy was I wrong. It was more to the story than the two of them just abandoning me. I'm grown now but that shit used to fuck with me mentally and physically. I can't change the past, but I love our current situation; I wouldn't trade it for anything. I love how they love me.

I try so hard to stay strong and positive, but with all the obstacles I'm facing my heart can't fuckin' take it. I'm not that fuckin' strong. On the outside looking in I appear to be. I know my breaking points and I'm at my breaking point. I don't know how much more I could take. I'm about to fold and break down at any given minute.

I'm so serious, but I can't for the sake of my girls. The two of them are precious diamonds in this crazy world. I know they're depending on me. I'm all they have left. I got to shake this depression for the sake of my girls. I keep pushing because of them. Ever since their father got killed a few months ago, shit has been more than rough for them. Every day they're asking questions about him. I told them just remember how your father loved you and he's always watching over you.

Griff and I were together for seven years. He was everything to me. The moment we met my life changed for the better. Griff and I traveled so much it felt like we used to change the weather. He moved me out of my grandmother's house and into a nice brick three story home in College Park. My life started to make sense. I was no longer boxed in. He loved me unconditionally. In return, I gave him all of me. We created two beautiful daughters that I cherish and adore. He left me in this world carrying his precious baby. I can't wait to spoil and give him the world.

The day they took Griff away from me, my life changed for the worst. We were supposed to get married. We never got the chance to say I do. Those stupid ass muthafuckas robbed me of that too. He proposed to me on our anniversary. I reminisce about it constantly. My whole world came crashing down. Damn, why did they have to turn my world upside down? I loved him so much. It's like I couldn't breathe without his touch. I had a slight heart attack the day after he died. It felt like I died with him. He took a piece of my heart with him and I didn't want to live anymore. Just the thought of not having my soul mate with me killed my heart to the core.

Griff was in the streets heavy, but I didn't know how heavy until the day the streets took him away from me. Griff never brought his work home with him. Of course, he made sure we were straight and out of the way. The moment he died a lot of things started to come out about him. I couldn't cope with it. I didn't know he had a wife. How could he, and we had a beautiful life? She showed up at the home we shared, with the Sheriffs and attempted to put me and my daughters out on the street. She was so fuckin' weak for that. It took everything in me not to beat her ass, with a fuckin' bat. She wanted everything but little did she know that the home we shared my name was the only one on the deed. She was a heartless bitch trying to get rich. I saw right through all that shit. No matter how bad people treated me I could never treat them the same way.

It's this thing called KARMA, it always comes back to play.

I depended on Griff for everything, but I always worked. Even though he didn't want me to. He made sure I stacked my money and saved all his. I've been working hard these past few months, so I could give Camina and Cariuna a Christmas that they were accustomed to. My mother and father told me that I didn't have to work because they owed me a nice life since they weren't around. I wouldn't accept anything from them but every week I had huge deposits in my savings and checking account courtesy of them.

"Mommy, are you going to buy us a new Christmas tree," my youngest daughter Camina asked. If she asks me about a Christmas tree one more time, I know something. I told her I would get us one and I would. Since her father has been gone, she's been giving me a hard time. I know she's acting out because he's gone. Even though I want to spank her I can't. I haven't even told her that I'm pregnant with another child. I wasn't sure if I wanted to keep the baby or not because Griff is gone. I'm already having a hard time with two. It was too late to have an abortion anyway. It's safe to say I was keeping him.

"Yes Camina, I'm going to get us a tree today," I beamed. Camina was smart and she wasn't buying it. She was spoiled and I blame her father. I really didn't need a new Christmas tree. It's just the old one reminds me of Griff. Every year we looked forward to putting our Christmas tree up together. This would be the first time in seven years that we wouldn't be able to do that.

"Please Mommy, can we get some toys to put under the tree also," Cariuna asked. I wasn't looking forward to Christmas this year. I had a lot to be thankful for, but I missed Griff like crazy. I don't even know where they buried him at so I couldn't visit him. I just want to talk to him. I would give anything just to see him. I couldn't even spoil him. I had to spoil my girls and our newest addition that they know nothing about.

"Sure, baby we can grab a toy or two." Cariuna grabbed my coat and car keys. She gave Camina her coat and zipped it up. I guess they were ready. I made myself a hot cup of tea before we headed out. It was the beginning of November and it was already cold outside. I grabbed a hat and scarf. I needed to redo my hair. It's too cold to wash it and my dandruff is getting the best of me. I'll wash it tonight.

Camina hopped her little tale up front. I told her about sitting up front. It's a habit she can't break. Her father always allowed her to ride up front with him. She thinks she can do that with me, but it wasn't happening. "Camina in the back now!" I pointed to the back seat. I have plenty of pictures of Griff and her on my phone.

"Mommy can I see your phone," she asked. Every day she would grab my phone and look at pictures of her and her father. I knew she missed him and I'm sure he missed her. I miss him too despite all the bullshit I've been going through since he's been gone.

"Sure Camina," I beamed. I swear she loves her father. I know it's hitting her the hardest because she can't see or be with him every day.

♡

We finally made it to Walmart. I hated coming here. It's always packed, and I end up buying more things than I planned to. We picked out the big green tree with the white frosted tips. It was expensive but it's nice. We grabbed a few Christmas ornaments while we were here. Shopping is therapeutic for me. I had plans to stop by Bed Bath and Beyond on our way home to get some stockings for them.

“Mommy can we go to the toy section now,” Camina whined.

“Sure baby, but one toy okay? Mommy brought just enough money for the tree, decorations, and the both of you a toy,” I explained. I had to put that out there because they would pick out everything they wanted for Christmas. Then I wouldn’t be able to surprise them with anything. We headed to the toy section and they went crazy grabbing the highest shit possible. I wasn’t surprised. I shouldn’t have agreed to let them go to the toy section.

“Pick another toy out and we'll come back and get that one.”

“Mommy, it'll be sold out, these are the only ones left,” she pouted and whined. I swear they get me every time. I could never tell them no. I need to start because whatever they wanted, they got.

“Okay, come on let's get out of here.” Everybody was out Christmas shopping. Walmart is the worst fuckin’ place to be around the holidays. I grabbed the girl’s hand and our way to check out.

“Mommy did we forgot the lights?” Camina asked.

"The tree already has lights built in, so we don't need any."

"Okay, mommy." We continued in the direction of the check out when I felt a slight tap on my shoulder. I turned around to look and see who it was. It was a man and what the fuck did he want with me? I don't like people walking up on me especially while I'm with my daughters. I grabbed their hands as tight as I could. Damn, he was fine and I'm not even into light skinned guys. He had a nice thick build low haircut and a bottom grill. Let me stop looking at him. I need to keep moving because I met Griff the same way and it's only one him. I'm not looking to date anyone right now or replace him.

"Excuse me Ms. did you drop this," he asked. I looked to see what I dropped, and it was a wad full of cash. I couldn't accept the money, because it wasn't mine. If somebody lost their money around Christmas time, I would feel bad for them because they needed it more than me.

"No sir it's not mine," I explained. I turned around and I continued to walk off. He tapped me on my shoulder again. I turned around and gave him an evil look. Don't fuckin' touch me because I don't even know you. I'm trying to check out and he's holding me up.

“Take it. It yours now and pay for your stuff,” he explained. I don’t need anybody paying for my stuff I’m more than capable to do so. I placed the money back in his hands.

“I can't take it,” I explained and walked off.

“You will take it shorty. It’s not up for debate,” he explained. He tugged on my coat and put the money in my pocket and walked off. I didn’t like him in my personal space. Okay if he insists.

“Thank you, Mr. Mommy, we can get more toys now,” Cariuna asked. I can’t believe Cariuna. I just shook my head and headed toward check out. No more toys. I’m not buying anything else in here. I’m ready to leave. I want to eat lay in my bed and reminisce about Griff. Damn, I craved him.

“No Cariuna we’re going home. I still have to cook, and you need a bath,” I explained. She started to pout and whine like Camina. I wasn’t having that shit. I gave her a don’t play with me look. We made it to check out, paid for our stuff, and headed to the car.

I tossed Cariuna my phone and told her to order us a pizza from Marcos on my cell phone. I placed them inside of the car while I put our stuff in the trunk. It's cold as hell outside. Damn, I just want to cuddle and lay up under Griff. I made sure my doors were locked. It's too many snatch and grabs going on and people sliding in your car and pulling off. I didn't want that. I would go crazy if someone took my car with my girls in it.

"Shawty you need some help," he asked. I looked over my shoulder to see who was talking to me. It was the guy from earlier so I turned back around. I wasn't trying to entertain him just because he tossed me a few dollars that I didn't need.

"No thank you," I stated. I just wanted to go home eat and relax. The tree was harder to get in the trunk than I thought. I was out here struggling for at least five minutes. I felt a tap on my shoulder. I looked over my shoulder and it was the same guy again. I was beyond irritated at this point.

"Shawty, let me help you, so you can get your shorty's home," he stated and laughed. I didn't find shit funny. I only folded because this tree didn't want to cooperate, and he wouldn't take no for an answer.

"Okay thank you," I beamed. I stood to the side with my arms folded across my chest waiting on him to finish. He put the tree in my trunk properly. I slammed my trunk door shut and he walked me to my door. I appreciated him being a gentleman.

"What's your name shawty," he asked. I had a feeling this was coming.

"Crimson." I sighed. I really didn't feel like being bothered.

"It's nice to meet you Crimson. I'm Ahmad and by the way can have your number?" he asked. I was a little hesitant, but since he's been so nice to me I gave him my number. A small conversation wouldn't hurt. "Take it easy Crimson I'll call you in a few." Ahmad and I went our separate ways. As soon as I slid in the car Camina and Cariuna couldn't wait to ask me questions.

"Mommy who was that man and what did he want," they asked. I'll be single until I'm dead fooling with them.

I was cool with that because I know I could never love another man how I loved Griff. They didn't want anybody in their space if it wasn't their father. I felt the same way.

"It was the guy that gave you guys the money. He just wanted to make sure we got in the car safe that's all," I explained. Cariuna and Camina weren't buying it. Ahmad sent me a text with his number. I might lock it in, but nine times out of ten I won't. I couldn't offer him anything, not even a small conversation. I wasn't interested. Carius Deon Griffey Jr. was the only man that had my attention and he wasn't him.

♡

The girls and I finally made it home. I couldn't wait to eat this pizza and take a hot bath. I swear this growing baby inside of me has me hungry as fuck. I'm always eating shit up. Thank God Cariuna ordered two pizza's one for me and one for them. I jumped in the shower and handled my hygiene. I knew if I ate first. I wouldn't take a shower and I hate going to bed without one. I had missed calls from my mother and Danielle.

I called Danielle back first because she's been acting funny these past few weeks, and I wasn't with it. I knew something was up with her and she wasn't ready to tell me just yet. I'm all ears even though I'm going through my shit. I still had time to help her get through her shit. Just like I knew she would she answered on the first ring.

"Crimson where have you been? I miss you best friend," she beamed and smiled through the phone.

"No, you don't. I miss you more though and you've been acting funny these past few weeks. I know something is going on with you. I'm all ears when you're ready to talk. You know I would never judge you and I'm here for you too," I explained.

"I know Crimson, but you have a lot going on. I don't want to burden you with my problems and add more stress. So, I've been keeping things bottled in. I'm trying to cope with it the best way I know how," she sighed.

"Danielle don't do that. Your problems are my problems. Since when have you ever went through anything alone?

I don't care what I'm going through. If you need me, I'm here. It's always been that way and it'll never change. Whatever you're holding in it's not good for you. I want to see you soon. As in tomorrow. We're well overdue for a link up, massage, good food, and a few black chick flicks. I wish I could drink but I can't." I explained. I miss my best friend/sister.

"Okay, cool it's a date. I don't know if I'm ready to tell you yet Crimson so please don't pressure me. I just want to have fun that's all. The reason why I called you is that my baby Cariuna hit me up on Facetime. She was telling me about some man you met in Wal-Mart that gave you some money. Guess what, I got the time and I want to hear all about that," she stated. See Cariuna talks too much. I would expect that from Camina but not Cariuna.

"Danielle it's nothing to tell since Cariuna told it all," I laughed and that was the truth. I had no plans on pursuing anything with him.

"Yeah, I heard Cariuna's side of the story, but I want to hear yours. I was surprised Cariuna was telling someone's business. I guess the little devil Camina is wearing off on her. Thank God you woke up because I was ready to reunite her with her father. God bless his soul because I can't deal with her. I think we need a DNA test for her. Ain't no way in hell you gave birth to that," she laughed. I had to look at my phone because Danielle was going in on my baby.

"Aye, lay off my fuckin' child for real. You got me fucked up, she's just misunderstood," I laughed. I gave Danielle the rundown on my little encounter. It wasn't anything worth telling because I had no plans to entertain or pursue it.

"Girl, you stay pulling a nigga at the grocery store or some shit. He might be the one. History may be repeating itself. You met Griff at the store and it's not coincidental Crimson," she explained.

"Danielle I'm not looking for ANYTHING at all. I'm cool by myself. Griff hasn't even been gone a good year yet. It's too soon to be moving on. I know I'll have to get there one day but today isn't the day. I'm good."

"I never said you were looking. I was just stating facts from your history. You said the same thing about Griff and look what the two of you built. No matter how hard you tried to fight and ignore it, what's meant, is what's meant. Just maybe God sent you something else to mend your heart or at least start the process of your new fresh start," she explained. I hate to admit it but Danielle might be right.

"I hear you, but I don't want that to be the case. It's okay to grieve in peace but I'm not ready for anything serious or temporary. I just want to do me with my three only. Now how would that look I'm pregnant with Griff's child and I already have another man? It's tacky as fuck if you ask me and I don't want anybody in my personal space."

"I hear you Crimson I do, BUT you deserve to be happy too. Nobody can compare to Griff and I know you'll love him past forever until you're able to see him again. People are going to talk regardless. Let them talk. I know Griff would want you to move on and be happy and live your life. If you don't move on that'll be selfish as fuck on your part. I just want you to be happy best friend. Griff was the only man you've ever been with and loved. Someone else deserves to experience what you have to offer. I'm not saying fall in love again, but I want you to live Crimson. Let your hair down and smile again. It's nothing wrong with conversations. It's up to you if you want to pursue it and see where the road takes you," she explained.

"Danielle this conversation was supposed to be about you and not me. You're telling me everything I need to do, but you haven't even disclosed to me what's going on with you? I don't want to talk about me tonight. I want to talk and focus this conversation on you."

"I don't want to talk about me and if I did, I couldn't talk about it openly in my house while my husband is here. Tomorrow, when we meet up, have your ears and antennas up. Make sure your cup is empty because my life and what I'm going through is sure to fill it up," she whispered. Damn. Danielle and I said our goodbyes. I'm looking forward to this conversation because whatever it is must be deep if it can't be said in front of Baine.

A MONTH LATER

Chapter-28

Rashad

Don't get me wrong I'm glad Griff is back and amongst the land of the living, but I need my nigga to let that shit be known ASAP. I don't mind being the face of our organization, but I'm ready to change positions. It's a lot of work and even though he's behind the scenes making moves. I'm not ready for his position, not now. I'm too wild and reckless to be the face. He has way more patience than I do. It's time we had that conversation. I just want to be the muscle and the enforcer. That's it. I hate putting on fitted suits every day.

"What the fuck you keep looking at me for nigga," he asked. Griff was on the edge like a motherfucka. More of the reason why I need to say what the fuck I have to say.

He misses being at home with his family and he doesn't have to be.

"Aye Griff, so when are you going to tell Crimson that you're alive? You know she's not fuckin' with me because she found out about Keondra and I don't have shit to do with that," I asked and argued. Griff's playing a dangerous game. He needs to tell Crimson what's going on immediately. I don't like being put in the middle of shit. When she finds out I'll still be in the middle of it.

"Rashad chill out. I'm about to make my presence known soon. I got to hit Keondra where that shit hurts, and then I'll let it be known that daddy's home. Crimson ain't going nowhere, trust me." He argued. Okay, I'll follow his move, but I'm not with it. I can't even go see Camina because her mother's tripping and her daddy is always with me.

"Okay, keep thinking that shit if you want to. Camina told me her momma had a boyfriend," I laughed. Even though I haven't been able to see them physically. Camina hits me up every morning to let me know what's going on.

I don't know how Griff missed that if he's staying in the house, but I had to put a bug in his ear, so we can get this shit in motion. He's at home but he's missing some very important shit at home. His kids need him, and Crimson needs him.

"You a muthafuckin' lie. Don't fuckin' play with me. Crimson ain't got shit. She can add a nigga to my hit list if she fuckin' wants too. I'm not having that shit," he argued and explained. I threw my hands up. He needs to be prepared to add this nigga to his list.

"Don't shoot the fuckin' messenger." He wouldn't even be tripping so hard if he goes ahead and tells Crimson. Then she could follow his lead, but he doesn't want to take my advice. "Shit I don't know why you're getting mad at me. I'm just fuckin' telling you. What are we waiting on? Shit, let's get the shit on the fuckin' road before ole boy swoops in and marry Crimson before you do."

"Rashad, stop fuckin' playing with me for real. I know you're not talking about coming clean. You let Baine marry Danielle and now you're her side nigga. How does it feel to let your woman go home to another nigga every night," he asked and laughed? I stroked my beard because Griff was fuckin' with me heavy because I told him what it was. "Shit what if she was doing you, how you did her?" Griff was on one for real that was low as fuck.

"Griff, I'm not even about to argue with you because you're my nigga. I fucked up years ago and I'm man enough to admit that. Danielle knows what it is between us and wherever I see her and Baine I'm letting that shit be known. She's mine and I don't give a fuck. If I got to body that nigga to get her, it doesn't fuckin' matter to me.

Don't make the same fuckin' mistake I did. You need to let Crimson know what's up. I don't even want to kill Baine. I just want to let that nigga know it's not hard to get what belongs to me. She may go to him every night, but I can guarantee you he's not fuckin' his wife. How much you want to fuckin' bet. Stop baiting me Griff, before you end up burying that nigga." I argued and explained.

"I hear you, but you know I don't want to hear that shit about Crimson. That's my soul mate. AND if it's any truth to that boyfriend shit, that nigga can go ahead and give it up, that's me right there. Ain't nobody playing daddy to my kids but me," he argued. Griff and I finished kicking it.

I don't how Crimson didn't know he was staying at home, but he was. I always dropped him off at home when Crimson wasn't there. Griff's a slick ass motherfucka. I haven't heard from Danielle since this morning. Let me call her to check in. I hit the Facetime button on my phone

"What's up with you? How your day been so far?" I asked.

"What's up," she asked licking her lips? Danielle was sexy as fuck too. I loved seeing her in her scrubs or her nurse get up.

"I'm good, what's up with you? I'm busy as hell. I have one more patient to see at 2:30 p.m. and I'm running out of here. What about you?" She asked. She was looking at me as if she was trying to figure me out. Since we've been kicking it I haven't stalled with asking her anything.

"Busy handling business. I miss you though. I've been thinking about you since this morning. Let me ask you a question," I commanded. Danielle sat up straight in her chair and gave me her full undivided attention.

"You know I love you right?" I asked. Danielle and I never stopped. Of course, when I saw her again, I was going to make my move. It was supposed to be her and me. Not her and him.

"Yes," she smiled.

"I just want to make sure that I'm not wasting my time. Do I have a fair chance or you're bullshitting?" I asked. Griff had me tripping when he said that reckless as shit earlier. It had me thinking hard as fuck.

"Rashad, what are you trying to say? You know I'm married and of course, I know we can't keep this up. I'll have to leave and it's easier said than done. I had no clue this was about to happen between us. It's not comfortable for me. I tried to cut you off, but you were persistent. I'm not a cheater and I'm cheating. Something I swore I would never do. Starting over is the hardest part. I wouldn't even feel comfortable keeping this business and I know he purchased it for me. I'll have to figure something out," she sighed.

"Are you still fuckin' him?" I asked. I looked at Danielle with a straight face.

"Rashad, what's up? Where is all this coming from? He's still my husband in case you forgot, but no I'm not fuckin' him. I can't have sex with two men at the same time. Are you fuckin' someone else besides me? I can't even believe we're having this conversation." She sighed.

"Danielle you're worried about the wrong shit. I care about you and I'll never have you out here without. If you're worried about your business. Give him that shit and start looking for a new spot. Have your realtor call me with the numbers and I'll cut the check. If he has a problem with you leaving than he can deal with me. Stop worrying about that. We'll cross that road when we get there. You're the only one whose guts I'm burying my seeds in."

"I hear you, Rashad. My patient just walked in. I'll hit you back when I finish."

"Okay but I want you to listen. No excuses. The world is yours," I explained. I know Baine will have a problem with us being together, but it is what it is. His issue shouldn't be with her but with me. He should thank God that Griff's alive because the same way I laid down his niggas, him and Ike were next on my hit list.

Mya has been blowing me up heavy but I'm not fuckin' with her like that. I've been dodging her. She's a good girl, but I can't commit to her. I got feelings for her and I can't lie I do love her but I'm not in love with her. I don't see me marrying her. I'm treading lightly with her. We're cool and we fuck but I haven't fucked her in a minute since I've been fuckin with Danielle. I wasn't trying to do that because shit is already complicated with us.

I know Mya isn't going to be happy about my choice, but the love isn't there. It's not her it's me. She's just not the one for me. I didn't commit to her for this reason. Hopefully, she'll take the high road and accept shit for what it is. I don't want things to be awkward between us. I had no clue Danielle and I would end up here. I'm not going to lie I did shit. I prayed for her to come back to me every day and I preyed on her when I laid eyes on her again. I wasn't about to let her get away from me again. It's been too long.

Danielle

I don't know what I've gotten myself into, but I'm in some deep shit. I love my husband I can't lie but I ain't never stopped loving Rashad. I tried so hard to fight temptation, but I couldn't. This secret is killing me softly. I haven't even told Crimson about Rashad and me. I can't. I'm embarrassed because I'm cheating on my husband and I shouldn't. I know Baine knows something's up because I've been denying him sex. I never deny him. I don't feel comfortable fuckin' two people at the same time. Sneaking around with Rashad is wearing me out.

The only reason I'm able to pull it off is that Baine leaves the house early to check on his business. As soon as he leaves, I'm gone too. I did take my vows seriously. It always men looking at me and trying to get up with me and I always shut it down. I didn't have any insecurities in my marriage. Rashad doesn't understand leaving Baine won't be easy. Trust me if he finds out that I left him for Rashad, it'll be a war. I never knew what they had against each other nor did I ask. I knew the world was shifting, but damn why I had to be in the middle of the shift. I just want to run and hide.

Leaving Baine is going to be one of the hardest things I'll ever have to do. I'm not sure if I want to leave him. I'm confused and torn in between the two. I know what hurt feels like and I don't want to hurt him. He's my husband and he's my best friend too. It's too late to take back everything I've done, and Rashad won't let me just walk away without being with him. Every time we have a disagreement or an argument it's about me leaving Baine. It'll probably be different if they didn't know each other or had a bad history.

I swear when it rains, it pours. Who would've known one night alone at Crimson's house with Rashad would've turned into this? My body, heart, and soul yearned for it. I love Rashad but he hurt me. I don't want to get hurt again or hurt nobody? It's a pain that I could never forget, and I don't want Baine to experience that because he deserves more than this. I can't point the finger at no one else but myself. I tried to stop him, but he wouldn't ease up. I should've known better. I've been beating myself up about it every day. Why did my heart want something that was foreign? The universe gave me a warning, but I was so smitten and ignored it.

Chapter-29

Griff

♡

Rashad hit a nerve. It was time for me to go home immediately. It takes a lot to fuck with me and my family means the world to me. It's not a muthafucka breathing that's going to keep them away from me. I know this little setup we got going on is crazy but it's only temporarily. I had to move like this to see who else was working with Keondra. It looks like she was on this journey alone trying to take me out. Crimson in the arms of another man isn't happening. My family isn't up for grabs at all. I didn't mean to spas out on my nigga, but damn I had to be slipping because I don't know how I missed that. I couldn't wait to get home to check our room to make sure she hasn't had another nigga lying up under her.

Crimson isn't that type of woman so I shouldn't even be thinking like this at all. Lying in the underground tunnel that I had built in our house is killing me because I want to be laid up under her and my babies. Every night when I know they're asleep. I creep in the house and watch them sleep. It's taking everything in me not run up in Crimson while she's sleeping. It's time to get this shit in motion. Losing my family isn't an option and whoever this nigga is that's sniffing up behind Crimson is making himself a target.

Keondra's been locked up for over a month now. I can't believe her dumb ass tried to deposit that money at the bank, but that's what she gets. She's caught another charge on top of the one she got from trying to take my house from Crimson. I don't know how I missed the signs, but this bitch was really a fuckin' liability. I'll have to make a few calls to get her released. She's been breathing for too long and now it's time for me to kill her and get back to my family. I know Camina and Cariuna are going crazy without me.

It ain't no way in hell I was letting Crimson move on without me. We already made plans for me to be her husband and she already agreed to be my wife. I sent one of my attorney's a text and told them to get Keondra cleared on the counterfeit charge. Keondra said she was a stripper and that was a perfect alibi. We were shooting a music video and she picked up the wrong bag of money.

Keondra

My luck has been bad lately. I can't win for losing. I've taken so many losses these past few months I don't know how I'm going to bounce back. I don't even have a plan B. I swear I mapped my plans perfectly. Going to jail wasn't a part of the plan. I know for sure Ike's going to divorce me if he hasn't already and Jacque is dead. The only thing I have access too is a few of his bank accounts if his mother hasn't seized them. My savings account is running low because of lawyer fees and court cost.

I could sell Jacque's Range Rover that was parked in front of the house, but I don't know what Ike did with it. I don't have anybody in my corner but Jermesha. Every week she puts a $100.00 on my books. She kept money on her phone so I could call her. She came to see me every week. I'm thankful she hasn't turned her back on me. My cousin Cutie wouldn't even accept a call from me.

I thought about the plan to execute Griff long and hard. I've been planning this shit for years. I just don't understand how all this shit backfired on me. I've done a lot of shit in my life, but I wasn't expecting everything to hit me at once. The day I got arrested my mother got killed. I wanted to die right with her. I never thought about living without her. I just hate that the last time we saw each other we weren't on good terms. If I would've known the money was counterfeit, I would've never taken that shit to the bank to try and deposit it. Griff was dead, so I knew he couldn't have been on too me.

I've been sitting in this cage for over a month now. I don't think I'm getting out. I can't believe I wasn't able to attend my mother's funeral or bury her properly. I begged and pleaded with the police to set me free. I had to be there for my mommy. Who would do that to her? She's the sweetest person in the world? Whoever killed my mother wanted me to know they touched something special to me. I'm not hard to find. They should've gotten at me.

I would give anything to get mommy back and to say I'm sorry. I swear sitting in this jail cell feels like hell. Many nights I've cried myself to sleep and thought about hanging my body from the bunk rail. I've had plenty of time to think about my actions.

I fucked up big time with Griff and now Ike. I'm so tired of fighting this fight. I thought once Jacque and I made it official and out in the open that simple things in my love life would finally be right. It maybe finally time for me to start doing everything right. I heard the officer open my cell. I looked to the right out the corner of my eye. It was a little after midnight. I don't trust these men or women officers. I've seen so much shit in the past thirty days that nothing surprises me. I closed my eyes and said a quick prayer hoping this sick muthafucka wasn't coming in here to try and violate me. We were on lockdown currently. I didn't ask any questions. I only spoke when I was spoken too. I laid my head on my pillow waiting on him to leave, but I never heard my cell door close.

"Deleon, pack it up you're free to go," the officer stated. He grabbed a handful of my ass and felt me up a few times. I was confused by his last statement. I jumped up so damn fast but if he said I was free to go then guess what? I'm getting the fuck up out of here. I guess there is a God. Every night I've been praying that God would set me free of all the negative things around me and surround me with positive energy.

Guess what, nothing was positive about me being in jail. He was removing me from this atmosphere finally. I'll have to move a little more careful because I don't want to land myself inside of here again. I didn't have anything in here that I wanted to take. I wanted to get out of here as fast as I can. It was too late to call Jermesha to come and pick me up. I'll have to catch an Uber home. I can't wait to go home and take a nice hot bath.

♡

Two hours later and I'm finally home soaking in my hot tub and sipping on a nice glass of wine. I had my Uber driver to stop by Walmart so I could grab me a few things to cook. I grabbed a pack ground turkey, steak fries, lettuce, tomato and pepper jack cheese and a bag of fresh Vidalia Onions. I wanted a turkey burger so bad I could taste it and it was good. I know I shouldn't care because I'm out of jail and the counterfeit charge was dropped.

I'm thankful for it but I was curious as fuck. I wanted to know who lied and said the money was from a video shoot and that I made a mistake and I grabbed the wrong bag. It was a lie and someone helped me out big time. I may never find out who it was but I'm thankful and I'm not going to worry about it anymore.

I've concluded that I can't live in this house. It holds too many memories that I would never forget. Jacque dying here was another factor. I'm going to sell it and find me something smaller and secluded. I needed the money anyway. I checked my savings account and I only had about $200,000.00 to my name.

I paid my cell phone bill as soon as I got home. Before I could get a decent charge, I was receiving text messages from Jacque's mom and his baby momma. They were coming back to back. I couldn't deal with this shit right now. I cut my phone off and continued to soak in the tub. I began to think about my next move. My next move had to be my best move. I didn't have anybody to help me I was solo out here on some good bullshit.

Hopefully, I'll come up with something. I couldn't go back to Griff's house because that would land me back in jail. Griff had Crimson living airtight. You couldn't even get on the premises unless you had the code, or you were the police. Fuck that safe, I'm not trying to go back to jail. I still couldn't believe the money was counterfeit. Griff got crazy money. I know he's not moving like that. Maybe I should try to hit one of his traps. I know they keep money there. I just had to find the right nigga that could get me in and to make sure Rashad was nowhere to be found.

Maybe I could go home and grab some of Ike's shit. He owes me too. I wanted Ike in jail. He's never stepped foot inside of a jail, but I've been twice. I shouldn't have put that brick in the car because I could've sold and got some money off it.

Hopefully, I can sneak in our house while he's not home and grab a few of them. Ike only kept consignment work at home. If it was ever a drought in his business, he had a few keys and bricks on deck to supply the streets. I knew he wouldn't be as generous as Griff was in the divorce and give me anything. I'm forced to take a few of his consignments to make sure I eat. I guess that will be my next move. Hopefully, Ike hasn't switched up his routine. I'll have to go there when he's not at home. Ike catching me wasn't an option. The last time we crossed paths with each other, it wasn't pretty. I wish I could forget it, but I can't. He was so ruthless and angry when he killed Jacque. It's forever etched in my mind. I have flashbacks about it frequently.

Griff

My attorney hit me up early this morning and told me that Keondra was released from jail last night. That shit was music to my fuckin' ears. It was time to dead her and get back to living my life. I hated to kill her mother, but she fucked up when she touched mine. When Dre told me that shit it brought tears to my eyes. I don't give a damn about shedding tears behind mine. I'm human and I'll always express my feelings. My mother, Crimson and my children are a weakness for me. A motherfucka can play on that if they want to and they'll see how ruthless I get behind attempting to fuck with something that's special to me.

I hit Rashad up and told him I wasn't leaving the crib today. I hit my attorney up and told her that I need her to send the letter I wrote Crimson certified within two days. I knew Crimson was going to be gone today. I ordered a nanny came from Amazon and it was scheduled to be delivered today. I need to set that up in our room because I need to know what the fuck is going on. Amazon just sent an email to my phone that my package has arrived. I made my way through the tunnel and up toward the basement.

Crimson cooked breakfast this morning. I could still smell the aroma in the kitchen. As soon as I made my way toward the dining room. I heard a voice.

“Mommy it’s a package at the door from Amazon did you order me something,” my princess Camina asked. I stood in the corner and watched my princess. She’s gotten so big. I can’t wait to scoop her up.

“Cariuna open the door and see what’s on the porch. I didn’t order anything. Camina you better not have ordered anything from Amazon on your iPad. I’m serious,” she argued. Cariuna came downstairs the stairs pouting. Anytime she pouts she’s in the middle of doing something and didn’t want to be interrupted. I miss my first love. She’s my heart. She looks just like her mother.

“Mommy it’s a package with daddy’s name on it,” Cariuna smiled and yelled. Damn what the fuck was today and why are they home right now? It is what it is. I’ll be home sooner than they think. Maybe it’s not meant for me to hear or see some shit I don’t need too.

Daddy’s home, if it is a nigga in the picture, I’ll make sure that nigga is gone. I know Crimson. I don’t even know why I’m tripping. I got one thing to do and that’s kill Keondra and she’ll be dead by the end of next week. I want her to get comfortable. I want to hit her the same way she hit me. Only I'm going out the same way I came in, harder than muthafucka. She wouldn't expect it to be me.

"Cariuna, where did you put the package," she asked. Crimson strutted down the stairs in a silk robe. My dick got hard instantly. She has gained a few pounds. I came from around the corner to check her out. I bit my bottom lip. I wanted her in the worst way. I wanted to pick her ass up and bend her over the couch and make up for lost time.

"Mommy, I sat it on the sofa in the family room," Cariuna smiled. I remember when we first had her. The moment she opened her eyes and looked at me. She smiled and I saw her little dimples.

"Mommy, daddy ordered something for me. Let's open it. I told you he missed me," Camina smiled. She rubbed her hands together and started jumping up and down. Daddy does miss you. I can't wait to see you soon princess. Crimson bent over to open the box. I'll have to make some arrangements soon. I need to slide up in that and feel her.

"Carius? Damn, I miss you so much. A nanny cam? I didn't order this. Camina did you order this and charge it to your credit card." She asked. I miss you to Crimson. I can't wait to hold you. I can't wait to say I do and make it official.

"No mommy, I didn't do it," she pouted and whined.

"Okay baby maybe it was a mistake." It wasn't a mistake. I just needed to see if you had anything extra going on that was a sign that I needed to bring my ass home.

"I miss my daddy. I can't wait until he comes back to get me," Camina whined. I tiptoed back to the tunnel. I couldn't listen anymore because I miss the fuck out of my family. I'm sliding back up next week it's not up for debate. Crimson started talking. I stopped to hear what she had to say.

"Camina and Cariuna trust me your daddy misses you too. I miss him so much. He watches over us every day. I can feel him. He loves you and never forget that. Nobody could ever take your father's place," she beamed and smiled. If she only knew how close I was. I can't wait to show them how much I missed them. I'm not going back to the tunnel. I'm kicking it in the basement.

Our house was so big Crimson wouldn't come down here anyway. I needed to be close to my family. Hearing Crimson speak confirmed everything I needed to know. I know mine and I knew she wasn't giving a nigga her attention or time. I worked hard as fuck to get her. Ain't no way in hell a nigga was sliding up under her that easy. I put in so much work to get her I knew she wasn't moving on that soon.

A FEW DAYS LATER

Chapter-30

Crimson

I only had to work four hours today. The only good thing about my hours being cut short was that I didn't have to pay for daycare. I was able to take Camina and Cariuna to school and pick them both up. I started to march my ass in my supervisor's office to see what's going on. The schedule was put out Sunday and I was confirmed for 44 hours this week. Later that evening they sent out another one that only had me scheduled for 30 hours this week. I wasn't a part-time employee nor a PRN employee. It's crazy because the muthafuckas that never come to work are scheduled for 44 hours plus. Something must give. I'm so tired of this fuckin' job. Every week my hours are getting cut shorter and shorter. I swear every day it's something different at this job.

If I wasn't pregnant I swear I would mop the floor with one of these bitches. I want to quit so bad, but I can't unless I have something else. I didn't have to work but I didn't like staying at home all day either. I love the hustle of getting out and getting it. I probably should since I'm pregnant. I'm not showing but this pregnancy is different than my others. I couldn't stand on my feet for too long because they would swell. I needed the few little coins that I do have coming in because I didn't want to touch my savings. I like adding and not subtracting.

My checks have barely been $800.00. What the fuck could I do with that besides put gas in my car and food on the table? Health insurance and my 401k and taxes were taking everything. My car was acting funny a few weeks ago. I had to get a water pump and the heater fixed in it. I wanted to call Rashad to take it to Griff's mechanic, but I wasn't fuckin' with him. The repairs were $1200.00. I've been driving Griff's G-Wagon. I swear his cologne is so strong it smells like he was just in it.

I think they're cutting my hours out of spite. I heard my supervisor whispering something about me. She was telling a co-worker I fuck married men. I was going to let the slick comment slide, but I'm tired of bitches thinking they can say whatever about me and think I won't say anything.

I smiled at them, bitches. They gave me a nasty look. Yep, it was time for me to check those bitches. I knew they had to be some kin to Keondra. I don't even bother anybody. Griff was the only man I've ever been with. It confirms it's someone she knew. I stood right in front of them.

"The funny thing about gossip is bitches always leave out the truth. The next time Crimson Rose Tristan is the topic of your discussion make sure that bitch tells you the truth. If he was her husband, I had no clue. He divorced her, that's the truth," I argued. They were looking at me as if I were crazy.

"Excuse me Crimson who are you talking too?" My supervisor asked. Now she wants to act clueless. Bitch, I'm talking to you.

"If you can who you can hear. I'm giving you the truth. You were talking about me, right? If you got some shit you need to say to me let that shit be known. If it ain't directed it ain't respected," I argued. I'm sick of these bitched. God better bless these bitches.

"You know what Crimson-," my supervisor stated. I wasn't about to let her get another word out.

"You know what Tracy fuck you and fuck this job. It's a difference between you two and me. I don't need this fuckin' job. Y'all do. I can go any fuckin' where because this isn't my only source of income. My name and degrees and credentials speak for itself." I argued. I threw my badge at her. I'm tired of bitches disrespecting and fuckin' with me because a bitch they know doesn't like me. I ain't got fuckin' time. I knew they were talking about me because as soon as I walked in on the tail end of the conversation, they both cut their eyes at me. I'm about to chill for a minute. I'm pregnant and I don't need the extra stress. I just get a bad vibe being here and I'm big on vibes.

I went home to do some much-needed cleaning. I laid out steaks earlier for dinner. I could go ahead and put them on. I stopped by the store to grab the girls some snacks and juice. Their snack pile has been getting low quick and it's just the two of them. I used to have to get on Griff about eating all their stuff. He's gone now and I know the girls are growing but damn. Cariuna and Camina can make a mess. I heard a knock at my door. I looked out the peephole and it was the postman.

“Hi, I'm looking for you, Crimson Tristan. I have certified mail for you. Can you sign here,” the postman asked. I signed my name on the slip. I took the thick envelope from the mailman. It had Griff's name on it. I took a seat on the sofa and ripped it apart. My chest started to cave in. I swear I couldn't stop the tears from falling. He wrote this the day he died.

Why am I just now getting this? Even during all the bullshit, Griff was still looking out for us. I knew he would never leave us without. I looked at the paperwork that was in the envelope. The divorce decree was attached and the last will of testament. Keondra is a big fuckin’ liar. Griff divorced her the day we first made love. I knew he would never do that to me. I’m glad I quit my job and gave it to them bitches raw. I grabbed the papers and locked the door. The attorney's office was in Atlanta. I had to go pick up Camina and Cariuna from school so I wouldn't be late.

Keondra did a lot of shit. She’s been plotting this whole time to kill Griff. Why didn’t he tell, me? She took a lot from me. I lost everything because of her. I got to find a way to kill her without getting caught. I can’t wait to tell

Danielle and mother this. I need to call my mother to see if she'll come with me.

"Hey Crimson. What's going on, shouldn't you be at work?" She asked.

"Yep but I quit today," I sighed.

"Good because if I heard one more thing about them fuckin' with you I was on my way up there. Is everything okay?" She asked.

"Yes but no. I need you to ride somewhere with me. I can't say it over the phone."

"Okay, where are you? Do I need to come to you?" She asked.

"I need to come to you where are you?" I asked. My mother was stalling. I knew she was with my father. She just didn't want to say it. "Momma I know where you're at. I'm on my way. You're too old for this."

"You know what Crimson. Come on because I'm not fooling with you. I know you're not talking. I was just picking up something," she lied and hit me with a laugh. My father loves my mother but she's trying to fight it. I wish they would just be together.

♡

I got my stubbornness honestly and it's her fault. My attitude is a combination of her and my father. I have two younger brothers who I haven't met yet. They're in Miami and they're supposed to be coming soon.

My father didn't stay too far from me, so I picked up my mother first. What I'm about to say I don't want Camina and Cariuna to hear me. I made to my father's house. I called my mother and told her I was outside. She couldn't even get out the door good because my father was all up on her. She swears she doesn't love him anymore, but she pushes her BMW X5 faithfully. I swear every time I look at her plates I laughed. I swear my dad is crazy. I love listening to my mother tell me stories about him. My mother jumped in the car and rolled her eyes at me.

"Pull off now Crimson before he comes out here. I'm going back to Cali I'm not about to play with your father period," she explained. I wonder what he did.

"No, you're not going back to Cali. I need you and I'll miss you," I beamed. I was laying it on real thick.

"Crimson you don't have to miss me. You just quit your job. Pack up and you can come with me. What's so important that you couldn't say it over the phone?" She asked. I tossed her my purse from the backseat.

"Grab the envelope and read." I headed toward the daycare to get Camina and I'll pick up Cariuna next. Her school is right down the street.

"Crimson, you know what, you need to kill this bitch. I knew she had something to do with his death. Don't you let that bitch get away with nothing and I mean that shit.

The same way she gave it, you better fuckin' serve it. Ain't no way in hell she pulled off that stunt by herself. Griff was a real ass nigga and I'm glad he was all yours. He left you straight and you shouldn't be working for anybody. This bitch got to go period," she argued.

"I know momma that's why I called you. I ain't never wanted to kill anybody in my life but Griff was a good man. She took that away from me and my kids. He was my soul mate. Can you help me?" I asked.

"Can I help you? I will fuckin' do it. I knew it was a reason I didn't like that bitch," she argued.

"I want to do it. It's on me."

"Okay," she stated. My mother and finished talking. We picked up Cariuna and headed toward Griff's attorney's office.

♡

We finally made it to the attorney's office forty-five minutes later. Traffic was stupid. I gave the receptionist my name and she escorted me back to the conference room. I kept sniffing because I could smell Griff's cologne. It smelled so good. God, I miss him. Why is his scent lingering in the air?

"Ms. Tristan it's finally nice to meet you. I've heard so much about you. It's finally nice to put a name with the face. I have a lot of documents for you. Hi Camina and Cariuna, it's nice to see you again," Griff's attorney beamed. Damn, how did she know my kids and I haven't met her? I signed my name on everything and she led me to a vault. It smelled just like him. It was so much fuckin' money, jewelry, diamonds, and gold in there it was ridiculous. I couldn't take it. I started crying. Keondra killed him because she wanted all of this. I had to get out of here because it's too emotional. "Crimson if you need anything just let me know. I want you to be careful because Keondra is crazy and she'll be handled real soon."

"Thank you and I appreciate that. I'll be in touch if I need anything." We left out the attorney's office. My mother grabbed my keys. I was in no condition to drive. I don't even want this stuff. I just want Griff. That's it. She took him away from me because she wanted his wealth. She's stupid. He fuckin' married you. You had all of this and you fucked up. I'll be less than a woman not to handle her and I know for a fact she killed him.

TWO WEEKS LATER

Chapter-31

Keondra

I've been out of jail for a little over two weeks now. I spoke with my auntie regarding my mother's funeral. Let's just say our talk wasn't good. I couldn't take it. Somebody killed my mother, and my auntie said it's because of me. My mother told her I was into some deep shit and she was getting death threats. My heart dropped immediately because she never told me that. She wanted me to cut all the extra shit out, but she was never specific. I wish I would've known because I could've protected her and possibly prevented it.

I had one last hit that I wanted to make and after that, I was leaving Atlanta and starting over for good. I wanted to hit Griff's trap, but I've been watching it for the past few days and there hasn't been any movement. I think they moved it. I guess Rashad switched everything up after Griff died. The next best thing was Ike. I've been watching him for a few days now. Our neighborhood was always quiet, and my neighbors wouldn't suspect me. Ike always left the house by 9:00 a.m. and he didn't return until about 11:00 p.m. I know he had cameras so my plan was to kill the breaker so the cameras wouldn't be running, and he couldn't witness me going or coming.

He changed the locks, so my key didn't work anymore. We had this small basement window in our backyard. I was going to break that and climb in. I only had one problem I needed somebody to drive. I knew I could be in and out of the house within an hour. I needed to pull off as soon as possible. I know when I flip the breaker switch back on it'll alert Ike. We had this issue when we had an intruder and the security system was down.

The only person I knew that was down to ride was Jermesha but these past few weeks she hasn't been herself. We haven't even seen each other since I've been out. I find that strange because she was the only one in my corner. I grabbed my phone to call her to see what's up and she didn't answer. I sent her a text.

Me - Hey best friend I miss you. I need a favor from you. I'm headed to your house.

Jermesha - Hey boo I miss you too. I moved and my man doesn't want anybody to know where we live. He's been tripping lately and I'm on lock. I'll try to get up with you tomorrow.

I didn't even respond because a nigga ain't never came between us. No wonder she was acting funny. I can't even knock her hustle. She was in her niggas bag and if he had money she was securing it. I couldn't wait until tomorrow to do this. I had to move on it tonight. I wanted to leave Atlanta tomorrow. I found somebody to buy the house. I accepted the offer and the buyer did also. Everything would be finalized in two weeks. I sold the house for $320,000.00 because I needed it. My mother left me her house.

I'm moving to California and I need Ike's bricks to help me make some big moves out in Cali. If I had to do this shit on my own than I would. I know for a fact ain't nobody got me but me. I suited up and dressed in all black. It was a little after 6:00. It was already pitch black outside and that was perfect. I had about four hours' tops to get this done and head to the airport.

♡

I made it to the house Ike and I used to share in about forty-five minutes. It started raining so traffic was heavy. I needed to do this shit quickly because Ike doesn't fuck around in rain. He would be home sooner than 11:00 p.m. I pulled up in front of our house and it was a car that looked familiar. Jermesha's fuckin' car. I knew her candy red Infinity from anywhere because it was sitting on twenty-twos. I know this bitch wouldn't play me like this. Nah not my fuckin' husband. Ain't no fuckin' way. We're not divorced yet. It's not going down like that. I grabbed my phone and sent her a text to see if she would respond.

Me - Best friend wish me luck. I'm about to go see Ike to see if we can work on our marriage.

Jermesha - Keondra leave him alone before he hurts you. I don't want anything bad to happen to you. You know you're not one of his favorites.

Me - You right best friend thank you for looking out.

You know what, fuck this. I can't believe this bitch is fuckin' my husband. I said that just to throw her off. I'm about to knock on that door, better yet I'll kick that bitch in because that's still my fuckin' house. I'm Keondra Deleon. I'm glad I didn't tell her my fuckin' plans because she would've told him. Not Jermesha. Not the last muthafucka I could depend on is fuckin' my husband. She played the fuck out of me. She kept my books laced with money and she kept money on the phone courtesy of Ike. No wonder she had it.

To make matters worse this nigga moved her in the house that we shared. After everything I've been through with Ike, she knew it all. Damn, when it rains it pours. I can't even believe that I'm crying. I threw some water on my face so they wouldn't be able to tell I was crying behind this shit. I did everything for this bitch. I fed her when she couldn't eat. I brought her clothes when she couldn't shop. I don't even know why I'm surprised because if she crossed her own cousin, she wouldn't hesitate to cross me. I checked my mirror to make sure my make-up was on point. I jumped out of my car and slammed the fuckin' door. I marched up to my house and banged on the door like I was the fuckin' police. I'm glad I wore my Timberlands because I started kicking this bitch in. The door swung open and it was Ike. He had a fuckin' AK pointed at my head.

"Bitch why are you banging on my door like you're the fuckin' police? Bitch you don't fuckin' live here. You fuckin' disgust me. Give me one fuckin' reason why I shouldn't leave your ass leaking on my front porch? You're trespassing hoe, and you got the nerve to come to my house after you set me up on some rah-rah shit? Guess what bitch, it ain't going down like that," he argued and cocked the gun back. My heart dropped instantly. I had no clue he was here. I thought she was. She told him I set him up.

"Ike, my fuckin' best friend though. Do what you got to do. Jermesha bring your hoe ass out here. You want to be me so bad bitch you couldn't wait to fuck behind me? I made you hoe. I did every fuckin' thing for you. If I had it you had it," I argued. I can't even lie but this shit right here hurts the fuckin' worst.

Jermesha appeared right behind Ike in some lingerie displaying all her curves. I tried to reach around him so I could tap her fuckin' ass. He wouldn't let me get at her for shit.

"No Keondra, I don't want to be you. I made myself. I've always been me and everything you've ever done for me bitch I repaid you. I held you down in jail and made sure you were straight. We're even. I had it, so you had it. I could've turned my back on you while you were in there, but I didn't. Get out your feelings cause it ain't no money in them," she argued. I tried to reach around Ike so I could beat her ass. Ike lifted me up off the ground and put me in a choke hold so I wouldn't be able to touch her. Tears poured down my face. He was really trying to end my life right in front of this bitch. I couldn't breathe.

"Calm your stupid ass the fuck down. It doesn't feel good, does it? You wanted to fuck Baine. You bragged about that shit. You fucked Jacque in my house, yeah bitch I saw that shit. You set me up to take the fall for Griff's murder and you know I didn't do that shit. You called the cops and dropped my name and shit. I had no plans to fuck her and fall for her, but shit why not, you did it. Why are you mad when you created all this shit? I'm fuckin' with Jermesha heavy and it ain't shit you can do bitch. You got about ten seconds to get the fuck off my property before I put an end to your life stupid ass bitch," he argued. Jermesha cocked back the AK and pointed it at me. Ike finally released me from the choke hold. I took off running.

Jermesha fired a shot I can't believe this bitch. My life flashed right before my eyes. I just knew I was about to die. Thank God it missed my eye by an inch. Damn, I've done a lot of shit, but I didn't think I deserved this. I jumped in my car and pulled off quickly. I ran the stop sign and a car rear-ended me. Another car hit me from the side. I locked my doors instantly. Please, Lord, don't let them kill me. My windshield was shattered. Someone approached the driver's window with a bat and busted out the window and glass shattered everywhere. I tried to hop in the passenger seat to make a run for it but my doors were being snatched opened. I was cornered and I couldn't move.

"Bitch, I bet you're surprised to see me," she stated. I recognized the voice, but I couldn't think to figure it out. I felt a huge punch to my head, and the next thing I know everything went black.

Chapter-32

Crimson

Tonight was the night. Mother Dear had the girls. I was putting an end to Keondra and all her little bullshit. This bitch had to fuckin' go. She's taken way too much from me to allow her to keep living and getting away with shit. I know I couldn't bring Griff back, but she didn't deserve to live either. I've been following her for about a week now to see what she up was too. My mother, Danielle, and I were following her right now. Rashad is sitting at the corner waiting to ambush her the same way she did Griff. We both agreed she needed to feel the same pain she inflicted.

I'm tripping because Danielle tapped me from the back seat and told me this was Ike's house. We were a few houses down from her so, I couldn't believe it. What was she doing here and why? I knew something was about to go down. My mother pulled a little closer toward Ike's house. She couldn't recognize us because the tint was extra dark. Jermesha's car was in the driveway. I knew some shit was about to pop off. I'm nosey as fuck. What, I couldn't help it. I raised the window down because I wanted to hear it all.

Keondra slammed the door hard as shit. I knew she was pissed but everybody knew why Jermesha's car was out here, and it ain't for you. It went down and I was in tears. I felt bad for her, but you are the company you keep. Jermesha was fuckin' this girl's husband. Danielle and I couldn't stop laughing. We heard it all. My mother just shook her head. Like mother like daughter. I swear Mona Scott should've been here to record this shit. Rashad and his crew had Keondra cornered in. It was time to get this shit on the road. I was ready to kill her and get this over with.

♡

We were following Rashad for a long ass time. I'm pregnant and I'm ready to eat. Normally I'm in bed relaxing and ready to drift off to sleep. These past few nights I've been having dreams about Griff. They seem so real to. I don't know if it was because I was horny or what, but the sex felt real I've been waking up wet as fuck.

I've washed the sheets every day this week. I didn't mind at all. I swear his kisses were everything. It's like I could feel him. I made sure Cariuna and Camina were in bed by 8:00 p.m. every night. I couldn't wait to dream about him. Ahmad and I have had a few conversations and I agreed to meet up with him later just to talk. I've been dodging him for months. We just talk on the phone that's it. He knew I was pregnant. I agreed to go to the movies with him after I leave here. My mother killed the engine. I guess we're finally here now. I unfastened my seat belt instantly. It's time. Danielle and my mother hopped out too. Rashad and this other guy in a ski-mask were standing at the door waiting on us. Rashad was staring a hole in Danielle. She tried to ignore it. I don't know who the other guy was, but he kept looking also. He didn't say shit.

"What's up Crimson," he stated. Rashad knows I wasn't a fan of his but oh well.

"Hey, Rashad, where is she? I got a date tonight and I only got an hour to spare." He looked at me and the other guy. I don't know what that was about. I'm just saying we're already in the middle of nowhere. I wanted to kill her and be done.

"Aye Crimson, I don't want to hear that shit. Dead that shit before I do, you'll fuck around and get your date killed," he argued. I wasn't about to argue with Rashad. I followed him in the building and Keondra was lying on the floor unconscious. I thought of a million ways to kill this bitch. It wasn't going to be quick or easy. I wanted her to feel me. I sat my backpack on the floor and I grabbed my blow torch out my bag. I lifted my foot up and stomped her in the face. She woke up immediately. I kept stomping her, but I wasn't ready to kill her just yet.

"Wake up bitch," I yelled. She could barely keep her eyes open. My mother placed a hot cup of coffee in my hand. I poured it in her face. Her eyes bucked at me.

"Where am I?" She asked. I had her attention now. My fist connected with her jaw.

"I bet I'm the last person you expected to see. You took a lot from me when you took my soul mate and my children's father away from them. You killed him because you wanted his money? The difference between you and me is that I wasn't with Griff for his money. I could give two fucks about it. We loved each other unconditionally. If he was dead broke, he's still where I wanted to be, but you took that away from me.

You fucked up my family, you denied me of planning his funeral and burying him. I was in a coma because you lied about still being married to him. The day you took Griff away from me bitch, you sparked a fire in me that won't be put out. You're going to feel me." I argued.

"Please don't kill me. I'm sorry," she begged and pleaded.

"Bitch, fuck you." I lit the blow torch. I held her face in one hand and I burned her fuckin' mouth. Her tongue was fuckin' gone but she wasn't dead yet. I dropped her head and it hit the concrete. The pain I feel in my heart she needs to feel it too. I took the blow torch and placed it in the middle of her chest. I wasn't easing up until I saw her heart myself and I watched that bitch burn to fuckin' pieces. Her eyes rolled in the back of her head. Danielle walked up behind me and grabbed the blow torch from me and I checked her pulse. Keondra was dead and no longer in the land of the living. This is my first time killing someone and I don't feel bad about it because she took Griff away from me. My mother tapped me on my shoulder.

"Crimson can you and Danielle ride with Rashad? Your father wants me to meet him, he's not that far from here," she asked.

"Sure." I gave my mother a hug. Rashad tossed Danielle his keys. We walked to his car but as soon as I walked past the guy with the ski-mask. It was something about his energy and his eyes that seemed familiar, but I shook it off. He was looking at me. I'm ready to get out of here and go home. Hopefully, Rashad doesn't take too long. I might have to cancel my date. I'm tired anyway. I'm glad this bitch is finally out the way. Now I have a little closure regarding Griff's murder.

Chapter-33

Rashad

Crimson murdered Keondra without blinking twice. I didn't think she had it in her but shawty put in work. I was surprised when she hit me up and told me she wanted me to grab Keondra for her. I told Griff what the play was, and he couldn't believe it. He wanted to be there so he could clean up her mess. He was about to blow his cover in his ski-mask eying her. When she said she had a date? I knew he was about to snatch her ass up. Hopefully tonight he'll come clean so he can put her heart back together again because she deserves it.

She brought tears to my eyes when she was explaining to Keondra what she did to her. Griff's eyes were red as fuck. I know he felt that shit because I did. He had him a real one and I'm not even mad at him now. I understood his moves. I'm glad he did it because he deserves to be happy. Slap and Wire cleaned up the warehouse. I hopped in my Benz. Crimson was sitting up front and Danielle was in the back. She had me fucked up. She knows what it is between us.

"Crimson, get your ass in the back. Danielle, get your ass up front now," I laughed. I was serious too. Fuck that sit back there with your husband. Crimson did as she was told. Griff smacked me in the back of my head. He couldn't say shit because his cover would be blown. I pulled off. I had plans to drop Griff off first. I don't know how he was going to sneak in the house tonight without her knowing. He'll probably fuck around and go through the front door.

"Hurry up Rashad I don't have time to play with you. I told you I had a date," she explained. Griff and I locked eyes with each other in the rear-view mirror. His eyes were red as fuck. I knew he was heated. Crimson was pushing it. I don't know if she knew that was him, but she was reaching.

"Crimson chill out with that date shit. I don't want to hear about it. Don't you think it's a little too soon to be trying to date someone? I ain't feeling that shit at all. If you need me to do something just let me know and I'll do it. I'm not going to sit here and act like I'm okay with it because it's disrespectful to me and my nigga," I argued. I hate being caught up in Griff's shit.

"Griff wants me to date again," she laughed. We locked eyes with each other in the rear-view mirror. I just shook my head. Crimson is going to snap on his ass I can feel it.

"Yeah right. Trust me he didn't mean that shit. He's waiting on you in heaven. Crimson my nigga will stalk you from his grave before he lets you be with another man," I laughed. I locked eyes with Griff and Crimson rolled her eyes at me.

"Whatever Rashad. Who is this crazy person you have riding with you? Do you talk and why do you have your ski-mask still on? What are you looking at?" She asked. Griff didn't say shit. He leaned in her face and just stared at her. "Move and get out my face because you're creeping me out. Rashad hurry up and take me home. I don't appreciate you having me ride in the back with a psycho," she argued. Griff scooted right next to Crimson and she was hot. If she only knew who was up under that ski-mask she would go crazy. Danielle sucked her teeth. I knew she was about to come to Crimson's rescue.

"Excuse me psycho since your friend won't say nothing. Can you back the fuck up off my friend," Danielle asked and argued? Griff shook his head no. I laughed in Danielle's face and she didn't like that shit all.

"Stay out of peoples business and worry about me when I'm all up in your face later. I hope that nigga no you ain't coming home tonight because I'm kidnapping you," I argued and explained. Danielle sucked her teeth and mumbled something up under her breath. She heard what the fuck I said. If Baine was expecting her, he'll be in an empty bed tonight.

A FEW HOURS LATER

Chapter-34

Griff

Tonight is the night. It's about to go down. I can't wait to be reunited with my baby. I miss the shit out of my babies. I had Rashad call Mother Dear and told her to bring Cariuna and Camina to the house. I've been away from my family far too long and yesterday was the last fuckin' day. I can't wait to hug, kiss, and spoil them rotten. I already know Crimson is about to trip but that's just some shit I'll have to deal with. These past few nights I've been in our room and we've been making love every night. She thought she was dreaming but, in a few hours, she'll see it wasn't. She was pissing me the fuck off talking about her date and shit. I wasn't having that at all. I unhooked the battery from every car. She wasn't about to meet no fuckin' body tonight, but me, Carius Deon Griffey.

Crimson is a savage for real. I thought she was going to just shoot and kill Keondra, but she terrorized the fuck out of her. She held her own. She brought tears to my eyes when she admitted to Keondra about how she felt about me and what she took from her. I got a lot of making up to do. I'm sorry for all of that. Her mother looks just like her. I'm glad she finally got the chance to meet her. It was a little after 1:00 a.m. and I knew everybody was asleep. I didn't have to tiptoe through my shit anymore.

I headed upstairs and I stopped by Cariuna's room first. She was asleep when I kissed her on her forehead and whispered in her ear. I told her that I loved her and I'd see her tomorrow. Next stop was Camina's room. She was tossing and turning in her bed. I climbed in right behind her and held her. She finally got comfortable and stopped moving around. I kissed her on her cheek. I missed her and tomorrow she'll see exactly how much. Next stop was my bedroom. I went to the bathroom and took a hot shower. I had plans to wake up Crimson. I wasn't about to prolong it. I handled my hygiene, stepped out the shower, and dried off. I brushed my teeth because I had plans to fuck and suck on Crimson all night.

It was all or nothing now. I pulled Crimson's body to the edge of the bed. She was naked as the day she was born. My face was eye level with her pussy. I ate her like she was my last meal and she was. Her hands roamed my body and she was riding the shit out of my face. Her eyes were closed because she didn't want to open them because she knew it was a dream. I raised up and started sucking on her breasts. Her nipples were hard as fuck. I through her legs over my waist. Crimson was wet as fuck and her pussy was tight as hell. It took me a minute to get in but when I did, she gripped my shit and I couldn't move. I started stroking her long, deep and hard. The only sounds throughout the room were soft moans and my grunts.

"Please don't stop Griff. I want you. I need you. I thought you promised you would never leave me," she moaned. Crimson did this every night for the past few nights, but I never said anything back to her, but tonight all that was about to change. I leaned in and kissed her and sucked on her bottom lip.

"Crimson, baby I adore you. I just want to spoil you. I want you and I need you too. I'm sorry I had to leave you, but baby I came back just for you." Crimson's hand roamed my body. I traced my tongue on her lips. I slid my tongue in her mouth and she returned the kiss. I continued to beat her pussy out the frame. Her hands caressed my face. I place my hands on her cheeks. She finally opened her eyes and they were trained on me. She closed them and opened them up again and she was still looking at me. I leaned in and kissed her.

"Griff, get the fuck off me. Is this some sick ass joke?" She argued. I wasn't raising up off her at all. She can forget all about that shit. I know she was upset with me. I could feel her chest heaving up and down.

"Nah, it's not a joke. I'm sorry Crimson. Can you find it in your heart to forgive me?" I asked.

"Griff, I'm going to ask you one more time to get off me or I'm going to get you off and I fuckin' mean that shit," she argued. Crimson was tripping hard. I knew she would be mad but not this mad.

"You know I'm not about to do that. Calm down before you wake my kids up. Can I explain myself, Crimson, can you allow me to do that? It's a reason for my actions."

"Your kids are already awake. Camina and Cariuna daddy's home," she argued and pointed to the door they were standing there looking at us. Crimson knew we didn't have any clothes on she was wrong for that shit.

"Daddy, daddy we missed you," they beamed.

"Daddy missed you too more than you'll ever know. Step out for a minute so I can put my pajamas on." Camina and Cariuna stepped out of our room. I grabbed my pajamas out of my drawer. Crimson put her robe on. My eyes were trained on her, she avoided eye contact with me. "Crimson this conversation isn't over."

"Griff, yes the fuck it is! We don't have anything to talk about. You faked your motherfuckin' death. Do you think I want to fuckin' talk to you? Once again, the joke is on me. Guess what though, you don't have to fuckin' worry about me anymore. I didn't sign up for any of this shit. I'm glad you're alive and you can help me raise our kids. It ain't no you and me. You were the motherfucka that was in the car with Rashad. No wonder you didn't say shit because you knew I would cut up on you. He didn't say shit either when you were up in my face. I'm fuckin' done. Goodbye Griff and keep you're lying ass away from me," she argued.

"I know you're mad and I'm sorry. I'll let you cool off but it ain't never over between us." Crimson is crazy as hell. Not even ten minutes ago she was telling me how much she loved and missed me and now she's done. She stormed out of the room. I don't know where she was going but she wasn't leaving here tonight. Camina and Cariuna ran in the room and hugged me. I picked them both up and carried them to the family room. I brushed my teeth and grabbed some blankets. Crimson wasn't about to ruin my night with my girls. They laid up under me and watching a movie. She walked past the guest room and we locked eyes with each other.

"I love you Crimson."

"You need to fix my car or whatever you did to it. Now all the cars ain't working," she argued and slammed the door.

"You're not going nowhere Crimson you can forget about it. We're going to work this shit out."

Chapter-35

Crimson

I can't believe Griff pulled that shit on me. It's like I don't even know him. Carius and Griff are two totally different people. I'm just supposed to accept it and not say shit? It's not going down like that. Fuck him. Where has he been for the past three months? I thought we were partners. He could've let me in on it. It never felt like he was dead to me. It felt like he was just gone for a minute and he was. I don't even want to know. He's the last person I want to see right now. I'm so good on him.

I came to Mother Dear's to get away from him. I couldn't be anywhere near him. As soon as I stepped out the car, they ceased the talking which leads me to believe they were talking about me. I'm so glad my mother is here. I couldn't wait to talk to her. I wonder where she went last night, was she in on it too? Cariuna and Camina love her. If I would've known that was Griff last night in the car, I would've fought his ass. Why would you do that to me? I meant to ask Mother Dear why she at my house with the girls. I don't fuck with Rashad anymore either. He knew Griff was alive and didn't say shit?

“Hey, Mother Dear and Ms. Gladys. Hey mommy,” I smiled. As mad as I am, I don’t even feel like talking to them. I’m sure Camina has called everybody and told them her father was alive. I walked right in the house and into my old room. I closed the door right behind me because I didn’t want to be bothered. Griff took the girls with him. It was perfect. I had no plans of going back to the home we shared. Mother Dear and my momma were right on my heels. I pulled the covers back and climbed in the bed. I had so much shit on my mind. I couldn’t even say a prayer if I wanted to. I heard my room door open and I knew it was Mother Dear being nosey.

“I didn't ask for any company. Can I relax in my room Mother Dear and momma? I'm good, trust me.” I sassed and sighed. I didn’t feel like being bothered. I wasn’t for the questions.

“Crimson Rose Tristan you can relax in your own home. I raised you not to run from shit. Take your ass home to your fiancé and work it out. Yo ass ain't been running over here so, don't start now. That little nigga that got you smiling that ain't Griff, dead that shit too,” she argued and laughed. I swear I can't stand her sometimes. I couldn’t hide my smile if I wanted too. Mother Dear knew too much. I got a lot of reasons to smile and trust me it's not because of him. We didn't even get to have our date. I wasn't trying to date anyone anyway. I would've called him sooner if I would've known it would've brought Griff back from the dead.

"Mother Dear, I'm not running from him. I just don't want to be bothered with him. Why can't I come over here and lay in my old room? Everybody can come back here but me, why is that a fuckin' problem? Momma, why are you always running behind Mother Dear? Can both of y'all leave?" I argued and asked. I don't want to see Griff nor talk about him.

"Crimson Rose Tristan. I haven't raised you but these past few months have been everything to me. I love you and just hear him out. Listen to me. We all make fuckin' mistakes. I made plenty of them but I'm learning from them. Go home and work it out. You laid in a coma for over a week because you missed him that much. You yearned for that man in your sleep. Shit, you're carrying another child of his. He came back to you and your children. Crimson you don't have to miss him. I'm your mother and you're so much like me it's crazy. I rubbed off on you bad and it’s funny to see my mini-me in action. Go home and forgive him. Go make love to him like you’ve been doing because Camina already told us you were screaming about her daddy in your sleep,” my mother laughed and explained.

“Momma, I’m not doing it. It's not that's easy. I got to stand for something. You saw what I went through, and he did too, but why not give me the heads up? He knew I was in a coma for a week. He was somewhere living his life. I went through too much while he was gone. No, I don't want to talk to Griff nor see him. He stayed away from me for three months. He can add another two months. A person can't fuck me over and just come back like shit is all good that goes for him too.” I argued. I’m not ready to talk to Griff.

“You’re a spoiled brat Crimson. Between Mother Dear and Griff, they've created a fuckin' monster. I know you how you feel Crimson and I understand that. I wanted to earn your forgiveness and trust. Don't be too hard on him. Trust me you’re standing for a lot. I figured that was him last night because he didn’t say anything. His eyes stayed on you,” my mother explained. So much for coming over to here to clear my thoughts. Everybody was team, Griff.

“Go home Crimson, he’s worried sick about you.” Mother Dear explained. I’m not going home. He can continue to worry sick about me. He needs to feel how I felt.

“No Mother Dear, I’m not going home. I’m good on Griff. I’ll see him in two months. I’m glad he’s not dead but the thought of losing him for good almost killed me. I don’t know how to deal with him being back. I refuse to deal with him. His children missed him. He can enjoy their company.” I argued. I made my bed back up and grabbed my purse out the chair.

I had to get out of here too. I don’t want any lectures on how I’m handling Griff because the only way I’m going to handle him is to not deal with him. He handled me by faking his death because his ex was so caught up behind him. I should’ve known it was more to that bitch. No wonder Jermesha was going was so hard for her friend.

“Crimson don’t be that way, hear that man out. It’s a blessing that he’s able to come back to you.” She stated. It’s a blessing that he faked his death and abandoned me and his children? I swear black people a trip. Mother Dear loved Griff and she can continue too. Mother Dear wasn't talking about shit. My momma was laughing and smiling at me the whole time. I don't have anything else to say.

"I heard enough Mother Dear. I'm thankful Griff's back but I can't deal with him right now. I refuse to go back to that house and be up under the same roof with him. I'm sure the girls won't miss me. They have him back. I'm leaving and I'll see you soon. Bye ma." I explained. I need a break from him and the girls. The moment he came back Camina had no problem saying I told you my father was coming back. I wanted to beat her little tale, but I couldn't because she was right. I wasn't going back to my old townhouse because he would know I was there.

I went to the old townhouse that Danielle and I shared. I parked my car in the back so he wouldn't recognize it. I couldn't deal with him. We can co-parent. I'm okay with that. My phone was ringing, and it was Danielle. I couldn't go to her house either because he would go there too.

"Mrs. Mahone, what's up?" I laughed. Danielle is playing a dangerous game and I don't want any parts of it. I don't like trouble at all. I hope she didn't stay with Rashad last night. I'm not even about to ask because I don't want to know. The less I know the better.

"Cut the bullshit Crimson, you know that man is looking for you. He came by here with Rashad and his babies. My heart dropped when Rashad and Cariuna came to the door. He fucked me with his eyes lustfully and told me he'll be back. Camina already acting funny. She was sitting up front with her daddy. I waived at her and she rolled her eyes at me. I swear she needs her little tale whipped. Girl, thank God Baine wasn't home because it would've been some shit. I'm glad Griff is alive but don't ever let Rashad know where Baine and I lay our heads," she argued. I told you she's playing a dangerous game.

"Whatever Danielle. Stop entertaining Rashad before Baine hurts you. Stay away from him and I mean it. He needs to stay away from you. I don't like how this shit is turning out. I don't want Baine thinking I hooked the two of you up because I didn't. You got Griff's number tell him what you told me. I'm not fuckin' with Griff the Ghost." I laughed. I'm not a fan of his right now. I love him but I'll love his ass from a distance.

"Crimson, you're tripping hard on that man. Let my boy live and be great. He's sorry. Griff the Ghost said bitch you know you're his BOO," she laughed. Danielle got jokes for days.

"Whatever Danielle, I thought you were on my side? I guess not. I'm just supposed to forgive him and not ask any questions? I'll pass. We can co-parent that's it. I'm moving out. He ruined us the moment he pursued me. He NEVER and not once mentioned he was married to that bitch. I had to get my hands dirty because of him and that crazy ass lunatic. I'm good. The best thing he ever gave me was my two daughters."

"Crimson don't forget to mention the child of his you're carrying now. When are you going to tell him about his mini-me? I'm not saying that you have every right to ask questions. He made a mistake he should've told you I agree. You're letting Keondra win by acting like this. Just a week ago you couldn't wait to go to sleep and dream about fuckin' him. Now you ain't got to dream bitch, you can fuck him with no remorse. Griff a fool for that one. I knew you lost your damn mind when you were telling me about your dreams," she laughed.

"Fuck you Danielle, and bye I'll talk to you tomorrow. You're laughing at my expense." I argued and laughed. She wasn't in any position to laugh at me. I don't know what her and Rashad got going on but it's dangerous and I don't want to be in the middle of it. He shouldn't be knocking on her door with Cariuna at all. Rashad is a crazy motherfucka.

"Go home Crimson, please." Danielle knew me better than I knew myself. She knew I wasn't going home. Griff knows that, and he should expect it. The moment I woke up and found him lying in between my legs and it wasn't a dream. I've hardly said three words to him. The girls were happy he was back when they walked in the room this morning. I was too but he would never know that. I know we had to talk but I wasn't ready to talk about it today or tomorrow.

♡

Two hours later I finally made it to my destination. I drove around for hours debating if I wanted to go back home or not. I chose not to go back. I should've grabbed me something to eat on my way in, but I didn't. I'm hungry and the only thing here was some lunch meat and a few slices of bread and a bag of chips Cariuna or Camina left. I miss my babies. Cariuna hasn't even called me. I swear this cold cut sandwich was everything.

I didn't have my kindle, but I had a paperback book **Our Love Is the Hoodest** by **Nikki Nicole** sitting on my living room table. I couldn't wait to read it and see if it weighs up to **Journee & Juelz**. The reviews said it was better. I took a hot bath and put my phone on silent. This book was good so good that I had lost track of time. I stepped out of the tub and dried off. Griff called my phone at least four times and I refused to answer. I was tired between this baby and finding out he's not dead. I'm beat. I put my phone on vibrate and do not disturb. I didn't want to hear it ring. I was tired and sleep was finally ready to consume me. This is the first night in months that I don't have to cry myself to sleep because I missed him so much.

I was sleeping well. I felt somebody staring at me. I opened my eyes and it was him. I turned on my side. I couldn't look at him. He tapped me on my shoulder hard as fuck. Not today Griff. Please just let me be I'm in my feelings and I have every right to be.

"Crimson are we really doing this? I swore I told you to get rid of this townhouse years ago. Why do you still have it? Why the fuck aren't you answering your phone? You can't fuckin' hide from me. Can we talk about this like adults? You haven't even heard me out. I'm sorry, come on and let's go home," he argued.

"Where are my kids Griff, if you're here? We can talk but not now. I don't have to answer my phone for you. You haven't called me in 90 days. I'm just supposed to answer my phone because you're calling me?" I argued.

"They're with your mother. She came to get them since I couldn't find their mother. Get up and let's roll because we're not doing this. That nigga that got you smiling that ain't me, dead that shit because daddy's home. Ain't nan nigga taking my place. You heard what the fuck I said Crimson, let's go. You can do it my way or learn the hard way," he argued.

"I'll meet you at your house, Griff. I'll see you later." I turned back around. Praying he would leave. He pulled the covers back and touched my legs. "Don't touch me."

"What the fuck is that supposed to mean? Bring your ass own Crimson. I swear I'm not trying to go there with you but you're trying the fuck out of me. I know I'm in the doghouse but damn I don't mind being there as long you're at home. I missed the fuck out of you. You know I can't sleep without you." He explained. He picked me up and threw the cover over me. I could've sworn I told him don't touch me. I missed him too and he knows that. I just want some space from him.

"I need my purse and my phone. I can drive myself to your house. I can walk Griff." I argued. I swear he's doing the most. I was coming to his house. My mother needs to pick a side it's either me or him. It can't be both of us.

"I know you can, but you're riding with me. I don't want you driving this late. I had your car towed to the house. This little hideout will be empty by tomorrow just so you know." I can't deal with Griff right now. He was doing the most. His hands roamed my body. Damn his touch feels so good. He smells good too. I saw a U-Haul truck pull up. He sat me in the passenger seat of his car. I watched him give instructions to his workers. I put my hands over my mouth to stop the smile from coming out. Griff opened the car door and slid in and pulled off.

I turned my head toward the window and closed my eyes. I refused to look at him. He grabbed my hand and I snatched it from him. He grabbed it back I didn't even put up a fight because his touch was calming.

"Crimson." He stated. I refuse to answer him. "Crimson Rose Tristan, I know you hear me talking to you? Why are you playing with me? Do I need to pull over on the side road so we can hash it out right now?" He asked.

"Keep driving Griff, and take me to your house," I argued. I was tired. What would make him think that I wanted to stop on the side of the road and talk this late at night? He already woke me up out of my sleep.

"Our house? Anything that I own is yours and it hasn't been my house in a while," he argued. He's doing the most I swear. I know we needed to have a conversation but he's not ready to hear what I have to say. The remaining of the ride was quiet. No words were spoken between us.

It was so much tension between us I could feel it. Griff and I have never been in this space before. I swear this felt like Deja Vu. He pulled up to the gate. The moment he killed the engine it's on. I'm taking off and locking myself in our room. Griff killed the engine. I tried to unlock the door, but it was locked. Griff laughed at me. I know he didn't put the child lock on my door. He walked over and unlocked the door. He stood in front of me. This was the first time I was able to take him in since he reappeared. God, I missed him so much.

"Can you please move Griff?" I asked him nicely. If I had to ask him again it wouldn't be nice.

"Look at me when you're talking to me Crimson!" He yelled. I don't know who Griff think he's talking to. Since he rose from the dead I couldn't look Griff in the face because I'll go against everything I fuckin' believe in. I refused to do that with him. I'm not going against shit.

"Griff, I got to throw up, can you please move?" I asked. He backed up and gave me a little space. Got him. He picked me up and carried me in the house. I closed my eyes and rolled them.

"What's wrong Crimson?" He asked.

"Everything." I kept it short with him. He carried me upstairs to our room. He tossed me on our bed and hovered over me. He bit his bottom lip. I looked at everything but him. I swear this baby is making me nauseous. I jumped up and ran to the bathroom. He was right on my heels. He grabbed my hair. I threw up the whole sandwich. I guess he didn't like the sandwich.

"Excuse me, can you back up?" I asked. I needed to brush my teeth and wash my face.

"What's wrong with you Crimson?" He asked.

"Nothing, I'm pregnant." I sighed.

"You're pregnant. I'm sorry Crimson what are we having?" He asked.

"Carius Jr."

"Swear baby?" He asked. What the fuck did I have to lie for? I pushed passed Griff and went into our room. He was right on my heels. He grabbed my waist and held me in place. I broke down crying. I couldn't hold it in if I wanted to. My feelings and emotions were a wreck and they were bound to collide sooner or later because of him.

"Move, please. You hurt and broke me. You took a piece of me when you left," I cried. The moment I woke up from the coma and I found out I was pregnant. I was sad again because the thought of Griff not experiencing the birth of our third child done something to me.

"Stop crying before you upset my son Crimson. I know you hate me, but I'm sorry. I love you and it's nothing in this world that's going to keep me from you and my kids. I don't regret anything I did because I'm going to protect my family at all cost. I'm hurt too because you're shutting me out. I thought our reunion would be bittersweet. I guess a nigga was better off dead since you're acting like this. You want me dead too Crimson? I swear it feels like I'm dead since you don't want me to touch or hold you." He argued.

"Griff don't say that. How the fuck, do you think I feel? Don't twist this shit on me. I laid in a coma for a week because I couldn't deal with the thought of not seeing you. My heart stopped beating because of you. I abandoned my children because of you. It fucks with me because you're not dead. Where the fuck have you been for 90 days? You never mentioned you were married, Griff. Did you ever think that was some shit I needed to know? I'm happy you're alive. Your children need you and I need fuckin' space from you."

"Space, it ain't no fuckin' space. I'm sorry Crimson. Yeah, I should've told you I was married to her, but I didn't because we wouldn't have gotten this far. You would've cut me off immediately. I divorced her and before I took it there with you, I made sure of that. These past 90 days I've been living here. I can't change the past, but our future looks very bright. We got to move past this Crimson. It's killing me that I hurt you to the point you don't want to be around me. Can I love the hurt out of you?"

“You're not sorry Griff. I thought there were no secrets between us, but you got plenty. I don't trust you and if it's not about my kids then you don't have anything to say to me. I'm leaving this house. Please don't come after me. We'll talk about co-parenting later.” I argued.

“I am sorry Crimson don't put fuckin' words in my mouth. I made a mistake and I'll own up to it. I wanted to come back earlier, but I couldn't. I had to hit that bitch where it hurts. I should've killed Keondra a long time ago, but I didn't. Allow me to right my wrongs. That's all I'm asking.

It ain't no fuckin' co-parenting. We've been raising our kids together and nothing will change that not even you. If you need space this house is big enough but you ain't leaving this muthafucka to lay anywhere else,” he argued. It was pointless to even have a conversation with Griff. He wasn't even trying to hear nothing I had to say. I climbed in the bed and he climbed right in behind me. He wrapped his arms around my waist. He started whispering sweet nothings in my ear. I tried to hold in my tears, but I couldn’t. Griff turned me around to face him. He wiped my tears with his thumbs.

"Crimson, I'm sorry and you know that. I never meant to hurt you. I'm not trying to upset you because you're pregnant with my son and I don't want anything to happen to the two of you. I should've been honest with you, but I didn't want you to worry. I had it under control, but if I'm living, I will never let anything happen to you or my children. I'm not asking you to forget but I'm asking you to forgive me. I'm fucked up behind this too. She killed my mother Crimson. So yes, I did that because if she would've come for you and my children, this place we called earth would no longer exist," he explained. Griff's eyes were red. I know his mother was a touchy subject for him.

"I forgive you, Griff. You know I can't stay mad at you forever, but don't EVER do that to me," I explained. I loved Griff with everything in me. It pointless and a waste of my energy to stay mad at him. I love him. I missed him. He made love to me. I said a quick prayer thanking God for bringing him back to me.

A WEEK LATER

Chapter-36

Danielle

Since Griff's home I won't be seeing any more of Rashad hopefully. Why do I care? I shouldn't because maybe I can get my marriage back on track. I keep asking myself that same question over and over. I care but why? It was the insane sex sessions or maybe it was the flirting or him threatening me to leave my husband. Maybe it was the thought of throwing my marriage up in his face whenever he made me mad? I haven't seen this man in years, but it bothered me that I wouldn't be able to see him again. It's like all my feelings that I had for him resurfaced because we were around each other a lot due to Griff being gone. It was the dick that has me sick. The thought of not seeing him again was fuckin' with me mentally. We've been creeping around for months and I swear each time was the last time but that was a lie.

For some odd reason, my heart was aching and begging to escape the tight grip I had on it. I shouldn't even care because I'm married and it's nothing that he could do for me. I kept telling myself that, but it wasn't the truth. I think it was the kiss we shared that has me mesmerized. Ever since we kissed the first night a Crimson's I've been hooked. I shouldn't have crossed that line. I should've stopped him the moment he started. I wanted to see if he was bold enough to do it. Boy was I wrong I should've known better. Baine would kill me if he knew that happened.

I guess that's one thing that I'm taking to the grave with me. Sometimes I trip on how happy we used to be, but he fucked that up and now I'm married. Ugh, I got to shake the thoughts of him quick. Damn, I was in love with him. I would've done anything for him. Why am I reminiscing about him? Please, God, help me shake these thoughts and memories of him. I heard a knock at my door. I was in a daze and had lost my train of thought when it comes to him.

Thank God because I needed to shake these thoughts of him quick. I wasn't expecting another patient until 3:30 p.m. I wonder who it was. I knew my husband wasn't stopping by. We stopped taking walk-ins after 1:00 p.m. Maybe it's the medical supplies I ordered, and I needed to sign off on. I'm enjoying my lunch trying to get my mind right.

"Come in Michelle." I beamed. Michelle was my receptionist. She handled the front desk and she was my assistant. I'm on lunch and I don't feel like being bothered. I had a lot of shit on my mind. I really needed to get these things off my mind. Baine knew something was up with me, but he didn't know what. I'm trying to sort that out. It's gotten to the point where I didn't even want to be around my husband because of Rashad.

"Boss lady you have a patient that's demanding to see you. I told them they would need to schedule an appointment because we're done taking walk-ins for today." She stated and smiled. I looked at Michelle like she was crazy. Rules were rules. Who was demanding to see me? I wasn't expecting anyone. I would politely tell them to make an appointment as a walk-in and I'll see them tomorrow.

"My next appointment isn't until 3:30 p.m. you can assign them to another nurse if they have the availability to take a walk-in patient." If it's not on my calendar it's not getting seen period. Its protocols in my facility. I'm the boss and I make the fuckin' rules.

"I tried to do that but he's not listening," she sighed. Who was he and why wasn't he taking her word? Michelle was good at her job. It had to be a serious problem if she's consulting with me. She can handle her own. I had my game face on because I don't know who this man was.

"Send them in." I sassed. Michelle smiled at me. I swear I really didn't feel like being bothered. I had two hours before it was time to see my patient. I just wanted to relax for the next two hours.

"Thank you, Boss lady, I appreciate that. He was really giving me a hard time." She sighed. I had to have the patience for whoever this patient was. Michelle escorted them in. Speaking of the devil. I was just thinking about him. My smile instantly turned into a scowl. Are you shitting me? I can't fuckin' believe it. It was Rashad, Cariuna, his son I'm assuming, and a bitch. It had to be his son because he looked just like him. We locked eyes with each other. I know he didn't bring a bitch with him in my place of business. What type of games is being played? I guess this was the sign I needed to stop whatever this lil shit is. Why they are here and what do they want with me?

Rashad fucked me with his eyes. The chick he was with looked a little uncomfortable. I knew they were fuckin' around because it's the same look I used to give him whenever we were out together. It's the same look I'm giving him now.

On God why does this nigga continue to try me at work of all places? I've had this clinic for years and he's never stepped foot in my practice with his son. Rashad was fuckin' with me. He wanted a reaction out of me, and I refused to give him one. He must think I'm a joke. More of a reason why I need to focus on my marriage and what Baine and I have going on because Rashad is trying to interfere with that.

I swear this nigga is funny as hell. I'm glad he got a bitch though. Where has she been, and you've been running down on me? I've been fuckin' you every day for the past two month's right here in my fuckin' spot. Something's never change. I wish I could tell this bitch to tell him to stay up out of my face. Leave me the fuck alone because I'm married. I walked around from my desk to see my Goddaughter Cariuna. I pulled her in for a hug.

I swear I wish he would stop using her to get at me. I'll be sure to let Crimson know that. I haven't seen her in a few days since her father's back home. I need to text her mother to tell her I'll keep them this weekend because she and Griff need a lot of alone time. She's probably driving him crazy. I know how she is. Cariuna is a beautiful child. She looks like Crimson and Griff but that damn Camina looks just like her father and he has her spoiled rotten. She's a fuckin' monster. She's bad as hell.

"Hi, I'm Danielle the lead nurse, how can I help you?" I asked with a faint smile. I was waiting for them to say something. My time is precious, and I refused to be in the room with Rashad and this chick.

"God mommy Danielle this is my cousin Rashad. He sprained his ankle playing baseball. Can you fix his like you fixed mine," she asked and smiled? Rashad better be glad I love Cariuna and I don't discriminate against kids or else it would've been no. Anything for my baby.

"Sure, Cariuna I can do that. Hi handsome! I need his mother and father to fill out the paperwork and I can get started. Do you want some apples and grapes? Can he have some too?" I asked. I gave Rashad the paperwork.

He filled out the paperwork and his baby momma didn't say shit. Oh, baby, I'm not your issue, he is. Take that up with him. She knew we knew each other but she didn't know how. I grabbed Cariuna and Rashad's hand and led them to my station. I felt his eyes trained on me.

Rashad and his baby momma followed behind us. I sat Lil Rashad up on my examination table to check out his ankle. He was so handsome. His ankle was starting to swell. I applied a little pressure to it. I hope I didn't hurt him too bad with it being just a small sprain.

"It hurts," he whined. I wish I could take the pain away, but I can't.

"I'm sorry handsome," I whined and pouted. I gave Lil Rashad and Cariuna a pop cycle. I wrapped his ankle up and he was good to go. "He needs to stay off his ankle for a few days. If it hurts and he can't tolerate the pain give him Motrin. Here's a prescription for Ibuprofen and Tylenol. He's young so don't give him the whole thing just a small piece and he'll be just fine." My job was done and the four of them can carry on.

"Thank you, how much do I owe you?" He asked. His soul was trying to speak to mine, but I wasn't giving in. I wish he would've kept his mouth closed. Ugh, his voice fuckin' irks me. He knew he didn't owe me shit that's why he came with Cariuna. I can't stand him. He just reminded me why I hated him in the first place.

"It's on the house take care Cariuna and Lil Rashad. You can stop by the second window on the left. His discharge papers will be there and an excuse from school if he needs one." I explained. I walked back to my office and locked the door. I was reminiscing about this nigga. Rashad didn't owe me anything. The only thing he could do at this point is to leave me the fuck alone. At this point, I hope he never shows his face again. Stay away from me and I meant that shit literally.

I couldn't wait to tell Crimson about her brother in his little Shenanigans. My next appointment wasn't until 3:30 p.m. I grabbed my phone to call Crimson. I had an hour to spare before my patient arrived. I hope she was in a better mood than she was a few days ago.

"What's up Danielle, I haven't heard from you in a few days? Are you abandoning me too?" She asked and beamed. I could tell by her tone that she was feeling better than what she felt a few days ago. Hopefully, she blessed Griff with some makeup sex.

"Good Afternoon to you too! I haven't heard from you all day. You must have had a long night. Can you talk?" I asked. I needed to vent bad and Crimson was the only person I could talk too. She was my personal diary and that would never change. I hope she wasn't laid up with Griff, because there's no telling when we would be able to have this conversation again.

"Good Afternoon. I had a long night but it's not what you're thinking. He can't even smell lick or fuck this pussy if he wanted too," she argued and laughed. I swear I'm not beat for her shit today. She should be happy the love of her life is back. I heard Griff saying something in the background.

"Tell Griff I said what's up. I'm praying for you friend. Do you want to talk about it?" I asked. I know Crimson is going through a lot so I'm here if she needs me. My little dilemma could wait if she needed to get some things off her chest. She needs to move on and forgive him. I understand why he did it. Keondra was crazy but we could've handled that bitch years ago if she was that stupid.

"No, I don't want to talk about it. What's up with you today?" She asked.

"Excuse me, BITCH, I was just being concerned. Anyways I thought you would never ask? First, where's your husband? Can you talk, talk?" I asked. Griff and Rashad were close, and I don't want him to run back to

Rashad and tell him what I told Crimson. Men talk just like women.

“Yes, I can talk. He's right here. I'm not MARRYING SOMEBODY I DON'T KNOW. Fuck out here with that shit.” She argued. Crimson is hell. I already knew she was giving Griff a hard time that's why I haven't heard from her. He knew Crimson was crazy he just didn't know how crazy. I heard Griff laughing in the background. “Can you please step out the room Griff? I need privacy while I'm talking to Danielle. Feel free to stay gone for 60 days or more,” she argued.

“Stop Crimson, please.” I laughed. She’s stupid. I hate to say it, but it’ll be a while before he gets in her good graces. She said she forgave him. I think she’s just throwing shots at him. She missed the fuck out of him. She’s not going to let him live that down. Crimson holds grudges. I’m glad she forgave her mom. I wish my mother would come back. I want what Crimson and Cheree have badly. I need that right now.

“What I do?” She laughed and asked.

“Listen you know what the fuck you just did. Let me tell you about this fuck nigga. How about Rashad, Cariuna, Lil Rashad and his bitch just left here. Crimson on

God it took everything in me not to show my ass, even though I own this motherfucka. I wanted to knock his fuckin' head off. Stop playing with me because I'm not bothering you. Please stop letting him use your kids to see me." I argued. He got me so fucked up. He better be glad I'm not the bitch I used to be. On everything, I love I would've clowned his stupid ass.

"Danielle say what now? I know you motherfuckin' lying. I ain't never met Rashad's baby momma nor have I met a chick he's dealt with since I WAS dating his friend. He's on my shit list too. You know sneaky niggas flock together. He knew all about this nigga being alive, but he didn't say shit. I'm going to tell him and her FATHER, don't be having my daughter around people I don't know. Bitches were already trying to kill their father because they can't let go." She argued and laughed. Crimson was going in. Ever since she caught her first body, she hasn't been the same. I like the new Crimson, but I miss the old one. She did have a point. I don't want anybody around my goddaughter. I'll kill a bitch dead behind her.

"Bitch I wish I was lying. You know we don't take walk-ins after 1:00 p.m. Girl they were demanding to be seen. I was already on go because they tried Michelle.

When they walked through the door I damn near lost it. He had the nerve to be smiling." I argued and explained.

"Danielle, what's going on between the two of you? You sound like you've started something you can't shake. Did you forget that you're married to Baine? Whatever the two of y'all got going on I don't like it. I'm going to be honest if you're leading him on and he's leading you on it's going to end badly. I don't want to see you get hurt or Baine." She explained. I needed to check myself quick.

"Nothing is going on between us Crimson. He's just sniffing up behind me and doesn't need to be. I'm married and he has someone. I love Baine and I'm not about to ruin that for someone who couldn't be faithful in the beginning because. If he would've been honest from the jump we wouldn't even be here. His son is a reminder of what he did."

"You can keep it real with me. If it's something there don't cheat on Baine, walk away first. I love Baine. He's a good man and I was so happy when the two of you made it official. Rashad is my brother too no matter what. I hated that the two of you couldn't work past the little bullshit, but it is what it is. Don't break up your marriage over a fling. Make sure it's the real thing. If it's not anything there then let Rashad know to move around, you're not circling back. I don't like the way it looks, because this wouldn't even be going on if a motherfucka didn't fake his death. You feel me," she asked and argued? Baby Crimson was throwing slugs at Griff.

"You're right Crimson, but practice what you preach. Make up with your husband. As much as you missed that nigga bitch, the only thing you should be doing is fuckin' and sucking'. He's sorry. It killed him as much as it killed you. Fuck and makeup already. Griff isn't to blame because it takes two. The moment he picked me up and carried me out your bed and into the guest room I shut it down. I really should've gone in on him because he shouldn't have done that. I'm married and he should've respected that."

"Danielle, I don't want to talk about me. Don't tell me how to handle him. At least you're owning up to your mistakes and you're recognizing what's going on. Leave Rashad alone, he's nothing but trouble. I'm not going easy on him because if I do, he'll do it again. Fuck him. We shouldn't be together if he can't be honest about everything.

He knows the real me. I don't know the real him and to be honest I might not want too." She argued. I heard

Griff yelling in the background. “Move Griff. Leave me alone and give me my phone back.”

“Aye Danielle, she got to call you back because she got me fucked up,” he argued and hung up the phone. When it rains it pours? I pray Griff and Crimson can move past this. Michelle sent me an email confirming my 3:00 p.m. patient canceled. Cool, I was going home for today. I cleaned up my desk. As soon as I hit the light, I heard a knock at my door. I opened my door and it was him. I rolled my eyes because he was the last person I wanted to see. I attempted to push past him.

“Excuse me were closed.” I spat and sucked my teeth. I tried to lock my office door and Rashad pushed me inside. “Look you shouldn't be here. Keep your hands to yourself go tend to your child and your child's mother. I need to tend to my husband,” I argued. I meant that. I couldn't wait to go home and cook him a nice meal.

“I don’t give a fuck about you being closed. You need to watch your mouth. What's wrong with you? I thought we were good. She's not my child's mother. You should ask before you start assuming shit. You're not going home. Tell that nigga something came up.” He argued.

"Look Rashad I'm not doing this with you. I don't give a fuck who she is. I'm not bothered because I'm spoken for. You should be there and not here. Make this your last time coming here. See you." He walked up behind me and wrapped his arms around my waist and started kissing me on my neck. I tried to move from his embrace.

"Danielle, I love you and that'll never change. You love me too, but you keep fighting that shit and you don't have too. You can leave that nigga voluntarily or I'll make you leave him involuntarily. I swear that's a fuckin' promise." He argued and revealed.

"Stop Rashad. I can't do this with you. I won't do this with you. You cheated on me. Don't do that to her. It proves you're no different now than you were then. Be a different man for her Rashad than you were for me." I pushed him off me and ran to my car. I had to get away from him fast. I had to stop cheating on Baine. He deserved more than that from me. He's been nothing but good to me. He didn't deserve me creeping with Rashad behind his back.

I ran to my car as fast as I could. I damn near breaking my ankle, but I had to get away from him. I finally made it to the car. My heart was beating fast because I haven't run this fast in years. I kicked my heels off and threw my shoes in my briefcase. I refused to fall victim to his bullshit. I hit the unlock button on my car. I threw my bag in my backseat. I felt a pair of hands around my waist. He knelt and bit my neck.

"Move Rashad, please. You can't do this I'm married. If my husband just so happens to pull up it's going to be a problem. I don't want any problems." I argued.

"Danielle, I don't give a fuck. If it's a problem I want them. Baine already knows what it is with me. You fuckin' belong to me. If he wants smoke, then we can shoot it out and I'll air his bitch ass out. I don't give a fuck so what the fuck are you trying to do?"

"I'm not trying to do anything Rashad. I'm married. Do you understand that? I'm not available and where is she? Go fuck up her life and leave me alone please."

"Danielle do you understand that I don't give a fuck. Understand that your marriage doesn't mean shit to me. I'm telling you now dead that now or else I will. Why are you so worried about her? I care about shawty I ain't gone lie but I can't commit to her, because I could never give her my heart. You got my heart and I don't want it back. I just want to right my wrongs and love the fuck out of you." He argued. He closed the gap between us. He wrapped his arms around my waist and snatched my keys out of my hands. He whispered in my ear. “Let's go. I told you, you're rolling with me tonight.” He’s coming on way too strong.

“I can't Rashad,” I cried. He removed his hands from around my waist. I turned around to face him. He cupped my chin and wiped my tears with his thumbs. I don’t need this right now.

“Why can't you Danielle? What are you crying for? What the fuck are you trying to prove? You’ve already proved that you could move on, so we've been there and done that. You made permanent decisions on temporary emotions. Tell me something new. If you can look me in my face and tell me that you don't love me and have feelings for me, I'll walk away right now. I won't even chase you, Danielle. I'll let you be. I'm waiting for you to tell me what the fuck I need to hear. Don't let me get away this time,” he argued.

“Give me my keys Rashad please,” I cried. I can’t do this with him. Baine could ride by anytime and my whole world could come crashing down all because of him.

"Stop crying. I'm not giving them to you Danielle until you answer my question," he argued. He was all up in my face. Our mouths were damn near touching each other. I couldn't take a step back if I wanted too. I tried and he kept closing the gap between us.

"Why do I have to validate anything for you? I can't be standing out here with you like this." I explained and cried. He's doing too much. My life is over if Baine rides by here and sees this shit.

"You need to Danielle because if you're crying it's some shit on your chest that you need to get off. I'm not letting you leave here until you do. I don't care if he pulls up, I want him to," he argued. I had to make this shit quick because I could already tell I wasn't leaving here without telling him how I feel. Maybe I did need to get this off my chest.

"Rashad let me keep it real with you. Yes, I still care about you and I love you. I never stopped. I can't lie even if I wanted too. I'm married and I just can't walk away from my marriage. It's not that easy. We've been married for years and we haven't had any problems. If we were married would you want me to do this to you? I can't just up and leave him because you're telling me to. You have some issues that you need to handle. Can I have my keys, Rashad? I told you what you wanted to here." I cried.

"If you loved me Danielle, WHY the fuck did you marry him? Why you do that shit? Did it take you all these years to fuckin' say that? You've been hiding from me for what? I fucked up and I can admit that. I wouldn't trade my son for anything in this world. You wouldn't even give me the chance to right my wrongs. You're stuck but that's not where your heart is. I can't even commit to another female because you hold the keys to my heart. I can't even love another female if I wanted too. I tried but it didn't work. Give me my fuckin' heart back." He argued and tossed me my keys.

"Don't leave now Rashad. I told you what the fuck you wanted to hear. You couldn't handle the truth. You asked for this and you're the cause of this. Take your ass on." I argued and cried. He looked over his shoulder and gave me a smug look. I swear it felt like my heart caved in. I slid in my leather seats. I couldn't move and I started shaking. I grabbed my phone to call Crimson. I couldn't call Baine he would demand to know what's going on. I couldn't give him the truth. Thank God she answered on the first ring.

“I need you,” I cried. I couldn't hold it in. Tears flooded my face and my heart was aching something serious. I couldn’t stop my body from shaking. I can't believe he did all that just to hurt me in the end. What the fuck did he expect from me? He wanted me to be honest and I gave him that.

“What's wrong Danielle?” She asked. I couldn't even form the right words to tell her what's wrong because my heart hurts so badly. I finally let go of what I've been holding on for so long. Just to get my heart broken again. I told him everything he wanted to hear and as soon as I did it’s fuck me again and he stomped on my heart. He could’ve kept his comments and his feelings to himself. I hate and I still love him.

“A lot,” I cried. I wish I could stop the tears from falling. I wish I could stop my heart from aching. I wish I could stop my body from shaking.

“Where are you?” She asked. I tried to stop crying so I could tell her where I was, but I couldn’t. I was hyperventilating. I needed to get myself together quick.

“I'm at the clinic in the parking lot.” I sobbed. Snot was dripping down my nose. I grabbed the Kleenex from my glove department to clean my face and nose. I should've kept my thoughts to myself. He didn't even deserve the truth from me, but I'm a different breed. It felt good to get it out, but I wasn't expecting that from him. He asked for it.

"I'm on my way." I know Crimson was going through her own shit, but I didn't have anybody else to call. I needed her shoulder to cry on. I needed her ear to listen. I needed her to tell me that everything would be okay. I guess that's what I get for listening to my heart. Damn, I should've never revealed that part of me. I should've kept that secret to myself and maybe I wouldn't be dealing with the aftermath of how we both felt. I banged my fist up against the steering wheel. Rashad peeled out of the parking lot driving reckless. We locked eyes with each other. I'm sure somebody saw us. I just hope no one that knew Baine saw us. I couldn't explain this.

♡

Crimson and Griff finally pulled up. Why did he have to come? His friend is the reason why we're here. Crimson hopped out and grabbed my keys. I got out and slid into the passenger seat. Crimson pulled off. She looked at me and I looked at her. I broke down crying again. I couldn't help myself. Rashad exposed me and I didn't like that.

"Where to?" She asked. I don't care anywhere but home or here.

"Our spot." I sobbed. Thank God Crimson and I kept our spot for days like this when we both wanted to get away and escape from our reality. I just wanted to hide from the world.

"Girl I don't know if we still have that. Griff packed that up the other day. Let's go to my mother's townhouse. If not, we can go to Mother Dear's." She laughed. Who told Griff to pack up our shit? I needed to vent and be comfortable in my own shit.

"Just drive. I can't go home." I cried. If Baine were to see my face like this. He would have a lot of questions that I couldn't give him the answers to. I can't believe he done that to me. I should've expected that from him. It felt like we broke up all over again.

He just gave me an explanation this time. I should've never given him the benefit of the doubt. I shouldn't have even allowed him in my space just to fuck up my life again. It took me years just to put myself back together after he fucked me over. We finally made it to Mother Dear's house. Griff packed up all of Crimson's hideouts. My grandmother and Mother Dear were on the porch. I kissed my grandmother and Mother Dear on the cheek and walked in the house and headed straight to Crimson's room. I didn't feel like talking. I kicked my shoes off and laid across the bed. Crimson climbed in and laid right beside me. I swear I missed days like this when we could kick back and chill with no worries and stressing over the men in our lives. I would give anything to turn back the hands of time.

"What's wrong Danielle? Are you ready to talk about it?" She asked. I was ready but I wasn't. I didn't want to hear I told you so. I gave Crimson the rundown of what happened and why we're here. She looked at me with wide eyes. I turned my back toward her. I didn't want to be judged. What I just repeated shouldn't have come from my mouth. I couldn't keep my feelings in check if I wanted too.

"Please don't judge me, Crimson." I sighed and wiped the tears that fell from my face. My feelings and emotions are all over the place. I finally confessed my love for him, and this is what I get in return? What did he expect? He wanted me to keep it real and I did just that. She tapped me on my shoulder. I refused to turn around and face her. I'm so embarrassed.

"Danielle, come on now, you know me better than that? I would never judge you. So, you've been holding in this secret for all these years? How does it feel to finally let it all out? Bitch, you can keep a secret? Why? We're all human and we make mistakes? I'm not judging you, but you should've never married Baine if you were still in love with Rashad. He still loves you too Danielle. I think he was hurt just to hear you say that after all these years.

The biggest question I have for you is what are you going to do about it? You and I both know it doesn't end here. It's just the beginning. I feel so bad for Baine. He's about to lose his wife." She laughed. Crimson ain't shit. I swear what makes her think I'm going to do that?

"Yes, I've been holding it in Crimson. Some things are better left unsaid and now I wished I would've kept that to myself. What do you mean what am I going to do? He basically demanded me to leave Baine and I told him I can't do that. How can I leave my husband Crimson and we don't have any problems? I love Baine and I never thought about leaving him. I'm just supposed to leave Baine and be with Rashad and see where he takes me? Get the fuck out of here." I argued and laughed. I don't think I could do that. It's the reason I've been prolonging leaving because I had no plans to. I couldn't tell Crimson that Rashad and I've have been fuckin'.

"I hear you, but you still haven't answered my question. How are you going to move forward because clearly, it's something there or else we wouldn't be here? If Rashad is anything like Griff, he's coming for you. I don't want any parts of it. It's just too messy for me. I love Baine that's my brother and he loves you," she laughed.

"Crimson, your only concern should be me. It's not about to get messy because Rashad made it clear that he didn't want me anymore. He said he wanted his heart back and I'm okay with that. He can have it back. I'm not leaving my husband. I'm going to do what I've been doing and that's to steer clear from him." I explained. Staying away from Rashad was easier said than done. It was a knock on Crimson's door. We weren't expecting anyone. Crimson looked at me and rolled her eyes. "Bitch, are you going to say something?" I whispered.

"Hell no, we're not expecting anyone. We're sleeping." She laughed.

"Crimson and Danielle. I know y'all fuckin' hear me knocking? Y'all can't whisper for shit. Griff and Rashad are on the way up here. They're on the porch talking to Ms. Gladys and my mother. Y'all think I'm fuckin' playing. Y'all need to find somewhere else to hide out at besides here. These pussies whipped ass niggas be doing the most.

Danielle, I thought you were married, girl. You're playing a dangerous game. Why is this man that's not your husband running up behind you?" Ms. Cheree asked, yelled and laughed. If she only knew? My heart dropped. Rashad needs to go on, I can't take any more today. Crimson looked at me with wide eyes.

"Bitch, you nervous as fuck. I can hear your heart beating." She laughed. I pushed Crimson. We heard the door open we both acted as if we were sleeping.

"Crimson, I know you ain't sleep, let's roll," Griff stated and tapped her on her leg. Damn, we haven't been here a good two hours and they're already pulling up. I felt somebody tower over me. My heart was damn near beating out of my chest. He leaned in and pressed his lips against mine.

"Danielle, I know you ain't fuckin' sleep. We're going to try this shit again. Call that motherfucka up and tell him you ain't coming home tonight or else I'm calling him," he argued. I refused to acknowledge him. I heard him dial a number from his phone on speaker and Baine answered. I jumped up quick and snatched his phone. He was laughing. I didn't find shit funny. He's getting a kick out of making my life miserable. He doesn't run shit here.

"Rashad leave me the fuck alone you play a lot of games but don't fuckin' play with me. You said you wanted your heart back and you can have it back. My husband ain't got shit to do with you and I. Leave me alone. I'll tell my husband myself that you don't get the picture that I'm married, and you won't leave me the fuck alone." I argued. I pointed my finger in his face I'm sick of him and all his shit. "Go run up behind the bitch you were with earlier."

"Oh yeah, you're still tripping off that shit from earlier. Let's call Baine up and see? I want smoke with that nigga and it ain't that kind of smoke you're thinking about? Our beef is way bigger than you. Danielle, you just added extra fuel to it. You'll fuck around and be a widow fuckin' with a nigga like me. You don't want to fuckin' try me. If you want to do shit your way you're going to lose big time." He argued. I wasn't about to argue with a confused ass nigga that wasn't mine. I snatched my keys off Crimson's dresser and walked to my car.

Rashad was on my heels. I opened my car door and he slammed it shut. I turned around and gave him a smug look. I folded my arms across my chest and grilled him. He didn't say shit. I swung my door back open.

I jumped in my car and peeled off. I wasn't doing this with him. He doesn't run me. He needs to run that bitch he's with. I don't know when I'll see Crimson again. I'll call her tomorrow. I should've never let his stupid ass get in my head and in between my legs. I hope Baine isn't home when I make it there.

A MONTH LATER

Chapter-37

Mya

He always says I'm tripping but I'm not. I laughed that shit off every time. It was him and not me. Give me one reason not to trip and we wouldn't have any problems. I have a lot of reasons to trip and he's the reason why. I guess that's what boys tell their women when they can't think of a decent lie to tell. I should've been fuckin' with a man instead of a boy. I'm sick of it and I'm ready to get to the bottom of it. I know Rashad has some shit going on and he doesn't want to hurt my feelings. I would rather him be honest with me than tell a lie and continue to lead me on.

I've invested so much time in Rashad it's crazy. I've tried to leave him alone numerous times, but he always came back and made things right between us. Time isn't something that you could get back. My time is valuable. Everything was perfect between us until his friend Griff faked his death and came back to life. Rashad and I never put a title on what we have but he's made me some promises he hasn't kept. If it's someone else just say that. Don't leave me in the background. I have options too. I could be committed to someone else instead of waiting on him, but that's what hurts the most. I asked him could I fuck someone else and he had a problem with it.

You can call it a women's intuition or trusting your gut. Rashad had me fucked up at Griff's funeral. I've been looking at him sideways ever since the day he ran to her side and carried her bridal style. I looked at him differently. I swear that was so disrespectful. He lied and said it was Crimson. I knew it wasn't her because I looked her up on Facebook. Lying ass motherfucka. I couldn't see the chicks face, but her eyes told it all. I would never forget her eyes long as live.

The way her eyes looked at him and me I knew something was going on between the two of them. I knew something was up because he had an attitude when I asked him about it. He got upset and dropped me off at home. A few weeks ago, we had the same fuckin problem when his son hurt himself playing baseball. I locked eyes with those same set of eyes. The tension between her and Rashad was so thick. It was hard to ignore, but I played that shit cool. I didn't want him to know that I was on too him.

Let's just say we were supposed to chill after his son was situated, but he dropped me off. The only reason I didn't cut up was that his son and his niece were in the car. I didn't say anything, and he was surprised. He asked me was everything okay. I nodded my head yes. I made sure I slammed the fuck out of his door. I'm tired of coming second when I know I could be first. I hopped in my car and I waited about five minutes after he pulled off before I pulled off behind him. I wanted to be a good distance behind him before I followed him. He dropped his son and goddaughter off to his mother's house and he headed straight back to the clinic. I was pissed instantly.

I trusted my gut and it led me back here. That was the first red flag. The clinic was set up in a huge plaza with medical office space. It's kind of hard to tell who's going where and who's watching. I sat outside for about twenty minutes and she finally came out running. I knew something was going on. I felt the tension. I sat and watched it. It took everything in me not to bust him out.

He was running up right behind her. The exchange between the two of them broke my heart because it was something between them that I couldn't even compare too. Had I known he had this going on I wouldn't even be out here looking crazy. I should've left the moment my feelings were hurt, and my heart started to ache, but I couldn't. I couldn't move and I continued to watch the two of them.

Something happened between the two of them that day because when he finally pulled off it was reckless. Crimson came about ten minutes later. She jumped in Danielle's car and they drove off. I wanted to know more about her. Who was she and what the fuck was she doing with my man? I followed her. I didn't have to work that day so; I followed her home after she did all that running around. Danielle Mahone was her name and Baine Mahone was her husband. Married and she was fuckin' with him.

What would Rashad want with a married woman? For a few days, I would ride by there to see if Rashad car was there, but it wasn't. I stopped riding by and brushed it off because I knew who she was. I started riding by early in the morning and guess whose car was up there, his. Every fuckin' morning between 8:00 a.m. and 9:00 a.m. he was there, and it went on for months. I barely saw him or heard from him.

I fell back because I didn't want to feel like I was sweating him. He came back around, and I assumed whatever they had going on was over, boy was I fuckin' wrong. Rashad made his way back between my legs again and I let him. My hands roamed his back and my manicured nail traced the scratches on his back. To say I was pissed was an understatement. I would've never slept with him if he was sleeping with someone else. As soon as we finished having sex and he was asleep. Rashad always laid on his stomach. I looked at his back and it was scratched from a woman. She marked her territory. I asked him about it, and he denied it.

Today was the day I was confronting the two of them. I just had to. I just wanted him to be honest with me. I hope Danielle stays in her place because this has nothing to do with her and everything to do with me and him. I pulled up to Danielle's clinic and like clockwork, he was there. I tried to get myself together because the last thing I wanted was for this nigga and his bitch to see me cry over him.

I approached Danielle's building and the door was locked. I wasn't surprised because if you're married and fuckin' someone else's man it should be. I made friends with the cleaning company that owns this building and I swiped the key to Danielle's building in the process because I knew I would need it. I knew what Rashad was doing, I just wanted to see it for myself. I wanted to catch him up. He didn't have to lie to me. I made my way through the clinic.

It was spotless. I headed straight back to Danielle's office and they weren't there. I walked through the facility and it was quiet. I heard some noises coming from down the hall. I walked a little closer so I could hear what they were saying. I stopped right in front of the door with the crack. I heard grunts and soft moans. I could tell he was about to bust a nut. I peeked in the room and Danielle was lying on her back and Rashad was nailing her pussy to the wall. I could hear their bodies smacking up against each other.

"Danielle, how long are we going to keep this up? I'm tired of fuckin' creeping with you. Dead that shit TODAY, not tomorrow," he argued and grunted. "I'm this close to coming to your fuckin' house to let him know what fuckin time it is. It won't be nice. You'll be a fuckin' widow." I've waited so long to be with him, and I never had a fair chance.

"Rashad leaving him is hard because we don't have any problems. You and I just happened again," she moaned. Again, oh so they've fucked around before this isn't the first time. I wonder why he never told me about her.

"You don't need an explanation to leave. Just fuckin' leave," he argued. Oh, this nigga really wanted to be with this bitch, but he's stringing me along because she's stringing him alone. She's about to leave her husband for him. They deserve each other. I didn't even realize that I started crying. I wiped my eyes with the back of my hands. I fuckin' hate him. I will not cry over him. I was going to do a courtesy knock, but he doesn't even deserve a courtesy.

The door was cracked open. I stood in the crack of the door neither one of them were paying attention. I zoomed in with my cell phone and got a picture of the two of them. It was perfect because she raised up to kiss him. I got the perfect picture of the two of them. I wanted her husband to see this shit. I opened the door and I started clapping my hands. She clawed his back up good pissing me off even more. Lie after fuckin' lie. Rashad turned around and looked at me. Danielle gave me an evil look. I gave her what she gave me. She knew I was fuckin' him. I had no clue he was fuckin' her. I couldn't hold back these tears even if I wanted too. I cared about him that's why it hurts so fuckin' much.

"Watch your fuckin' hands Mya and why are you here?" He asked and argued. He pulled out of Danielle and threw his shirt over her to cover up. He was fuckin' this bitch raw and he swore I was the only one he fucked raw. I ran up on him and smacked him in his face. Danielle jumped up instantly and put her clothes on.

"You know why I'm here. I just had to see this shit for myself. Out of all the men I've been with I swear I thought you were the most real? I just knew you would've never fucked me over, but you did countless fuckin' times. A month after month I asked you was it someone else and you said no., I heard your whole conversation. You're making plans to be with somebody else. Why couldn't you fuckin' tell me that?" I asked.

"Mya, are you my woman? We were just fuckin' around. I care about you I'm not going to sit here and fuckin' lie. I cared enough to spare your fuckin' tears. I never committed to you because I didn't want to hurt you. I didn't want to see you crying because of me. I didn't tell you because I didn't think I had to. It's out in the open now are you satisfied," he argued.

"No, I'm not your woman Rashad, and it's not about that. You've made that clear on a numerous of occasions. You weren't seeing anyone. You wasted my fuckin' time and I could've given myself to someone else, but I was waiting for you. Is it fair to me that you've been fuckin' the both us? I tried to move on and stop fuckin' with you, but it was you that came back to me. I asked you about these scratches on your back and you fuckin' lied.

To make matters worse she's fuckin' MARRIED. I knew it was something up between the two of you. She's the same chick from the funeral. You had me in her face, and you've been fuckin' her the whole time. I knew I wasn't tripping because I could feel the tension between you two. It's cool though. Danielle, you can have him. Rashad, I wish you nothing but the fuckin' best. Thank you for wasting my fuckin' time," I argued. I left out the same way I came in. I wasn't done yet. I had to pay Mr. Mahone a visit. I wanted him to know what his wife has been up too.

I thought hard about what I was about to do. I wasn't in the wrong. Danielle didn't owe me any loyalty and I didn't owe her any either. Mr. Mahone wasn't too hard to find. All roads lead to **Nik & Skeets Bar and Grill** his Maserati was parked out front in VIP. He was very easy on the eyes. I can't lie but I'm good on niggas right now. I followed him one night to see if he was up to the same shit his wife was but he wasn't. I sat by his handsome ass all night and, he never said a word to me, but his partner Ike wanted me. Ike wasn't my type. Everything about him screamed he was a hoe, so I stood clear of him.

Tonight would be different. I had no plans to sit by him without an actual conversation. I decided to get dolled up. I'm single and free to mingle. It was the beginning of winter so of course, I wanted to bring my mink out. I had a cute fitted red Chanel dress. I couldn't wait to squeeze in it. These past few months I've picked up a few extra pounds fuckin, sucking and feeding my face. I flat ironed my hair bone straight. It draped down my back. I made sure my perfume would hypnotize him. I gave my face a nice nude beat with a red lip. Christian Louboutin's adorned my feet.

Nik & Skeet's Bar and Grill was the new hot spot on the Westside. If you were looking for a nigga with some major paper or bitch with some money this was the spot. They catered to wealthy. It was $100.00 just to get in and that included an appetizer and complimentary drinks. Anything else is prepared to run up a tab.

I would've never known about this place if I wouldn't have followed him. It was right off H.E Holmes. It was a cute little setup. Monday night that motherfucka always went up. I looked in the mirror and checked myself out before I made my way inside, and I was on point. I gave the bouncer my $100.00 I made my way toward the bar and Mr. Mahone was sitting there tossing back a few shots. I took a seat right beside him. The bartender took my order for the drink. All eyes were on me. I grabbed my phone out of my clutch just to toy with it until she brought my drink back. A few niggas were in my face trying to holla, but I wasn't impressed. I was only here for one thing and that's Mr. Mahone. I dropped my phone I knelt to get it, but he beat me to it.

"Here you go Ms. Lady," he stated. He has a nice voice and very attentive. I see why Danielle didn't want to leave.

“Thank you.” I beamed. I grabbed my phone out of his hand. I turned around and faced the other way. I could feel him staring a hole in me, but I brushed it off. He stood up and leaned in my personal space. I could smell his cologne, damn he smelled good. He sent chills through my body when he spoke.

“What’s up? What’s your name?” He asked. I could feel his beard tickle the nape of my shoulder. I placed some space between us because he was too close to me. I couldn’t allow him to be this close to me because he’s making me nervous.

“I’m Mya, can you back up please?” I asked.

“Yeah, I can do that. I’m trying to see something. Ms. Lady every time you come in here you sit right beside me. Do I know you or something?” He asked. Oh, he has noticed me. I didn’t come to conversate. I just came to drop a bomb that’s it.

“I don’t know you, but I know of your WIFE,” I sassed. I had his attention now.

“You know my wife,” he smiled. If he only knew what I knew about his wife.

“Yeah I do, we’re fuckin’ the same nigga,” I smiled and laughed. He bit the inside of his jaw, just the reaction I was looking for.

“Aye shawty, I think you need to watch your fuckin’ mouth and stop speaking foul on my wife,” he argued.

“I wish I could, but I can’t. I just wish our nigga would’ve kept it real. I got proof you want to see it? I never state facts without proof.” I argued.

“Nah I’m good, you can keep it. Whatever you do in the dark always comes to the light. I never go looking for shit. If what you say is true it won’t be long before it lands in my lap. I’ll see you around though,” he stated. It didn’t go how I expected it to but at least I put that bug in his ear. I tossed back one more shot and headed back outside to my car. I had to walk past his car to get to mine. I knew he was looking at me. I could feel it. I slid in my car and pulled off.

EPILOGUE 5 MONTHS LATER

Chapter-38

Crimson

I've been tossing and turning all night. I couldn't sleep. I wasn't scheduled to have lil Carius until August 5th. Every other day these contractions are getting worst and I've been going to the hospital on a false alarm every other day. It's only July 26th, I think it's for real this time. I didn't want to drag Griff out tonight because he's had the girls all day. I've been tired, but Lil Carius is hurting me, and I can't take it. I raised up and placed my hand on hip. My contractions were the worst, but I've never felt a pain like this before. It was so bad my feet felt numb.

I knew that was different, this is my third pregnancy and normally I could shake the pain but not this. It felt like something was wrong. The pain and contractions kept becoming more intense.

"What's wrong baby?" He yawned. I love to hear him talk. His voice is deep and raspy.

"Nothing," I whined. I can't take this. Something has to give. He has to come tonight.

"Baby come here, what's wrong? If you're in pain lets go check and see if my son is okay. I don't care what time it is, wake me up," he explained and yawned.

"Okay," I sighed. Griff jumped up and cut the light on. I could feel the sweat pouring down my face.

"Crimson, you're in labor. I can tell, you can't be doing that. Sit on the bed and don't move. Let me wake up the girls so we can get out of here," he argued. I knew it. I just knew he was tired, and I didn't want to wake him because it may be a false alarm. Griff got the girls ready. My bag was already packed. I sent my momma a text and told her I was headed to the hospital. She said she was on her way.

Griff and I made it to the hospital an hour later. My mother and father were both in the waiting room waiting on us. The nurses got me in a room instantly. When they checked my cervix, I was dilated at six centimeters already. My son was ready to make his entrance in the world.

My contractions were speeding up. I couldn't get an epidural because we got here too late and Carius Jr. was ready to meet his parents. Griff laid in the bed right beside me. I guess he knew I wasn't feeling good because I held onto the side of stomach tracing the many stretch marks that have appeared. I can't take these contractions at all. They're killing me. My son was doing a number on me.

"Baby what's wrong, are you okay?" He asked. Hell no I wasn't okay! His son was killing me. I guess he wanted to see us as bad as we wanted to see him. Griff grabbed a face towel from my bag and ran cold water on it to wipe my face. I was sweating badly and I was hot. He fed me a few ice cubes. Camina and Cariuna sat in the corner watching me. My mom was snuggled up in my dad's arms.

"Not really, the contractions are killing me. It's nothing I can do about it." I pouted. I had to take one for the team.

“Okay, breathe as they taught you in your prenatal classes. Come on baby you got this. We’ve been down this road before. Just a few more hours and you’ll be just fine. Let me get the nurse to check you again. It might be time to meet our prince.” He explained. Griff went to go page the nurse. The doctor and the nurse came into the room to check me. I couldn’t take these contractions anymore. I couldn’t do it, they hurt so badly. I’m sure they look at my face and could tell.

“Ms. Tristan, you’re at nine centimeters. It’s time to get you prepped for delivery. Little Carius is ready to meet his mommy and daddy and his big sisters!” She smiled. Thank God, because we couldn’t wait to meet him.

Griff looked at me and kissed me on my forehead. I wasn’t nervous anymore. I knew this would be over in a matter of minutes or an hour. I have a low tolerance for pain, but I would have to deal with this. Griff was right by my side for the third time and he hasn’t left it since we met. The girls and my parents cleared our room. It was just the two of us now. He held and kissed my hand for reassurance.

“Crimson Rose Tristan, I love you and thank you for having my third child. I got you now and I’m never going anywhere." He explained. I know he ain't, we have three kids now.

"I love you too baby." The nurses and my doctor finished setting up the room. I squeezed Griff's hand for support because I needed him.

"Ms. Tristan on the count of three push for me. 1, 2, 3." I started pushing. My doctor instructed me to push again and I did.

"One more push." My doctor yelled. "He's coming, one more push Ms. Crimson. I think he's a little bigger than we expected." I bet he is. I had to push one more time. Hopefully, this is the last one. "He's coming!" My doctor yelled. Thank God. I don't think I had too many more damn pushes in me.

Carius Jr. came out screaming. He had a set of lungs on him. He was mad at the world and the only thing we wanted to do was spoil him. He weighed in at nine pounds and nine ounces. Griff cut his umbilical cord. My doctor and nurse started cleaning me up. He was still screaming exercising his lungs. Griff wouldn't let the nurses clean him up, he wanted to do it. Carius Jr. was so handsome. Griff held him in front me, he looked just like his father and

Camina. I'm not surprised, he had Camina's attitude already.

The only features he had of mine were my eyes, head, and my hair that's it. I couldn't wait to hold and kiss him. I'm ready to hold my son. I can't wait to shower him with love and affection.

A MONTH LATER

Griff

"I've been waiting on this day to come for as long as I could remember. I knew she was the one the moment I met her. Crimson Rose Tristan the moment I laid eyes on you baby I knew I had to have you. It was your smile and those two big dimples in your left and right cheek. The first day I met you, who would've known our souls would meet and create a ton of memories. Our road getting here wasn't easy, but I wouldn't want to take this journey with anyone else but you. I chose you then and I choose you now. Thank you for giving birth to all three of my children. The only thing in this world that would make my life complete is the two of us getting married. You gave me a lot of gifts and I've given you plenty. The last gift I want to give you is my last name, Griffey. I asked you to be my wife and you said yes. The only thing left to do is for you to say I do." I explained.

Crimson was crying but she knew I meant everything I've said. I wiped her tears and cupped her face.

"Carius, stop you're messing up my makeup. I thought we both agreed that you wouldn't make me cry today. The day you asked me to marry you, I already had my vows written. I knew what I would say to you? Over the years a few things have changed but one thing that's always been consistent and that's how much I love you. I know I'm a spoiled brat and that's because of you. I was scared to love, but I don't ever regret being submissive and allowing myself to be comfortable with you. I love, loving you. I cherish waking up to you.

Carius Deon Griffey Sr. I don't ever want to stop loving you. In this crazy world, nothing makes sense, but we make sense. I thank God every day for you, you're my soul mate. I'm forever grateful for our worlds colliding. Who would've known seven years later we would be at the alter saying I do. I'll be here crying letting the world know how much I love you," she stated.

"Carius, do you take Crimson Tristan to be your wife?" He asked. Hell yeah, she's been, my wife. She already knew what it was between us.

"I do."

"Crimson, do you take Carius Griffey to be your husband?" Of course, she does.

"I do," she smiled and beamed.

"I now pronounce you husband and wife. You may now kiss the bride," he stated. He didn't have to tell us twice. I finally married the love of my life. I grabbed Crimson's hand and led her into the banquet hall for our reception. Our family and friends were all in attendance. Rashad and Danielle did their toasts to us. Crimson was sitting in my lap. I couldn't wait to get out of here. Our honeymoon starts in a few hours. I'm taking her and our children to Griffey Island. It's a small island located off the coast of Trinidad and Tobago.

Everybody was enjoying their selves dancing and celebrating with us. I noticed a commotion coming from the dance floor. It was Rashad and he was standing in front of Danielle and Baine. Crimson turned around and cupped my chin. She placed a kiss on my lips. Rashad has been tripping ever since he saw Baine here with Danielle. I'm riding with my nigga right or wrong. I didn't agree with him sleeping with Danielle while she was still married but I don't have anything to do with that. I knew it was going to be a problem, but it is what it is. He said wherever he sees them at he was letting it be known.

"Baby, Rashad is about to fuck up our reception. Go out there and get him, please. Don't let him make a scene," my wife begged and pleaded. Crimson stood up to let me go get my nigga. I didn't want to be in the middle at all so I wasn't saying shit. Baine and I grew up together and our fathers were best friends. He was family. I stood by Rashad. He looked at me and smiled I already knew what time it was.

"Can I cut in?" He asked Baine looked at me then Rashad and rubbed the bridge of his nose. Danielle looked like she was about to shit bricks. Hey, she knew how Rashad gave it.

"You want to cut in and dance with my wife? You're disrespectful as fuck if you would think that I would allow that my nigga," Baine argued. All eyes were focused on what was unfolding right here.

"Rashad, please don't do this here and ruin Crimson and Griff's moment," Danielle pleaded.

"Danielle, you already know what it is with me? I've been telling you this shit for months. Wherever I see you at with him I'm letting that shit be known. I told you that you could do it my way or learn the hard way. I gave you the option to leave but you were stalling. Crimson and Griff had their moment but now it's my fuckin' moment. You got two fuckin' options and you better pick right the one. You can continue to be with a nigga or you can leave this nigga and let him know your marriage is a wrap. What's it going to be?" Rashad asked. My wife was walking toward me now. Damn, Rashad aired that shit out. I felt bad for Danielle. I swear I did.

"Hold up, Danielle please tell me you haven't been cheating on me with this nigga? I'm not even surprised, but I should've known better. I met this lil chick name Mya a few months ago at a bar. I guess it's his chick huh? She said my wife was fuckin' her man and she had pictures and everything but I didn't want to see that shit. I knew you wouldn't do me like that. I gave her my number and she sent them immediately, but guess what I never opened them. If I open this message I swear to God it better not be you," Baine argued. He opened his phone and went to retrieve the message. Danielle took off running and Crimson ran right behind her.

This is the end of Crimson and Carius story. I left Danielle and Rashad's story open for a reason. I'm not finished with them it's the beginning of something new. I know y'all nosey ass want to know what's going on. Y'all know my messy ass will drop some tea at discussion in a few weeks. Join my mailing list to get the tea for this drip that will be dropping soon.

THE END

Pushing Pen Presents now accepting submissions for the following genres: Urban Fiction, Street Lit, Urban Romance, Women's Fiction, BWWM Romance Please submit your first three chapters in a Word document, synopsis, and include contact information via email @Nikkinicole@nikkinicolepresents.com please allow 3-5 business days for a response after submitting.

CONTEST ALERT

E-Gift Card and Cash App Giveaway! I Wanted to Announce It Here First. Read, Review on Amazon and Goodreads! Post Your Review in Your Favorite Reading Group on Facebook or Instagram. Tag Me In It (Nikki Taylor) on Facebook or Instagram (WatchNikkiWrite) Twitter (WatchNikkiWrite) Email Your Entry To NikkiNicole@Nikkinicolepresents.com.

The First 50 Reviews I Get I'm Going to Draw A Name. You Pick the Gift Card It'll Be For 30.00 or Give Me Your CashApp Name I'll CashApp You $33.00. I Do Things in Real Time! I'm Not Holding It Until the End of The Month. If I Get 50 Reviews on Day 1 Of This Release. I'll Draw A Name the Next Day and You'll Get The E-Gift Card of Your Choice or The Cash App. For Each 50 Reviews I Get I'll Draw A Name. You Can Get A 30.00 E-GIFT-CARD or 33.00 CashApp. I'm Giving Away 3 Prizes.

CPSIA information can be obtained
at www.ICGtesting.com
Printed in the USA
LVHW041541270619
622553LV00003B/482

9 781070 370484